PRAISE FOR W W9-CTD-347

"Wood clearly knows the ... system."

—Publishers Weekly

"William P. Wood, a former prosecutor, knows well how to surprise and engross us."

—Vincent Bugliosi, Author of *Helter Skelter*

"A natural storyteller!"

—Norman Katkov, Author of *Blood and Orchids*

GANGLAND

"Compelling...A bloody showdown between manipulative killer and dedicated prosecuter from which no one emerges unscathed...Wood knows the intricacies and ironies of the legal system."

—San Diego Union

"Suspense-filled...Realistic, fast-moving...Molina is the kind of criminal you love to hate."

—Daily Press (Newport News, VA)

"A unique legal thriller...Wood knows the ins and outs of prisons, courts, government witness programs...*Gangland* demonstrates graphically the tensions, frustrations, and personal dangers often endured by the families of crime victims."

—Deltona Enterprise (FL)

STAY OF EXECUTION

"Wood delivers a compelling moral tale disguised as an intelligent thriller."

—Publishers Weekly

MORE PRAISE FOR WILLIAM P. WOOD!

BROKEN TRUST

"A tour de force of compelling courtroom drama and spellbinding storytelling."

—Gus Lee, Author of *No Physical Evidence*

"Wood combines colorful, behind-the-scenes details with a non-stop plot."

—*Library Journal*

"A spellbinding tale about the men and women who dispense justice from the bench."

—*Associated Press*

RAMPAGE

"One of the better courtroom dramas in years."
—*The New York Times Book Review*

"From the first to the last, *Rampage* is superior."
—*Cleveland Plain Dealer*

"A taut courtroom drama… Hard to put down."
—William J. Caunitz, Author of *One Police Plaza*

PRESSURE POINT

"What Joseph Wambaugh did for law enforcement, William P. Wood will do for the judiciary."

—*Tulsa World*

"Wood, a former prosecutor, really shows his expertise of writing about the legal system with this spellbinding, gripping novel."

—*The Best Reviews*

A KILLER UNDER GUARD

Molina's shoulders bunched briefly under his black coat, drawing it tight. "I know these people. They're my relatives. They don't do anything, especially not at her funeral. I had to explain it to my friends." He nodded his head a little to the right at the feds grouped nervously around him.

Molina tried to scratch his nose with his handcuffed hands. He had no more interest in Swanson. He said toward the casket, "I would've got something better, they let me do it." Then he turned to go.

In front of him and the men guarding him, the young men flowed on coiled muscles from the cars toward the gravesite.

The two groups faced each other, Molina still near the casket, his hands clasped together in a metal prayer. He turned to Swanson, his face bright with brute pleasure.

The old man marched straight ahead, while the younger ones paused. One of the feds called out, "Stop right there. I don't want you any closer."

An adjuratory hand was raised, the fed holding it up like his own form of benediction. But the old man ignored it and marched forward, his gaze set on Molina. Most of the words were caught up in the wind and Swanson only heard him say daughter, killer, murderer....

GANGLAND

WILLIAM P. WOOD

LEISURE BOOKS   NEW YORK CITY

For William Friedkin,
with high regard and gratitude

A LEISURE BOOK®

October 2007

Published by

Dorchester Publishing Co., Inc.
200 Madison Avenue
New York, NY 10016

If you purchased this book without a cover you should be aware that this book is stolen property. It was reported as "unsold and destroyed" to the publisher and neither the author nor the publisher has received any payment for this "stripped book."

Copyright © 1988 by William P. Wood

All rights reserved. No part of this book may be reproduced or transmitted in any form or by any electronic or mechanical means, including photocopying, recording or by any information storage and retrieval system, without the written permission of the publisher, except where permitted by law.

ISBN-10: 0-8439-5705-0
ISBN-13: 978-0-8439-5705-1

The name "Leisure Books" and the stylized "L" with design are trademarks of Dorchester Publishing Co., Inc.

Printed in the United States of America.

Visit us on the web at www.dorchesterpub.com.

GANGLAND

"...dost thou not perceive
That Rome is but a wilderness of tigers!
Tigers must prey; and Rome affords no prey
But me and mine...."

Shakespeare, Titus Andronicus

"Perhaps it is upon the instant we realize,
admit, that there is a logical pattern to evil,
that we die...."

William Faulkner, Sanctuary

CHAPTER ONE

First the doorbell rapidly chimed twice, and even before the soft notes faded, a harsh steady knocking began. Then the chiming doorbell sounded again.

Angie stepped away from the washing machine as quietly as she could. She dropped her armload of clothes to the linoleum floor, and realized her heart was beating quickly from surprise. I'm safe, she thought, I'm safe now, as the chiming and knocking went on and on.

She stood still, then tiptoed from the alcove off the kitchen that held the washer and dryer, over to the living room window. By standing against the wall and just barely pushing the curtain's far edge, she could see out to the brick steps and the front door. Two men stood at the door. Like mechanical pieces on a medieval clock, one pushed the doorbell, while the other, with a bored yet insistent raising and lowering of his knuckled fist, banged on the door itself.

She didn't know either of them. They both wore suits. Not very good ones, she thought. They looked like salesmen, maybe Jehovah's Witnesses.

The first rule was to watch for strangers; that's what Swanson told her. The second rule was always to ask for identification. The third rule was to call him. That was how she had to live for a while.

She held the curtain tightly. "Who is it?" she impatiently called out over the noise.

Like a signal, the chimes and the knocking stopped. "We're investigators from the D.A.'s office," said the younger one to her right, "and Mr. Swanson would like to see you right now."

The other man had his hands on his fleshless hips and he kept turning his upper body right to left, peering at the neighborhood. "It's real important," he said.

"Hold up some ID," she said.

The younger man reached into his coat and took out a black wallet-sized case. The other guy did the same thing. They held gold badges, stamped with the seal of Santa Maria County, toward the black slit between the window and curtain. In the spring morning's adamantine light the badges shimmered.

It was the same kind of badge Swanson had showed her, the kind he had. She unlocked and opened the front door.

The two men smiled at her. "Are you Angelica Cisneros?" asked the younger one. He used her real name, not the phony one she told everybody in this new city and wrote on checks and charge slips. She could have her real name back when this was over.

"What do you want?" she held the door by the handle, ready to close it quickly.

"Mr. Swanson says he's got to see you," said the younger man. They were both young, in their twenties, with white shirts, plain ties, and dark suits. The younger had sandy-colored hair and slightly protuberant eyes.

"I'm not supposed to come down until day after tomorrow," she shook her head angrily. "I'm busy now. I got plans today." Swanson had done this to her before. Come down now, he'd say, we have to talk. "Let's go over something you told me yesterday," he'd say with his breathless enthusiasm. Like a kid with a new toy.

The younger guy was casual. "He said it was very important. He said there's some problem with your testimony."

"I haven't testified."

"Your statement, whatever. What you've been saying about Hector Molina. Mr. Swanson said something's come up. He's got something for you to look at."

"Something big," said the other one, still looking around.

"He's going to make another arrest? He's got somebody?"

"We don't know. He just said he has to see you."

The other guy stopped looking around and stared at her. He had a thick neck and she noticed how the reddish-blond hair was combed carefully straight back, like half the cons and homeboys who came to visit Hector when he first got out of prison.

Her heart still beat too fast. Never going to be scared again, she had vowed, and now she stood in her own doorway, frightened because these two guys had come for her. She wasn't going to live like this much longer. Swanson had promised. Once they got Hector, it would end, finally.

"I haven't seen you two before," she said.

"We got thirty-six investigators. I'm Max," said the younger one as he pointed with his thumb. "This is Les. So. Can we go? We're supposed to hurry it up. Mr. Swanson's orders."

She stepped back from the door. Hurry it up. That was Swanson. Always in a rush. "Come in," she said irritably. Just two messenger boys. "He could've called. I'm going to call, tell him this is a bad day. I got a lot to do."

"He's out," Max said quickly. "We got to bring you to him. That's why he needs you right now."

She dialed Swanson's direct line at the district attorney's office. Max threw his hands up and Les moved his head left to right, taking in her living room and its clutter. "When's he coming back?" she said into the phone. "You don't know how long it'd take for him to get to a phone?" Max was pointing both hands at himself and mouthing, "We'll take you," with exaggerated faces.

"No, I'll see him myself," she said, hanging up. Max smiled.

"We'll take you right now."

"Everybody thinks they can come and tell me where to go

when they feel like it," she said. "That's the way Hector does things, okay? Angie come here," she mimicked, "Angie bring me this. Angie get rid of this. I got to take it from you guys, from Swanson?" They don't care, she thought, watching their faces. The boss said fetch. "You mind if I change? That's okay?"

"Sure, that's okay," Max smiled.

She tromped to the alcove and picked the clothes off the floor and shoved them into the washer. Might as well get them done while she was out. Funny guys, she thought. All my life it's been funny guys.

But *he* wasn't funny. From miles away, another state, from a place she didn't even know, he could still reach out and disrupt her life. He would always do that. Until she stopped him. The sick longing crept over her again, as it had ever since she first went to Swanson. I'm hurting Hector, she thought, I'm hurting him bad.

She heard channels being changed on the television, rapid flipping of the dial, Max doing all the talking and his pal Les saying something low, short, tense. Funny cops.

In the small bedroom she shrugged off her old sweater and jeans. One of the few friends she'd made in this new city was old Mrs. Powell across the street. Maybe she should tell Mrs. Powell she'd be gone for a couple of hours. So what could she say? Lie again? The old lady didn't even know her real name. The lying stopped there, but she couldn't tell the truth. My husband kills people and I'm telling the D.A. everything I know? No, not even old Mrs. Powell with her five cats and empty bottles of cream sherry lying around would stay friends after that.

The guys in the living room were arguing. She thought she heard an open palm smacking something.

She finished dressing, brushing her hair quickly, tight hard strokes that pulled some of the black strands away.

"Okay? Let's go? I'm not waiting for you guys," she said. They stood in the center of the room. Max had one shoulder up, like he was about to block a smack from Les. Instantly, they turned to her.

"Don't you look nice. Very nice," Max said with a nod. "Don't you carry any money, a purse or something?"

"You got me rushing so much," she said, flustered. She was embarrassed that her eagerness to hurt Hector had been so nakedly exposed. She hurried back to the bedroom and plucked a brown purse from the disordered bureau. Now they were joking with each other when she came out.

"Can we go?" she asked sharply.

Max stayed with her as they stepped out and she locked the front door. Les walked briskly to a green two-door Impala parked in the street and got in the driver's side.

"He left the motor running?" she asked.

"Real big hurry, gotta go," Max answered like a little kid as they got into the car. He held the front seat aside so she had to sit in the back.

"You taking me home, too?"

Les finally spoke without turning his head on that thick neck. "We'll get you back. Can we go? It's our ass if we're late."

Angie slid as gracefully as she could into the backseat while Max hopped in beside Les and even before he had closed his door, the car jerked loudly away from the curb and jounced quickly down the street.

"Jeezum, I almost didn't get my leg inside," Max complained, bending down to check his shoe.

"Oops," Les said.

"You guys been together long?" she said to break the vaguely unpleasant atmosphere.

Max didn't answer immediately. "Three years. That's how long I've been with the D.A."

"Three years, four and a half months. We're like brothers, right? We act alike, we talk alike." Les shook his head. "What a crazy pair."

"I remember that old song," she hummed a little.

Max grunted and pulled a very wrinkled bag from under his seat. He took out an orange and began carefully picking bits of peel from it with a fingernail parer on his keychain.

"Got these fresh, out near where Mr. Swanson's waiting. They've got these fruit stands, bags of stuff, all fresh stuff," he said, his mouth a little twisted as he concentrated. "You want some?"

Angie shook her head. "I just ate."

"I like oranges, better than apples even. You get more juice in an orange. They're messy, don't get me wrong. Take an apple if you want to be neat and clean. Orange tastes better, though, 'cause of all the juice."

A thought struck her. "We're not going downtown? Swanson's not downtown?"

Les answered, "Look at him. Like a girl picking at that orange. Why don't you just peel it like everybody else? Stick your finger in it and peel it, don't play with it for Christ sake, look at that."

"Where's Swanson?" Angie felt nervous again and made a silent prayer that this fear would melt away someday, a sign that Hector's last and most secret power over her had finally been broken. "Where we going?"

"Out in the boonies, over the river." Max gestured vaguely with the fingernail parer. Half of the orange was exposed, a pulpy brain-like mass glistening in the broken peel. "He's out in the field."

"I want to stop at the D.A.'s office," she said. "I want to go there first."

Max turned in his seat so he was staring at her, holding the orange in one hand. "Why?"

"I just do."

"Sure, right. We'll go there."

Les nodded his head rapidly. "You want to tell me why we're going there?"

"She wants to."

"So we get our asses chewed for hauling in late?"

Max sighed. "We'll go, if you really want to, but we're going to take a lot of grief from Mr. Swanson for being late. You know him."

She bit a nail. Damn the panic that made her afraid all day, in the supermarket, even walking over to see Mrs. Powell. Hector can't hurt me now, she repeated, he's locked up, he's gone. I'm dancing on him. "Forget it then. It can wait."

"No, no, you want to go, we'll go. You tell me where to go," Les said.

"Take me to Swanson. Forget it."

Max munched on sections of the orange, squishing the pieces in his mouth with squeals of pleasure.

Angie put her head back. Leave these poor guys out of it, they're just errand boys, they don't need your problems, too.

She opened her eyes and noticed that the backseat floor was littered with stale bits of popcorn and torn Kleenex tissue. A child's broken yellow plastic cup rolled indolently at her feet. She leaned forward.

"I thought these cars had radios in them."

Max pointed at the radio. "You want to hear something?"

"Leave it off," Les said. "I'm enjoying the peace and quiet."

"I mean radios you talk into," she said, "like cop cars."

"He doesn't like music." Max finished the orange, took out a very large white handkerchief and wiped each of his fingers.

"That ain't music, buddy boy, that's hard on the ears, is what it is. He's got this racket going day and night, day and night. It gets on your nerves, right?"

"You guys sound like you're married," she said, because they sounded so silly, bickering about peeling oranges and playing the radio. "That's the way my husband and I used to fight. Except he'd hit me."

Max grunted again and Les chuckled. "Well, see, this is a county car, not a cop car, so we don't get that kind of radio," Max said with a shrug.

Outside, the streets passed in an unrolling procession of green lawns, tall stately old elms and oaks, squat new houses, and three-storied Victorians crowded together like displaced great ladies. Angie couldn't keep track of the street names flowing by as Les drove through every yellow light, slowing down only the slightest for stop signs. He weaved through the sluggish traffic, changing lanes constantly.

"You're going to get a ticket, you drive like that," she said.

"We'll fix it," Max waved it off.

Even with her window rolled down, in the confines of the car, the smell of the sweetish balm holding Les's hair slickly in place and the ineradicable tobacco smoke driven into their clothes made her a little ill.

"Swanson must have told you guys about Ralph Orepeza," she said, biting another fingernail. She liked talking about Hector's affairs, revealing them to the world and letting the world put an end to them.

"Sure. Everybody heard about him. Ripping off a drug project, big bust, lots of new stuff," Les said.

"I didn't know he was yours," Max said with real interest.

"All mine, every bit. I gave him to Swanson. Mr. Orepeza's an associate of my husband, I mean, he's going to be my former husband soon's I can divorce him. I told Swanson all about this guy, he's running this drug rehab place, he's snagging all the money, you know, grants and state shit, and he's giving it to my husband. I nailed him up and down."

Max whistled and shook his head, "Well, Mr. Swanson didn't give us all those details, of course. Jeezum, you're a pretty brave little lady."

"Right, give me a break."

"No, I mean it. She's pretty brave, isn't she?" Max asked Les intently.

"Sure, sure, she's brave."

"I'm not surprised, you know, he didn't give you the whole picture," she said. "I figure he trusts you guys, but he's always telling me, this is just between us, don't blab to anybody, just me. He's a real funny guy, he's always asking how my kid's doing, like he cares about her, how she feels. Sometimes, you know, I don't get him, okay? He's like this big overgrown baby boy. Then he's all serious and asking about my kid." But it wasn't Swanson who filled her thoughts. It was Hector. "Either of you two married?"

"Not no more," Les said.

"So, listen," she said, leaning to the front seat, her head almost between the two of them, "tell me if this sounds right. I can't even get a divorce from that bastard. He's some kind of special witness or something and they've got him somewhere with a new name and everything and I can't even find out where he is. I know he's snitching off everyone. Makes me sick. See, I'm not a snitch, it's different with me."

"Way different," Max agreed. "Way, way different."

"So they won't even tell me where they've got him now. So my kid, she's six now, her name's Cecilia, I got her living with my folks in L.A. He wanted to see her. They were going to make sure he could see her, and I go, fuck that. He's not having anything more to do with my kid."

They passed rapidly through the downtown bustle of Santa Maria, old office buildings, and the brown anachronism of the Elks Building like sorrowing sentinels among the tall glass boxes and concrete bunkers. It looks so much smaller down here, she thought, having seen the city from the air when she first flew in. From above, it looked enormous, spreading blue-gray and stony for miles among the green tiles of the geometrically precise farms all around it. As though this city was growing, actually moving too slowly for her eyes, but still dynamic, halted only at the banks of the slow, thick American River that bore crookedly through it. Swanson said it was over a hundred years old, from the gold rush days, all the eager ones going to the claims, and the disillusioned ones coming back made Santa Maria. Three hundred thousand people in the city, almost a million in the county, so foreign to her because only Los Angeles had been her world. They got Okies and Japs everywhere, whites, like they all want to be farmers or play in offices. The big inland valley of northern California, too far from everything, everybody a stranger, she thought, except an old pal like Ralph Orepeza and because of Hector, here I am. She looked behind the gray-and-white office buildings into the unearthly blue brightness of the sky, like glass, empty and imperious in its perfection.

Enough, let him go, she thought. Stop thinking about Hector. She tried to change the subject. At Max's pale throat, teasingly just below the level of his white shirt collar, she saw a blue-green line. "You got a tattoo there? On your neck?"

"Something I did in the Navy, stupid thing. You know, you're a kid and you do stupid things like that."

"Toot, toot," Les imitated a ship's horn.

"Leave me alone," Max complained.

"My husband," Angie said, "he's got tattoos on his arms, his chest, he's got one on his back, Jesus with a long beard. He's got a Sacred Heart, flowers, all that gang junk with bloody knives, like that."

"I didn't like getting this one. Hurts when they do it. I don't think I'd like so many."

"Looks like it'd hurt." She saw something under Max's arm, "You got a gun?"

"Sure I got a gun." Max pulled his dark coat open and showed her the brown-handled gun butt in its shoulder holster. The leather gave out a dry groan as he shifted in the seat.

"Show her mine," Les said.

Max opened the glove compartment. Inside, Angie saw a dark metal shape, bigger than what Max wore. "It's a .44 Special," Les said proudly.

"That makes me feel better, you got that stuff," she said. "If I'd had one, I'd a used it couple of times. You bet I would've, like when he started hitting me and the kid."

"Yeah, well, we're ready for anything." Max aimed two fingers out the window. "Pow. Pow, pow."

"We're married eight years," she said, shaking her head, "and he's out of the joint for seven and a half months. You believe that? Seven months out of eight years."

"Turn here, here, here," Max said suddenly, and Les swung wide, heading out of town.

"Much farther?" Angie asked.

"Nothing much, we're almost there," Les answered.

She thought of nights before they were married. In the imperious blue spring morning, she remembered nights when Hector held her in the darkened bedroom behind her father's barbershop. There was one small high window in the room, and through it came stale evening air and the deep hiss of cars on the nearby freeway. Hector held her close, their bodies heated together, his legs between hers, dancing in the dim room to the alien sounds around them, humming music himself as he pressed his face against her cheek, then her mouth. Sometimes he took her up into the hills so that they made love in the car with a sparkling dark expanse spread below them, the whole city twinkling green, white, red, orange in the night. The hunger rose again with the memory of those nights. The hunger and the shame and anger that gave it substance. I loved him, she thought with wonder and bitterness, Holy Jesus, I loved him and I didn't even see him.

The car bounced roughly several times, grinding querulously as it hit the bumpy parts of an ancient concrete-and-steel bridge over the great slow-moving river that ran beside Santa Maria. Green metal struts, a latticework with rusted rivets, made a shadow play across her face as the car picked up speed over the empty bridge. Behind them was the city, and ahead she saw fewer buildings, some large lit neon signs for cheap motels and truck stops competing with the vaporous blue brightness of the sky.

"You look jumpy. You feel nervous?" Max asked solicitously.

She jerked away from the memories. "I guess I'm a little jumpy, yeah."

"Just the thing right here, just the very thing for that," and Max brought a pint bottle of amber-colored brandy from under his seat. He held it for her, grinning and raising his eyebrows.

"You don't get in any trouble?"

"Don't worry about us, you're the one who needs calming down." He moved the half-empty bottle toward her.

She took it. "Thanks. A little's a good idea." She closed her eyes briefly, letting the rich, heavy liquor go down in one swallow. "That was nice. Join me?" She tried to hand the bottle to Max.

"No, take another, you need it." He lowered his voice. "But don't give any to that guy. He gets mean." He nodded toward Les.

"I do. Shame on me, but I do get nasty sometimes," Les sighed. "Maybe I shouldn't."

"Go on. It's kind of like health food."

She took a short drink. "It does help."

"Sure you don't want another?" Max shook the bottle in front of her when she gave it back to him.

"That's enough for me, I get drunk real easy. I feel this already."

What would Swanson be wearing this time? It was a game she played. He was becoming more informal every meeting. Last visit he had on this baseball cap, no tie, jeans, just like they were old friends getting together. He was a little like her first priest, Father John he wanted to be called. Very easy, like it was simply a matter of saying yes and God did everything after that. Swanson was like a priest and she was confessing. That was why she wasn't a snitch. And he showed her pictures of his kids, all three, two girls and a boy.

"Hey, that's where I got the oranges," Max pointed. "I want to stop on the way back for some corn." The road ahead narrowed to two lanes. She saw fruit stands, the first of the year, sheltered under thick green canopies of eucalyptus and elms. Oranges, melons, and vegetables were spread out in uneven rows. A little boy in a chair at one stand waved frantically at the speeding car.

She felt the familiar hunger and nervousness. If I get so nervous just talking about Hector, what happens when I have to go up in court? How's Swanson going to save me there?

"If we got time, we'll stop," Les said. "Grown man getting excited about some damn apples and oranges." He blew a raspberry.

"He's out in the middle of no place, isn't he?" she said. There were almond trees on either side of the narrow little road they sped down. They had passed the city and the fruit stands and even the farmhouses. Now there were only mute legions of almond trees. "Like where are we going, like exactly where?" she pushed forward until she was just behind Max.

"Half mile in there," Max pointed into the trees. "It was such a pain finding this place. We got lost twice, we had to go back. Boy, I gave him good directions, but he still screwed us up." He poked his thumb at Les.

"Blame it on me, okay," Les said. "It's the fucking wilderness, okay?"

The car swung sharply to the left, going off the uneven asphalt onto a smooth dirt road that led into the heart of the grove of trees. Around them were branches laden with buds, the tips like a multitude of tiny dark green lights.

"And what's he doing? You didn't tell me, like exactly what's he doing out here?" She turned her head quickly to either side. There was nothing but green interwoven branches.

"They dug up this old box, bank box with some stuff in it, papers and stuff. You're supposed to look at it."

"I don't know anything about a bank box," she said.

"So you got to look at it," Les said.

Curiosity suddenly leached away her fear. Maybe Hector buried some records, or Ralph Orepeza did. Swanson must think she knew about it. Like buried treasure, another kid's game.

"It's pretty anyway," she said. Max and Les were suddenly quiet. "You can see the mountains," she said in surprise. Through a wooden tangle of branches and leaves and tremulant green buds, she saw the gray-white mountains in the distance at the horizon, as though the peaks were rising up to meet the blue sky. Like torn lips, she thought, all cut and jagged. Like the times Hector came home with his mouth bloody. He pushed past her and cleaned himself at the kitchen sink, gently dabbing at the bruised flesh. Sometimes he let her clean the blood off his swollen lips or face. He was never mad. He would get mad, frighteningly enraged later, but when he cleaned himself or let her hold and bandage him, he was coldly silent.

Max tapped his fingers against the window and nodded his head to the vague tune he whistled softly.

They stopped. "Everybody out. End of the line," Max said brightly.

Angie got out as Max held the seat for her. "I don't see him. I don't see his car." She couldn't hear anything, either.

"I think this is the place. He's got to be around here," Max took her arm firmly. "I left a trail of breadcrumbs."

"Oh, riot," Les said behind them.

She squirmed, "You find him. I'll stay at the car. I don't want to go looking."

"She'll stay," Max glanced back at Les.

"Riot," Les said.

"Maybe you're lost, there's nobody here." She twisted in Max's grip. "You're making me trip. I can walk myself."

"I got to hold you up, lady." He put another arm around her waist. "Touchy feely."

They had stepped a little deeper into the grove, away from the road. The ground was alternately hard and spongy and she kept stumbling, even with flat-heeled shoes. When his arm pulled around her, the fear burst open, lanced and putrid. She pushed forward violently, ready to run, in panic, shouting for Swanson, for anyone.

Max's leg caught her sharply in that first arching movement, his arms released her, and instead of bolting away, she fell heavily to the ground, face first, the shout reformed instantly into a cry.

"There he is now!" Max exclaimed. He pointed up.

Reflexively, she jerked her head upward, and knew at the same moment that Max lied when she felt the hard metal thing touch the back of her head, almost tickling. There was, she knew instantly, no time to cry out or even turn away. There was no time for Cecilia or Swanson or anybody.

In that moment she felt regret at her own foolishness and vanity and Hector's guile, and looked along the invisible line Max pointed out, leading like an unspoken prayer, from the almond grove up into the indifferent glassy blue sky.

Four shots snapped through the silence of the grove.

CHAPTER TWO

"Before you say anything," Swanson warned Detective Richard Weyuker, "I swear to God, if I can make Hector on a second murder in this county, I'm going to do it. And Jesus Christ, the damn feds aren't going to save his ass this time."

"I'm really sorry about her," Weyuker said. "She was doing a hell of a job."

"She was. She really was." Swanson had not gotten over the shock of hearing that Angie Cisneros was dead. There was a first time for everything and this was the first time a witness in one of his cases had been killed. People died all the time, an old man beaten with a coffeepot lived to identify his attacker, but gave up before the trial. The victim in an arson case got hit by a truck during the lunch recess of the preliminary hearing. An elderly couple was looted of all their silverware and the mementoes of a lifetime and both had heart failure within two weeks of the burglary.

But he had taken precautions for Angie Cisneros. He had hidden her with a new name and address. Only a few people in his office knew who she was or what she was doing. On many reports, to judges for search warrants and other district attorneys in California, she appeared as a CRI, a confidential reliable informant, known but secret.

There was his own pride, too. He couldn't truly believe that one of his witnesses would be picked out and killed.

"So who are these jerks?" Swanson asked. He and Weyuker were at one end of the police department's Homicide Bureau, a crowded collection of desks and typewriters, teletypes and bulletin boards with layers of flyers and wanted posters stuck to them. Three other detectives talked so loudly on the phones that it was hard to hear over them and the clanking, clacking of the teletypes. He raised his voice.

"Number two's in there." Weyuker pointed at the door behind them. "I stashed number one up the hall," he said loudly.

"So who are they? Can we tie them to Molina?"

"Maybe. Number two's Maxwell Dufresne. I bet my kid he's got a B number because I made a couple of very chic tattoos on him and he looks like he might have been in the joint for robbery. He's going to be the talker."

"How about the other one?"

"That's Lester Narloch. He's the asshole, I bet. Not one damn word, not one sound, nothing at all. He just sits there, he's got his arms folded."

Swanson only had on a thin white shirt and dirt- and grass-stained white shorts. He had added an old tweed sport coat, but the spring evening's chill made his skin prickle. That was how the worst news always came, while you were with your family, refereeing a soccer game and your kid was trying to make a goal he'd practiced all week. In the middle of the game, the small gray box at his waist had given out a high piercing cry. Something had happened. The beeper never summoned him to a phone unless something dire had happened in Santa Maria County.

Instead of the five-minute walk from his office on the third floor of the district attorney's building, along tumultuous tree-fringed streets downtown to the aging stone fortress of the police department, he'd had to rush into the city from a soccer field on his afternoon off.

"They don't want lawyers? Neither of them?"

Weyuker shook his head with such a snap Swanson feared his toupee would leave its moorings. "Narloch won't say anything, and Dufresne's just started talking, but I haven't heard the magic words and I've given them their rights and the guys who brought them in did, too."

"I'm praying," Swanson crossed his fingers. "See that? Please, let these two guys give me Hector Molina dead solid. Pretty please. And keep the fucking feds away from this homicide."

"Amen," Weyuker said.

"Okay. Let's see number two." Swanson rubbed his hands together.

Weyuker brought out a fat keychain and unlocked the interview room door. Over the door, a red light glowed showing that the room was in use. Swanson followed him inside.

Swanson was tense, although he didn't show it. He was a blustery, heavy man who always seemed confident. His black hair contrasted with the paleness of his face and legs.

Unavoidably, as he walked behind Weyuker, he had a good look at this latest toupee. It sat uneasily on his round head, a faintly curled graying mass of hair. In Vice, Weyuker wore a tanner, sportier model. Earlier, when he was in Auto Burg, it was a blond almost military cut. But now, graduated to Homicide, the most prestigious city bureau, the middle-aged detective affected a conservative look. He was painfully thin, from Swanson's point of view, yet he had a double chin and freckles.

Over the years, he and Weyuker had worked all kinds of cases when chance brought them together, as it had on this one. But chance did not keep them on the case, nor did it bring them both to the interview room. This was where Hector Molina forced them to be.

It was a small room, lined on all sides with white fiberboard that muffled every sound. Sokol, another detective, sat in one of the chairs around the mottled brown table. At the far end, farthest from the door, sat a man. His white shirt was torn open at the collar and a tie hung very loosely around his neck like a gaudy noose.

"This is the D.A.," Weyuker said to the man.

The man looked at Swanson and started to laugh very fast, as though burping.

"What's so funny?" Swanson asked, sitting down.

"Nothing's funny." The man stopped his burping laugh.

"Why you laughing then?"

"I always laugh when I'm really nervous. I guess I'm really nervous." He grinned, and started the burping sound again.

Sokol waved to them.

Swanson's legs were a little cold so he briskly rubbed his hands over them. "You're Maxwell Dufresne?"

The man nodded. He had a small fresh bandage over his left eye and Swanson saw several cuts, recently scabbed, on the hands that drummed fretfully on the table. "Yup. That's me."

"What happened to his shirt?" Swanson asked Weyuker.

"What happened to your shirt?" Weyuker asked Max.

Max shifted uncertainly, nervously watching Sokol. "It got ripped." He burped twice, then pressed his mouth shut tightly and took deep breaths through his nose.

"Max and I had a disagreement about how he happened to be in the car that got into a three-car pile-up and he's got a dead woman in the trunk," Sokol said.

Normally, Swanson liked interrogations, even though he didn't do many, even in a crazy unit like Special Investigations where one day he'd investigate the mayor's assistant for selling coke, and the next have to find out if a fleeing robbery suspect really did turn and fire four shots at the police officer who killed him with one bullet. Most cops, Weyuker excepted, were wary around him. Someday he might be looking at them. Dick Weyuker didn't seem to care.

Swanson didn't like this interrogation because it wasn't normal even by those cockeyed standards. There was no fun in this one. Angie was dead.

She trusted him and had been persuaded that coming to Santa Maria from Los Angeles would free her forever from Hector Molina. Swanson had a murder hanging over Hector and Angie could provide evidence that even while he was a protected witness helping the feds make cases against his former gang associates, he had been committing crimes. Hector would be taken out of the witness protection program, the murder case could go forward, and Angie could divorce him and get custody of her daughter free and clear.

Max, sitting down the table, was vivid proof that trusting Mike Swanson had not been good enough. It's a talent making people trust you, Swanson thought, like tennis or playing the piano. You find out you have it and you work it, make it better, refine it. He had discovered his talent during the summers selling cars at the old man's dealership. Swanson Pontiac, twenty-two years at the intersection of Sutter and Benedict downtown. The old man was grudging, but finally impressed with the way young Mike handled customers and moved the iron. Oil and water, the old man said, but it worked. Take a loudmouthed tyrant like the old man, and then the soft-spoken, persistent, logical, sentimental son and the cars sold. There was a terrific feeling when he got a reluctant customer to go for a car, like a hesitant witness or suspect finally agreeing to talk.

He had no regrets about those summers. He learned about what he could do with other people. After work on the hot weekends there were girls from his class or the class a year younger to take down to the riverbank in the evening. You only had to bring along beer and a blanket. Charming Mike. Mr. Smooth. He met Diane one of those summer weekends and spent more than a few nights with her by the soft, sibilant-sounding river.

All in all Santa Maria was a good place to grow up in, go away to college and law school, come back to, marry a girl you had known for years, and raise a family. It was for all of those reasons that this interrogation unnerved him. An enemy, unseen and vicious, had once more come into the city.

When he spoke, he ignored Sokol. "Do you want a lawyer?" he asked Max. Those eyes, like unlit lightbulbs, smooth and protuberant, stayed on him.

"Is there some kind of deal we can talk about? Something, you know, between us, so I can tell you and you work it out?"

"Just a second, Max." Weyuker sat opposite Swanson. He had his steno pad out and unclipped several pens from his shirt pocket. "Now, you know your pal is down the hall? You know we've got two guns from your car. We know it's a stolen car. We've got the dead woman, the one you guys shot, and we've got her wallet in your coat pocket." He reached into his own pants pocket and brought out a slim, red wallet and gave it to Swanson.

"We can do something," Max said, his fretful glance going back and forth between Swanson and Weyuker. "I can do something for you, give me a chance, I can."

The slim wallet unfolded in Swanson's hands. The wide-eyed, empty-faced driver's license picture gazed back at him without any of Angie's vivacity and none of the brutality she lived with. Proud and hard and desperate, she had violated every code of behavior she'd been brought up with to come to him. The license was still in her married name, Angelica Molina, and gave her address in Los Angeles. I let you down, he thought, forgive me.

"Poor Angie," he said aloud, looking at her picture.

Max burped his laugh abruptly.

"You think it's funny? You think anything at all about this is funny?" Swanson said slowly.

"No, sorry, sorry, just nervous."

"I'm glad you're nervous, Max."

Swanson felt something sharp and cold go through him almost painfully. Molina had reached out, from somewhere, and plucked his witness away. Just like that. Like God.

"Maybe we can do something," Weyuker went on, "but I want Mr. Swanson here to know everything about you and bozo brains down the hall before he decides to make any deals, and I want you to hear everything I tell him." He reached into his shirt pocket and took out a black leather rectangle and slid it to Swanson.

The sharp coldness was deeper. Swanson knew what the black thing was even as he opened it and the gold Santa Maria County badge, cobalt blue on its borders, glimmered for him. Underneath the badge was stamped "District Attorney Investigator."

"Did the other guy have one?" he asked.

Weyuker nodded. "And this guy had a gun in a shoulder holster."

"Where did you get this?" Swanson asked.

Max swallowed and drummed his fingers harder on the table. "I want some kind of deal. I'm not saying anything unless we get a deal."

"Fuck a deal," Sokol said violently, coming out of his seat as he threw his pen down and it skittered to the floor. "We used to have a hole in the fucking wall, right there," he shouted, pointing at the unblemished fiberboard, "from two guys just like you. Their fucking heads made that hole when they started acting just like you're acting." He reached for Max, who huddled back in his chair, putting his hands in front of him and wiggling them as if to make Sokol vanish in a puff of smoke.

"He's going to hit me again," Max yelled.

Swanson didn't move. He held the badge very tightly. Weyuker, now leaning so his body was across the table, held Sokol back with both hands on his chest, "Hey. Hey," he said emphatically as Sokol pushed against him. "Get out of here if you can't handle it."

Swanson looked at Sokol, his face set and angry. The other detective snapped away from Weyuker and pushed against the wall behind him. "Forget it," he said, then to Max, "right there, bud, their fucking heads made a hole in the wall." He thumped his chair to the table and grabbed his papers. He swore, slamming the door.

Max touched the bandage at his head. "He hit me. He hit me right there, right where I got hurt by the steering wheel."

"You make him very angry," Swanson said. "That's why we want him to stay outside, so he doesn't cause any trouble. It was entirely wrong for him to strike you."

"You tell me, Max, and I'll write up a complaint on him," Weyuker said.

Max blinked his bulging eyes. He pulled his white sleeve across his mouth and cheeks. "No, I don't want to file anything. I don't want him to hit me anymore."

"Right," Swanson said, "you're right. Okay now. Tell me where you got the badge."

"I want my deal first."

Swanson rubbed his legs under the table again to warm them. The room smelled of pine cleaner and sweat. Angie's killing was bad enough, but the implications of that badge on the table were worse. He held it tightly once more.

The badge went right to him. It represented his job and the people he trusted.

"This is the only, and I stress that, Max, the one and only deal you get from the district attorney's office, you understand?"

The fearful, fretful face quickly nodded.

"You will answer all the questions I put to you or Detective Weyuker puts to you. That's the first thing. The second thing is you will tell the truth now and you will tell it in court. If you don't tell the truth now and in court, I will make sure you are tried with your buddy. He isn't going to like you at that point and you're going to have a snitch jacket."

"I want to be protected," Max interrupted. "I want to do my time in Security Housing."

"Where'd you do time before?" Weyuker asked.

"Couple of places."

"Where?"

"Folsom. And Deuel. I was at DVI first."

"For what?"

"Some bullshit."

"What kind of bullshit?" Swanson broke in. "I mean, I can get your rap in two seconds and I don't like playing twenty questions for starters."

Max laughed. He breathed through his nose again as if the air had abruptly become quite thin. "Robbery, two robberies in L.A. and a car thing in Bakersfield."

"Armed robberies?"

"Right, sorry," he said swiftly, "yep, two armed and a car I took from this guy, but he really owed me for it, so the car isn't a good rap, but the robberies, yep, they're okay."

Swanson reluctantly let go of the badge. Where did this guy get it? Who could get hold of two badges and give them to killers? How did he know where she lived, her new name? First take it step by step. Play this guy. "We'll work on getting you into Security Housing someplace," he said, "that'll be part of the deal. The rest of it is that you'll plead to murder one with special circumstances, and I'm going to tell the judge that you should go to the joint for the rest of your life instead of getting the death penalty. That's because you're so helpful and cooperative."

"Can't I get a voluntary?"

"Max. I could walk out of here now and take you and Lester to trial and convict both of you and get the death penalty. But, you're going to tell me how you got this badge. How you knew where Angie Cisneros lived. How you got her to come with you, right?"

"Right. I'm going to tell you everything." He paused. "You are Swanson, that's what I heard?"

"Yes."

Max violently broke into his burping laugh. He began shaking his head. He put his hands on his sides and slowly steadied himself. Swanson and Weyuker simply waited until the gasping breaths quieted. Max put out his scabbed hand. "Shake my hand so I know it's all okay."

Swanson took his hand and shook it. Like kids in a tree house, he thinks this makes it all fair and square, a guy who has been to the joint for armed robbery and just come from killing a woman. He made Weyuker shake on it, too.

"Here's what we'll do," Swanson said. "You'll sign a Miranda waiver now. You'll give us a full statement. Then we'll get a public defender to stay with you through the plea in court. I want you to have your lawyer right through everything."

Max minutely examined the grease-soiled cuffs and sleeves of his white shirt. He seemed much more composed. "I'll tell you stuff. I don't know about murder first. I mean, I didn't shoot her. I'm not giving Les up, okay? You've got his gun so you could show who shot her. I didn't. That was Les." The pleading bulbous eyes were on Swanson. "So, I think I should get something for that. Jeezum. Life in the joint. That's too much, man. I didn't do that much."

"I told you the proposition."

"I'm going to give you a lot, man, believe me. A whole fucking lot that's going to rock you. I should get something."

Swanson stood to avoid the chance Max's fretful hands would touch him. The dulled sound in the room wrapped around him. Time to make the sale.

"Well, it doesn't look like we can do business after all, Max. I can see that now. You really don't want to help yourself. So, I'm going to get out of here and let Detective Weyuker and Detective Sokol finish their business and then I'll see you in court."

He turned away. More than anything he wanted to know what Max had to say, but he wasn't going to let Max know that.

"Oh, Jeezum, Jeezum," Max whined. I can read your mind, Swanson thought as he looked back at the youthful, vapid face suffused with self-pity. You're thinking about all those years and never getting out. You'll feel better soon. You'll never have to worry about the awful minuteness of every moment of your life. Even with the prospect of life in prison and a life of protection from vengeful cons, he knew Max would find serenity in the endless predictability of events.

"I guess that's it," Max conceded finally, blowing air through his mouth. He sniffed and drew his sleeve past his nose and stared down at his hands like an agitated child.

"Good. That's the thing to do," Swanson sat down again. "First, sign the Miranda form, Max," and Weyuker pushed it to him. As Max carefully took the pen in one scabbed hand, Swanson saw the blue-green tattoo that spread across his throat just below his Adam's apple. It was a trademark of some kind.

"What's that say?" He pointed at Max's throat.

Max signed the form and self-consciously raised his chin a little higher so the words were visible. "It's the Harley Motorcycle brand thing. I got it at Deuel."

"Must have hurt like a son of a bitch to get a tattoo on your throat like that."

"Yeah. It did," proud and smug because he had endured the pain in order to have something unique among the other cons.

Suddenly, Swanson chuckled. "You know it's misspelled?"

"Where?" Max demanded, his eyes instinctively lowering.

"Hell. I didn't notice that," Weyuker exclaimed brightly. He traced the letters in dull dark ink that crossed Max's throat. "It's got motorcycle spelled 'm-o-t-o-r-c-y-l-e.' That sure ain't motorcycle."

Max rubbed his hand over his throat as if to feel the letters, or rub them away. "It's spelled right."

He can't spell. I bet he can't even read very well, Swanson thought. That's what some of the bogeymen are. Not all of them. The one who set this up isn't simply pathetic or vicious. Or even simply homicidal.

"Now the next thing you're going to sign is a contract the detective here will have typed up. You know what a contract is, don't you, Max?"

"I know what it is."

"Okay, so this contract is going to have every agreement we just talked about in it. You sign it. I sign it. That means you are legally bound to tell the truth and tell me everything. If you break your contract you don't get sued or anything like that. You go on trial for murder one with me doing everything I can to make sure you get the death penalty. You understand?"

"I understand," Max said quietly.

Swanson spread his hands on the table and looked at Weyuker, whose pen was ready over the steno pad. "Okay, Max, let's just take one or two preliminaries. You and Lester hooked up in Folsom?"

Max nodded. "We all hooked up there."

"Spell out who that is."

"Me and Les and Hector. The three of us. And some others."

That sharp cold point again. Angie hadn't known of any of this. "What others?"

"Some guys who're Brothers. Hector's pals."

"You in the Brotherhood?"

Max shook his head, a little ashamed. "I was going to be, but I got out too soon. Les made it."

"How about the Nuestra Familia? These guys you got in with, they NF?"

Max nodded.

"Aryan Brothers and NF guys all together, Max? You think I'm going to believe that?"

Max looked at Weyuker for help. "It didn't make any difference. We're all Hector's guys, that's what counted. It's just him and us. Still is. Right now, right here in your town." He smiled, genuinely, for the first time.

"My basic problem here is that I don't buy two gangs who hate each other with a passion working together. For anybody. To do anything, I don't care what."

"Hector got it to work," Max said with a sage nod. "Some guys saw what he was talking about. It made sense."

Weyuker shrugged at Swanson.

"You know Hector killed a kid here a couple years ago, Max? You know about the robbery he tried over at Tice's Market?"

"Man," Max wheezed breathily, "that's what this is all about," and he waved his arms, drawing the last word out into a long burping laugh.

Swanson had first read about the killing in police reports early on his tour in Major Crimes. It was not a spectacular crime. But it became the case that wouldn't go away. He interviewed Frank and Hannah Tice, heard from them how their family had been cleft suddenly, irrevocably. For the first time, Swanson encountered the pain Hector Molina caused as he moved through the world.

Two and a half years before, Hector Molina had come to Santa Maria to see an old friend who was running a drug rehabilitation project. He had stopped at Tice's Market on its tree-shaded street around four-thirty in the afternoon, a dog day of a hot summer. It was a small store that served the immediate neighborhood and mostly sold ice cream, cigarettes, and beer.

For some reason, Molina decided to rob the store. Perhaps he was short of gas money, or couldn't resist the impulse when he saw only the Tices, their son, and another customer inside.

He made the Tices open the cash register. His gun was some sort of big automatic, the Tices couldn't say more. At gunpoint he herded the four people into a back storeroom. The Tices went first, then Edgar Rolly, the customer, a fat, minor fence in the neighborhood, and last, the Tices' son Donny. Before Donny got to the storeroom, Molina shot him, once in the upper back, then again in the chest, from a downward angle as he lay on the floor. The back wound was not mortal, according to the stilted, unfanciful medical report. It was the second shot, as the boy must have stared, for that brief, scalding moment, at the gun and his killer, that blew out part of a lung and his vena cava, the large vein going to the heart, and killed him. It was unclear why Molina killed the Tice boy. Perhaps an impulse, perhaps an insult that the kid had been unable to contain. He locked the three others in the storeroom and left.

It was a good case, Swanson knew, dependent entirely on the observations of the three survivors. No one else had seen Molina come or go. He left no fingerprints or other physical evidence. But the indelibly burning testimony of those witnesses was more than enough.

Angie and the dead Tice boy and two prison gangs who fought each other like wolverines, all somehow wrapped up in the person of Hector Molina. Swanson picked up the badge again. "Where's Molina now? Do you know where he is?"

"They got him over in Carson City. It's a bitch whenever we had to see him, you know, get in the car, drive over to Nevada, come back, you waste a whole day and sometimes Les wanted to go to Vegas or Reno. Just a bitch."

So it begins, Molina talks to the feds, Angie talks to me, Max snitches Les off, an unbroken circle of betrayal and punishment, Swanson thought.

He went to the door with Weyuker. "Stay put, Max, we'll be right back with the contract and you can sign your life away."

"Gotcha, chief," Max made a faint salute.

The noisy normality of the Homicide Bureau crowded out the deadening closeness of the interview room. Swanson touched his toes, groaning a little and arched his back as he straightened up. Two detectives threw a soda pop can back and forth like a baseball and laughed about who would have to open it.

"You believe that about NF and ABs working together?" Weyuker asked.

"They're not. It's kind of what I thought, based on Angie's information. Molina's got renegades from the gangs, just like Max and his pard."

Weyuker rolled paper into his typewriter and flexed his fingers. "Let's see, let's see, how about party of the first part and party of the second part and we've got to have a sanity clause."

"There isn't any Santy Klaus," Swanson said.

"I know the joke."

"You know the big joke? This scuzzy guy is going to blow Hector Molina out of the witness protection program, just like Angie wanted. And there isn't one damn thing the U.S. Attorney can do about it. All over. Bye, bye."

"You got a bigger joke, I think," Weyuker pecked away without looking up.

"I guess I do," Swanson said with a cold sigh. "Molina's got a pal in the D.A.'s office."

"Appears so."

Angie's killing shocked him, made him angry. The knowledge of how it had been done unsettled his world entirely. The corruption was close at hand; someone he worked with, joked with, perhaps even knew very well, had delivered a witness to her murderers.

He concealed his feelings by calling out to Sokol across the room, using his nickname. "You're too brutalizing, Ricardo," and Sokol shivered in mock terror.

When Weyuker finished the contract, they went back inside with Max, bringing him a Seven-Up and a Snickers candy bar when he asked for them. Swanson asked Max what had happened.

"You won't like it. Believe me, you won't like it." Max thought it was funny as he chewed the Snickers with gusto.

CHAPTER THREE

Diane Swanson told her youngest child Megan to stop kicking the table leg and settled Lizzie at her place with a plate of fried chicken and salad.

"Would you try Matt again?" Di asked Robin Cantwell, a large woman who wore gold-framed glasses and was helping to bring food to the table. "My vocal cords are raw from shouting at the game."

"He's up in his room?"

"That's where he usually sulks. He's like Mike when things go wrong, he blames it all on himself, on not doing something right and he gets mad."

Robin nodded. "I'll bring him down. Fortunately for us, the twins are about as athletic as pancakes." She wiped her hands on a paper towel.

Lizzie spoke up. She had a piece of lettuce in one hand, casually held in the air. "I always make a goal in field hockey at school."

"Don't tease Matty about not making a goal," Di warned. "I mean it. I do not want to hear any teasing at the dinner table."

Di sat down and made sure Meg could easily get at the pieces of chicken. They were eating in the kitchen, at a small round table covered with a brightly colored yellow-and-white oilcloth. It was past seven and crackers no longer controlled Meg's appetite.

"Is Robin eating dinner with us?" Lizzie asked.

"Yes, she's staying over because Bruce is working late. It was nice of her to say she'd help us out with dinner, wasn't it?"

"I suppose so," Lizzie said laconically.

"Put the lettuce back on your plate."

Gratefully, she heard Robin coming down the stairs. A wash of blue twilight had fallen outside the louvered windows. Joggers husked guiltily and righteously around the large park across the street and somewhere too close at hand the seductive tinkling of an ice-cream truck was making its way toward them.

Matt, who was ten and still wearing his grass-stained soccer uniform from that afternoon, sat down silently at his place. Robin sat beside Di.

"Thank you," Di said.

"It was no trouble. Matty and I had a fine chat about school." Matt took a deep breath.

Meg had picked up a piece of chicken and was about to drop it into her wide open mouth.

"You know that's not right," Di said.

"We have to say grace," Matt grumbled.

"Maybe you'd lead us, Matty?"

Another deep breath. Matt bowed his head, his eyes only partly closed. "Thank you Lord for this food and everything today. Amen."

Robin had a small smile. "Amen," she said, "Thank you, Matty. We don't say grace at our house, but you could come over sometime and do it."

"Maybe I will," Matt grudged, eating a chicken leg methodically.

"Daddy never says grace," Meg announced to Robin.

"He says it in his own way," Di replied. "We've discussed that before."

"They don't miss one thing." Robin began eating. "Bruce

tried to whisper something to me, and Amy, from across the living room, heard him and said, 'I don't think daddy's too fat.' I nearly fell over."

"What's Bruce doing? I missed it the first time, sorry."

"He's got two houses up and something has to get closed tonight and so he's coming in around nine. I sent the twins to Barb's and so here I am."

"Well, I'm glad you could come. I hate it when Mike gets one of these late calls. He's on a rotation deal at the office, everybody in his section gets beeper duty about once every three weeks. And I have never known it to fail that the beeper doesn't get him and me up at two in the morning or on his afternoon off."

"He left in the middle of the game," Matt said morosely. "I saw him go."

"Nothing happened after he left. Your team didn't do anything," Lizzie said blithely.

"Honey, remember." Di raised her finger. She turned to Robin, who was nearly finished with her plate. Robin lived three doors up the block on the quiet street and had been the first friend she'd made when they moved in nine years before. Robin's twins were only a year older than Meg and the two families often spent time together.

"Where did Mike go?"

"He didn't tell me. He got the call and then had to go. And it's so stupid sometimes. Sometimes it's just a policeman with a question he can't answer. One time it was a whole big bunch of them and they wanted his permission to pull the whole door off an after-hours bar."

Robin was filling her plate again. She was a large woman who moved easily. "Oh, my gosh. What did he tell them?"

"He told them to go ahead. They pulled the whole front off this building with a tractor."

When Robin hooted, Meg dropped her fork and joined her, kicking the table leg enthusiastically. Di put out a restraining hand.

"The real estate business is a lot less colorful." Robin sat down and sighed happily, "Well, here we are, a couple of work widows and isn't it great?"

The scraping and chewing and scratching of forks on the plates was calming, even if Matt was still in a sour mood and Meg too rambunctious because she was eating so late. It was very right, Di thought, very ordered.

"I've still got my lesson plan to finish for tomorrow," she said. "The fifth graders this time, we call them the Ferocious Fifth at school."

Robin shuddered. "Nevermore for this one. I wouldn't set foot in a classroom again."

Di heard the clock in the living room tone out the quarter hour. "Mike usually calls when he's going to miss dinner. I wish he'd called tonight and let me know how late he thinks this thing will go."

"Let's just enjoy this." Robin patted Meg's slender tanned arm, and brushed a hand over the dainty green ribbon tying the little girl's hair. From outside came the sound of several car doors slamming at the same time.

Di was eating salad as Robin looked through the window toward the park and the street. "I see two police cars outside. It looks like a couple of policemen are coming here, Di."

The tall man spoke to one of the four Sacramento County deputy sheriffs guarding the steel door and was let inside. The door shut and locked behind him. The room, which was to have been a recreational center for the main jail, was spare with only two metal tables and a scattering of plastic chairs on its linoleum floor. High slatted windows let in the light and even further bleached the fading pictures of yachts scudding across greenish blue seas bolted into the walls.

One man, in a light blue jail shirt and baggy denim pants, both stenciled with his number, sat at a table. He was writing in a small artist's tablet. He looked up when he heard the door close. He stopped writing and stood, remaining where he was until the tall man came to him. He put out his hand.

"Thank you," he said formally. He sat down again. He was

thickly built, his hair combed back and acne scars gouged deeply into his face.

The tall man looked around. He wore a three-piece suit and fiddled with the lowest button on the vest.

"They tell me you won't go to court tomorrow, Hector. You said you won't go on with your testimony. Am I understanding things correctly?"

Molina nodded. Carefully, with surprising gentleness, he closed the tablet and put his nibbed pen alongside it. He held his hands together. "Look at it, Mr. Massingill, you tell me. You tell me what I should be doing because of what you guys are doing, okay?"

The tall man sat down and crossed his legs. His thin-framed, round-lensed glasses made his eyes look magnified. He brushed a thin, nicotine-stained finger over his brown moustache. "Before we get into anything, you're going into court tomorrow. That was our deal. You've got to live up to your part of the bargain."

"I have lived up to it. I've been testifying in seven trials so far. Check it out, Mr. Massingill, you know what I been doing."

"Then you'll be in court tomorrow."

"No. Not now."

"It's not something we can discuss." He pointed a thin stained finger at the man across the table. "No more deals, no more arguments. If you don't go in tomorrow, Hector, you're out. I swear to God you'll go right into the general population in the nearest prison I can find with your old pals in it."

Molina nodded. The brown-pitted face was impassive. "That's what you're doing to me right now."

"What are you talking about?" Massingill suddenly stood up, looking down at Molina.

"I go to the shower this morning before court, right? I come out and find six, eight other guys in there and I don't know any of them. They could know me. Nobody's supposed to be in there, right? Any of them could be NF or Brothers. And I get this when the guy puts my food through the slot." He reached into his pants pocket and brought out a matchbook.

Massingill looked at the front and back of the matchbook and the name of the obscure motel printed there. He opened the cover. Inside was written YOU'RE DEAD in neat square printing. He closed the matchbook slowly and put it away. "It doesn't mean anything. You've got guards outside here and you've got guards around you in court. You're in isolation when you're not in court, aren't you? Nobody can get to you."

A whisper-like chuckle and smile came from Molina. He leaned back in the plastic chair, balancing on its rear legs, his thick body pressed into it. "You have to be realistic here. I did it. I did this guy at DVI in the yard right under the guard tower. There were four guards, ten, twelve yards from me, but I still did this guy."

Massingill said, "I remember the Deuel hit."

"Sure, sure, I copped to that one. I'm just reminding you how guards don't mean everything." He slammed his chair forward so that the legs banged to the floor. "You told me my protection as a witness was guaranteed. So how come I get messages from Nuestra Familia associates with my breakfast and I get left alone, all fucking alone, in a shower with six guys who could've killed me right there?"

"I'll check on it. I'll make sure the staff is more careful."

"No. No. That's not it. I'm compromised here, man. I want you to get me out of here. I want you to move me to some other jail, I don't care where." His jaws pressed tightly. "Because I'm not saying one more thing for you unless I get protected like you promised."

"You can't be moved. That would delay the trial."

"Fucking Diaz isn't going anywhere. I'll nail him. I gave him the contract on Jaime Linares."

Massingill lowered his lanky body into a chair. He took out an unfiltered cigarette and since there were no ashtrays, cupped his left hand and tapped the rapidly accumulating ash into his palm, like he was taking holy communion. This is what I gave up everything for, he thought, so I could sit here and get yelled at by a hit man trying to go straight. No wife anymore, no kids, just a job that hangs on what this guy does in court. And he knows it.

"I could have sent one of my assistants over," Massingill said. "You know you've got some juice, Hector, when the U.S. Attorney for the whole Eastern District of California cares enough about you and the evidence you've been giving to come over here and listen. You wanted me and I came. You wanted to be housed out of state, and I did that for you. You get visiting privileges other protected witnesses in the joint don't even dream about. I mean," he tried a grin, "you've got to admit that I've given you a hell of a lot of service."

"And I'm giving you twenty, maybe more, NF members and associates."

"You've got to trust me. When I say you can't be moved, it's the truth. When I say you'll be protected, I'm telling you the plain truth."

"I can't testify." His arms, heavy in the pale blue shirt, folded across his chest. He blinked several times before staring at Massingill.

The ashes in Massingill's cupped hand were light, ephemeral, like the light-headedness he felt when he talked to Hector. There would be nothing if he didn't give in on this point. Molina was a rock. He knew what he had to bargain with and who he dealt with. What a deal I made, Massingill thought. He held his shortened cigarette in his lips as he tried to figure out the mechanics of moving a prisoner from the Sacramento County Jail at seven in the evening to another jail and then bringing him back in time for the Diaz trial over in federal court at ten in the morning. Special transport, special cells, restricting access to Molina, guards, the problems for handling this most-protected witness had to be subdued or there would be no testimony tomorrow. And after he finished testifying in this trial, move him gently back to prison in Nevada until the next case came up on the court calendar in Los Angeles or San Diego or Bakersfield or any of the dozen other places Molina could name names. Massingill exhaled slowly.

"How can I feel safe here?" Molina still watched him. "They send in a matchbook, they can shank me with a knife on the end of a long broom handle, they can throw something on me and light it, they can get me with a zip gun."

"All right." Massingill held up his hand to stop the recital. He ground out his cigarette on the edge of the metal table and put the pile of ashes neatly beside the butt. "I'll get you out. But, we can't keep doing this, Hector. You've got to trust me."

The arms unfolded and Molina smiled briefly. "Hey, Mr. Massingill, this is for you, too. You got seven convictions so far. You want the rest, okay. You keep me safe. You keep me guarded."

I was a conscientious objector during Vietnam and I graduated in the top five percent of my class at Boalt Hall, Massingill thought as Molina went on joking with him. I worked for some good pols and some bad ones before I got appointed United States Attorney and somehow it all added up that I'd be in a stuffy storage room in a jail with a guy who's coldbloodedly killed maybe fifteen people. And the weird part, the truly peculiar logic of this whole thing is that he's really trying to change his life. Maybe Swanson, that D.A. from Santa Maria County doesn't think so, always calling, complaining, saying he's got a case showing Molina's still dirty. What a monumental pain in the ass. The same D.A. who almost destroyed the complicated, delicate bargain made between the U.S. Attorney's office and no less than five other jurisdictions in California where Molina had committed murders.

I'm responsible for thirty-two counties in California, right up to the Oregon border, everything civil or criminal that the federal government might be interested in, Massingill thought. So one lone D.A. in one stupid county held out so he could prosecute some diddly grocery store shooting Molina did, and that was supposed to be worth losing the unbelievably valuable testimony only Molina could give. Every other county saw the wisdom in the bargain. You give up the murders in your county, we give Molina immunity and he testifies against the whole hierarchy of these prison gangs. Everybody benefits. But this D.A. Swanson wanted to keep his little homicide to himself and it almost, almost kept Molina from buying into the deal.

Molina ultimately did agree that one murder case hanging over him wasn't all that bad. It could be disposed of satisfactorily after he finished testifying in all the NF cases. The D.A. in Santa Maria County was bound to be more reasonable when he saw the gold Hector Molina had turned over in the form of hard convictions of gang leaders.

Massingill also thought something else. I've lived and worked with this guy for the last two years. He's trying to atone. He really is trying to change and I've chosen to help him and I can't back out now. He won't let me.

He stood again. Molina carefully flipped open the tablet. Massingill saw rows of elegantly curved black letters, curlicued and decorated, across the page. Molina picked up his pen and with several assertive, brisk strokes, made a capital M on the page.

"I'll do up a monogram for you, put it on your briefcase or shirts."

"No, thanks. The calligraphy's coming along."

"I got nothing better to do before I go on. I bring my pad and a couple of pens and I can sit back in the judge's chambers and do something."

As usual, he thought, Hector wins another round. Massingill was about to knock on the door to be let out when the knock came from the other side. Molina, he noticed, quickly put down the pen and watched the door.

"Okay," Massingill called out.

The door opened. One of the four deputies looked first at Molina oddly, then at him. "I need you for a minute, sir." He held the door for Massingill.

"Somebody'll clear your cell and move you in a couple of hours. Then you're back here at nine tomorrow. You finish your testimony." He gave Molina a thumbs up.

Molina nodded, still warily watching the door.

Stepping outside into the shiny, waxen corridor lit by harsh bulbs in little metal cages, Massingill was surrounded by the four deputies. They watched him deferentially. He listened to what one of them told him. All he said was, "Christ," in a distracted, angry whisper as the deputy talked. He absentmindedly took out another cigarette, rolling it between his thin, stained fingers without lighting it. He avoided looking at the deputies, seeing instead the main jail's flat hard walls, smelling its ripeness.

"Let me back in," he said finally, steeling himself as the door opened. This was bad. This was very bad.

Molina hadn't gone back to his tablet. He was just below one of the high, inaccessible windows, standing in an oblong of paling early evening light thrown on the floor. He faced the door.

Massingill stopped at the metal table. Hector's got to be more than the five seven on his rap sheet. He looks five nine. Christ. First the matchbook and the shower and now this.

In the slanting pillar of spring twilight, Molina's scars and years appeared to be merely transient corruptions. He looks like a teenager, Massingill thought, and I'm his old man now.

"I've got bad news and that's all there is to it," he said. "Your wife is dead."

Molina stepped immediately out of the light; his face pitted again and his features darkened as though age and corruption had been waiting to seize him. "What do you mean she's dead? What do you mean?"

"She was killed this morning, Hector. I just found out. She was shot."

"They got her. They found her."

It was impossible to bring news like that to another human being, no matter who it was, and not feel queasy at the ruthlessness of the words. Hector's going to fold up on me completely, Massingill thought. He won't say another word.

Molina didn't move for what seemed long minutes. Then suddenly, with a jerky trembling of his hands before his face, he began crying. It shocked Massingill because he had never thought of Molina shedding tears, particularly for someone he rarely spoke about. One trembling hand covered his eyes and he said something over and over again in Spanish.

"I'm sorry, Hector." Massingill couldn't think of any more to say.

The imploring Spanish went on, the hand pressed against his

face more tightly so that his fingertips whitened, and tears dripped down the sides of his mouth.

"I'm sorry," Massingill repeated. The deputies watched curiously from the open doorway. He motioned them away.

There was a deep, shuddering intake of breath from behind the hand still pressed to his eyes. Molina said bitterly, "Where did it happen? Where did she die?"

"In Santa Maria."

"That place. That's a jinx, I knew something'd happen to her there. I know Swanson's responsible. It's his fault, he made her come up there so he could get me, and she dies."

"I don't know who's responsible. It's too soon."

"Oh, we know. They were trying to get me. To make me stop. Swanson's fault because he made her go there and they got her." Molina brought his other hand up, wiped his eyes with his knuckles. "Cowards. Fucking cowards. They can't make me stop."

"I'll get the details as soon as possible. Is there anything I can do for you right now?"

Molina shook his head and turned slowly to the table, sitting down. He put his head on his arm as if he was about to go to sleep. This was the woman Swanson said was giving him so much about Molina, all the deals he was still doing, the takeover of a drug rehab project down there in Santa Maria, all so unbelievable. Hector can't feel very close to a woman who'd do that to him. If it wasn't so grim, Massingill thought it was almost comically theatrical. Hector does his grieving husband routine, he thought. But, no, this woman was his wife, mother of his only kid. Of course he would grieve. He's different from the way he was, that's what I keep telling the blockhead Swanson.

"I don't want anything," Molina said. "Just get me out."

Massingill said something more about the transfer and, feeling foolish and confused, said he was sorry once more. He went to the door and knocked sharply. It can't be so, he thought, Swanson can't be right. As he stepped out, he saw Molina sitting upright at the table, alone in the gray fading room as the disintegrating early evening twilight fell about him in indistinct pools.

CHAPTER FOUR

Di caught the phone before the second ring had died away. "What's going on, Mike? Where are you? I've been calling all over trying to find you for the last half hour. There are two policemen in the living room and a couple sitting outside. Your friend Dick Weyuker is here with me. What's happening?"

At the kitchen table she could see Detective Weyuker sitting uncomfortably. He had been looking at his watch every few minutes and clearing his throat nervously. Through the windows, framed with buttery yellow curtains, she saw squad cars outside on the street. On the table were the dinner plates, the food lying cold and forgotten.

Mike started speaking, but she was so confused, it was hard to understand him. And there was something in his voice. Fear? Tension? He spoke with an edgy directness she rarely heard from him.

"I've been trying to get through, hon, but the line's been busy."

"I was calling everybody. I tried your office, the county operator, the police department. Mike, what is going on? These men have just dropped out of nowhere."

"Take it easy. It's nothing we can't handle. I'm coming home real soon. There are a few things I've got to take care of first and the guys will stay with you until I get there."

"Do we just sit here?"

"No, no, put the kids in bed like usual. Do whatever the guys tell you. You might start packing simple stuff, toothbrushes, some clothes, nothing much, for overnight. For you, me, and the kids."

He was very tense, she thought. "Are we leaving tonight, Mike?"

"Probably," he said slowly, "go to a motel for the night. So, we just need the basics to tide us over."

"This is very serious, isn't it? Why can't you tell me now?"

"Not over the phone, hon," he said softly. "It's okay. Believe me. I'll get there just as fast as I can."

"You've scared me," she said. "I don't want to scare the kids."

"Hang on a little longer, that's all and then we'll be together. Can you put Dick on, please?"

"I'll see you soon," she whispered. "I love you."

Mike's voice sounded tighter than she had ever heard it, as though he had trouble sounding so casual and mundane. "You, too, Di. Always and forever."

She turned back and held the phone out for Weyuker. "Mike would like to talk to you."

Weyuker bounced from his chair and took the phone. She heard Matt laugh joyously and from upstairs came the heedless babbling of the television. Her breath was short and she felt as though some calamity had taken place, and the world had just shifted groaning on its axis.

"You made it all sound very enigmatic," Susan Utley said to Swanson as he hung up. Susan was his supervisor in Special Investigations, a tall woman, growing heavy, with a sharply pedantic and sarcastic manner so she often seemed more a strict school teacher than a senior deputy district attorney.

"I'm not going to tell her there's a hit team coming after me and the witnesses in one of my old murder cases." He sat down heavily in a high-backed colonial chair. "This has not been one of my better days."

Joe Gleason hobbled back into his living room, putting a glass of ginger ale by Susan and coffee by Swanson. The room was too starkly full of prop furniture—a dry sink, pewter all over, an ornamental butter churn—to be anything other than an idea of an eighteenth-century American living room. Since he and Helena had moved in six months ago, he poked fun at rattling around in a showroom. He was the District Attorney of Santa Maria County and had been so for almost sixteen years, a record matched only by Samson Wilhoite at the turn of the century. To Swanson he always looked like a dour cattle rancher, spare and rumpled, with white and gray hair and thick glasses. His right foot was bulky in a cast because he'd broken it two weeks before on an untried horse. He rode ahead of the mounted sheriff's deputies in every Fourth of July parade.

He picked up his third Seven and Seven, half finished, "What's Weyuker say?" he asked, his fury barely contained.

"The county jail's making arrangements now," Swanson sat forward in his chair. "They're going to clear cells in the basement and close it off."

"How about our people? How close are we to getting them in safely?"

"SMPD has squad cars out at the Tices' market and their home. They're both okay. Another's going to Rolly's place for him. I'm hoping he hasn't decided to take off again without telling me. That buttons up all the witnesses."

"Who's going to pick up the Tices?" Susan sipped from her ginger ale, crossing one leg. She was the iciest of them, Swanson realized, and maybe she could see more clearly. Both he and Joe were pestered by devils.

"I'm going to do that," he said. "I owe them that."

"What'll you tell them?" Gleason eased himself into an easy chair beside the fireplace, his leg stiff in front of him. The easy chair was a little soiled where his head had rested over the years.

It was obviously not part of the showroom. He brought out his cream-colored cigarette holder and resumed chainsmoking.

Swanson reached for his coffee and drank with a ragged breath. He put the cup down on a disorderly stack of different-sized papers roughly jammed into a file folder at his left. "I'll say that the man who killed their son is planning to kill them. I'll tell them two guys are coming to kill them, guys' names are Raymond Alves and Narcisso Rivera. One woman was killed this morning. I'll tell them Molina wants to make a clean sweep, the witnesses to his murder, and the guy who wants to prosecute him for it."

"Yeah, by God," Gleason said, "make sure they know this involves you."

"What estimate do you give them for how long they'll have to stay in protective custody?" Susan asked.

"I don't know. I'm going to tell them it'll be as short as I can humanly make it."

Swanson was with the only two people he could unequivocally trust in his office. The knowledge of a betrayer inside the D.A.'s office hurt more than the pain of losing a witness, or his own peril. It was hard to avoid becoming emotional.

"I got raps on everybody so far," Swanson said. "The two guys in the bucket and Alves and Rivera." He swung the heavy file onto his lap and dug into it, reading from a yellow teletype page. "So here are the players. Raymond Alves, d.o.b. 1957, he's got four a.k.a.s like Insane, Roy Avila, so on. Been to the joint twice, once off a voluntary that started as a murder one, second time for a two-forty-five. The victim ran away, I guess, so Raymond didn't get a chance for his second homicide. The weapon was a claw hammer. He's got a conspiracy to commit murder, dumped two years ago. No victim. And he's got a couple of felony assaults, no convictions."

"Where?" Gleason asked tersely.

"Kern County, L.A. I've got requests going down there for the files so we can get a better handle on this twerp. Rivera, Narcisso." Swanson slid one page behind the other. "You really want to hear about this guy?"

"Yes," Gleason muttered.

Swanson held one end of Rivera's yellow rap sheet and let the other drop to the floor. The whole criminal record was three feet long.

"I did that once at a bail hearing. It's a great trick," Susan said. "What are the highlights?"

He folded up the rap sheet. "Assault, an involuntary he went to trial on, car clouts, more assaults, robbery with armed and use allegations in Los Angeles. One arson. The key thing is that all four of these pukes were together at least once, up at Folsom. All four were gang members or associates. They dropped out, they ran with Molina."

Gleason deftly pinched off the lit end of his cigarette, tossing the butt into the fireplace. He glared at Swanson. "You're going to see Brother Massingill first thing tomorrow. You're going to shove this in his face," he said angrily, "and this time you make him give us his pride and joy. Putting our own people in jail? God. Can you imagine the smug, self-satisfied audacity of that little con, bribing his way into my office, trying to make us dance to his tune? Well, it's not going to be. I've got news for him."

"I'm going to take care of it, Joe," Swanson said. First I've got to make it through the agonies tonight, he thought, Di and the kids rushing into his thoughts. There was so much to do before he could go to them.

He put his notes, written in a hasty, scrabbling hand, from the Dufresne interrogation in front of him. He stood up. "I'm going through the chronology once, for old times. You mind? It helps me get this new stuff in place."

"Ancient history, Michael," Susan said. She squinted disapprovingly at his grass-stained shorts. "I hope you had a good time."

"I left too soon, I don't even know how the game came out." He stared cursorily at the first notes, reassured by the papers he had grabbed to bring over. After Max Dufresne's revelations, he had made calls around the state. He had enough now to answer most of Gleason's questions. Susan had started taking notes of her own with a slim gold pen in a slim brown pad.

"Okay." Swanson used his hands, as he always did in public, whether he was in front of a jury, or in a bar, or selling cars. "We go back two and a half years, August 16th. Molina comes to town to see his old gang pal Ralph Orepeza. Ralph's running a drug rehab thing called Make An Effort, Inc. He gets federal money, state, too. It's something like a 60-40 split. He's been head guy for a year, okay? Only the money doesn't go to the poor and helpless assholes, it goes to Molina. They ran together in L.A. in the Locos, one of the top ten gangs. Ralph did time at our good neighbor Folsom down the road, and on his way back home when he gets out, he likes it here and stays."

"I don't see him," Susan said. "Do him again."

A deep breath, a man formed out of statistics and charges. "Orepeza's like thirty-eight, nine. Fairly bright guy, got through most of high school in bits and pieces. Same basic story, early problem years, so forth, so on, then graduation from juvenile detention to hard time. The basic career criminal, lots of upward mobility. The big items on his résumé are a very, very bad two-eleven with a knife that got pled out as a grand theft person. Don't ask me why. Victim was cut to shit, a complete stranger, a tourist. Ralph does three years on that, gets out, gets busted for an eleven-three-fifty. Something like half a pound of coke, shades of his later career."

"I don't remember any other drug charges," Gleason said. "I remember he was a violent son of a bitch who studied real estate when he was in the joint."

"He got his realtor's license, that was off this second prison commitment," Swanson said.

"What do you mean, his later career? This is new?" Susan paused in her careful note taking.

"Yeah, all new. Just a second, I'll get into it."

"Half a pound of coke sounds like a lot more than personal use, Michael." Susan pointed her pen at him.

"It started off as a possession for sale, but the snitch didn't show up for the prelim. It got bargained out as simple possession, Orepeza goes back to the joint on that and he gets his ass violated on the grand theft person because he was still on parole. Total joint time is like five years, I guess."

"What happened to the snitch?" Gleason hadn't taken his eyes off Swanson. He gave the impression of heat rising, like a fire burning for years in a coal vein.

"What do you think?"

"Well, Joe," Susan said slowly, making a tiny, dark-blue doodle on her pad, "it doesn't require much wattage to guess what happened. Witnesses don't stay around these guys. I like to think most of these no-show witnesses just had something better to do."

"Okay," Gleason jerked his head at Swanson. "What else?"

"I've had the gang unit in L.A. red-tag all their cases on Orepeza," Swanson said, "but this is all they had on that one."

As Gleason was about to swear, Susan waved some of his thin, strandy smoke away. "Are we going to be in the way when Helena comes home?"

"People sitting around the house who don't want to talk to her, she's used to it. She's a politician's wife." Gleason lit another cigarette.

Swanson started off again. I like it, he thought, even now, I like being the center of attention. What a fool. He hastily poked through the file for something, found it, and said, "Here we go. So, Orepeza's gotten the tour, he ends up at Folsom on this last commitment and he runs into Hector Molina, asshole buddy from the good old days in east L.A. He hasn't seen Hector much, nobody has, Hector's inside most of the time. He leaves his wife," he paused, "he leaves Angie outside. But, Orepeza's heard a lot about his old bud, everybody has back home. Since he's been in, Hector's gotten tight with the NF, he's a big guy with the gang. Like numero four when he was really cooking. Very high up. He's the brains, too. And the muscle. They want guys hit, Molina does it, inside, when he gets out, anyplace. He doesn't get caught and he's nasty so everybody stays afraid."

Swanson held a hand up, pulled a half-torn legal-sized page

from the clutter. "Before I forget, I checked with Special Services over in the Department of Corrections right after I got away tonight. I wanted to check on Molina's status, see if Dufresne was jacking me around about everybody wanting Hector. Special Services says the contracts on Molina are still out and collectible. The NF wants him dead, the Mexican Mafia, and they get some blab that these hot dogs, the Texas Syndicate, are trying to be big guys saying they want him, too."

Gleason threw his ice cubes into the fireplace. "Who'd you talk to?"

"Hartsfield. I always talk to Hartsfield."

"He tell you where this intelligence comes from? Did he even give you which prison?"

Susan broke in. "Nobody in Special Services tells anybody anything about any of their snitches inside the joint, at least lately. I mean, Joe, we couldn't even get them to show me a file I swore to look at only in their office, as they watched, and I wouldn't write anything down, no notes. Nothing for a defense attorney to get."

Swanson agreed. "They won't give up any more. They wouldn't even do it for a court order, Hartsfield says. People would die. It's like they're in a fucking foreign country."

"All right, all right. I'm glad somebody else besides us wants the little bum dead." Gleason grinned fiercely. He turned peremptory. "Get to the meat."

Swanson nodded, taking a last, quick drink from his cooling coffee. He noticed a stuffed duck, supposedly transfixed in flight, hanging over Gleason. "The basic skinny is that Molina and his old bud Orepeza come to an understanding. Ralph gets out, he settles down and becomes very straight. It's great timing. Hector's no dummy, he sees the wind blowing and it's time for rehabilitation and group gropes and money. So Ralph Orepeza's got all these community contacts down south, and they got friends in Sacramento, blah, blah, blah. Ralph gets to head his own drug rehab project. He's got twenty-two patients or whatever they call them, on the books, staff of six, annual budget from the taxpayers of about $200,000."

He wondered, even as he heard himself, why prosecutors and cops so often start calling the worst defendants by their first names. There was a macabre bond, never to be admitted or even thought about, between them.

"What's cute," he said, gesturing for them, "is that Molina's doing all this while he's still carrying weight for the Nuestra Familia. See, he's freelancing, getting Orepeza set up, while he's supposed to be a company man all the way. The little gang he gets together, this is all really, really dangerous, going private."

"I assume he's greedy," Susan said.

"Sure he's greedy, but it's something else. Hartsfield says he thinks Molina had some kind of falling out with the top guys in the NF, something that would've gotten him burned good sooner or later. Molina started his own business so he'd have something when the roof fell in."

"He made it fall in," Gleason rumbled. "He went to the feds."

"I think that's backwards, Joe," Swanson said, not bothering to moderate his bluntness since he and Gleason had no need for courtly posturing. "Molina gets the bad word from the NF, maybe he sees he has no future. He's shrewd enough to start making arrangements. Hector went to the feds so he'd be protected from the NF."

Susan didn't look up. "And their price of admission was his testimony in gang cases."

"Sure. It's a very happy arrangement. Now what Orepeza is, he's Molina's banker. Like three-quarters of the rehab budget goes to an account at the Inland Valley Savings Bank in Manteca. The account's serviced by Orepeza, the Make An Effort, Inc. is padded with people who don't exist, stuff that wasn't ordered or delivered, it's pretty basic embezzlement. Ralph's using his real estate license, also acquired at taxpayer expense, to start dropping the money into two ethnic restaurants, one Thai, one Italian. He buys into a housing project. This is north of us, up around Yolo County, you get more for your money. We got the auditors in, they documented all this shit."

"Who gave Mr. Orepeza that community service award?" Susan raised her eyebrows at him.

He sighed. "The Downtown Santa Maria Business Association."

"Don't crap on them," Gleason said with a wry scowl. "I'm probably going hat in hand to them next year when I run again."

"Right now, we got Ralph on an embezzlement complaint. He's out and about on a $75,000 bond."

"What're you doing about him now?" Gleason demanded.

"Weyuker's making up an arrest warrant for him, conspiracy to commit murder. He'll call me here when it's ready, I'll check it out, we'll get a judge to sign it and authorize night service on Orepeza."

"Weyuker's got someone watching the house?"

Swanson nodded sharply. "He's got the place under surveillance so when Orepeza comes home, we can make sure he doesn't go anywhere until the warrant's ready. We could've used Dufresne's information to revoke his bail on the embezzlement, but a new charge is better."

Partly satisfied, Gleason held his cast tenderly, moving it nervously on the carpet.

Swanson felt a pang. "We got everything so far from Angie. She burned Molina good. We got good search warrants for Make An Effort, Orepeza's house, the bank records. She did a lot in a month, names of other guys Molina had working for him. We got two D.A.s watching them. She hurt Molina. She got to his banker."

"Now what's going on?" Susan asked him. "Tell me what we didn't know."

"Drink?" Gleason pointed at him.

"No. Nothing." Swanson sat down. He put aside the hurried notes on the steno pad because he knew how they fit. He closed his eyes. He grabbed his thumb. "Okay. Okay. One. Big secret Molina kept from Angie. He recruited fringies from the Aryan Brotherhood and the NF. I don't think he told the whole truth to anybody in his life. What kind of recruits? Same short timers like the NF, vicious little pukes, but the kind who'd mess up sooner or later and their own people would take care of. The guys who weren't going anyplace."

"How? What was the pitch?" Susan's voice came to him.

"You'll get rich, you'll be big guys with me, here's what I got in mind. Jesus. I wish I had that interview transcript." He wanted them to get some sense of the boasting, weeping, self-touting, bored waves that lashed over Max as he talked. But, even those memorialized emotions didn't begin to lend vitality to Molina's persuasive arguments. He came to Max and his cellmate Lester three times at Folsom, gently, then vigorously, with flattery and hard visions of wealth.

Swanson looked at Susan. "Molina had a terrific rep in the joint. Everybody, ABs, Black Guerilla Family, the whole crew, he's the tough guy, the smart guy. It's got to be a big charge when somebody like that says to you, hey, we can do things together."

"He's very selective? He chooses these targets carefully?" Susan asked.

"Nasty and then loyal, that's what he wants. He worked for eight months and he rounded up about ten guys. That's the whole thing. Between Angie and Max I can give Massingill almost all the names."

He closed his eyes again and grabbed a second finger. "Okay. Two. I ask Dufresne, 'Why the ABs? I mean, why didn't he stick with his own jerks if he wanted to set up a private thing?' Here's Max. 'It's crank,' he tells me, 'the NF isn't into crank. Aryan Brotherhood's got bikers outside, pals, people who run with them. So if you want to get into methamphetamine, you want real money, you go to the ABs who get you in with the bikers who cook the stuff and move it.'"

He heard Gleason shuffle, getting out of his chair. It was like he was talking to himself in the still room. "So I ask him, 'Why're motherfucking white racists going to work for Molina?' Here's Max again, 'They get help.' What help? 'Sometimes they want things to happen, they don't want it on their hands,' he's so colorful. Like what things, I ask. 'Like a hooker isn't paying out when she's supposed to, somebody needs a lesson, whatever.' Killing? Max says, 'Whatever they want. We take care of business.' "

"My God, he's doing dirty laundry for bikers." Gleason swore. Swanson looked at him, standing behind his chair, hands loose, ready to blow. His cold stare was fixed on a point just above the fireplace.

"Three." Swanson now held a small bunch of fingers tightly. "We're talking about a hell of a lot more money than Angie knew about. I did a little addition, Weyuker checks it out, and if it's straight, Molina's got Orepeza handling three, maybe four hundred thousand dollars a year. There've got to be other bank accounts and who knows what he's gotten that cash invested in. See why he went nuts when we arrested Orepeza on the embezzlement? We cut the money tree, no drug rehab scam, no biker dope. So he hits Angie to stop any more damage from her, end the possibility of a trial here. He hits the witnesses and me on the Tice killing so that isn't hanging over him anymore. He can go back to business, sitting in Massingill's lap."

"Mr. Orepeza is our prospective snitch on all these items?"

He closed the disarrayed file folder slowly. "This guy will bury Molina deep, deep down. He'll back up Dufresne. Molina gets the bum's rush out of the witness protection program."

"Michael," his supervisor said calmly, "we're now talking about a great deal more than one homicide. It might be fair to ask how far we want to go on the Tice case."

How far? Swanson had never asked that question in any case as long as the witnesses and evidence combined properly. His interest in Hector Molina's machinations while a federally protected witness extended only to getting him out of federal custody. It was the murder of Donny Tice, and now Angie, that mattered.

"We've got two homicides." He knew Susan posed the question largely to hear his reasons. "Both committed in this county, and we've got good evidence, tonight anyway, on both. We can make the Tice murder now. It's getting staler every month Molina doesn't stand trial. The Tices are an older couple, Edgar Rolly is a problem witness because he takes off. We've got to go as soon as possible."

"As far as I can see, most of this other crap doesn't involve this county," Gleason snapped, "but these two murders, yes they do. A kid in a grocery store? I'm going to prosecute that case and Mike's right. I don't care who's stacked up between us and that prosecution. We're going on it."

"Well, don't bark at me." Susan put away her neat pen and pad. "I'm only raising the issue now."

Gleason limped from behind the chair, his manner softened. He was awkward momentarily, "Mike, can I do anything for you and Diane? You need any kind of help?"

"Don't be shy if I can do something," Susan said.

She had been a prosecutor two years longer than him, a bright, acerbic woman whose cross-examination skills were always observed by younger deputies, like medical students raptly following the hands of a brilliant anatomist driving deftly into the heart of earthly existence on a dissection table. Susan had never married, and her semi-annual change of partners had ceased to be special office gossip. Swanson only thought of those impatient, unsatisfied relationships with sadness. He had seen Susan's delight with his kids. The woman who was merciless pursuing a hostile witness played for hours on the sofa with Meg.

"I appreciate it," he said. I'm too embarrassed and frightened to say anything else, he thought. "I want to find out who's passing information to Molina. I want to find out who took those badges and gave them to Orepeza. He handed them over to Max and Lester. There's an interesting little wrinkle here." He spoke bitterly to Gleason, standing stern and adamant near the fireplace.

"God, I'll bust a gut if I think about this." Gleason shook his head. "I know everyone in that office. Hired them all as I built the place up year by year. Now one of them's selling us out."

Susan tugged at Swanson's shorts. "What's interesting, Michael?"

"Max says, 'Yeah. We meet Ralph at this parking lot, blah, blah. He gives us the badges. He gives us her funny name, where she lives.' Max has this goofy way of showing he thinks something's unusual. He kind of laughs, but it's not a real good laugh. I ask him, 'What's that for?' He says, 'He was pissed, Ralph was pissed, he had to get the cunt's address himself.' 'Why?' Max asks him. 'Because,' Orepeza says, really pissed, 'his connection would only swipe these fucking badges. Couldn't even ask for something like Angie's new identity. The connection would go ape.' So, Orepeza had to do all the legwork himself, getting her identity." He looked at Susan. "The asshole in our office has some scruples. Makes you wonder."

"Perhaps Orepeza's spy didn't know Angie's new name and address."

"Dufresne was definite because it seemed weird. The connection couldn't even be asked about Angie's location."

"We're going to find that individual," Gleason said with brutal certainty. Swanson understood his raw sense of betrayal. Gleason had cajoled money from capricious and stingy politicians on the board of supervisors and made the D.A.'s staff bloom to three hundred people as the county itself swelled. From his fifth-floor office he could look out onto the palm-lined business district and the white, beached whale hulk of the county courthouse across the street. He looked down from his accomplishment with satisfaction.

Then he was fifty-eight and the years had passed and suddenly he found there was a worm inside the lovely thing he had built.

"And next year, I'm up at bat again and this is just the kind of thing that could do me in," Gleason said. "Spies in the D.A.'s office. Old Joe's losing his grip, isn't he, doesn't even know what's going on. And say, this guy Molina took over a drug program, didn't he? Killed a witness, too. What the hell is the D.A. doing?" He grimly pushed off from the chair, limping a few steps. "There are guys in the office waiting for me to fall. I know it." He swung to Swanson. "But don't you make any decisions in this case because you think it'd help me. I'm going to make it or

I'm going out because my deputies handled their cases the way they thought they should be handled. No politics."

"Word of honor, Joe," Swanson said, "I wouldn't do it."

There was, he admitted, less truth in his declaration than there seemed. He was willing to do a great deal for Gleason. "The first move's to make a list of anyone who knew Angie Cisneros was talking to me. The badges, anybody could've picked up. They're just down there in the office administrator's locker. Do we number them?"

Susan stared at her toes briefly. "We don't. We do have a record of investigators and deputies who turned them in."

"Lot of people keep their badges, they retire, new job. We haven't gone after them."

"It never mattered before," Gleason muttered.

Since Max had started talking, Swanson ran up mental lists of people who knew Angie was meeting with him. "Almost anybody could've known about her," he said. "Secretaries, whoever was on the switchboard, everybody in our unit, the gal in Victim-Witness downstairs. It's wide open."

"It isn't anybody. It's one person. One out of three hundred," Gleason contradicted him angrily. "And you keep that in mind."

"All right, Joe. I'll narrow it down."

Susan stood up, yawned once, and crossed her arms. "Once you get a list, we've got to march the usual suspects through Bobby." Bobby Norman was an investigator who used to be a police sergeant. He was the office's polygraph operator.

Swanson looked at his watch covertly. Had he only talked to Di twenty minutes ago? She was probably starting to pack because they were being driven from their home. No, don't think that way. Ice, like Susan, that was the only hope. Even Gleason's bitter anger only led to despair. Don't think about the Tices or Angie. Only the family mattered. His family.

He was startled by Gleason's next suggestion. "Mike, tomorrow you get a gun from Bobby or Weyuker. I want you to carry one from now on."

"I don't have a permit. I barely know how to shoot." He turned to Susan for support.

"Joe's right," she said. "I'd feel better."

"It's a precaution. I've never had a deputy shot and you will not, I repeat that emphatically, be the first of my lawyers who gets shot." Gleason winced slightly putting his weight on the cast. He often spoke with candid paternalism to Swanson. He had hired Swanson right out of law school and from the start treated him like a more seasoned deputy. It didn't hurt that Joe Gleason and Swanson's father had been fellow Kiwanians and acquaintances for twenty years.

Something else might have been behind Gleason's concern, he thought. Two inset bookcases bracketed the fireplace. They held few books. Gleason and Helena had moved from their old home when it came to feel too big for them after nearly thirty years.

The top shelves of one bookcase were filled. Photographs, some in frames, some simply stacked, some pinned to the sides of the bookcase, were all of Gleason's only son Alex, killed in Vietnam. The one time Swanson saw his chief's public mask drop was that year. Gleason, as usual, welcomed the new deputies at a group meeting. He wept by its end.

"Okay, I'll get a gun. Maybe it's a good idea," he said.

"Do it before you see Massingill tomorrow and read him the riot act. I want this little bastard back in Santa Maria."

I want to go home, Swanson thought, I want to get home where I belong so my family isn't surrounded by strangers.

But he still had obligations to fulfill before he saw Di again, and they made him resentful. At that instant he hated Gleason and Susan and the Tices, everybody who kept him away from his home.

The phone rang and Gleason went for it, hobbling along on his good and bad legs.

"Maybe Weyuker's got some word on Orepeza," Swanson said.

Ralph Orepeza wished his sister Elisa would be quiet. He wished she would be quiet and stop handling everything breakable in the airport gift shop.

"You're coming back to L.A. in a week," he said again. "You're not going away for ten years."

"Get away. You call me; you go, okay we're leaving now, right now, pack up, and I come along. So leave me alone if I want to look at things, okay?" She picked up a fragile glass sculpture of the Hollywood sign with such force Orepeza nearly groaned. He put his hand on hers and gently settled the glass piece back on its shelf.

"I would've given you time, really, baby. I just hear on the news that my two guys are caught, they've got this woman in the trunk, and it's time for me to go. I mean, they're coming for me right after they get my guys. I couldn't wait around."

She went for a glass ball with the skyline done inside of it. "All's I know is I wouldn't like a scary guy like Moonman coming after me."

"Put that down."

"Hey. You can afford it. You got money."

"Put it down. He's not coming after me. He won't know where I'm going. You don't know. Nobody does." Moonman was Hector's old gang name.

She didn't seem impressed. Like always, snotty, always acting like he was some kind of bug and she was a ballerina twirling around.

"You owe me," she said, "like for my time and trouble. Maybe I won't hear from you. You won't send me any money. I should take what I can get now."

Orepeza was at his imagination's limit. It started with the hurried departure from Santa Maria as soon as he realized that Max and Les were in custody and that soon Hector would begin thinking everybody was against him. That left the other two guys, Alves and Rivera, wandering around someplace, but they'd have to take care of themselves. If Hector still wanted them to waste some people, fine and good for him. But, he was getting away.

He'd seen it coming, ever since Angie showed up and started talking and he was arrested. It was only a question of time before Hector decided he would try to deal his way out and have him hit, too. Like he did Angie, like he wanted all those other people. Hector was ready to settle scores. He was getting anxious with his cash stopped.

"I'll write. I'll send you money," Orepeza said, taking her hand and leading her away. "Don't make people look at us."

She laughed out loud. "We're not even out of the fucking L.A. airport and you think people are watching you." In fact, he felt reasonably safe among the incurious, endless crowds rushing from gate to gate on the international side of the large airport. Nobody looked at anybody and the stream of people just went on. He was transparent, except when his sister started grabbing everything like she owned it.

Now it was over. The twice weekly runs to Carson City to see Hector, the meetings with the pig bikers who cooked the meth, the whole runaround with the drug project. No more dealing with Hector's pet snitch who gave out the word on what Angie was telling that D.A. Swanson. Orepeza wasn't sorry his time with Hector had come to such an abrupt end. And he did have enough money.

She didn't quiet down even when their flight was called, prancing ahead, making him cringe. She stood haughtily beside him as the guy at the Mexicana Airlines boarding gate checked their tickets.

"Two aisle seats for you and your wife, Mr. Fuentes," he said with a smile.

CHAPTER FIVE

Swanson and Weyuker, on their way to the Tices' house, drove in silence. It was past eight and night had fallen utterly over the city. The high-shadowed falseness of the streetlights on the stores along the street only made it obvious how dark it was everywhere.

"We missed him by an hour, maybe a little more. Wherever he's going, he didn't take much."

"The point is, we missed him. He's gone. All I've got left is good old Max sitting in the jug. This whole thing's gotten away from us, you know? It's not ours anymore. It's Molina's. He's calling the shots."

"I wouldn't look at it that way." Weyuker had turned the heat up too high and made the inside of the car clingingly hot. Swanson had taken off his old sport coat. "If those two chumps hadn't started fighting about where they were going to stop for lunch, they might have seen that stoplight and those cars. They'd have dumped the body in the river and we wouldn't know what was going on."

An hour or less and Orepeza was gone, irretrievably and irrevocably. Swanson knew there was no hope of finding him, barring something as farcical as two hit men getting into a tiff about which place to stop to eat. Poor old Max didn't notice he was headed right for cars waiting at a stoplight. Instead of getting rid of Angie's body in the inexorable current of the river, the trunk of their car had burst open like a jack-in-the-box, revealing her to everybody.

Two such accidents were not in the cards.

"How was everybody holding up?"

"Pretty good, all I could tell. You get a bunch of cops dropping in the middle of supper, and most people would've taken it poorly, but Diane was cool as a cucumber. Everybody's doing fine."

"I want to get back to them as soon as we can take care of this. I don't want to hang around."

Weyuker wiped his forehead and tried to lower the heat. It was a fairly new unmarked police car, but the miles had all been hard and things had a tendency to be unreliable. Even the Mobile Crime Computer bolted to the dashboard like an extravagant television spit back strange answers when a suspect's license or physical description was punched in. "I want to get home myself. The wife doesn't know anything." He glanced at Swanson again. "You want to do the talking?"

"I guess I better. It's my responsibility. They're my witnesses."

"I hate this part," Weyuker said, his eyes dead ahead on the street. "Sometimes you think the world's gone crazy. These folks lose their boy, they get held up, they don't know when or if the guy who did it is ever going to trial, and now they've got to go to jail because guys are coming here to kill them. *They've* got to go to jail. How long? We don't know. What about their business? We don't know. We don't know much of anything, I guess." He shook his head and whacked his open palm against the heater under the dashboard. "After all this time, nothing much bothers me, you know? Blood and guts, I don't care. Getting bored, wasting my time, I don't care, I'm still putting in my hours and still getting closer to retirement, you know?"

"Right."

"But what still gets to me, really gets under my skin, is feeling that everything's upside down, all topsy-turvy like now. Like we've done something really wrong trying to follow up a murder case. Like you messed up because you want to get a guy in custody. It's like it's all crazy."

Swanson watched the buildings pass by in the night. He had heard complaints like this from Weyuker fairly often. The Tice case first brought him into contact with Weyuker, who had a daughter almost ready for college and a wife named Sarah who seemed bored all the time.

He and Weyuker had nursed the case over all the unexpected chasms and delays in the legal system. They had followed similar careers, both rising to handle murder cases, he in the district attorney's office, Weyuker in the police department. When he moved on to Special Investigations they let him keep the Tice killing because nobody knew more about it or Molina. In their parallel advancement, Swanson saw much of himself in Weyuker. He didn't share Weyuker's vanity or edgy ambition, but they did look at the world in the same way, with one major difference.

Weyuker, as far as Swanson knew him, was a fallen idealist. Most people who look for justice eventually harden to its recurrent absence. Weyuker never had. He felt cheated that evidence frequently went bad, memories failed, and passion often meant more than right or wrong. There were stories over the years about Weyuker's tenacious attempts to make a case come back from the dead when everyone else was throwing dirt on it. Someplace in the back of his mind, Weyuker held onto an idea of real justice, a true symmetry of act and judgment.

After all their time together on this case, Swanson trusted Weyuker. It was hard not to. Swanson took people as they seemed, or as his experience expressed them to him. He gave up trying to fathom motives after his first felony trial, an argument about who should use the pump at a gas station. The victim was sprayed with gas and set afire. Swanson reckoned externals from that time on. He had no ability to read into the devices and desires of the human heart. It was one of the few lessons he took with him from his early churchgoing years.

What he and Weyuker shared was a stubborn optimism that the Tice case would be the bright exception. The killing was brutal and without mitigation. Molina was clearly guilty. Because they had worked so long together, were so alike in background, he knew Weyuker drew hope from his pursuit of Molina. In a shifting, uncertain world, it was simple and easy to hold onto. Even Molina's deal with the feds hadn't changed that.

Under the great shade trees along the street, the city smelled of lemon blossoms and honeysuckle, and the faint earthen richness of the rice fields just beyond the last house. There was fear in the midst of what he'd always taken for granted about his job because now everything was suddenly, terribly different.

"Swing by the market once, will you?" he said. "I'd like to get a look at things."

"It's all quiet."

"I just want to see it myself."

Weyuker turned left and picked up speed. Swanson decided, abruptly, that he would send Di and the kids away. As much as he wanted to hold them close, to shield them himself, they would be better away from the city and whatever was to come.

Tice's Market was glass-fronted with a few large paper signs declaring sales on pork and tissue and aluminum foil. The lights were on, but the front doors had their rusted grillwork pulled into place and the trays of ice in the windows that held meat and fish during the day were dully empty. It sat on the corner with a small park on one side and a senior citizens residence on the other. Swanson saw nobody on the sidewalk. An old woman with a shivering little dog walked slowly from the residence toward the park. She didn't even look at them as they drew up to the curb.

"One car over there?" Swanson pointed at the darkened squad car hidden in the deep well of shadow of trees several yards down the street.

"If our guys show up to look things over, we'll see them before they see us."

"I'm going to take a look." Swanson got out. He put his sport coat back on and noticed that the light sweat on his face had become oily and cold suddenly. Weyuker also got out and fell in alongside him as he went up to the market's grilled front door and squinted inside. So small, really. Nothing fancy or even interesting, three little aisles and half-full shelves, an old-fashioned freezer near the cash register that held the ice-cream bars most kids came for during long summer afternoons. A few magazines in the rack, all well thumbed, the windows grayish and faintly specked. Hard to see, but near the very rear, at the end of the last aisle, in a dark pool of its own shadow, was the storeroom and the place where Donny Tice had died.

It all started here, everything that brought them to this night and this fear. The reverberations of those gunshots were raging silently out of the past at him.

"Nobody home," Weyuker said.

"Nope. All dead and gone. Let's see what the guys have to say."

They walked down the sidewalk into the shadows. Two patrol cops sat in the car. One was writing, in a crabbed style, on his clipboard.

"Hi, fellas," Swanson said. He had his badge out, but they knew Weyuker. "How's it going?"

"Nothing. Real slow action around here. This is like a dead end." The cop at the driver's side had his elbow on the window. "It's looking like a very quiet night."

"Right," his partner said, chewing gum and writing.

"Maybe not." Weyuker looked at the street and houses, the garbled jollity of a television program hanging in the dusk. "Maybe you'll be the lucky ones. Maybe they'll come right by you."

"Right, sir." The cop finished his report, checked his watch and added the time to the top of the page. "I don't think we're going to see anybody but the little old ladies and the little old men."

"Take it easy." Swanson slapped the car roof as he turned away. He and Weyuker walked back to their car. The slightly damp, slightly chill spring night enfolded him. The city was Joe Gleason's responsibility and his. He knew what a prosecutor was after having been one for ten years. A prosecutor felt wrongs done to others as wrongs done to himself. He felt the pain of the Tices and their frustrated anger, as if they were his own. He had never met Donny Tice, knew him only from pictures and remembered good times and police reports, but he would track the killer of that boy forever as if that killer had struck at Matt or one of the girls.

He ached with fear for them. Yet it was still a spring night, indistinguishable from any other spring night, from the first night after he and Di were married while he was still in law school and she yearned to come back to Santa Maria.

"Dick, can you get me a gun, something I can carry without looking too obvious?"

Weyuker was at the car door. "Sure. What do you want?"

"I don't know. What do I want?"

"A .38 would probably do it for you. I didn't want to say anything, but I think it's a great idea. You don't have one at home?"

"Nope. We've got an old police baton behind the front door. That's it."

They both paused. Swanson said, "I never really thought I'd need anything else."

"A .38," Weyuker said confidently, "that'll do it. I'll see if I can't grab a decent one before we split up tonight."

"No, don't knock yourself out. Tomorrow's fine." The thought of the gun bothered him and he wanted to put it off. It wasn't going to be easy to explain to Di.

"Well, I guess we can't duck this anymore." Weyuker got into the car.

"Yeah, let's go," Swanson said as they moved away from the curb back up the street. The old woman stood solitary and motionless, at the edge of the empty park with her small shivering dog held tightly to her chest as they drove by.

Hannah Tice put her face against him, her arms around him. "What do we do, Michael? What do we do now?" She was only as tall as his shoulder so he could see the top of her head and the dandruff in the dark blond hair, smell the shampoo she last used. She wasn't crying, only pressing her face to him as though he could say something or do something and it would all change.

"It's only for a little while," he said softly. "We don't have enough men to protect you if you stay here. We just don't have enough men, that's all."

She raised her head, "I don't know what to do, I don't, I don't. Oh, my dear God, I don't know what's happening."

Swanson saw Frank Tice watching him with dislike. It was a mutual feeling. As much as he tried to feel even sympathy, there was some unbreakable hostility that came from Tice and stopped everything else. Tice was a man who looked as though he had been taller and then squashed, his figure rounded and roughened, his body squat and heavy. He had an underslung jaw which thrust out at the world. Weyuker was with him and they all stood in the tiny living room whose every light was on and whose open windows let in a faint breeze that ruffled the thin white curtains.

"So we're going to jail," Tice said loudly. "Isn't that fine? You can't think of anything better to do, you put us in jail."

"It's the safest place. Unless you left Santa Maria," Weyuker said. He looked utterly uncomfortable and kept glancing around the room.

"What about my market? Who runs my market? I'm supposed to close the market? I don't have the money. We don't even take vacations. I'll go belly up, doing what you're saying." He glared truculently at Swanson.

Swanson acutely knew how ludicrous the whole thing must look. He was tired and wearing his shorts and sport coat, as though he'd just stepped away from that soccer game. Tice had dropped a newspaper near his sofa, the paper draped and limp like the discarded wings of a great insect. Everything interrupted, caught in mid-breath.

Hannah went to him and smoothed her hair. "We don't have a choice, isn't that right, Mr. Weyuker? They're trying to help us, that's all. Just helping."

Tice remained rooted, ignoring her. "You tell me what I'm supposed to do, I lose my business now, okay? Is the county going to bail me out? How about this Massingill son of a bitch? He's going to bail me out?"

"Frank, I honestly think it'll only be a few days. You've got to face it, you're too exposed at the market. You're right out in the open."

"And I'm all alone, don't I know it." He squeezed his eyes shut and a clenched fist rose in the air. Hannah took it and stroked his arm.

Over the sofa was a landscape. A stone cat sat in a corner. They had nothing expensive. On the mantelpiece was one framed picture of Donny, taken when he was a junior in high school. A thin, shy face in a dark suit. He had never been captain of anything, won any awards, or achieved any particular success beyond being liked by his classmates and destined to work in the market or some other job like it.

"We wouldn't be in a regular cell," Hannah looked at him. "It wouldn't be like we were in jail for something we did."

Weyuker shook his head vigorously. "Not a bit. It's more like a hotel, the way we're getting it ready, and believe me, everybody's going to be standing around looking out for you."

"A hotel," Tice snorted.

"It doesn't sound so bad." Hannah had cried some time soon before they arrived. Swanson didn't know how these two people went on day after day as the days became years and the injustice done to them hung over everything they did.

"It's bad," Tice said loudly, taking her in his hands and shaking her. "They're putting us in jail because they can't even get the guy who killed Donny. That's what's happening to us now."

"It's my family, too," Swanson suddenly shouted. "We're all at risk, not just you. It's Edgar Rolly, and you, and my family. I know it's bad, and I wish to God there was another way to do it, but there isn't. Okay, Frank? There is no other way."

His outburst made Tice stop. He looked away from Hannah and a bewildered expression appeared on his face. "I guess that's right."

"My love," Hannah said, putting her arm around him, "we'll

get a good night's sleep and then we'll pack and spend a few days away. That's all."

Weyuker looked at Swanson and cleared his throat.

"I think you better pack tonight," Swanson said more calmly.

"Do we have to?"

"I think that's safest. I'm moving my family out tonight."

She nodded. "Yes, yes then that's what we must do. We'll pack a few things to make ourselves comfortable." She smiled slightly. Tice had not moved from her embrace and he was a much older man than he had been. "We'll have TV and newspapers and things like that."

"Sure, anything we can do, you name it," Weyuker said. He tried to grin.

"And I won't have to cook," Hannah announced brightly. "I'll have somebody else making all the lunches and dinners." She kissed Tice.

The market was a family business and she worked as hard at it as Tice did.

"Everybody's being so good to us," she said, taking Tice by the hand toward the bedroom. "They've done so much."

Tice held her hand tightly. He didn't look back at either Swanson or Weyuker. "I'm tired, Hannah," he said. "I want to go to bed early. I'm really so tired."

Chapter Six

"You're pooping out on us." Someone snatched Swanson's almost-empty vodka and tonic and waved it in the air for the waitress. "We got to cheer you up."

He tried to grab the glass. "No more. I've hit the line."

"The guy's been sitting here moping for a half hour," a woman at his right complained. She nudged him in the ribs. "Lighten up, Mike. Life goes on. You aren't the first guy who lost a witness."

Swanson had tried all the old tricks. He tried jokes and talking brashly fast, keeping up with the other deputies, cops, and assorted courthouse crew who filled the bar, along with the insurance and stock brokers from downtown offices. But it didn't work anymore. A loud, shrill crowd pressed against every table, which sat like islands in the bar. At one end of the bar, almost lost in the febrile chatter, a piano on a raised platform was banged for a melody.

The waitress appeared. "Again, Janey," said the guy who'd taken his glass, making a circular motion. "Swanson's turn to ante up." He put an arm around Mike.

The waitress, in her casino dealer's outfit, vanished into the noise and smoke.

He told himself that this wasn't really breaking his solemn vow to Di. He wasn't drinking, really, it was just the one, and he wasn't taking anything home with him. He was doing it all here, where it should be done.

"I hate snitches," the woman by him said, pushing some hair out of her eyes. "Working a snitch is such hard duty. They always make you feel nervous, don't they, because you never know when they're going to sit up there on the witness stand and go sideways. I had one, he snitched off his co-dee in a two-eleven, attempt one-eighty-seven. They shot an old man, hit him with the rifle butt, stole his wallet. Couldn't tell who did the shooting. Everything's peachy until trial. Then my snitch sits there and says, 'Yes, ma'am, I did it. I shot him.' I looked at him and I said, 'You told me differently, didn't you? Didn't you tell me something that was completely different?' And he says, 'I lied.' I lost the attempt murder."

"You got the robberies?" Swanson asked.

"Sure. Two armed robberies. Whoopee."

He looked around the little table, littered with glasses and napkins, bits of popcorn and matches. He knew everybody, and that was why he had fled here after seeing the Tices. It was why he couldn't go home, even though that was what he had been burning to do ever since Max revealed the deepest and most dangerous secret to him. Now Weyuker was hand holding the Tices and settling them into their cell in the jail and having a cop sit in Edgar Rolly's apartment until he showed up. Swanson closed his eyes, the noise soothing him, ending thought and emotion. He was safe here. He didn't have to think about Di and his own family. At least for a moment.

"Tell the graffiti story," someone said urgently to him. "That'll cheer you up."

He managed a smile. He could still fool them. He was Mike Swanson who treated the whole thing like a romp. He could drink with them, laugh, even tell them a little about the killing, but he couldn't admit them to the greatest secret, that there was an informer in the D.A.'s office, because it might be one of them.

For the first time, he was cut off from the renewing and revitalizing company of these other deputies.

"Okay," he tried it boisterously, "this is right after I got on Special Investigations. I got these gang cases, street gangs, the Hoovers, El Locos, that whole nine yards. And I found out they put these chicken scratches or hex marks or whatever you call them all over walls to mark their territories. They spray paint these squiggles everywhere with their marks and gang names, Crazy, Bad Man, Pygmy, it's one big joke." Everyone was listening, like they always had. "SMPD and everybody else was having a real hard time making any gang cases, you know, nobody would come forward, witnesses folded up, the whole drill.

"So the first thing on the unit, I got a briefing about these gang problems. And I found out these guys would call each other out, you know, challenge each other? They painted over someone else's chicken scratches, putting a big X through it. That meant you were dog meat. That's when I got the idea."

Swanson saw them waiting for the payoff, even the ones who had heard about this escapade before. My own guilty knowledge, he thought, I don't know who I'm talking to anymore.

"About a week later, I went out late at night to the area SMPD was having the most trouble. I had my trusty spray painter and I just did some dabbing here and there for about an hour. Nothing too fancy, just the usual big Xs and call outs."

Another woman asked, "So what happened?" taking a sip of her beer.

"Disastermundo," said one of the men, turning to see where their waitress was in the crowd.

"It got a little wild," Swanson admitted cheerfully. "For the next two weeks, SMPD got real busy. They picked up eight, nine of these little weenies trying to cut each other, shoot each other, set fire to cars, you name it. Everybody thought everybody else had called him out and they were going to avenge it. I took four cases to trial out of all that. Three of these weenies went to YA for sixteen months. The other one got locked in his room, I think."

"Juvie strikes again." There was appreciative laughter.

Just clowning, Swanson thought, nothing to it.

He rose.

"Big Mike, you can't leave before the drinks," the man said, still casting around the bar for their waitress. "This is your round anyway."

Swanson left money on the table. "Got to go home," he said. "I should've gone home a long time ago."

If he stayed, he would have another drink and couldn't afford it, now more than at any other time in his marriage. Across the room, near the piano, in a small space cleared away for a few jerking dancers, he saw a woman who waved at him. He turned and began working his way out of the bar, paying no attention to the various lawyers and cops who called to him.

He knew the woman, her name was Karen, and on a night superficially like this one a year ago, they had gone to her place. He had a vivid, guilty recollection of waking up in bed with her, both of them hung over and disappointed in the unforgiving morning. He didn't see her again. But there had been several others, a teacher like Di, a sad little aerospace public relations consultant who had just lost her job. They went to the Cabana Motel on the county border, along the same road that Angie had probably been driven that morning.

For a little while, he thought of it as a restless game, played after years of faithful marriage. The memory of those stolen nights embarrassed him and Di had never known about them.

It was after the Tice case began that he gradually, grudgingly, lost the engaging delusion that rules were temporarily suspended for him alone. There were no suspensions.

He had to get home.

The flashlight in his eyes made him squint and put his hand up. "I'm Mike Swanson," he said, trying to cut off the piercing light. "I live here."

The cop holding the flashlight lowered it. "Just checking,

sorry." He was a young guy with a barely visible moustache. Behind him, still in the squad car, Swanson saw his partner talking into his radio. The front door of the house opened.

"How's everything out here?" he asked. He actually sounded cold about it.

"Okay. We've got another car checking the neighborhood every ten, fifteen minutes. Nobody's come by here." The young cop shook his head. "Hell of a deal."

"Thanks. I appreciate what you're doing."

He was already headed up the walk to the front door. Another cop stood there. Two squad cars parked outside of his house, another patrolling the neighborhood, as if the brightly lit tennis courts at the park across the street were not filled with cursing, jumping players and kids on bikes didn't careen around the corner shouting after each other. Where am I? he thought.

He had put the walk in himself two years before, each stone cut laboriously during a hot summer. The house itself was set in the older heart of Santa Maria, where elms and oaks rose tranquilly along the street. Nine years he and Di lived there, their home braced on either side by restored Victorian eminences, painted, plastered, and embellished into a guilty modernity. Nine years of piecemeal restoration for them, a slow and random effort rather than the systematic demolition and resurrection around them. There was a deliberation in Di's way of doing things. Unless they had more kids, and neither of them thought that was a good idea, this was their home for all, and she felt they could afford to patch it, add a fence or garden, plant trees, or paint it a different color at leisure, taking delight from the tasks themselves, Matt helping him cut the stones for the walk. There were summer picnic dinners under the elm in the backyard near the playhouse he'd built first for Matt, but which Lizzie and Meg had appropriated.

That morning, he thought, in some wonderment, they'd talked about getting bids for an addition to their second-floor bedroom. Only that morning.

"How are you, Mr. Swanson?" asked the stooped, older cop

with sleepy eyes who greeted him as he came in the door. Swanson had never met him before.

"Okay, thanks. Where's my wife?"

"She's upstairs, the kids are upstairs. Roy and me are holding the fort down here." He pointed at the other cop sitting on the couch with a *National Geographic* open on his lap. Swanson recognized him from some cases back in Felonies or maybe only because he'd seen the guy playing charity football every year for the police league.

The older cop stood to one side and lowered his voice, "We've got your doors covered, nobody in or out."

"Tell your guys we're going to be leaving very soon," he said. "Probably about thirty minutes."

He sensed Di even before she touched him or the older cop reflected her coming down the stairs and into the living room. Her arms went around him in a silent, tight embrace. She kissed him and then let him go. He reached out after her hand.

"Come upstairs," she said.

He let her lead him, and turned to say, "We'll be ready soon, okay?"

"I've got it," said the cop.

There was a strange feeling in the room with these men in uniform, coffee cups on the end tables and even on a bookshelf, the walkie-talkie on the couch making grating, scratchy sounds. It was the scene of a party that had never started, leaving its trailings and nothing else.

Di had changed clothes from that afternoon. She was wearing jeans and a sweater and her brown hair had been combed straight down.

The upstairs hallway was dark, light slitting from under Matt's door. They only spoke again in their bedroom, the door closed.

"I'm not frightened," she said. "I was when you first called, but that was surprise mostly, having policemen show up." She laughed slightly.

He dropped his sport coat and went into the bathroom with

the half-crushed toothpaste tube and herbal shampoo on the glass shelf just below the medicine chest. He ran cold water into the sink.

"Now you've got to tell me," she said.

He looked at her. Behind her, on the neatly made bed, was a travel-worn suitcase laying open with clothes heaped into it.

He washed his face in the cold water and told her.

They sat on the bed, shoulders touching, the hard metal edge of the suitcase at his back.

"I've been telling everybody all day long that I knew what to do," he said, holding her hand, "but I don't."

"You're not Superman."

"People who trust me are dead. They're in jail. I've put you and the kids in jeopardy."

"We don't have time for self-pity," she said gently, "that's right, isn't it? There are things we have to do."

He looked at her. "Joe wants me to carry a gun."

"Then that's what you better do."

"I'll make it up to you."

"There isn't anything to make up. You did your job, you did all you could for the Tices. That part is over and done with, Mike. We've got other things to do now."

"I've got to find us a place for tonight, then sort it all out tomorrow."

She let go of his hand and began folding some of the shirts and underwear into the suitcase. "I made a reservation at the HoJo's. It was the easiest place to go."

It would do. The motel was set among other motels at a busy intersection of two freeways. Travelers were the commonest people, numberless and indistinguishable.

"I'm dead right now. Is this all that's left to pack, our stuff?" He pointed at the suitcase.

"The kids are all done. I put Lizzie and Meg to bed, so they're probably asleep, but Matty's been fussing around, so I think he's up." She stopped packing for a moment. "I prayed for us."

The usually unspoken, untouched part of their marriage, Di's belief and his lack of it. Twelve years together had not changed them at all in that respect. He kissed her. "Can't hurt," he said.

"We have to make a promise together, too," she said gravely. "I don't want the family separated. That gives this man, these people their victory. We've got to stay together, Mike."

"If it looks too dangerous . . ." he began.

"It's always going to be that way. I've thought about it. The men downstairs and Dick Weyuker convinced me. The worst danger for you and me and the kids is splitting us up."

He held her again. It was time to go. "I'll try, hon, I'll do everything I can."

"Superman," she said.

"I'll get the kids."

They were on their second drive through the large parking lot encircling the Howard Johnson's Motor Lodge. The orange-and-white building was always in view as they seemed trapped in its orbit.

"You're making me nervous," Di said, turning the wheel of the old VW van to round a sharp corner, "Stop now?"

"Stop, right now," Swanson said.

She brought the van to an abrupt halt near the opaline green swimming pool shining brightly against the darkness. Meg roused herself in the backseat and wanted to get out while Matt and Lizzie sat stonily silent.

"Okay, drive around once more and park," he said. He vaguely remembered something like this from the six or so stakeouts he had been on, but he wasn't sure if this was the right way to see if anyone had followed them to the motel.

"I don't think anybody came after us," she said, starting to drive slowly through the parking lot, "except that man I almost hit."

"He shouldn't have had his butt stuck out like that."

The drive hadn't been bad, Di had been direct and careful. No, the bad part was leaving the house, everybody holding hands, lights out, their suitcases awkwardly tugging them as they hurried to the VW with two cops in escort. Neighbors they knew up and down the street went on with their evenings, televisions blaring, people chatting over drinks, someone out in his driveway noisily fixing the outboard motor on his boat. The Swansons hurried from their home like furtive exiles, and nobody noticed at all.

The cops were going to stay in the house through the night, acting as though the family was still there.

Swanson registered at the main desk in the lobby, still and hard as a plastic tomb. Trucks went grinding and grating endlessly on the freeways in the night outside. Di held Meg's hand, a white little suitcase filled with two dolls and a coloring book in Meg's other hand, tiredly dragging on the rust-colored carpet.

"How many nights?" asked the clerk, a college kid who had never finished college. He had on a short-sleeved white shirt and was very tanned.

"I don't know right now. Maybe just tonight."

"If you stay over a week, we have some rates that might be better. Looks like you had a long trip."

"Pretty long," Swanson said, leading Di and the little procession away.

They met no other people in the feverishly lit place. Swanson and Di held each other, Di held Meg's hand, and Matt and Lizzie walked together. They went around corners, down stairs, through smoky cool corridors to their two rooms. Di took a key from him. "You stay with me tonight, Matty."

"Where we going?" he asked deliberately.

"No place tonight. We're all going to bed now."

He held his own small suitcase tightly. "I'd like to know what I'm doing."

Swanson kissed Di. They were reluctant to let go. "Sleep tight," she said. He waited until he heard the room door lock. The curtains were drawn already.

He took Meg and Lizzie into their room. Two double beds, night table, bureau with a glass top. Wearily, he tossed the key down and dropped his suitcase. Lizzie looked dubiously. "I'm not sleeping with Meg, am I?"

"Just for tonight, sweet, that's all. I don't want to argue about it."

"She kicks, Daddy," Lizzie complained, Meg darting into the bathroom with a laugh.

"That was only when she was little. It'll be okay for tonight." He took off his sneakers and supervised getting the girls into bed. Unfortunately Meg seemed revived by the trip and was giggling. "We on a vacation? We going to see Gramma?" she asked repeatedly. She was obviously overtired.

"No, it's not really a vacation, just settle down and go to sleep, I'll be right here. You sleep well." He turned out the light and went into the bathroom to change. Unpack in the morning, everything in the morning, Massingill and Molina, and everything else. God, it shouldn't be possible to feel this weary.

He stood for a moment in the darkness, barely making out Meg and Lizzie in their large, strange bed. Every night at home his routine was unvaried. He went to their room. First he heard light breathing, the sound of his children asleep. He closed the door, enclosing himself in their darkness. Meg and Lizzie's bedroom had a slightly cloying smell from the invisible, inexpungable bits of crackers, sour milk, cheese, and myriad other residues of their habitation. He would sit down slowly on the edge of their bunk bed, Lizzie asleep just above him.

In the reassuring, mystifying darkness at home, he thought he could see Meg. The covers were usually tangled about her legs as she lay on her stomach. Her face would have fallen off the pillow and she would sigh faintly with her mouth open. He sometimes touched her hair, fine and golden and straight, with wonder even after five years. His touch was always gentle.

He tucked Lizzie in, too, but she slept so lightly it was hard to keep from stirring her. Through the bright, flower-decorated curtains at the window came a splash of lemon light from the street, so faint that it only outlined in the softest, ancient light the toys carelessly discarded on the floor, the unused crib in one corner, a rocking horse's flared and battered mouth, all part of a primordial cave where the young were tended and protected.

He got into bed as quietly as he could. This was all different, the pillows doughy and sullen, the bed half-empty. Even though it was cool, the air conditioner still hummed its lulling tune.

He raised up on an elbow and gently lifted the phone receiver. He called Weyuker and told him where the family was.

Sometime in the night, with the trucks clanking and clashing, the bed underneath rigid and hard, Meg crawled under the covers with him. He had been half-dozing, half-dreaming violently, when her heavy, perplexing warmth slid next to him for comfort. He drew her closer. Not long afterward, he found out that Lizzie was right, Meg did kick.

Swanson let his hand touch the wall separating him from Di. She was that close and that far away.

Pray for us, he thought.

Across a hundred miles of sleeping landscape, Hector Molina had finally gotten to his temporary cell in a county correctional center outside of San Jose.

Molina sat on the edge of his bunk until the sounds of men milling about outside the door faded and he was certain the oblong slot in the door would not unexpectedly slide open. They had probably been told it was better for him to sleep. He got off the bunk and threw the sleeping pills the jail doctor had given him into the steel sink and ran the tap.

His eyes were rimmed, red and moist. Periodically he had wept for the last three hours. The chaplain at the jail he had been brought from found his distress so painful he offered to ride with Molina in the small gray federal marshal's bus to the new jail. Molina turned him down tearfully. The chaplain, anxious to do something, fished out his rosary beads and gave them to Molina.

During the tedious ride over the nighttime freeways, glowing with lights from the cars and cities they passed, Molina cried. Or he sat bewildered, holding the beads. When he cried he bent forward, his head hanging over his jail sneakers, and tears fell onto the unfeeling metal bus floor. He had two marshals with him and two riding in the front. The marshal on his left offered him a piece of gum. He could not even look at Molina. After they had driven for an hour, without any other words spoken among the three of them, the marshal said suddenly, "Sorry for what happened," in a too-bland voice.

"I can't stand this," Molina said, his head barely rising, moving from side to side in anguished bewilderment.

"Well, like the pastor said before we left, you got to try."

His companion, watching Molina with clinical discourtesy said, "He's faking."

"Shut up," came the terse command. "You haven't been around long enough to say that."

Molina raised his head. Tears washed freely down his face. He looked at the marshal sitting beside him, a paunchy older man. "Who would do this to her? My enemies, they'd do it. My enemies."

"Beats me. I ain't heard anything, but I'll tell you man to man, I think it stinks."

Since no one on the bus had any more information, Molina fell into silence. On occasion he cried again, but without much force. He clutched the rosary beads.

His cell, as he surveyed it with a knowledgeable eye, was meant for special prisoners, probably local judges or cops or prominent people who got picked up for drunk driving or other crimes and couldn't be put in with the regular jail population. It was a comparatively spacious cell as he paced it off from the bunk bed cemented to the mustard-colored wall to the steel-bowled toilet and sink on the opposite side. Sometime during the night, more often than usual, he assumed the slot at eye-level in the door would open to see if he had tried to hurt himself. Massingill would order such a watch.

There was about an hour left before lights out. Molina went to the bunk and carefully pulled off the heavy salmon-red blanket and bundled it into a ball. He took it to the toilet and lowered it in. Using his fingers he pushed the quickly sodden blanket farther and farther into the steel bowl until all of the water had been soaked up. He paused to roll up his sleeves and then reached in, picking up the heavy, dripping mass and dropping it into the sink, forcing the water out.

The toilet bowl was dry. He glanced up again to see if the door slot was closed. Probably no one would check for a while, until after lights out. He bent to the bowl, one ear to the hole that connected into the main water system. At first, he heard nothing. Then faintly, with a sepulchral echo, he heard the anonymous voices. Two, three, then four and five, like a party line. Some Spanish words came to him, but the rest was in English. It was the usual gripes about the canteen being lousy in this jail, somebody getting ripped off, a fierce pledge that a slight would be paid for in blood, some gossip, and something about a meeting the next day of homeboys in the Crips gang. That at least sounded interesting.

He was on his knees, hands on either side of the steel bowl, leaning and listening even when the light, high and protected in mesh overhead, went out. He stayed there for some time. You could never tell when the word might be passed. But there was nothing about any newcomer or a snitch being brought in. Nobody lay claim to the NF contract on him. He wasn't even there.

Molina got up, rubbing his stiff knees. In the darkness he laid out the wet blanket on the floor. He flushed the toilet to bring water back into the bowl and then undressed. His things, the books and tablets and papers, were neatly stacked for him at one end of the bunk. He put his folded shirt and pants on top of them. He held the bunched-up rosary beads.

Although it was hard to hear much of what was going on beyond this special cell when he lay down on the unyielding bunk, he made out, either in imagination or reality, the bopping radio music and dissonant singing riding over it elsewhere in the jail. It had been a weary day, court, then Massingill, then the chaplain, the bus ride. There was a great deal to worry about with no money coming in. Certain things had been set in motion to free him from old worries. The news of Angie's death meant some of the things had worked; he hoped the others would as well. His alliance with the bikers, and many of his own people, depended largely on a reliable flow of cash.

Lazily, he saw again why those alliances had to be made. He

recalled the moment when he knew his life was about to transform itself.

Gilbert Villagrana was the Nuestra General. It was just before lunch, a dusky late fall morning at San Quentin. The two of them stood in the shadow of a cell block, rising around them like the walls of a castle. Confinement was essentially a mental perspective, he learned, and Gilbert Villagrana thought of himself as the lord of a fortress rather than an inmate.

It was about a month before Molina was going to be released.

"We done big things," Gilbert Villagrana said, his hand patting Molina's shoulder lightly. "You want a reward, okay. You going to get one, you believe me. How about the whole Valley, north of Ventura, it's yours. You believe me? You got four captains now. They're your guys, you believe me. You going to do big things."

Molina knew the often-repeated question was rhetorical or an involuntary twitch. Gilbert Villagrana didn't want an answer. He was much older than Molina, in for life and rejected for parole eight times so far. On his cheeks he had tiny white whiskers, like frost thrown on him, and as the two of them walked slowly, Gilbert Villagrana rolled a little from side to side. He only had two toes on his right foot, the others having been lost to a shovel during his warrior days on a farm near Fresno.

A lesser man would have been flattered, fooled, by the apparent elevation Gilbert Villagrana offered. Molina was dismayed and bitter. He was a city fighter being given the rural part of California. It was not his expected promotion. It was a slap, cleverly concealed. He would have great trouble managing this territory and with four captains under his command, the entire Nuestra Familia would soon know he had been brought low. The word would pass quickly. He was to be disgraced and discredited.

He thanked Gilbert Villagrana for this generosity. Two NF soldiers idled close by, keeping watch. The shadowed strip by the cell block was deserted, though, the air redolent with a smoky haze.

Molina had done great things for Gilbert Villagrana. He was

the future of the NF, a marriage of its farm-country past and city promise. He took a ragged extortion gang inside maximum-security prisons and changed it into an organized, ruthless manager of privileges, drugs, and murder. His latest triumph had been the creation of the New Family. Gilbert Villagrana cackled over this as they slowly walked. All of the suspected traitors and weaklings were being forced into the New Family where they could be watched and eliminated. The Nuestra Familia would remain pure, dedicated.

Abruptly, Gilbert Villagrana stopped, said something obscene in Spanish to one of the soldiers, who grinned. He stepped to the cell block wall, back to Molina, and briefly urinated. Gilbert Villagrana's inability to hold his water when he was excited was widely known but never mentioned. Molina had seen his leader quickly relieve himself a dozen times during a tense meeting.

He concealed his anger and hatred for the Nuestra General, waiting coldly as the older man jiggled, zipped himself, and roll-walked, an arm going on Molina's shoulder.

"Someday, I'm not doing this anymore, you believe me. I get tired, I want to sit down, take it easy. That's what I'm going to do. Let the young motherfuckers run around. You believe me? You do it, Hector. You can have it. It's going to be yours, you believe me."

It was at that exact instant, the grinning, white-stubbled face genially drawn near his, that Molina knew certainly he was doomed. Gilbert Villagrana would never willingly release any of his power, as those who flew too close to him, or appeared ambitious, had discovered in their final gory moments.

He couldn't kill Gilbert Villagrana, who as Nuestra General was too powerful, and Molina reckoned that Galoz or Rubio or Hernandez would sooner kill him than the old man. Rivals and enemies were inevitable in a rise like his, Molina knew.

It was then that he began drawing malcontents, the restless ones, to him. He had no future in the Nuestra Familia, so he had to create his own. And he had to secure his future in some way, protect himself from the jealousy and ire of Gilbert Villagrana. That came later. . . .

He rolled the rosary beads in his hands. Angie. He would have to go to her funeral. It was important he insist on being there. He would tell Massingill.

Another memory stirred him. He thought with instant pleasure of the usual Wednesday night dessert at Deuel, thick dark brownies that had to be thoroughly chewed. He ate them first. Dessert was always eaten first and a little hastily from habit. Somebody might take it otherwise. He could get as many brownies as he wished. He felt a pang at their absence now. He genuinely grieved at the loss of those Deuel brownies.

CHAPTER SEVEN

"I've got two cases on the front burner. Both tough for different reasons."

"I may have to take one," Susan said.

Swanson leaned his head back. "First is Judge Haata and his trip to the alley two days ago. I've got the arresting officer and an almost-eighteen-year-old whorelette for witnesses. The cop followed the judge's car into the alley—"

"Why again?"

"High area of two-elevens and prostitutes. He thought it was either some kind of rip-off or something. We've got him seeing the whorelette get into the car, it's a big clunky old Lincoln, then go into the alley and park."

"Don't use that word, please."

"Whorelette?"

"That's the one. It makes her sound like a munchkin and I might drop it in court."

They were in Susan's office, a blue day burning through her windows on the third floor. She sat behind a heavy oak desk. There was a dirty large Bozo clown doll on the floor near her in a corner. He didn't know if it was evidence or an old toy.

"I haven't talked to her in person." he said. "Her name's Shalimar."

"Like the perfume?"

"I guess."

"Oh, God." Then quickly, "Is she black?"

He closed his eyes, trying to see the face sheet of the police report. "Nope. Female Caucasian. I talked to her yesterday morning about coming in today," he looked at his watch, "at nine. She says she knows what this is all about. I said, what? She says, the charges are pimping and pampering, right? I said, no. No pampering."

"My gosh."

"She's not worried about testifying against the judge. She didn't know who he was, but she's very, very worried about her toaster and her alarm clock."

"Her what?"

"When they busted her and the judge, she had this large bag, purse, whatever. It had her prized possessions in it."

"The toaster and clock?"

"That's it. She would like them back as soon as possible."

"Oh, my God."

"Real fast. The cop gets out of his car, comes up to this Lincoln parked in the alley. He shines his light into the front seat. He sees Judge Haata and Shalimar. His pants are open. She's working on him."

"He is such a disgusting little prick."

Swanson yawned involuntarily. "Anyway, we've got good observations. We've got a statement from Haata at the scene."

"Refresh me."

"Arresting officer gets his ID. Sees he's got a Superior Court judge with a hooker. We can say hooker, can't we?"

"Yes, don't be a wise guy."

"So the judge zips himself up. He says to the cop, 'I was just doing this for laughs.'"

"That's our boy."

"You know the best part about Shalimar, right?"

"Yes, yes, I do," Susan said. She looked at him. "You look pretty tired."

"Well, it wasn't one of the best nights I've ever had. Di's watching the kids. I'm hoping Massingill will make life easier for us all today."

Susan sighed and picked at the last of the glazed doughnuts that had been sitting in a paper plate on her desk. "I'll confess that I didn't sleep too well. Did I ever introduce you to Ed?"

"No. I don't think you did."

"Maybe he's too recent. Poor Ed had to hold my hand for half the night." She wouldn't look at him. "I don't think Ed's the domestic type."

"I appreciate the thought, Susan."

She took a deep breath, again solid and sarcastic. "What's the other hot one I've got to baby-sit for you?"

"The clerks at the muni court. I've got two that're very good prospects."

"How many in-custody cases did they release on their own?"

"The final count is two hundred and twenty-six."

"I don't believe it. I don't believe two clerks in the municipal court could sign release orders for in-custody felony defendants in that many cases without someone finding out."

"There were rumors, but they took a long time to percolate up to the right people. This is going to be as tense as Haata's case. He's claiming the cops set him up because they're after him for some rulings on police brutality cases."

"Oh, bullshit," she said. "If he wasn't such a greasy little jerk, Haata would've been one of our best sentencers. I always used to get the best sentences from him, the most time, conditions, everything you asked for."

"Well, that's what he's saying. He wants a trial. He won't plead to the six-forty-seven-b or anything else. He says he's going to expose this conspiracy. The other case, same thing. Very high visibility, a lot of attention. We'll look like dumbbells because it went on for so long."

"They're not our clerks. They're court clerks."

"I think it'll rub off, some. It's going to be a rough investigation."

"What's the motive for these releases? Do you have anything on that yet?"

"Well, I've got a preliminary idea. I got the printout yesterday for all the cases these two let go." He slid the computer listing of names of defendants and charges to Susan and sat back. She read very quickly, flipping the pages with growing impatience.

"Eleven-three-seven-seven, eleven-three-fifty, a few robberies, a car theft, now we're back to eleven-three-fifty-one. They're all drug cases, Michael. Every single one of these things is a drug case."

"So bribery is the obvious motive. I think that's the one that'll pan out." He gave her another list. "That's what I came up with this morning. Everybody I could think of around here who knew about Angie and what she was telling me."

Susan took it without reading it. "Well, while you're fiddling around with Mr. Massingill, Bobby and I will start checking through this." She had a small television on the far corner of her desk. In the late afternoons, alone, she watched reruns of Mary Tyler Moore and ate cheese crackers. "I'm not looking forward to this."

He looked at his watch again. "Last thing. We still can't find Rolly. I got Weyuker looking at a few places he hangs out, but Dick thinks Rolly'll show up at his apartment. We still got one cop there. Would you keep an eye on it? I better hit the road if I'm going to make Sacramento."

"All right, all right," and for the second time that morning and perhaps only the second time since he had known Susan, he saw her vulnerable and worried. "Tell Di hello, please. Tell her I'm thinking of you all."

At the door, as he was half in and half out, she said in her old way, "I don't want to be coy about it when she shows up. When is Shalimar's baby due?"

"About a month, she told me."

★　★　★

The nicest thing about the Kiels, Di thought, was their eagerness to be friendly. They were two of the most chatty old people she had ever met.

"I've been teaching for about seven years," Di said, "I took some time off when that one was born—" she pointed at Meg splashing water in the shallow edge of the Howard Johnson's swimming pool, "but I've done all of it. Except P.E. I've managed to avoid that."

"This is the most astounding coincidence. Mr. Kiel spent all those years as school superintendent in Columa. Now we come all this way and we end up sitting around a pool with a teacher."

"I teach at a private school."

"It's the profession," said Mr. Kiel, chewing slowly on what looked like a bread sandwich. "It doesn't change. A teacher is a teacher."

Di could see Matt and Lizzie and Meg in the pool. It was almost eleven in the morning and there was nobody else with them. She and the Kiels sat under a white-and-brown beach umbrella at one of the empty glass-topped tables. The Kiels were eating early.

"It was the worst possible thing," Mrs. Kiel was dry and brown and her hands moved gracefully, "for a vacation. Do you have vacations like that? The car gives up in a strange city, you don't know when it will be repaired, you don't know what to do. You can't travel. This has been very unsettling."

"We're on vacation ourselves." Although the lie was easy, it seemed rude. "Lizzie. Don't run. Walk around the pool."

"Very nice children," commented Mr. Kiel, a small crumb of moist bread falling from his mouth. A litter of tiny white crumbs covered the glass around his plate.

"Do you have any children?"

"We had one," said Mrs. Kiel.

"Our Andrew."

There was silence among them. Di had finally relaxed a little after Mike left. Breakfast with the kids had been difficult, but they were easier in the water. There was a peculiar cant to the morning, as though she was going to snap awake at any moment. We're all playing hooky, she thought. She had told the school that a stomach bug had gotten them all down.

"Andrew was also a district superintendent," said Mrs. Kiel with a thin, proud smile.

"One day he fell dead over his desk. Just fell over dead."

"How sad. I'm very sorry."

"You never think you're going to outlive your children. It never seems right." Mr. Kiel swept the crumbs into one hand and popped them slowly into his open mouth.

"We travel a great deal. We drive and fly."

"Around the world twice," said Mr. Kiel slowly.

Di felt a slow prickling begin down her neck. Meg was coughing a little, the trucks and cars were still driving all around them, the white concrete-aproned pool was safe. Yet there was this uncomfortable feeling, like ants on her, and it grew worse each moment.

"You're new in Santa Maria?"

"Well, yes. We've only been here a day and a half. Our car lost its transmission. In the middle of the freeway. It's a frightening thing."

"Gears."

"What?"

"Lost its gears. Can't shift anymore. Just grinds."

Di almost felt like squirming in her plastic chair.

"Is there something the matter?" Mrs. Kiel frowned and leaned toward her.

"Why? What do you mean?"

"You're staring. You were staring at Mr. Kiel."

Mr. Kiel smiled widely.

Two people sought her out at the pool. They made the overtures. They sat down and began talking, trying to be friendly, getting closer to her, asking where her husband was, how long they were staying, always questions, questions. Di turned away. The kids bobbed around in the blue-green water under the sun.

"I'm sorry. I was thinking."

"The hazard of teaching. Thinking too much. I believe it killed Andrew, so much thinking and worrying." Mr. Kiel spoke softly and slowly.

Di saw a man in a windbreaker come from the parking lot. He leaned over the chain-link fence around the pool and smoked a cigarette. Gradually his eyes came around to her. He was short, dark-haired, with a heavy moustache and he was smiling at her.

"Do you know who that is?" she asked quietly.

"We don't know anybody here," Mrs. Kiel said. "We're just waiting to hear from the garage."

"Mechanic."

"He's watching me."

"Is he?"

"I'm sure he's watching me," Di said, suddenly standing up. "I think we better go inside now." She shouted, "We're going back to our room. Now. Everybody out."

Lizzie protested and Matt ignored her. She strode to the pool, down the short steps into the shallow water, soaking her jeans. She had Meg by one arm. "Matt, Lizzie. Out now. I mean it."

The man was staring arrogantly, lazily, blowing rings of smoke. He was grinning at her.

"Would you like a dime?" Mr. Kiel said to Meg. He dug in his loose gray slacks.

"No, thank you, thank you. It was very nice." She hastily dried them all, got their sandals on. She herded them quickly out of the pool. "The best of luck. I hope you don't have any more trouble."

"Here's a quarter for you, little miss." Mr. Kiel held it out, holding it toward Meg's eager hand, which was instantly pulled away as Di tugged the children away with her. The coin fell to the concrete with a hollow tinkle and the man smoking at the fence finished his cigarette and dragged coils of plastic tubing and a vacuum to the water to start cleaning the pool.

CHAPTER EIGHT

Swanson found Claude Massingill talking to several FBI agents outside a courtroom on the fourth floor of the gray, blocky Federal Courthouse in Sacramento. Federal marshals, dressed in bright blue blazers that gave them an unexpected jaunty appearance, loitered in the vast corridor or guarded the closed double doors of other courtrooms.

"Molina had his wife killed yesterday," Swanson said. He and Massingill had argued about Molina for so long that greetings or courtesies had vanished.

"I don't think so."

"I got the guys he sent to kill her in custody. One's talking. Here's what he said." Swanson pushed a thick file at Massingill.

"This must be the famous transcript Joe called about." Massingill hefted the file without opening it.

"Police reports are there, too. I've got the gun. Molina's threatening the lives of witnesses in the Tice case. He's got your witness program turned inside out."

Massingill tucked the file under one thin arm. The FBI agents watched them. "What do you want me to do? Exactly."

Swanson was curt in return. "Turn him over to me."

One of the blue-blazered marshals tapped Swanson's shoulder. "Excuse me, would you step over here?"

"What for?"

"Just over here, please."

Swanson saw a second marshal coming toward him.

"What's the problem, Jack?" Massingill asked.

"I'm going to have to find out if this man is carrying a weapon," the marshal said.

"I am. I've got a .38 Special in my coat pocket," Swanson said irritably. He had been unnerved by it all morning as he drove to Sacramento. Weyuker gave him the gun with instructions on how to use it, but he had no confidence in his own ability to get the thing out, aim it, and hit whatever he was aiming at. The gun weighed oddly in his pocket. There was no holster for it. Swanson continually felt like he was off balance, always aware of the solid thing against his hip. Weyuker promised a better set-up, but this was all he could do on short notice. It was one more reminder that things were very wrong.

"Yes, sir, that's what I thought. I'm going to have to take charge of that weapon while you're in the building."

"You're carrying a gun, Mike? Since when?" Massingill was a little amused.

"Yesterday. When I found out that Molina's trying to have me killed. He's got someone in my office and he used my name to get Angie."

"Will you let me have the gun, please?" The marshal's wide hand was out, and he had come closer to Swanson.

"It's okay, Jack." Massingill waved him away. "This man's a deputy D.A. He's with me."

"I still have to take custody of that weapon."

"We'll leave." Then to Swanson, "Let's see what we can do, all right? We'll talk when we get outside."

Swanson saw alarm on Massingill's face. Claude didn't like talking about his best witness when other people were nearby. He was very proprietary about Molina's security.

Massingill said something quickly to the FBI agents and then walked with Swanson. "The guys are very careful. Since we started the gang cases everybody's gotten death threats. You didn't know? All the judges got them; I did. The judges get twenty-four-hour protection. I make do. I haven't needed a gun."

Massingill wasn't going to get a rise out of him this time, Swanson pledged to himself. "Joe Gleason thought it was a good idea," he said pointedly.

They passed through the first-floor lobby, crowded with milling people, like a great disaster had overtaken Sacramento. Men, women, children were everywhere, some collapsed on the few wooden benches, sitting on suitcases, babies rocking in their mother's biding arms. Some of the crowd, chattering in an agonizing welter of languages, was being drawn slowly into the white-lit void behind the doors of the Immigration and Naturalization main office.

Swanson pushed through the people, made ill at ease by the eyes that fastened on him.

They walked around the park that encircled the state capitol, a white plaster façade like an overgrown butter-creme cake decoration in the sunlight. Massingill stopped suddenly at a dark iron monument to Junipero Serra in a green copse of trees and ferns.

"Let me have him." Swanson faced Massingill. "Read the transcript. It's over, you can't use him anymore."

"Of course I'll read it." He had the file squeezed tightly under his arm, as if trying to press it into his side. "I'm not going to end an important series of trials based on what some yo-yos you pulled in are saying. First you came to me with information from his wife about this guy Orepeza. Orepeza wouldn't say anything. We couldn't make a link between him and Molina. You're still going to try him for embezzlement?"

"We've got an arrest warrant out. It's in the transcript there, one of the shooters makes the link."

Massingill grunted slightly. "Based on what? All you've got are some guys who would say anything to deal their way out. Mike, you and I both know Molina's got any number of folks who'd like to stop his testifying for us."

"I've got a dead witness and three people in protective custody."

"But is there more?" Massingill pressed. "Is there something else besides the word of this guy?" He moved his arm so the file shifted a little.

It was coming again, every old argument, every obstacle placed in his path when he told Massingill what Angie had seen and heard. The FBI was supposed to be investigating it all, but Massingill hadn't reported any progress in three weeks. Swanson agreed with Susan's view. The U.S. Attorney, she said, had bought a bad painting, a phony, and now either couldn't or wouldn't admit it because the damn thing had cost so much. He would insist on its genuineness.

The problem was more subtle, though, since Molina was a good witness.

"We're going to extradite him from Carson City," Swanson said to shock Massingill. "I'm going to get the records of his visitors in prison. You've been letting guys like the shooter have access to Molina and you wouldn't even tell me where he was."

Massingill's angular face became inscrutably empty. "That's a very sensitive piece of information. The location of a protected witness, especially this one, is supposed to be very secret. I'm wondering how you got that information."

"From Dufresne, one of the shooters. It's there. Check it out. He's got a great record, and you let him see Molina."

Massingill patted his shirt pocket, then inside his coat, and more urgently, his outer coat pockets, finally groping in one and bringing out a cigarette which he lit, his cupped hands shielding the guttering match, which he threw into the murky pool around Junipero Serra's corroding statue. As he did so, the file was kept tightly wedged against him. "That's an interesting item," he finally said.

"He's been dirty ever since he got into the program. He killed his best friend so you'd trust him."

"I think I've got a better fix on Hector than you do, Mike, with all respect." His eyes were baggy and small through the round glasses. His three-piece brown suit hung heavily on his thin frame and he expelled an acrid, nicotine smell like a bellows when he moved. He reminded Swanson of a big cricket. "When Hector went into the program, he was cut off. He wanted to see some old friends. That's only proper for a man living in another state, in strange surroundings, without any way for normal visitors to see him."

"These guys, they're ex-felons, for Christ sake. They work for him."

Massingill smiled a little. "A guy like Molina, what kind of friends do you think he'd have? We checked all of the names he gave us. This man Orepeza, of course he had a jacket. But he's a community leader now. Everybody seeing Hector is searched. They're not bringing him anything."

"They don't bring it in," Swanson said, "they take it *out*. He's running them. He's got your goddamn program as a shield and he's killing people."

"Mike, I'm frankly skeptical. I don't see any proof of a major criminal enterprise being run inside the witness protection program. Hector was devastated by what happened to his wife. I saw the man myself. Devastated."

"Are you going to let me have him?"

"I wish I could convince you of what Molina's done. He's testifying right now, today. He's doing something no one else has been able to do. Here we've got one of the founding fathers of the Nuestra Familia when it really got cranked up. When he was in Quentin, he helped write their goddamned constitution. Everybody in law enforcement who does gang prosecutions has read the damn thing with all the ways you can put out a contract, and the captains and lieutenants and regiments. Hector's going to give us Villagrana, the Nuestra General. He's giving us all the leaders. I'm telling you again, we're going to close down the NF as an effective prison gang in and out of the joint."

Massingill sucked on his cigarette and spoke forcefully. He believed it, absolutely.

"The hit on his wife isn't important enough? The Tice kid? Getting inside my office isn't important enough?" He didn't check his anger.

"Bring me credible witnesses, credible evidence, and I'll help you put Hector in the gas chamber. He's only got immunity for crimes committed before we made our arrangement."

Swanson brought himself back under control. "I've got a live snitch now, and my witnesses are still safe. I need him now."

"Let's try to be mutually supportive for once, Mike? Okay? Who does the most good here? You or me? I bet anybody who stands back and takes a look is going to say my trials. Three years, maximum. I'm finished then and we all get what we want."

"I can't keep my snitch and witnesses alive for three weeks."

"That's a little far out."

"You guys get threats," Swanson said. "My people get killed. You got to restrict who he sees, look at his mail, listen to his calls. You got to get a leash on this guy. Then you got to let me have him."

Massingill's thin, purplish lips clamped around another cigarette. "I'm not getting the message to you obviously. His wife lied. This guy," he let the file fall into his hand, "I'm sure he's lying. Hector's a man who's turned his whole life around. I don't have any illusions about him. He copped to killing twelve people, not counting yours. He's been to DVI and Folsom and Quentin. He's run with some of the worst East L.A. gangs, but he's changed."

"You don't even know what you're talking about."

Massingill ignored him. "The warden at DVI, he tells me Hector kept the peace there. They're very high on him at DVI. When there was trouble, guys getting shanked all over the place, guards shaking, Hector stepped in and made the peace and made it stick. You know how?"

"Jesus, I don't care."

"The warden's a dumb asshole. Molina was the peacemaker because he had every troublemaker hit. Cut their heads off. So ended the trouble."

"You're going to keep protecting him, no matter what."

"With a snitch, you either have a good twist or something else to use on him, don't you? In Hector's case, it's the contract the local NF made him fill on his best friend. You don't believe it made a difference. I do. Kind of a crisis of faith."

Swanson looked away, at the sidewalk of people with papers and briefcases, all the self-important parts of a state government. Massingill wouldn't help, even now. "It was a setup. Angie laid it out for you."

"A lot of innuendo from a bad marriage, Mike," Massingill said. "The substance is that he came to us right afterward, confessed, offered to give us the NF on a platter. And he's doing it."

"You still trust the son of a bitch." Swanson strode from the tree-darkened obscurity of the park, the white mass of the capitol rearing in front of him, the gun heavy in his coat.

"It's insulting," Bonita Hustis broke in again, making Bobby slap his hand down and Susan drop her pen slowly. "I've worked in this office for almost ten years and this is the first time I've been treated like this." Her mouth trembled and Susan was afraid she would cry.

"Bonny," she said pedantically, gesturing at the woman who sat corseted to the polygraph in Bobby Norman's small third-floor office, "I'm not accusing you of anything. This is an investigation. I've got to ask these questions of a lot of people."

Bobby stared disgustedly at the paper trail dripping from one end of the machine to the floor. He held it up like a dirty bandage. "Spoiled. Spoiled. She did it again."

"Every time you do that you make Bobby lose his place and he gets very angry and we have to start over again, so can we please just go ahead and you and I can take this up with Joe some other time?" She tried to soothe and reason, but her tone was caustic. Do I always sound like this, she thought with mild dismay.

Bonita tugged at her blouse collar with an unfettered hand. Her large bulk was squeezed uncomfortably into a rigid wooden chair. It had been, Susan guiltily admitted, funny to watch the cranky Victim-Witness coordinator get wound with electrical contacts in a constricting belt over her large bosom, taped with electrical leads to the fingers of one hand, and cuffed to measure her blood pressure on one flabby white arm. Bobby sat beside her, running the machine, its little lights and flicking needles scritching over the unwinding roll of paper as Susan asked prepared questions.

"I'm going to the Civil Service Board," Bonita cried. She fanned herself with one hand. Bobby had one of the dreadful windowless offices. The air in it sat like mattress ticking over them all.

"Well, that's your privilege, but we're going to finish this now," Susan said.

"This is harassment."

"Then, Bonny, I'm harassing people right after you, and I've harassed people before you came in today."

Bobby tore off the strip of paper from the polygraph. He had his sleeves rolled up and was sweating a little.

Susan began again. This was terrible. A morning with the eight-month pregnant whorelette who did talk more about her toaster and clock than about the judge. She was not going to be a good witness. Then these interviews which took an hour to do properly. It was painful to ask intimidating questions of people you worked with, even if you didn't like them, like Bonny Hustis, who was a piggish bore and barely competent. The final list from Mike had fourteen people on it. Any one of them could have betrayed Angie Cisneros. If there were positive answers in this airless room, then bank records, telephone records, whatever paper evidence could be found would be hauled in, sorted through. Joe didn't want a conviction so much as he wanted the source dried up.

Like metal spider's legs, the polygraph's recording needles moved unerringly over the paper as Bobby watched, marked each place, and checked the gauges. It would be so much simpler, Susan thought, to throw all fourteen into a lake and see who floated.

"All right," the questioner's rhythm slipped back into her voice. "Did you at any time in the last two weeks give any property of this office to anyone outside this office?"

"No. I did not. I resent that. I did not steal anything."

"Have you discussed any pending investigations with people outside this office in the last two weeks?"

"Like who? Like my neighbors? Like cops I know? Who?"

"Bonny, please, just give me a yes or no answer."

"Yes. I did. Is that what you wanted?"

Susan sighed. She would not say anything and prolong the interview. Perhaps a break after this one. She could get out and breathe again.

"Do you know a man named Hector Molina?"

"No. Never heard of him."

"Have you been paid any money or received any kinds of valuable consideration for information about investigations in this office?"

Bonita's screech of indignation made Bobby wince and look up. She made angry, gargling protests. He said to Susan, "Remember I told you that one's no good? It's two questions. You've got to break it up for me."

"I forgot," she said.

"First I'm a thief, then I'm some kind of . . . of?" the words decomposed into snorted excoriations. Bonita began tearing at the leads on her fingers, pulling at the cuff on her arm. She rose like a great balloon, taking the wires and the machine with her.

"Bonny," Susan said sharply, "Bonny, please, Bonny."

CHAPTER NINE

Molina saw the courtroom's heavy high doors open briefly and Massingill, crabbed over in a comic effort to be inconspicuous, come in and sink into a seat at the very back so that only the top of his head and the round-lensed glasses could be seen.

None of the jurors noticed him. Nor did any of the blue-blazered federal marshals who stood at the doorway and protectively beside the jury and by Molina's side in the witness stand. Their restless, bored, and always inquisitive eyes seemed to be looking anyplace other than where normal interest would cause a glance to linger.

The audience section of the high, baronial courtroom was crowded and marshals stood by each row. There were marshals near the table where the assistant U.S. Attorney and two FBI agents sat and the table alongside where Molina's own lawyer, plump, moist, and keen, listened intently to what his prize client said.

Apart from them, with a larger group of uniformed marshals, sat another lawyer, his woman assistant bringing papers and large files tied with brown string to him, and Diaz, whose restless hands had been handcuffed at the judge's direction when he stood up, shouting bloody revenge, and wildly pointed at Molina sitting on the witness stand. Every so often, the woman assistant would reach over and pat Diaz's arm as he stared at Molina, his mouth moving in constant, almost imperceptible curses.

Molina heard the assistant U.S. Attorney ask, "Was there a formal ceremony when you joined the Nuestra Familia at Deuel Vocational Institute?"

"I took an oath. The organization wasn't really all put together at that point in time, so they used an oath and things like that when you joined. I made them give it up later."

The assistant U.S. Attorney was sleek where Massingill was slender. His somber dark-blue suit was almost black. He wore a large class ring on one hand like a bishop. "How was this oath given to you?"

"In my cell. With two other guys, the one who sponsored me, who's now deceased, and the squad leader, that man there, Mr. Diaz." Molina barely raised his arm to point at Diaz. The woman held him soothingly.

"Tell us, Mr. Molina, what was the significance of that oath? What did it obligate you to do for the NF?"

"Anything I was ordered to do. If they said kill a warden, I killed a warden; if they said sell drugs, I sold drugs; if they said kill my best friend, I would kill my best friend. It was for your whole life, okay, the organization was everything."

"And you did some of those things?"

"Objection for vagueness," the attorney muttered, still moving one thick stack of papers from one file folder into another.

The judge smiled agreeably. "Yes, I sustain that."

Molina knew this routine well. It was a silly ritual, like the oath at Deuel, hollow and pointless. Everybody had games to play. Except him. He knew what mattered, what had to be done, even if it hurt sometimes.

The assistant U.S. Attorney needlessly returned the judge's smile. "Can you tell us why you would do whatever the gang told you to do, Mr. Molina?"

Molina answered first in an empty voice, which gained solidity as he spoke, growing slower in pace. The jury sat as though watching a play.

"First you do it because you believe in the organization. It is your family in the joint. It protects you. It gives you things. It's your mother, your father, sister, brother, everybody. Then you believe the oath means something, right? I stood in my cell just before lights out, I raised my hand. I don't even remember the whole thing, but it was things like, 'If I go forward, follow me. If I hesitate, push me. If they kill me, avenge me. If," he paused. He looked at Diaz with cold clarity. "If I am a traitor, kill me."

"The fear of death makes you work for the NF? Is that the answer?"

"Some, yes. You fill out an application before you join," Molina turned his heavy upper body to the jury, "and you list all your family and relatives on it. They make you give them pictures of your wife and your kids."

"Why is that?" The assistant U.S. Attorney tried to tuck his gut in a little as he stood up.

"If you don't follow orders, then you get killed. Or maybe it's your family. They know what everybody looks like and they've got people in the community who can do this. They can kill your wife." He hesitated, his acne-scarred face rigid.

He thought that would scare them. The judge said nobody was to mention Angie's death in front of the jury. Forbidden. He wanted to see what they'd do when it looked like he was getting close to saying it.

Alarmed, the assistant U.S. Attorney quickly asked, "Now, Mr. Molina you did carry out one of those crimes yourself, didn't you? I'm referring to the murder of Aurelio Archuletta. Was that your contract killing?"

"Your honor," Diaz's lawyer pushed aside his library of files and papers, "I will object to the exploration of this man's extensive criminal background because it is irrelevant. There is no suggestion that this murder is connected in any way to Mr. Diaz."

"It's foundational, your honor. It goes directly to the heart of this witness's participation in the crimes for which the defendant is on trial."

From his seat Diaz swore out a quick flurry of oaths in Spanish, hard, hot like molten bubbles.

"You be silent, sir, you be quiet," ordered the judge in a rare burst of directness.

Molina watched and listened, stopping once to blow his nose in a white handkerchief taken from the stiffly pressed pocket of his black suit, when they went on. He couldn't see Massingill's hooded eyes on him at the back of the crowded courtroom. All he knew was that this scene had been repeated in every previous trial. It would be done over and over again in all the trials to follow, like a mediocre play doomed to be staged night after night.

"Did you know this man you were ordered to kill, Aurelio Archuletta?" asked the sleek assistant U.S. Attorney.

"Yes I did."

"Did you know why you were to kill him? Did you know the reason?"

"It was explained to me that he was disloyal, he was making drug deals on his own."

"Did you know him well?"

"He was my best friend. We were kids together."

Memory could never be taken away in a strip search, no matter how thorough, and no device, however cleverly contrived, could probe into its hidden compartments. It stayed with you, vivid and inexhaustible and immanent.

Molina had never disciplined his memory as he had every other part of his life. It fed him over the years in prison.

He remembered that night. It was fresh each time he told as much of it as he wanted to. He remembered Angie and Flaco.

Flaco Archuletta, his long skinny arms drawing first around Angie, then lifting little Cecilia over his head so she hung there, squealing happily, kicking her short legs rapidly, was happier than Molina had seen him in a long time.

"I should have married you," Flaco said to Angie, as he put the child down, "instead of letting you meet this guy." He grabbed Molina, the jumpy thin arms pulling him closer. "Look at him. How could you marry this guy instead of me?"

"Don't blame me," Angie said. "It was a long time ago." She was smoking again and there was a pinkish flush on her cheeks. She wouldn't look at him. She had started doing that, holding the kid to her, keeping the kid away from him.

"We're not having dinner here," Molina said, as Flaco let go and threw himself onto the stained sofa. Cecilia ran over and began grabbing at his skinny legs. Molina had never known anyone as skinny, even before he started using crank.

"No, no, come on, Moonman, I want a real dinner, not some cheap shit stuff." He fended off the little girl's charges at his legs. Both the radio and television were running, sounding antiphonal responses as the commercials played against each other, thudding music dancing over huckstering voices.

Flaco used Molina's gang name, Moonman, given to him because he always seemed to be in outer space, thinking more than the others.

"I'm buying dinner." Molina glanced at Angie who lunged and seized Cecilia, hoisting her up, the kid squalling suddenly in frustration.

"Hey, hey, a party, right? You're a good guy, Moonman, that's just what I need," and Flaco's skinny arms were about him again. "Angie, we'll have a party," and he whistled and clapped his hands.

"She can't come. She's got to watch the kid," Molina said, already going for his worn denim jacket.

Flaco groaned and stroked the kid's small arm to stop her from making so much noise. "You can't come? I've been in the joint one hundred eighty fucking days, no good time, and I want to see you guys, and you can't come to a little party?"

"He says I can't," she answered, swaying a little with the kid. Maybe Flaco heard the wary bitterness. Maybe he even saw the way she looked at him, like he was some kind of prowler, an intruder in his own house. Molina laughed at that one. His own house.

"Let her come," Flaco said.

"Just us, nobody else tonight, man," he made his voice jovial, with the same conspiratorial bounce Flaco would know after their years in the gang.

"Okay, man, we'll go alone, but I wish you were along. I should've married you. I was an asshole for getting you two together." He bent swiftly to Angie's flushed cheek and pressed his sharp face to hers. He pinched Cecilia's leg and kissed her. "I see you later, honey," he cooed.

"When you guys coming back?" Angie stood in the dull, rubbed-smooth living room, the kid's head on her shoulder, the kid silently watching the two men.

Flaco must have been deaf if he didn't hear that. She was getting to be such a pain.

He put his hand behind Flaco's bony neck and held it closely. "This guy's getting a great big dinner, so we won't be back, don't worry about it."

"I just like to know when you're coming back," she said stubbornly.

"We'll be here when we're here, okay? Don't worry about it." He half-pulled Flaco to the door. "We got to jam now."

Flaco blew her a kiss. Molina was through the door and into the loud, indistinct hallway. He didn't look back but heard the door slam with bitter force. He hated that apartment and its fading, used furniture, the kitchen crushed into the small living room, the bedroom a dark little box whose only window looked out onto the upper floor of a parking lot. Her father, the barber, paid the rent out of consideration, he said scornfully and bitterly, for his daughter and granddaughter. She was married to a man who could not get a job and who spent his years in jail instead of taking care of his family. It was no life. If he, the brave barber father, didn't pay the rent, the child and his daughter would be on welfare, on the street.

That was the gall Molina had to taste every day with Angie.

He strode down the dim hallway with Flaco babbling beside him. His father-in-law did not grasp that he was a powerful man, whose word mattered in places where life and death were measured entirely in how much power you could command. Someday soon there would come a reckoning between them.

They were out on the street. It was a warm, engulfing night, kids running along the sidewalk chasing each other, cars being fixed in front of grimy buildings blasted yellow by the street lights. Over all, over everything, was the tinny aggressive music from radios in open windows and propped up on fenders.

"We'll use your car," he said to Flaco.

"I got this dink P.O. this time," Flaco said, speaking in that half-gurgling sputter he used when excited, "who grabs me yesterday when I get out and says he's going to watch me every second and bust my ass, violate me. He's going to violate me if I snatch a car, violate me if I do crank, he really liked saying that." They stopped at a new Cutlass. Flaco opened the door and Molina saw that the car was hot-wired. "I got this a couple hours ago on Crenshaw," he said, slipping behind the wheel with pleasure and bouncing up and down a little on the springy seats.

"When you going to get rid of it?" Molina asked as the car grunted to life and jerked into the street, Flaco's pinwheeling arms cranking the wheel.

"Tomorrow. I don't know. I got this guy who'll give me a couple hundred for anything this year, last year's model."

They sped through alternating strips of fierce yellow street-light and blackness, past snaggly buildings whose partly lit windows were like badly preserved teeth. He told Flaco he had no money for the celebration dinner.

"Moonman," Flaco said with chagrin, "what're we doing?"

"We get some," he said.

They drove to Union Station, around which Los Angeles had surged and receded, leaving city government buildings, high offices, and grim hotels and bars and warehouses. Like the old days, Flaco said, up high again, his hands inside the pockets of

the light jacket which flapped around him, Molina and Flaco
going to the bank, whichever bank they happened to spot first.

"You still got Peewee?" Molina asked as they stood searching
the faces and bodies that sluggishly moved past them in the
apricot-colored cavern of the great old train station.

"I never lost him. I go in, I hide him. I never get rid of this
guy." Flaco still had his little .22.

Molina saw him first, an older dude with a too-heavy suitcase that he had to drag along the shiny floor. He and Flaco fell
in behind him. They were following so closely they could hear
the sighs and weary moans as the stooped man pulled the frayed
handle of the suitcase with both hands.

The three of them groaned and plodded their way outside to
the palm courtyard where the train station flowed into the
street and became part of the city. The old guy stopped, put a
shaky hand to his forehead and they heard him gargle and spit.
He sighed deeply and clenched and unclenched his hands. He
straightened up a little, suddenly more alert about where he was
going. There was no one else in the spacious courtyard behind
the station. The only sounds came from the throaty rumblings
of buses idling a few yards away, and the muted announcements
from inside the station that wafted out like urgent promises.

Flaco was in front of the old man, a sloppy grin on his sharp
face, his hand drawing out the little gun.

Molina was behind the old man, who from instinct already
reached down to clutch the heavy suitcase that weighted him to
this place and made escape impossible.

"Give me your wallet," Flaco demanded, reaching forward,
his skinny arms jiggling a little. He pushed the gun into the old
man's face, almost into his eye.

The old man didn't really speak. Molina only heard incoher-
ent grunts, high-pitched like he was jumping from sharp
thumbtacks. His shaking hands fumbled into his brown suit,
past a heavy shapeless sweater.

"Come on, come on." Molina poked his fist impatiently into
the old man's back.

The wallet, large, black, and without any contours, held together by two thick rubber bands, was fumbled out to Flaco. Molina instead reached around and grabbed it. The surprise momentarily made the old man turn slightly, his phlegm-colored eyes widened. Flaco squeaked joyously and swung his arm in a wide arc, bringing it against the old man's head. The gun hit him. Still half-turning in surprise, the rhythmic grunts caught in one sustained groan, the old man tottered over, fell onto his suitcase, both of them tangled together on the pavement. His mouth was wide open.

Flaco and Molina ran. They scampered past the great bovine shapes of the waiting buses to the Cutlass parked a half block away. Their breath heaved in unison. When they scrambled into the car, Flaco pounded the steering wheel.

"We're a team," he yelled out, the car merged swiftly into the nighttime traffic, lost to view in a few seconds. "Moonman does it again," he yelled hoarsely, and praised Molina in a mixture of eager Spanish and English.

Molina quickly snapped off the rubber bands, and from the inner pocket of the wallet pulled out nearly forty dollars. He gave a short cry of triumph.

They ate contentedly at a restaurant far from downtown Los Angeles, close to the great winding highway that clings to the coast of California. Molina bought drinks for Flaco and they talked about old times in the neighborhood. More drinks, beers with them for Flaco. He was sad, he told Molina, to see bad feelings between Hector and Angie. He worried about them, thought about them and the kid, almost every day he was in county jail. Almost in tears, he said he loved them all, loved the kid like she was his own. After all, she might have been his if things had been a little different. More drinks for Flaco.

He flirted with their waitress, and Molina joined in a little for appearances. She didn't seem to like Flaco, but as he drank, she grew warmer. A small mariachi band banged and clanged staccato bursts of singing and music like metal pieces in the air.

By the time they left, Flaco had made a date to get together with the waitress when she got off at two a.m. He was not even going to do any meth, he told Molina, the night was too good all by itself.

Hector drove. For every beer and whatever else Flaco had, Hector barely sipped something of his own. He seemed, though, to be nearly as loopy as Flaco.

He drove them farther west, down to the Pacific Coast Highway and turned, heading along the rim of the land with the ocean, featureless and immense, lying forever beside them. Flaco sang most of the time, hanging his silly, happy face out of the window to let the warm salty air rush by it in the darkness. He didn't seem to mind that Hector said almost nothing now.

"You know, man, your name is bad even in the county. Guys in there heard about you, they had friends up at DVI or some-place, I said you and I were," he pressed his palms together, "like that and, man, I had it good." He laughed loudly. "Man, you scare them." Flaco laughed again.

Cities, indistinguishable and continuous, lined the highway and the oceanfront. White and green neons, bars repeated end-lessly. Because it was so warm a night, the sidewalks were busy and traffic heavy.

Molina drove them all the way to Manhattan Beach and parked along a stretch of beach closed to the public. Even though he couldn't swim, Flaco had an affection for the ocean. Ever since they were little, runty Flaco Archuletta had rhap-sodized to his best friend Hector Molina about the sea and its romantic violence.

The sea rushed against a sorrel-colored beach, bounded by brown heights. There was no one around, only the highway and the indifferent cars going someplace else.

"This is beautiful." Flaco jumped onto the sand, teetering in it, his arms spread open. "This is where we should live, you know, right down here, right at the edge. You go swimming, you lie on the beach, you got women when you want, you roll over and you fuck, you have a beer, whatever you want." They walked down a sandy embankment, under wire, and onto the beach itself. Across the water, lying almost invisibly, was the black mass of an oil tanker. There were no lights anywhere.

Molina sat down. He sounded like he was very drunk and very tired, his limbs boneless. Flaco talked about the first girl they shared, the year they dropped out of high school. That was Flaco. He always missed the big things because he spent so much time on the little ones. Like now. "Sometimes, you know, I think about her." Flaco grinned. "I mean, she wasn't so great, okay? Am I bullshitting? She had great little tits, but she wasn't so great. I just think about her, that summer. We had a lot of fun, man," and he fell back to the sand. He looked like an aquatic creature, beached and dried.

"You know I'd do anything for you, you know that?" Molina said, his words slightly slurred, his arms around his knees. "That's how much I trust you. Trust you more than any guy, anybody." He gave it a summary nod of profundity.

"You can't trust too many guys. I don't know anybody as long as you, Moonman, so I don't trust anybody else. I don't. You ask, check it out. I'm not bullshitting."

Molina tapped Flaco's arm. "You got Peewee?"

The gun lay in Flaco's small hand, black and inert.

"Point it at me," Molina said.

"Huh?"

The slurred voice was insistent. "Show you how much I trust you. Point it at me, right here," he pushed his chest out slightly.

Flaco gave a nervous giggle. "Bang," he said, curling his lips together. Giggling, he put the gun back in his pocket.

"Give it to me," Molina said.

"Okay, okay," and the black inert little object passed from hand to hand. But for the occasional sounds of the phantom cars on the highway, and lights from a slow-moving boat out on the otherwise dark ocean, they were alone. They might have been the only people on earth.

Molina could dimly make out Flaco's face. The sand was surprisingly cold beneath him.

"I get it," Flaco said with a rolling grin, his head wiggling. "Take your best shot, man." He pressed his eyes closed very tightly, the grin broadening.

Molina brought the small gun up to Flaco's right eye and pulled the trigger.

There was hardly any movement, a slight recoil in his hand. A tiny sound, instantly lost. As though weary, Flaco's body pitched over on its side, his head pointed toward the edge of the water where small curdled waves rolled and vanished.

For some time, Molina sat beside the body, the gun still in his hand, which lay lifelessly on the sand. He shook his head as if trying to clear it and then stood. From the distance came a bell at sea, dismally, dispiritedly clanging.

Molina walked the few yards to the edge of the water and then into the cold ocean up to his knees. The gun trailed under the water, when suddenly, with ferocious violence, he hurled it away, a small black thing arcing parabolically into the night, disappearing with a tiny hissing splash.

He walked back out of the water, his hands still limp at his side, past the skinny form crumpled on the sand, already melding with the sand and debris washed ashore. Molina did not look down and said with quiet fury, "You got the fucking beach forever," as he clambered up the sandy slope.

He drove home playing the car radio very loudly and parked the stolen Cutlass two blocks from his apartment. He left the windows down and didn't lock the doors. By morning the car would be stripped.

Inside the apartment he turned on all the lights, the lamps in the living room, the light in the small kitchen, flipping one on after another, then the television, the volume high as it showed an old black-and-white movie.

In between turning on lights he dropped his clothes as though shedding them, first his jacket, left on the living room floor, then his shirt, the damp pants, and he had to bend over to pull his shoes off, throwing them from him.

Angie, pale, was smoking a cigarette in bed, a newspaper spread over her lower body when he pushed roughly into the bedroom. She was wearing one of his old strap T-shirts and her heavy breasts hung down.

"What did I tell you about waiting up?" he shouted.

"What's wrong?" She froze.

"Didn't I tell you? Didn't I tell you not to do it?" He lurched for her.

"What's wrong? What's the matter?" she pleaded. He grabbed her wrists and pried the cigarette from her frozen fingers. Her eyes were opaque with fear, the old fear he'd seen so often. Of him. "You're going to wake her up," she said. The kid slept in a little room just off their bedroom.

He smashed the cigarette out, shoved the newspaper off her, and pressed her back against the pillow, panting at her. His mouth twitching and jerking, he kissed her roughly. She kept asking, "What's the matter? What's the matter?" whenever she could, until his lips and hands found her breasts and his body labored over her. They grappled across the bed.

Now Angie greedily pulled him to her, took his frantic, fierce caresses, and arched her full hips. Although she made groaning, pleasing pleadings, he was grimly silent, their flesh squirming moistly together, almost with the vehemence of punches.

They rolled apart, breath hard from both of them. She stroked his leg gently. "That was so nice," she said slowly, savoring the lingering and unexpected peace. He didn't answer. The television yammered loudly and Angie saw the brightness of the place.

"You turn the TV on?"

He stared upward as if trying to pierce the speckled ceiling.

"I better turn it off or it'll wake her," Angie got off the bed, her body shadowed and beautiful in the bedroom's glow.

Molina had one arm across his eyes. "I killed Flaco. I'm going to cop to it tomorrow."

She stopped moving, arrested as she was slipping on a pair of panties. She didn't move for several moments in the noisy, antic brightness. "You killed him?" she asked with a small smile, finishing her dressing. "You just killed him?"

"I'm not making it up. It's no secret." He was completely enervated, his words heavy and nearly unpronounceable.

He didn't see her begin striking at him, her fingers stiff as metal, her arms swinging at his face and body. Her voice was a shout.

Molina bolted upright, blocking her blows, his hands seizing her arms even as her unwillingly pinioned body continued to thrash and writhe in his grip. "You killed him," she shrieked, falling onto him. "You killed him, you killed him."

With a burst of fury, he flung her away. Angie hit the wall near the bed and began crying. The door to the small room opened and Cecilia ran out to her. She wailed loudly, Angie cradling the little girl and rocking her.

"Get her out!" he yelled, jumping from the bed and starting for them.

"You going to hit us again? Hit me, hit me," Angie cried in fear and anger. She struggled to her feet, holding Cecilia as Molina yelled. She backed up to the bedroom door.

The sight of them cowering away stopped him. Molina felt a great stillness fall over him. "You going to tell your daddy? Tell him I killed Flaco tonight and I beat you up, he's a tough guy. See what he does. Tell him I beat your fucking face in."

For some reason, perhaps because he stopped moving, Angie did, too. They remained separated by the bed, the TV gibbering, Angie and Cecilia crying, hushing, and crying again.

"I need protection," he said from that inner stillness, "for what I'm going to do. The guys who can give me protection will believe me now. Flaco's buying me protection. The best."

"What about us?" Angie cried. "What's going to happen to us?" Her face was swollen and contorted.

He turned from her, from his daughter. You can't control everything, he thought, like that grocery store. There was no good reason to go there, no good reason to shoot anybody, but he'd done it. Sometimes the control failed, the discipline gave way. He couldn't let that happen this time. Below him, from the open screened window, he saw the empty upper floor of the parking lot and the whole mute cavalcade of buildings that pressed against this hateful apartment bought for her, where he was feared as much as loved. Angie kept repeating, "What's going to happen to us?" then she said his name, then she screamed it.

Molina raised his eyes. The city seemed cold and stricken below him. He leaned his face against the rusted screen, sweat cold and thick on his body. He stared up into the great starlit concavity that receded into infinite darkness above him.

CHAPTER TEN

"I'm going out. I'll be back. I'm going to lock the door and don't open it for anyone, not anyone, until I come back. Do you hear me, Matt?"

"Yeah."

"I won't be gone long. Just be quiet, watch the TV." Di tried to conceal the panic that filled every moment she stayed in the motel room. Lizzie and Meg were bouncing back and forth on the beds and had strewn books, crayons, and cups all over the room.

"How long? I want to go out."

"No. Matt, you do not leave. You do not open the door. Just do what I tell you." Her voice was too loud.

He sat at the glass-topped desk, staring at himself in the mirror. He hadn't taken off his damp bathing suit, only putting a towel over the chair.

"Can't Dad do something?" he asked, half angry, half afraid.

"He is, right now. Don't worry about it, just keep an eye on things while I go out."

She said a quick goodbye, stepped out gratefully into the sunlight, and locked the door. It was, for a moment, like breathing again, to be able to draw in air without feeling it pressing against you from walls too close together. Di slipped on a pair of sunglasses and started walking. Her walk was quick, it could turn into a run. She felt like she was jerking back and forth, first rushing to the shelter of the motel room, then smothering in it and having to get out, no matter what.

The most terrifying part was that she had never felt this way in her life; it was new, uncontrollable.

The Howard Johnson's backed up against a levee road that ran, with abandoned railroad tracks, along a weedy path by the river. Everywhere around her cars passed on the freeways, people walked in and out of the other motels and fast-food restaurants at the intersection of the interstates. Di made for the levee road.

A deserted water-treatment station, colored by graffiti and rain, stood like a guardian at the start of the road. It was warm out, the clinging wet heat of spring, and she was sweating as she went by the station, down the road, the river slowly and impassively moving beside her. I could call Dick Weyuker, Mike said that was all right, but there's nothing to tell him. I can't tell him two old people scared me silly. I can't tell him I want to run, even if it means leaving the kids and Mike. I can't tell him.

Across the wide river, the bank was heavy and overgrown with green branches and trees, an impenetrable tangle. On her side, the road was raised up, bare and hot, under the sun. The road gave the illusion it would dip and continue into the river, as if the two merged somewhere in the heated distance. Where am I going? she thought. I can't go anywhere. I can't leave.

She walked closer to the edge of the road, where the dark brown water moved below. She was always the practical one. Diane's practical, she'll know what to do. Let Diane take care of that problem, she's got such practical ideas. All her life, she was expected to be useful, purposeful. When she met Mike and he took her out, along this river, then on their walks and the dances, she saw a similar resolution in him. It was going to be good to relinquish some of that burden to him, she'd thought.

She came to the edge of the levee road. Ahead was the broad

watery expanse of the river, sparkling in the morning. Di remembered the day she came home, it was right after cheerleading practice for the basketball team. Her last class had been Mrs. Cundey's geometry. All of that stuck. Just as it stuck that when she opened the door, Mom was laid out on the living room sofa, a white cloth over her forehead. The drapes were drawn. Two neighbors were standing, whispering, in a corner. The place was cool, strange. A small electric fan whirred on top of the television.

Mom raised herself off the sofa. Slim, nervous, with kind eyes, she looked so frightened. "Pop is dead," she said thickly. The neighbors stood, hands folded before them. "He had a stroke in his office and they've taken him away," and she went on.

The first feeling, oddly, was anger that no one had told her. The next was a pain that grew.

"I can't do anything, Di-Di," Mom said, stroking her arm as if to calm her, "You'll have to do everything for us. Your sister can't get back until tomorrow, so it's up to you. You'll know what to do. You will."

So she had to make all the arrangements to bury her father, vice-president of a small bank. There was no school for her, she cooked all the meals and took care of the house for the next two days, and met the lengthening line of friends who stopped by or took her aside in town. Pop belonged to so many clubs, committees, and civic groups that he was only home for dinner once or twice a month. It was a family joke how much he disliked Mom's food. Pop was the original backslapper, the club man who enlivened every party, and made everyone feel they were friends. As long as she could remember, he carried little promotional sewing kits from the bank and gave them to anybody he met.

They wouldn't even let me mourn, she thought, still hurt by it. Some events mark everything before and after them. It was so after Pop died. Before, she never thought about Mom's chatter, her various indulgences on expensive little silver things at home, the social affectation when she thought people ought to pay more attention to her. Pop went along with all of it. He didn't care. After he was gone, Diane couldn't tolerate the faint posturing and complaints.

Both her mother and sister let her do everything those few terrible days. They all got together every so often now during the year, but she never heard from Kathy except on a holiday and Mom stayed close to her youngest daughter. Pop used to tell her gently that Kathy and her mother were so much alike.

It was as though his passing unleashed a centrifugal force within them and they quickly flew from each other, driven away as much by time as indifference.

Let Diane handle it. She can handle anything. I can't handle this, she thought, standing at the edge of the river. What scares me most is if we stop being together. We stop being a family because of whatever is happening.

Across the river, on a small sand-and-rock strip people were fishing where the bank dropped off abruptly into deep water. Someone raised his hand and waved slowly at her. I must look like the figurehead on a ship, she thought, pointing myself out toward the water. The panic was fading by degrees. She returned the wave.

There was still the school, her teaching, their friends. They were together and would stay together. It was weak to think their lives had been upended so utterly.

But, there was that other time. It leant vitality to her bad dreams of the past.

Mike had started drinking, first with other deputies on late Friday night odysseys, then more at home. It was about two years ago, the time of the shooting at that grocery store. He began coming home later and later, Saturdays turned unbearable as everybody had to tiptoe around the house while he either slept or grumped it off. He was changing, perceptibly growing more childish, more petulant.

She had to do more and more each week; he was surrendering the kids and her. The moment came one miserable autumn Saturday. Lizzie was playing her badly tuned violin, practicing for the next lesson. The noise was irritating in the damp afternoon. It woke him and he shouted at her. Then he stomped out to work in the backyard and tripped going down the brick stairs outside the kitchen. He sprained a wrist and skinned his knee, raging like a small boy.

He grabbed his wallet, demanded the car keys. He was going to get out, away from this racket, this goddamn circus.

They faced each other in the kitchen. She had to pick up the pieces, as usual, as everyone expected her to. As much as you love someone, you can never know every secret or hope or fear. What she and Mike sensed, as they shouted and argued through the whole darkening, raining afternoon, was that they had come upon a line marking their lives before and after.

I would leave him, she thought, he knew that. I'd take the kids, and he knew that, and he knew that scared me and it scared him more than anything. And knowing, even as they shouted inanities back and forth, that Matt and Meg watched in silent, uncertain fear.

The shouting gradually grew softer. I had to make the stand, she thought, even if it was the most frightening thing for me. Mike did stop drinking, he made a promise about it, never in the house and no more on the long trips. Their life went on, until now.

You could stand there, staring out at the river and the city just off to the left, boats wallowing in the slowly moving water, all the people marking the minutes of their days without thinking anything could be very wrong in the world. Two worlds and we don't even know the other exists. She raised her head. Oh, God, she thought.

Every Sunday she took the kids to Good Shepherd Presbyterian Church near the high school. Mike came for a while, like he had to their other church in the old house. He even became an usher. But, he was clear about it. It was fine for her, fine for the kids, but God didn't have anything to do with his life. They didn't talk about it anymore, like washing the car or taking the kids to school. The difference was there and unbridgeable.

She looked at the little sandy beach, the motionless figures rooted in the brown water. It was time to go back, there were things to do. She turned from the river's beguiling middle distance and headed down the levee road.

Massingill convened the coordinators of his Task Force on Organized Crime at mid-afternoon in the conference room two floors above the courtroom where Molina was testifying.

He and Chris Rau, his senior criminal attorney, and Tommy Conn, who handled liaison with jurisdictions throughout the Southwest, grouped themselves in the middle of the long conference table. On the far wall, watching with posed benevolence, was the President's official portrait, framed in black metal.

Massingill and Tommy Conn smoked and shared a plastic ashtray from a local restaurant.

"Wow." Rau riffled the pages of the file in front of him.

Out of habit, Massingill gave them the ground rules for meetings on Molina. No notes left in the room, all papers brought in to be taken out, the copies of the file Swanson gave him to be returned and locked in his safe.

"Quite a tale," said Tommy Conn, grinning at Massingill.

"We've got a significant set of problems here," Massingill tapped his file, already dog-eared and circled with coffee-cup rings.

"Maybe," Rau said.

"The Santa Maria D.A. wants Hector's visitors stopped. He wants a close monitor on him."

"Can't do it."

"Let me hear it," Massingill said to Rau, who was a survivor of three previous U.S. Attorneys. Initial enthusiasm was not Rau's style. Only after he saw Massingill's conviction about Molina's value grow, did he too become an enthusiast. Molina now had no more fervent booster.

"Christ, Claude, we've all worked with Hector for what now? Two years almost? He'll put our feet to the fire if we start fooling around with his visitors. Jesus, Mary I can see him stalling everything."

"Like the coloring-book incident?" Tommy Conn smirked.

"He held up my Martinez, et al. trial for four weeks until he got the crayons and whatever shit he wanted to draw with."

"Yes. That's what he'll do. All right. We agree. Reactions to the allegations in the transcript?"

Rau leaned back in his chair. "Bullshit."

"All of them?"

"Who's this Max Dufresne?"

Tommy Conn interrupted, "He's the AB I told you about. New addition on Hector's hit parade of people who can come see him."

"Okay. Yeah. I saw his nine-six-nine-B package. He hangs out with, is close to, or just plain in with the AB. The wife's a contract hit to scare Hector, and ABs qualify for me. Maybe it's a personal grudge."

"Did we ever ask why Hector is seeing an Aryan Brother?"

"You ask him." Tommy Conn grinned again.

"No. We've got a lot of trust built up now. I will not have it jeopardized by half-assed accusations and slanders. Hector goes into a tailspin too easily."

"What are we doing?" Rau asked.

Massingill got a cigarette from Tommy Conn, leaned forward to have it lit, and settled back into his government-issue chair as though he were weightless. "I want to divvy up the material here. I want to get discreet investigations checking it out. But, this is critical. I do not want any inkling of this to get back to Hector."

"We're in the middle of the Diaz trial," Rau said. "We've got another set to go next month, and the rest strung out after that."

"I saw some of his testimony." Massingill pushed the file roughly. "Hector told his road to Damascus story again. I just cannot believe this." He pushed the file a second time. "He's right out there for us. He's giving us pure gold."

"Then let's not find out." Rau put his hands behind his head.

"No. I've got to know one way or the other if we've got anything here." A third, dismissive poke at the file. "We do it with deliberation." He looked at Rau and Tommy Conn. "We take every step very cautiously and deliberately."

"Slowly."

"Glacial," Tommy Conn snorted.

"Let's get through this series of trials with our honor intact."

"I'm just going to throw out a wild, wild idea." Rau slapped his hands down on the conference table.

"All right."

"What if it's all true? Hector's doing everything this butthead says he is. And the other stuff from his wife."

"I want him out."

"So he's going to put away enough NF killers, goons, and pushers to save, how many? A hundred lives? Maybe. Maybe, I don't know, how many million bucks in thefts that don't happen, drug buys."

"Swanson accuses him of murder. Future tense, too."

"And I say," Rau flipped his hands up, "so what?"

"Jesus," Tommy Conn chuckled.

"I was kidding," Rau said to Massingill.

"I know you were."

Massingill pushed the ashtray over to Tommy Conn, who beckoned for it between coughs. Of course, the suggestion had been in jest. . . .

Edgar Rolly rolled his eyes. "So I told this cop, I said, okay, you just get set and I'll follow you, okay? I'm right behind you. So he gets started, he gets down the street, and I'm waving from my car, and brother, I do a one-eighty and get the hell out of there." He jerked a fat thumb into the air to show he went the opposite direction. "I'm not getting locked up in no jail, no how, no way, no time, no sir." He finished another rum and Coke, upending the glass with a thunk on the table.

Across from him sat a little man with a pointed black beard. He listened, he laughed, he kept trying to get Rolly to leave the Barrel Club.

Rolly ordered another round.

"God, I hate that shit, yip, yip, yip, don't it sound like that?" He shook his head. The jukebox in the almost-empty bar was playing something by Michael Jackson. "You want another game?" Rolly started to heave himself out of his chair and head for the pool table.

"Naw, I don't want to play. That's a fag game," the little guy said with a toothy grin.

"Fuck you," Rolly muttered, sinking back into his chair. The drinks were ready at the bar and Raymond, the little guy, went for them. "No jail, Raymundo, not no how. I mean, what the hell for? I just haul ass out of town and that's it, fine and finito. Hell, I liked the kid, I guess, he's a good kid, kind of slow, he wasn't any rocket scientist, okay? But he was a good kid and it was fucking rotten for him to get killed. Like his folks, too. I just ain't going to make it my whole life, what happened."

Raymond dropped the drinks on the table and slowly drank his, while Rolly's pudgy jowls shook when he tilted his head back and downed half of his eighth rum and Coke.

"So I'm just going to stay way away from all that," he waved a fat arm around, "put a couple hundred miles between me and them and that's all and that's going to fix everything." Rolly scratched the stubble on his face. "Spend the heat of the day indoors, Raymundo, take my word for it. That's how you get to be ninety-two."

The Barrel Club was dark, largely empty except for empty booths. Along the false-wood veneer walls hung posters of old baseball stars. The clock over the bar, ringed around its grimy face in blue neon, said three-eighteen in the afternoon.

The door opened and a man almost as tall as Rolly walked in, his face moving around to adjust to the dimness. He spotted the lone occupied booth.

"Ray, Ray, there you are," he said, slapping the little man on the back and smiling. He wore jeans and a white shirt, the sleeves rolled up carefully. Blue-green tattoos of the Madonna and flowers curled up his forearm.

"This is Eddie," Ray said, "and this is Narcisso." He pointed at the man standing beside him.

"Call me Cisso, okay." He turned slightly. "I got that stuff outside."

Rolly finished his drink. He blinked several times and wiped his forehead. His hand came away wet with sweat. "This the guy you called, Raymundo?"

"This is the dude."

"Raymundo says you've got some stuff worth looking at." Rolly wiped his forehead again, the sweat from the alcohol still beading.

Cisso frowned.

"He's okay, he's a good old dude, right?" Ray patted Rolly's fat arm as it lay limply on the table. "We're buds, man. We been here for a couple hours. He's cool. He's okay."

"Hell, yes I'm okay. I'm just telling you, Cisso, I can look at merchandise and tell you what you've got and what you don't got. I don't ask questions, I just inspect. You show me, I can tell you if it's good, I might buy myself."

Cisso looked at Ray, then his lightly bearded face broke into a wide smile. He leaned to the table, "Check this out, I got a VCR, RCA. I got a twelve-inch color portable, I got CDs new. Check it out, man. All in the car outside."

Ray slid out of the booth. "I want to see."

Rolly slowly moved his bulk out, then got to his feet, wobbling a little. "Got to get my strength back there. Hold it. There. Yeah, that's the ticket." He braced himself for a moment on the table. He walked a little hesitantly behind Ray and Cisso out the door.

Only his car was parked in front. "Where you parked?" he said walking right beside Ray and Cisso as they turned around the building.

"In back. I don't want no street action, man." Cisso swaggered when he moved.

"I tell you, you go back to Santa Maria, you ask about me, and they'll tell you I've been doing this for ten years. Plus. I know what I'm talking about when I see stuff, no BS, no jacking off." A faded blue Buick, with dents and rust corrugating it, stood in the shadow cast by the building. An open garbage bin stank in the afternoon air.

Cisso briskly opened the passenger side door and bent low. Ray grinned up at Rolly.

"Let me get a look," Rolly moved lumberingly toward the car.

Cisso came out with a wooden baseball bat.

"You going to play some baseball?" Rolly asked.

CHAPTER ELEVEN

It was almost four in the afternoon before Swanson got back to Santa Maria. He tried to find Gleason, catching up with him onstage at Emerson Junior High School.

A small audience of older men and woman fanned themselves with programs. Gleason sat flanked by other county officials. Crudely lettered name tags perched in front of them. The county assessor was explaining why local tax rolls were shrinking. Gleason leaned back in his metal chair and his head fell to his chest.

By standing in the wing of the stage, by the light panel, Swanson could see Gleason. He began waving his hand.

Gleason yawned, one hand at his mouth.

The assessor finished and sat down. A younger woman stood up.

"Now we'll have a short presentation from the District Attorney, Mr. Gleason, on why the crime rate in Santa Maria County is growing."

The small audience clapped desultorily and Gleason smiled, standing at his place.

Swanson walked onstage and whispered to Gleason. Several

of the men and women perked up. Something was actually happening in front of them. A low murmur began swelling.

Swanson led Gleason backstage. The young woman had risen again. "I'm not sure what to do now," she said haltingly. "Maybe we'll skip to Mr. Hackett and his presentation on the mosquito abatement effort in this area." More limp applause.

"Massingill won't give him up," Swanson said.

Gleason swore loudly and repeatedly.

"Let's extradite Molina from Nevada right now. We get an extradition request before Massingill can figure it out. He thinks we'll stew, talk it out, he can take his time. Even if he thought we'd make the request today, he's going to assume it'll take a month, maybe longer, to get it up to Sacramento, through the Governor's office, over to Carson City, and he can fight it all along the way."

He spoke a little breathlessly. Through the P.A. system, the voice of Hackett droned on about mosquito breeding habits.

"How do you want to goose it?"

"I want to hand carry it. I want to walk it through the Governor's office. We can get this thing over to Carson City in a couple of days. We could have Molina in Santa Maria in a week."

"I'll start greasing things with the boys and girls." Gleason loosened his string tie suddenly. "Let's get out of here."

They walked out of the junior high school, Gleason favoring his cast. "This is what Weyuker dug up for me," Swanson slipped part of the gun out for Gleason to see.

"Looks good enough. I better get you on the Sheriff's list. You don't have a permit?"

"Joe, like I told you last night, I don't even think I can shoot straight."

A P.E. class was swatting baseballs energetically for practice at one end of the school's athletic field. Swanson felt galvanized by Massingill's obstinacy. They would have Molina by their own devices and the Justice Department wasn't going to stop them. The years of delay and frustration were over.

He told Gleason about two other stops he made after meeting with Massingill. At the California Department of Justice he went to the criminal division and got advice on the mechanics of a walk-through extradition warrant. Then he saw his counterpart in their Special Investigation section. He alerted him to the bikers Max had named and got a promise that a multi-jurisdictional effort would be made to round them up. If they had any sort of homes with electricity or telephone service, drivers licenses, bank accounts, or credit cards, Swanson would find out. At the very least, powerful scrutiny was being brought to bear on them. With luck, it would produce evidence against Molina.

Gleason sucked in a breath. "Can't we take charge of the little bum when he's in-state on one of these trials? How about that? I could have the Sheriff go down and bring him back and forget about extraditing him."

"It won't go. Molina's always in federal custody, no matter where he is. We couldn't take him. We can wait and the feds will just give him to us when they're done. We'll get squeezed to drop the Tice case because Molina's been such a great snitch. Angie was a tremendous break. She was making it certain we'd get Hector before the Tice case fell apart."

"We'll do it your way," Gleason rested his hand on his car roof. He seemed tired. "These kiss-ass meetings drive me crazy, but next year I've got to hit every damn one. Don't mind skipping today." He smiled a little. "Susan's narrowed things down some. She's gotten four off your list."

"So that leaves ten. I might have forgotten somebody."

"I know, I know." Gleason quickly closed it off.

One other thing had sat stonily in his thoughts on the long drive back to Santa Maria. He looked briefly at the kids yelling, swinging, running around the bases and Matt flashed into his mind. Swanson said, "I'm going to the funeral."

"Why?" Gleason was genuinely surprised.

"I owe her some kind of public penance. I should show some respect."

"He might be there."

"He might."

"Guess he has to be. He's the bereaved husband, heartbroken father. Massingill has to let him go."

"I don't care about him. I've got to go. For me."

Gleason had his cigarette holder out, fitting a cigarette into it. "Stay away from Molina if he's there. I want to keep this professional."

"I'm just a spectator, Joe."

Gleason blew a perfect smoke ring into the still afternoon air. It hung, suspended in front of him and he blew it away. "You could make it a round trip, the funeral and the extradition walk-through."

"I appreciate it."

"Di going to mind?"

"No. It's all a one-day shot. It's no worse than what's going on now."

A loud crack split the air. Both Swanson and Gleason turned to see a boy in blue shorts running past first base, a clear shot open for second and third and home. Swanson whistled. Gleason didn't look from the baseball diamond. He pulled out his string tie and completely opened his collar. "You have to find the funeral first, deputy, you can't wander all over the countryside."

"I'll follow the body," Swanson said.

It wasn't hard to get into the County Jail. Rising eight stories in the middle of downtown Santa Maria, it could have been an office building without windows, an office from which yells, laughter, crying, sometimes whole speeches, were hurled out to the people walking on the sidewalk below. The Santa Maria Police Department's old granite-fronted Victorian blockhouse and the jail were linked by a new covered walkway and fences surrounded the intake and parking lots.

Swanson went directly to the second floor and signed in at the reception desk. He could never see who manned the desk because it was set behind mirrored glass and the deputy sheriff on duty spoke through a microphone. Swanson slid his gold badge into the tray at the base of the mirror, saw it vanish and reappear a moment later. There were four other people sitting in the reception room, waiting to be called for a visit with a prisoner. Three of the people were holding hands. The fourth, sitting apart, Swanson knew. He was a fat man in a clerical collar who called himself Father Jones. He wasn't a member of any religious body, but insisted on ministering to certain prisoners. He waddled with a chrome walker and was suspected of passing drugs and information inside the jail. He looked up, smiled wetly, and went back to the little notebook he was studying.

The steel door buzzed, Swanson pushed through. He could see into the reception room through the duty officer's mirrored cubicle.

"I've got a gun," he told the deputy.

"Check it in, please," he held out his hand and took the .38, making a small notation and slipping the weapon into a locked metal box under his desk.

Swanson went down a gray-tiled corridor and up to the third floor. The light was thin, distant as it came through the shielded windows. He used to wonder what made a jail, almost any jail, so disheartening to enter. Hospitals, hotels, train and airplane terminals, all places where people crowded together had their own character, but none like a jail.

What made the jail different was the light, and the hidden windows and the way everything was solid, the walls, the floors, the doors. There was no real decoration because anything not bolted down could be torn off and used as a weapon.

On the third floor he went to the watch commander's office. The watch commander, according to the sign-out board was in the field, which meant he could be anywhere, doing anything. His deputy was about thirty-five, with a small potbelly and thick shoulders. His green uniform was a little wrinkled. He offered Swanson some of the coffee perking.

"We kind of like it to sit and age for a day," he said. "Gives it some bite."

"I want to see the witnesses in PC downstairs."

"Righto. Give me a sec here. How about you let me see your ID once more and check over with your office, 'kay?" He grinned and took Swanson's badge and ID card.

Nobody really wanted to work the jail detail, not for long anyway. The deputy commander's tiny office was littered with papers and flyers and cartoons clipped from newspapers. On his small desk was a framed picture of two boys on a horse.

"We got the floor sealed off, no prisoners allowed, only staff can see them. Meals we got coming by the guy on duty. No one gets to see them." He cheerfully led Swanson down the stairs, down to where even the faint daylight ended.

Swanson tried to be optimistic. His witnesses and snitch were safe, his family secure, and he was going to have Molina out of federal custody and in this jail before Massingill could react. Still, seeing the large gray-blue steel door, painted over and over so that it looked like icing, going through it and into the basement cells, depressed him. The deputy commander left him at the door with the guard.

There were only two cells. Both were large and into each had been moved mattresses, linens, and chairs. Hannah Tice was washing a pair of black socks in the old steel sink, her wide body hunched over. Frank Tice lay on the floor, on two mattresses stacked up and draped with a sheet. He was smoking a cigar and reading the newspaper.

"Hi, folks," Swanson said lightly.

The newspaper lowered and Hannah Tice turned from the sink. The door to their cell was open.

"Michael, how good to see you," she said, wringing out the socks, wiping her hands. Frank Tice remained on the mattress, one leg crossed over the other.

"Do you know they call this the Hole?" Frank Tice asked. He slowly got up off the mattresses. "The guy who brought us here last night he says, you're going to be living in the Hole. He made jokes."

"He was trying to be friendly." Hannah Tice smoothed her hair back carefully, a worried smile on her face.

"He tried."

"Well, you've fixed it up nicely," Swanson said. "You made yourselves comfortable." A small cross had been hung over the bunk and a picture of Donny placed on the washstand shelf.

Two open suitcases, like open mouths, gaped with clothes at the foot of the bunk. Magazines were stacked neatly on top of a small television sitting on two chairs.

"What's your news?" Frank Tice asked flatly.

He told them what was going to happen. "I think we're talking only about a week, that's all."

"Your family's safe?" Hannah Tice asked. She laid a reddened hand on Frank's arm.

"Fine, thanks. Everybody's making it okay."

"I'm glad to hear that." Frank Tice looked at his wife, then to Swanson. "We've been talking, we didn't get much sleep last night here. We talked most of the night. You know, even here, down here, you can hear all these noises? You ever heard the noises in a place like this at night?"

"No."

"It's like going to Hell."

"I'm very sorry. But, you're safe here and in a week you can go home."

"We will go home, that's what we decided."

"We just want to be in our own house, our own things," Hannah Tice said earnestly, "around the neighborhood, not like here. I've never heard things like this, like animals almost." She shivered a little.

"This is no place for us." Frank Tice chewed on his cigar. "You can't protect us? Okay. We'll protect ourselves."

Swanson had his hands in his pockets. How to reach these people who had been through so much and knew that more lay ahead? He walked over and picked up Donny's picture, a studio portrait.

"The difference now is that we're going to be in control," he said, looking at the picture. "It's going to be our turn and that changes everything."

"Does it?" Frank Tice watched him holding the picture. "Please put it down," he said more quietly than Swanson had heard before.

"Do you trust me?"

Hannah Tice looked at him intently. "Yes. We do, Michael. We always have."

"I'm going to make you a promise." He carefully set Donny's picture back on the shelf. "If I don't get Molina back here in a week, ready to take him to trial for killing your son and his own wife, I'll sit there in the store with you and we'll wait for them together."

"I've got a rifle, I keep it," Frank said. His cigar was cold.

"So we'll have your rifle and my .38, which I can't shoot worth a damn." He grinned at them. "How's that? Just us and them?"

Frank Tice looked at his wife, who said nothing. He put out his hand. It was a touching gesture from him.

"Thanks," Swanson said, shaking his hand.

They stood silently for a moment, an awkwardly emotional oasis in the depths of the jail.

"What's Rolly saying?" Frank Tice said finally.

"I haven't seen him yet."

"We thought you took him someplace else, to keep us separated," she said.

Swanson looked, with new eyes, at the empty cell adjacent to the Tices'. Untouched bedding and simple toiletries. Maybe Weyuker moved Rolly for some reason. He was suddenly worried.

"Where is Mr. Rolly?" Hannah Tice asked guilessly.

CHAPTER TWELVE

Where was Edgar Rolly?

"What's he running for?" Swanson had demanded of Weyuker after his jail visit.

"Christ Almighty. Who knows with Rolly. He just didn't want to come in."

"I can't get a decent night's sleep with him roaming around." Swanson angrily waved one hand.

"Look, the good part is, is if we can't find him, nobody else's going to. Rolly's good at hiding."

"Goddamn him. You been checking places he usually turns up?"

Weyuker nodded. "Out at that auto-wrecking joint on Greeley, the pawnshop, that all-you-can-eat place, they're supposed to call in, he comes in."

Over the years as a deputy district attorney, Swanson had dealt with witnesses like Rolly, but none with his perverse bad humor. Many witnesses wanted to avoid the inconvenience and upset of recounting things they had seen and heard. The longer a case went on, the more witnesses who became disenchanted, reluctant. And the ones who had been reluctant at the outset turned mulish.

During the two years plus since Donny Tice's killing, Rolly had disappeared for weeks at a time, without explanation, and returned without remorse for the disruption and anxiety he caused. He was unlucky enough to have been sitting, as he often did in the afternoon during the summer, on a milk crate just inside Tice's Market, gabbing and holding forth on the world scene, when Hector Molina decided to stop for cigarette money.

Many of Rolly's associates were small-time fences, too. Swanson held out little hope of help from them.

So where was Edgar Rolly and when would he decide to pop up again?

"You're not with us," Di said gently.

"I'm sorry. It's a slight witness problem," he answered, coming back to the Burger King and the open little boxes of hamburgers and fries littering the plastic table. He went on absentmindedly eating fries until Meg complained he had dipped into hers.

"Not those two older folks?"

"Nope. The other one." He cleared his throat for the kids. "He's playing hide-and-seek."

Meg wanted to play and only stopped when he caught her waist as she tried to bounce from the booth. He held her tightly. "And where do you think you're going, missy?"

Di shook her head, but smiled for the first time that night, a genuine smile. "We need to get a few more things from the house tonight. Lizzie needs her other shoes."

"My towel, my towel," Meg said.

"She needs her special towel."

"Am I going to practice this week?" Matt asked seriously. There was something poignantly older in his tone. Swanson didn't hear a kid asking the question.

"You don't play any better," Lizzie said.

"Knock it off." He held his hands up like a traffic cop. To Di he said, "I'll pick it all up on my way back."

"I thought we could go with you."

He pushed away an empty sandwich box and felt a sour belch rising. One of the fastest dinners on record, he thought, and with three kids neither he nor Di dawdled over food. "I'll be coming from the office, it's easier for me. Weyuker's meeting me at eight. We're going to do the extradition request."

"It would've been a good break for us."

"Not this trip, sorry."

Di nodded. She helped Meg clean up. Like Matt's new seriousness, Swanson noticed a different quality about Di. She didn't seem to waste time or effort, but all her movements, even her expressions, had dignity about them.

Back at the Howard Johnson's, they all moved into one room to watch television. The kids scampered in first, Di and Swanson right afterward. He shrugged off his coat and, as casually as he would have at home, tossed it to one of the beds.

The coat moved, as though with a purposeful life, the .38 coming out of the pocket, thudding to the thinly carpeted floor at the foot of the bed.

Matt turned, being nearest, and reached for the gun.

"Don't, Matty, don't touch it," Swanson said loudly, his voice harsh and raw.

Matt started in surprise, and pulled back instantly. Swanson stepped widely and scooped up the .38 by its butt. Meg and Lizzie, already at the television, stood in stiff bewilderment.

"Mike," Di said sharply.

He didn't look at her. "This is loaded, Matty, don't ever handle a loaded gun, you understand? Ever. This is very dangerous."

"I was only going to give it to you," Matt began. He was shocked and the tan of his face had whitened.

"Did you hear me?" he demanded.

"Yeah," Matt nodded several times quickly.

Swanson took a deep, unsettled breath. "Listen, this goes for everybody," he spoke to his three children who silently, nervously stared at him. "Nobody is to touch this gun. You're not even going to think about it. I'm sorry you saw it. But, it's very dangerous, you can't play with it, you forget about it. Everybody understand?" He waited.

They nodded. Matt had gotten back some of his color. As Swanson checked the gun, doing what Weyuker had told him to make certain the safety was on, Matt said, "Who's trying to hurt us, Dad?"

It was the youngster who reached for the fallen gun and someone older who spoke now. Swanson held the gun carefully. How do you explain Hector Molina to a ten-year-old or the absurd situation that protects him? How do you describe a menace that is behind bars and still abroad in the city? Or a betrayer among those who should be protecting that city? Or a woman shot dead in a grove of almond trees on a spring morning?

"What's important is that we're together and we're safe," Di sat on the edge of the bed, "and your father is doing his best to keep us safe."

"Is somebody going to hurt us?" Lizzie asked quietly.

"No. That's not going to happen, honey, never, never," he said. "We'll go home in a couple of days and this'll all be over. I'm going to keep us all safe."

"That's our promise. We don't make promises in this family that we don't keep, do we?" Di looked at each of them.

"I don't know," Matt said.

"Matty, I swear that everything's going to be all right. That's a solemn vow. You can't get anything better than that."

"You swear to God?"

"I swear to God."

"You don't mean it," Matt said.

"Yes, he does. He means it and so do I," Di said.

He picked up his coat and took the gun to his room. He hid it under the clothes in his suitcase and locked it. You can't forget, he cursed himself, you can't act like everything's the way it was yesterday morning. Things have changed.

When he went back into the motel room, the kids were in front of the television, absorbed in it. Di lay stretched out on one bed, her reading glasses on, a textbook open. She seemed to have stabilized everybody in the short time he was gone. She closed the book and took his hand when he came near the bed. "I want to talk to you," she said.

She led him into the bathroom and shut the door, pulled the lock. The fan started automatically. It was a little like the un-used cell at the jail, Rolly's empty chamber, the neatly folded towels and wrapped glasses, soap, and washcloths.

"I'm sorry I barked at you," Di said. She kissed him deeply. He pulled her to him and they both breathed a little heavily, leaning against the sink. "I've been edgy all day."

"You've been terrific. I messed up, not you. I keep forgetting why we're here."

"I got spooked this morning," she said. They stood against each other, their bodies pressed together, voices low.

"Bad?"

She laughed slightly. "How bad is it when you get paranoid about two old people on vacation and a pool cleaner?"

"That's bad," he laughed with her and kissed her again. "All day when I was on the road, I was thinking about you. I kept thinking, what's Di doing right now, this second? What's she saying? What's she thinking? And Matt and Meg and Lizzie? What're they doing? That's all I could think about." He ran a hand down her side, along her breast.

"We're fine. We'll be fine."

"I'll be gone until day after tomorrow. Got to leave early to-morrow and get to Sacramento."

"I'll take care of everything."

They moved and caressed each other in silence. Beyond the door the kids were shouting, lapsing into ominous quiet, shout-ing again over the television.

"There's no privacy," he complained, unbuttoning her blouse.

"Turn on the shower."

He leaned over and twisted the faucets in the bathtub. A roar of water sprayed out. They undressed quickly, as if there was no time, and stepped into the rush of water. Swanson panted. "Cold, cold," kissing Di, her skin, tasting the metallic water.

This wasn't any woman whose body he stroked and loved, but Diane, his wife, the mother of his children, the only woman who mattered. He paused and grinned at her, "I've got it all taken care of, Di. I've got this thing by the tail." He felt exultant, triumphant, for the first time since his world had mutated.

The world dwindled to the consuming watery loudness around them. Di held him tightly, everything became slippery flesh and movement.

There is a puckish demon which picks moments to wound and frighten, even as hope rises. Holding Di, an idiot voice began in his mind, a singsong reminder of peril. Three little pigs, it taunted. The kids shouted at each other in the next room, Matt and Lizzie and Meg, their children.

"Jesus, Di," he said in ecstasy and half-hidden fear.

Three little pigs. I'll huff and I'll puff, sang the voice.

CHAPTER THIRTEEN

Although he was in his office before seven the next morning, it took Swanson some time to get away.

Edgar Rolly still had not made an appearance. After talking with Weyuker, he went ahead and had a statewide alert put out for Rolly. Swanson also made certain they were continuing to look closer to Santa Maria.

There was paperwork, too. Along with the request for an extradition warrant, he prepared a diversionary pleading to distract Massingill. He was going to have Massingill served with a subpoena duces tecum, a court order for the production of all visitor records, notes, and physical evidence in his control relating to Hector Molina. The underlying compulsion for the subpoena was the murder of Angelica Cisneros. Swanson thought attacking this order might keep Massingill busy enough not to suspect that an extradition warrant was in the works.

He was on the phone to D.A.s in Solano and San Joaquin counties about Alves and Rivera. These offices were near enough to Santa Maria that they might have some information, but neither had any cases or records dealing with the two hit men.

There had been a story in the newspaper, and two TV stations had news crews camped in front of the building when he got there. The last thing he wanted was public comment and notoriety for Molina's men to follow. He had slipped in through the side door and climbed leaf-strewn stairs to his office.

People continually stopped by to ask what was going on. It seemed as though everyone was being dragged in front of Bobby Norman and asked questions about giving information away, selling out the office, committing various felonies.

A deputy named Bellman barged into Swanson's office. "I'm not answering any questions," he announced belligerently.

"About what?"

"Whatever this thing you got going. I'm not answering anything. It's piss poor." He waited, staring at Swanson, hands on his hips antagonistically.

Swanson went on re-checking the extradition request he and Weyuker had labored on until midnight. He kept checking the time. "You do what you think's right," he said. He swallowed a cup of hot black coffee quickly. Another fitful night, this time with Matt, and the next day seemed gray.

"Aren't you even going to do me the courtesy of telling me what's going on? Are we supposed to lock our files? We have a problem here or what?"

Theoretically an extradition request was one of the simplest things in criminal procedure. It was addressed to the Governor. It stated in supporting affidavits from Weyuker and Swanson, that a certain person, now incarcerated in Nevada, was wanted for trial in California on two counts of first-degree murder with special circumstances. This person, whose true and correct name was Hector Gabriel Molina, was therefore eligible to receive the death penalty in California.

The Governor would issue a warrant for the extradition of this person Molina from Nevada. The warrant would be served on the authorities in Nevada, who would then produce the person identified in the warrant.

It was all, in theory, very simple and very plain.

The person, Molina, could waive extradition and just come

back to California in the custody of police officials who would claim him for that purpose. Or Molina could contest the validity of the extradition warrant.

But, such a contest was not easy. All California had to establish in a Nevada court was that criminal charges existed against Molina and that he had been correctly identified. Fingerprints, prison records, the very brief testimony of Weyuker would be sufficient to do that. Contested or not, Molina would be turned over to California.

But, Swanson didn't think this simple process would either be quick or direct. Massingill would fight, somehow, to keep Molina from being taken out of prison in Nevada, out of the security of the Witness Protection Program.

And, perhaps unwisely, Swanson had told the Tices, himself, even Di last night, that he could accomplish this in a week.

He looked distractedly, annoyed, at Bellman. "You scheduled to be interviewed?"

"Shit no. I haven't done anything. I'm putting it on the record that I'm not going to participate in your little sideshow."

Bellman heaped compliments on himself, oblivious as Swanson packed his briefcase. "I'm sorry. Got to buzz out of here." He had his briefcase in hand, his phone was ringing, and the office page was sounding on all floors for him. Time, time, he didn't have any. "Tell Joe what you think about the sideshow. It's his idea."

He heard Bellman's angry expulsion as he pushed him aside. Down the hall, a few voices calling to him, greetings and entreaties which he ignored. He bustled downstairs to Bobby Norman's small office. Susan was there. "The funeral's in L.A., a cemetery in the Valley tomorrow."

"You should stay here and give me a hand. That would be the honorable thing to do."

"Too many errands, too many people to see." Norman came in, turned on the polygraph and set out his pens.

"Who're we down to?" Swanson asked. He jiggled his briefcase impatiently.

"As of this moment, I would say five possibilities and one or two odd ones, wouldn't you, Bobby?"

"Give or take."

"I'm right in assuming you're out the door?" Susan had worn a large red bow and she plucked at it to make sure it was straight.

"I've got to be on the road by ten to make it to Sacramento. Joe's lined everything up for me so I'll scoot from one office to another with the extradition request. If I'm lucky, everything really goes okay, I'll get it signed and be on a plane by five. Weyuker and a deputy are going to meet me in L.A."

"Michael," she said, hands folded in mock gentility, "we do not have our leaker. This office is in an uproar because people think we're running an inquisition in here. I'm very tired of questioning people I work with."

"I don't want to wait until we've got somebody tied down."

"Then whatever you do now can get right back to Mr. Molina."

"He's going to be in our custody so fast it won't matter."

She shook her head, "All right, on your way out, please send in the next victim."

He had one stop before leaving Santa Maria. It was time to see Max.

"My lawyer says I was an asshole for taking the deal," Max continued his methodical, mindless trek around the inside of the cage atop the county jail.

He was on his hour exercise period on the roof of the jail, enclosed on all sides and overhead by thick fencing so that even the sky looked like it was divided into a precise grid of little squares. Swanson gave him two packs of cigarettes and Spiderman and Teen Titans comic books with the staples removed.

"It's a little late, Max." He shielded his eyes against the inescapable morning sun. "You can't go back. I'm not going to force you to do anything. You'll do what you have to."

Max had rolled up the sleeves of his khaki shirt. His heavy

white forearms were crisscrossed with blue-green designs. He dropped the cigarette butt to the concrete floor and ground it out. "Maybe I should think about it a little longer is all." He squinted at Swanson.

The one person who doesn't mind being in jail because here he's safe and provided for, Swanson thought sourly. Think about it. Jesus H. "It won't make any difference, I'm telling you. You did the smartest thing under the circumstances, don't kid yourself. Now I'm going after Molina."

"He's a smart dude, man." Max grinned spontaneously. "He's one hard guy. I wouldn't fuck with him, my man."

As if he's already forgotten his own role, as if Max couldn't hold onto the fact that he would testify against Molina. The proturberant eyes were artless, perpetually vague.

Swanson said, "Once I get him back in California, you're going into court at the prelim or before the grand jury. It could be a couple of weeks, probably less."

Max's grin sagged. They trudged slowly around the roof. "I was thinking," he began.

"What?"

"How's Les doing?"

"He isn't saying anything. I don't know what he's doing. He won't talk to anybody, even his lawyer."

Max nodded, as though pleased. "He knows about me?"

"I guess. It doesn't matter." I'll write a book about the care and feeding of snitches. You had to know their moves before they did, measure out what soothed and frightened them. He knew what Max had been thinking.

"Maybe I could talk to him, okay? I could make him give up something."

Swanson shook his head. "I don't want him. I don't need him."

"Yeah. You got me." Resigned, matter of fact.

"I got you. That's right," Swanson said cheerfully. "You made the right move, not him."

"Yeah. I guess so. I guess I don't mind about Hector. He's hard, really tough. I don't mind about him. I've been thinking about Les." He avoided looking at Swanson, stopped at the fence, his hands pressed against the wire mesh so he looked like he was trying to squeeze himself through the tiny spaces into the blue day. "He's the only friend I got, you know? I mean, I ain't even got any family, real family, except him, and he ain't exactly family."

Swanson had his back to the fence so he could look at Max, the blue misspelled tattoo circled his throat, his face scanning the street far below. "This is day one, Max. You're starting all over, everything's new. First we clear away the old stuff, Molina and Les, these two clowns still out there," he pointed into the distance where Alves and Rivera were invisibly lurking, "then you start fresh. I'm going to help you stick to the right decision. You follow your part of the deal and I'm going to watch out for you. I'm going to be your family."

Swanson thought, the old man would've loved that pitch. Two hands on his shoulder for that and a bonus on payday.

"I was an asshole." Max straightened and began walking again. They walked in silence; Swanson pretended to look at the time casually. Around them, on all sides, lay Santa Maria, prone and invincibly ignorant. To protect it from predators like Molina, Swanson used people like Max. And Massingill used Molina. The difference was that he really had to become Max's new family. It was real for Max, not a scam. He had to protect Max like he would the Tices or his own family.

"You know I started wearing a gun? Wish I could show you, but I couldn't bring it in. I never wear one, never. But now I do," Swanson said.

"Oh, yeah?" Max's interest perked up.

"One time, I got into a situation, following a cop to serve a warrant, it wasn't even my case, I was just doing a favor, and this guy runs into the hallway. It's the guy. The cop's someplace else, this guy's got a piece pointed at me. I figured, this is it. I'm out. I'm gone."

Max nodded. He was following with great interest.

"So," Swanson spread his hands, "I did the first thing I thought of. I stuck my hands out," he made believe he was aiming a gun, "and I pointed at this guy and I yelled at him to put his hands up, I was going to shoot him, I yelled my head off."

"So what'd he do? Man, he could see you were bluffing."

"Not quite, it wasn't very bright in this hall. He dropped his piece and put up his hands. That was my one and only arrest. It was the one time, before this case, I wished I carried a gun."

Max grinned openly. "You were real lucky."

"Sometimes. Let me ask you, how do you rate Alves and Rivera?"

"Cisso's the tough one, Ray." He wobbled his hand and made a face. "He's along for grins mostly. He's good with a shank, jeezum bap, bap, bap, bap," he made rapid-fire thrusts, "holes all over before you know it."

"You're saying they're the A-Team?"

"They're okay. They're good guys."

"Max, you and Les got one woman to take care of and you fucked that up. Molina didn't give you me and four witnesses, right? He gave us to Alves and Rivera because they'll keep coming, right?" Swanson stared hard. "Right? Isn't that right?"

Max slipped a cigarette into his lips. "Yeah." He lit the cigarette, hands clawed into the fence mesh. "That's right."

CHAPTER FOURTEEN

Just the smells were enough, and the sounds, all the young voices and feet moving in the hall, the clanging bell announcing class changes, and the pungent sweetness of the cafeteria's usual Thursday lunch, creamed chipped beef on toast, hanging heavy in the air, made Di realize how much she missed the school. In only two days she felt exiled from it and her classes. Now she was back, actually walking down the brick-and-linoleum hallway, holding onto Meg, with Lizzie and Matt alongside. This was their school, too, and every so often Matt would call out to someone he knew. Like we've been away for years, she thought, like the prodigals returning.

It was one of the few times she enjoyed going to the principal's office.

She left the kids in the outer office, in the warmly lit, softly sounding room with two elderly secretaries who rustled papers and gently tapped at typewriters. Announcements for spring games and a dance were hanging on the walls.

Di went into Mrs. Crossland's office.

"Thank you for seeing me. I know it was short notice," Di said, standing in the doorway.

"I'm concerned," said Mrs. Crossland.

"Pardon?"

"I'm concerned about this story in the paper, Diane." She pointed at a newspaper folded into precise quarters on one corner of her small immaculate desk.

"I haven't seen the paper today."

"It's another story about a crime. Your husband's name is mentioned for the second time this week. It's a terrible crime and I'm concerned."

Di still hadn't come farther than a foot into the office. The soft sounds from the other room should have been calming, but they weren't.

"I want to tell you about that," she said. "I wasn't ill yesterday."

"I thought not. You're never ill."

"Mrs. Crossland, my family is hiding, we're under police protection."

The gray, smudged woman behind her small desk said nothing. Her black hair was swept back from her forehead so that she seemed to have a great white skull.

"What I mean is, I can continue my classes. I want to continue them. My husband and the police are handling the situation and I want to make certain that my children and I can live our lives as normally as possible."

The principal shook her domed head very slowly. The final bell for classes sounded, muffled, and the crash and shuffle of feet subsided suddenly outside. Doors closed. "I've said before that this sort of thing was bound to affect your work here. This whole violent world will come into the school environment."

The curse of a private school, Di thought, was the belief that it was a sealed bottle floating in a rough sea. "I can promise you that it won't. I only wanted to let you know what the situation was. I'll be picking up my fourth- and fifth-grade social studies classes tomorrow."

The principal sighed. It sounded like air leaking suddenly from a bicycle tire, tendentious and dry. "My major concern is safety."

"Pardon me again?"

"Unavoidably this kind of situation brings your husband into contact with violent, unstable people. I'm afraid that we could be caught up with them."

"I'm sure the school will be completely safe."

"There will be policemen? The students will know that something very dangerous is going on. God forbid there should be any sort of incident. I have to consider your welfare and the rest of this school, Diane. I have to."

Di had heard the same kinds of things for years, as though she and Mike were plague carriers and might infect the sterile precincts of the school. "I just want to teach," she said. "I want to come back to my classes. I want my children to see their friends and feel that life is going on."

Mrs. Crossland smiled. "You're a wonderful teacher, and you will come back. But I don't think just yet."

"What do you mean?"

"A leave is a good idea right now, I think. I've made arrangements for your classes to be taken over for the remainder of the semester."

"You're firing me."

"No, no, I'm making proper adjustments for a new and quite unpleasant situation. You appreciate that, Diane, I know you do. It's unfair to you and unfair to us for a close association to go on now."

Di wouldn't beg, but the pang she felt was terrible, a sick plunge without end. "I expected more," she said, opening the door wider.

"Please believe me. My thoughts are with you in this difficult hour."

"And my children? What do you have in mind for them?"

"They'll have to make other arrangements." Mrs. Crossland grimaced with sympathy.

"It's not fair. You know how unfair this is." Di's voice rose and she knew, with shame, that it could be heard easily by the elderly secretaries, hands now poised over the typewriter keys, who awaited the next words. The kids could hear, too. "You're making my children suffer for something that is completely out of their hands. You're punishing them."

"Diane, this is a private school. No child has a right to be here. It is a privilege." Mrs. Crossland sighed her squeaky sigh again. "The little wisdom age has given me is that life is seldom fair. Seldom." She shook her head.

Di had shut the door loudly even as the last words came after her. The secretaries hunched self-consciously over their typewriters. Matt stood by the group of chairs. Di gathered the kids up.

"Where we going?" Matt asked quietly.

She thought of the motel and its false cheer, the cramped rooms and worry.

"We're going home," she said, walking surely from the principal's office.

Susan didn't look at Bobby as he made the last wrap of the cuff around the arm of the woman in the chair. Almost noon, and Susan wasn't hungry. Bobby checked the wiring quickly and sat down at the polygraph.

"Why am I here again?" the woman in the chair asked timidly. Her brown arms were laid flat on the arms of the chair. She was a small woman, with dark hair and a small mouth and she sat very still.

She was the reason Susan had no appetite and Bobby continued to stare down at the gently humming machine.

"Well, Fran," Susan swallowed and knew she sounded cold, "we had some irregular answers the first time I interviewed you yesterday. We want to try them again."

"I guess that's all right," Frances Cameron said. "I didn't lie yesterday."

"I didn't say lie. I said the answers were irregular. The machine found something and Bobby needs to try again."

Susan put her hand out to the thin, brown arm resting on the chair. "That's a terrible bruise," she said involuntarily. "That's almost your whole wrist. How did you do that?"

Fran moved uncomfortably. "I banged into a door."

"Son of a bitch," Bobby muttered low, angry.

"Fran, Fran," Susan sighed sadly, "you can't let him hurt you like that."

"He didn't hurt me. I did bang into the back door, last night."

Susan tried to put it aside. Everybody knew about Fran's husband, the cannery worker who beat her up about once a week. A year before he had knocked out a tooth, and once kept her off work for nearly three weeks while the swelling from the bruises on her face and body went down. Poor gentle Fran, Susan felt cold and terrible inside, who answered all the questions wrong. It had to be her, of all the names on Mike's damn, damn list, it had to be poor Fran.

"Set whenever you want." Bobby cleared his throat and sat with half-lidded eyes. Fran had suddenly become just a squirrely subject.

Susan listened to the machine. God, it was stuffy in here. "You work in the Victim-Witness program, don't you?"

"Yes. With Bonny Hustis."

"Have you ever seen this woman?" Susan held up an enlargement of Angie Cisneros's driver's license photo.

"No. I don't think so." She shook her head. "No, definitely."

"Are you certain you never saw her come into the Victim-Witness lounge?"

"I never did."

Susan went directly to the most troublesome questions, the ones Bobby said showed the most dissembling on the lie box. "Have you ever given away property belonging to the District Attorney's office?"

"When I wasn't supposed to?"

"Yes. Have you ever made an unauthorized transfer of money or property belonging to this office?"

"I never did, no. I didn't."

Susan saw the slender brown fingers curling on the armrest and it was plain, no matter what Bobby's machine said, that this woman was scared.

"Have you ever discussed a pending case with anyone outside of this office?"

"Yes, sometimes, you know, just conversation."

"Did you take two badges from this office and give them to any outside person?"

Fran shook her head and twisted her head and her neck. "No. I don't have anything to do with badges."

For a half hour Susan patiently went through the questions, adding a few Bobby had suggested. The room closed in on them all, tight and insufferable.

Finally, Susan finished and Bobby unwrapped, unhooked, unwired shy Fran from the machine. Fran stood up. "Was that better? I haven't done anything, so there shouldn't be anything."

Bobby clasped his hands over the machine protectively.

"Thank you, Fran, I'm sorry we had to do this again." Susan waited while the door was opened and a little fresh air came in.

"Will you tell me if I passed?"

"I'll be in touch later. Please don't discuss this with anyone."

Fran left, slowly, quietly closing the door behind her. Bobby scanned down the long strip of paper, along the marks he had made where each question and answer began.

"I went through her personnel record yesterday and checked with CII," Susan said, hating the close, silent space. "She's been here three and a half years. I forgot she's got a brother in Folsom. It's a residential four-fifty-nine and he's doing the upper term."

That's all it would take, she thought, Bobby still studying with that pursed, sour look on his face. A brother in prison for burglary and any sort of pressure in the world could be exerted on Fran.

Bobby was blunt. "Lies. She was lying straight through."

CHAPTER FIFTEEN

In Memory of. Beloved of. Loving Mother, Father, Brother of. Those Who Have Gone Before. We Weep As They Are Uplifted. I Bring Them Unto Me. On and on in measureless rows, older stones, newer bronze plaques set flush into the hectically green lawn, names and dates Swanson ignored as he read the sentiments, while in one distant corner of the cemetery a sprinkler sent spidery gray traces of water in long lines onto the patient earth.

Behind a tall evergreen that swayed slightly and sibilantly in the cool, hard wind, Swanson hastily finished the last of four little vodka bottles from his flight the night before. He left the two little bottles he just drank on a worn tombstone as an offering.

All very appropriate, very right because Edgar Rolly was dead. Hang your head, old Rolly is dead.

He sniffed and sauntered back to Weyuker, shivering in the wind.

"Greatest invention in all human history," he said to Weyuker, patting him on the shoulder.

"What's the greatest invention?"

"Bite-sized alcohol." He peered at Weyuker critically.

"I didn't say anything. Damn, is it cold. It's supposed to be warm in L.A. So why's it cold?" Weyuker put his hand to his head every so often as the wind tugged remorselessly. "We're still clearing out before the guest of honor gets here?"

"Damn right. I don't want to be anywhere around when he shows up." Because I might do something, Swanson thought brightly.

"They going to stand around?" Weyuker pointed at two ostentatiously solemn young men who stood beside an almost-violet-colored casket that rested over a green baize-covered hole in the earth. The hearse, motor running, idled in the roadway snaking through the cemetery.

"Well, hell, I'll just find out." Swanson tromped over to the casket. He looked at it. "Hey. There's a goddamn price tag on this," he shouted.

One of the young men was apologetic. "It's not a price tag. It's disposition instructions."

"What the hell is it doing on there?" Swanson tore the yellow tag from the casket and flung it into the wind. It whirled aloft, flipping into the tree.

"I'm sorry if it offends."

"It does offend. You offend."

"All I can say is I'm sorry."

Swanson called out to Weyuker. "I had a case with undertakers, a couple years ago. Remember the gal who stole a hearse, guy in the back? She wanted to go off with him, only the bad part was he'd been dead for a while?"

"Wasn't mine." Weyuker licked the fingers on one hand and tried to smooth down an upstart curl of hair. "They're all flakes anyway." He nodded toward the two men in shiny black suits, buttoned up against the unappeasable wind.

"No, listen, Dick, this was all weird, I spent most of my time keeping it out of the papers. This lady undertaker, she's writing love letters to this guy. She was infatuated." He grinned and made a disgusted face afterward. "She had these bruises all over her arms, for Christ sake."

"Why she have bruises?"

"The lid. The coffin lid was too heavy." Swanson half-chuckled, the words coming fast and viciously. "It kept falling on her, you believe it? This crazy woman's getting all banged up trying to climb in and out of a coffin."

"That's true love."

"That's weird."

Four gunmetal-colored chairs had been arrayed on one side of the casket. Angie's funeral wasn't going to attract a big turnout.

"Okay, okay," Swanson drew himself up a little. "Tell me the rest about Rolly."

"I should've called you back last night."

"Tell me now."

"Well, Bakersfield P.D. made the ID on prints. They couldn't do a visual ID, their guy tells me it's like the basic split watermelon, the whole head. Body's sitting under some garbage bags in this big Dumpster behind a bar they have off the main drag."

"How long was he there?"

Weyuker shrugged. "There's no medical yet, so they just guestimate a day, maybe a little more. Car's still in the parking lot, they got his name off the license and the VIN, that's how they knew to run his prints so fast."

"Rolly wouldn't have been hard to find. I've got his CII rap."

"It's local action, a robbery, drunk roll, something like that, Bakersfield thinks. No wallet any place."

"Sure, local action." Swanson shook his head. "Like the Three Stooges. Moe bashes Curly. Get it? Molina."

"It could be a drunk roll." Weyuker clapped his hands to stay warm.

Swanson barged over him. "Don't your kids watch cartoons or anything? I can name you every cartoon show ever made. I've got Dangermouse and the Roadrunner, Care Bears, George of the Jungle. You know what gripes me? They cut the Bugs Bunny cartoons. Cut the shit out of them. They're supposed to be too violent. Bugs Bunny lights some dynamite, it never goes off, somebody swings a mallet, it never connects, just skip right over it. That's why everything's screwy, Dick, they're cutting the cartoons and kids don't know what's going on now."

He was inflamed by Weyuker's news, how powerless it made him feel. And Di unilaterally moving the kids back home. Everybody was ganging up on him, just when he was trying his hardest to save them.

"The theory is something heavy, blunt, wood, like a fence post or baseball bat, something like that," Weyuker said.

"Maybe a croquet mallet. Somebody's always getting bopped with a fucking croquet mallet in a cartoon."

"I feel bad about it, too," Weyuker started to say.

"You just make sure your guys watch my house until I get back," he said low, "I don't want anybody, anybody at all getting near my family."

"It's done, all taken care of."

He was in a panic when he got to the hotel in L.A. last night, called the HoJo's and found out Di had left. It was like a vise closed around the back of his head. He asked again. Yes, no question. Checked out around two.

Real panic, he called Weyuker. All was well, everybody back on the old homestead, cops inside, cops outside, cops scoping the neighborhood. He hung up even as Weyuker was still talking, so he didn't hear about Edgar Rolly until Weyuker showed up, surprise, surprise, at the gates to the Eternal whatever twenty minutes ago. He wanted to pay his last respects, too.

He called home. Di got it on the first ring. She's fine. Everything's fine except he almost had a heart attack. He can't argue with her over the phone, he can't turn around and come back because there is a sullen, inconsolable duty that insists he watch a brave woman be buried. So he clenched his fist and tried to stay calm. There were four little vodka bottles neatly watching him on the night table. His gun, wrapped neatly in its new holster, was beside them. And the extradition warrant he'd sweated blood for all afternoon was neatly laid out on his pillow. Just your average business guest.

Then Di finished up with the killer line. He was beside himself, he tried to sound a little upset, but not let her hear the panic. She wasn't as safe back home as she was at the unknown location like the HoJo. Di was really calm, solid, immovable.

She let him have the bedrock reason for her assurance everything was going to be all right.

"God's looking after us," she said just before they hung up.

He wanted to shout at her, he even held the buzzing, taunting phone, powerless and speechless for several minutes. Wake up, he wanted to shout, God's not looking after anybody. He didn't look after Angie or Donny Tice.

Now he knew God had let Edgar Rolly slip through, too.

But, try telling Di. Twelve years together, three kids, all the joys and pain, and still, still it was impossible to understand the lunacy that could lurk in another person. Like she was blind.

He hurried into the hotel room's small bathroom. Overhead, because he was so near to Los Angeles International, came the great thundering and abrupt pregnant silences of immense planes dropping through the night. He banged his hip on the sink. In the mirror, hard shadows muddied by the light, he saw an unlined fleshy face with a faint dark stubble. Would you buy a used car from this man, he thought. He was restless.

Two of the little vodka bottles gave up the ghost almost immediately and then he was ready for the hotel bar downstairs.

Time flies when you're having fun. . . .

Down the cemetery road, coming slowly, were three black cars, like great prowling cats.

"They're going to need more chairs," Weyuker said. He wiped his slightly running nose on the back of his hand. He kept glancing at Swanson as though he was playing babysitter.

The black cars drew up to the gravesite and stopped. Doors opened simultaneously and people appeared, an older couple, four young men with slicked hair and sunglasses, girls who held each other and wept. Behind them, getting out of the cars last, was an indeterminately aged man in a cassock and surplice. His stole flapped in the wind.

The others grouped themselves around the casket, the young men casting their blank eyes around, pausing momentarily on Swanson and Weyuker, who were shaded by a large pine and obviously watched them back. Over the wind in the restless branches it was hard to hear much of what was said. Swanson noticed the oldest man, paunchy, stern, dressed severely, motioning angrily, and the two young undertakers frantically trying to find more chairs. They did not. Swanson heard angry exhortations from the old man.

"You want to get closer?" Weyuker whispered.

"Right back here's fine."

"I thought you'd like to hear what they're saying, maybe say something yourself."

"I don't have anything to say to them." Nothing that wouldn't seem a self-pitying profanation anyway.

"You know any of them?" Weyuker looked at them all.

"Nobody special, just family. The pukes with shades are her cousins."

"They in with anybody?"

"The usual street gang shit, nothing much." Swanson stared down at his guilty shadow, pine shadows brushing over it. "Get everybody else away, run Hector in, crosses himself, looks sad, get him out. Very romantic, just him and Angie alone again."

The priest began. Heads bowed, only the girls were seated. The priest's hands were raised over the casket, the white surplice and stole gamboling around him.

Maybe he'd tell Di the story about the minister and the jail sodomy trial. That might help her understand. That's what popped into his mind when he saw the priest intoning over Angie.

Five years back, a jail gang-bang, seven on one and he took it to trial. A new minister, from one of the mainline, do-good churches ended up as foreman of the jury. A friend of Swanson's belonged to this guy's church. Every Monday he rattled off the new minister's pieties, sermons about our social failure and collective responsibility, the mess of America, crime because people aren't given self-esteem in more government programs.

Swanson watched this minister during the trial. He was an affable, smiling guy. He sat in the jury box scribbling notes all the time. He scribbled most when the various defendants described why they thought it was such a great idea to bone a frightened blond kid in county jail for writing three very bad checks. No details were omitted. A blanket was hung around the lower part of the bunk, the kid held down and raped. Again and again until four-thirty in the morning. He liked it, they all said. Everybody had a fine time.

Slowly, Swanson began hearing on Mondays that the minister's sermons were changing. Small things at first. He didn't smile so much. He didn't talk about generalized, social guilt. He talked to his congregation about retribution and the need for just punishment. He actually began talking about good and evil.

The trial ended. The jury went back to deliberate. Two hours later it returned. The minister stood up and firmly announced that the jury had reached verdicts on the defendants. Guilty, he said, seven times. He preached that Sunday about an individual's conscience and the law.

So maybe this was a way to get past Di's blind spot. Tell her that he'd shown this minister something new, something he had never believed possible in another human being, the capacity to inflict continuous suffering for pleasure. Swanson would say, I let him see my world, a little.

This man would survive better now, he'd say to Di. But, I wouldn't survive any better by seeing his world. Or yours. It was difficult to draw out into words. Perhaps unbelief was his protection. He had to willfully reject the specter of a God so small, so cruel. It was no improvement on the minister's trendy platitudes before the trial.

If I believed, he could say to her, like you do, I'd only make terrible mistakes in my world.

"Hey, hey, hey," Weyuker said urgently.

A white sedan came quickly down the roadway, followed by a blue sedan. The two cars pulled ahead of the black cars and stopped.

"How many can you see?" Swanson watched closely.

Weyuker squinted, "Can't make them out. I think six. One, two, three—no, looks like eight."

"The little bastard showed up too early." He grinned wolfishly.

"They should get out of here."

The cars didn't move.

"What do you want to do?" Weyuker asked.

"What do *you* want to do?"

"I want to get nine miles away because there's going to be trouble if those guys stay, and I didn't sign on for that."

"I want to stay."

Weyuker groaned.

"They've spotted him."

"I thought you wanted to get out of here."

"I lied."

At the gravesite it was obvious to Swanson that the young men, their sinister black sunglasses identical, were no longer interested in what the priest was doing. Their faces pointed at the two new cars clumsily waiting.

"Move," Weyuker muttered. "What the hell are those guys doing?"

Even the older man was watching, and Swanson could see him more clearly. The gray moustache was the color of steel. The face was set in marble. He was Angie's father.

The old man wasn't even paying attention to his wife, sobbing beside him. He was fastened on the two cars.

"I see a situation here." Weyuker pulled his coat closer to cover his shoulder holster. "We can just back up before anything happens."

"No, I'm supposed to be here." That thought was sharp, certain. He was a witness and a participant.

Hands raised in benediction, the priest intoned and the wind carried off everything he said, leaving only the tableau of crying girls in black and men poised. One by one they began moving, sorrowing figures circling the casket, touching it, shaking their heads. The old man held his wife up. She was drooping, no longer crying but actually sinking into herself as though some hydraulic mechanism that gave her a frame was failing. But the old man wouldn't take his eyes from the cars sitting nakedly in the cold, bright morning. One of the young men murmured to him. He shook his head with a peremptory snap.

"He wants to rush them, right? You take the left, I take the right, we meet, we take them down. Bet that's what he's telling the old guy," Swanson said. "This asshole wants to rush them."

"Yeah, but everybody's clearing out," Weyuker said, relieved.

The women were helped into the line of black cars. The priest hugged two of them, like a great insubstantial snowman in his billowing vestments. He got into a car and the engines of all three started. Only two of the young men and Angie's father, his face set in frost, paused at the car doors.

"I want to go down," Swanson began walking toward the gravesite, his hands deep in the pockets of his overcoat.

"Put on your badge, put on your badge," Weyuker said and they both slipped gold badges onto their coats.

Swanson suddenly felt absolutely clearheaded, the casket a few feet in front of him. This is what Molina meant, loss and pain and grief that never ended. He made his own sort of peace with Angie.

Even as he did so, he heard car doors opening, sharp commands. He looked. From the white sedan came four men in white shirts and ties and charcoal suits, their hair cut in a similar military closeness. They stood, in a phalanx, around the blue sedan. From it, Swanson saw four more men get out, two dressed like the others, and two from the backseat who were arguing. Swanson recognized one of them, the squared-off thickness in his black suit, like a shadow stamped over the sky and green lawn. He was handcuffed. The man who held him by the elbow was pointing, shaking his head.

Leading the man at his elbow, as though pulling a tethered horse along, the handcuffed man strode defiantly toward the gravesite. Instantly, the phalanx formed behind him.

"He's telling them what to do," Swanson said with wonder. "They do what he says."

A man trotted ahead to them.

"I'm going to ask you to clear this area," he ordered.

"We're family," Swanson replied.

"Stand clear to the right."

"I'm a cop," Weyuker said irritably.

The man moved forward to push them away. Swanson didn't

bother with him. The odd pair and their escort had reached the metal chairs. The man in handcuffs walked casually to the casket, looking at it with curiosity.

"Now, you're moving back." The charcoal-suited fed angrily pushed his hands out at Swanson.

"It's okay," the handcuffed man said. He sighed deeply.

"It's not okay," the fed didn't stop.

"I know this guy," he looked up.

The fed stopped.

Swanson said, "Hello, Hector." It was the first time he had spoken directly to Molina. I could touch him, Swanson thought with slightly drunken calmness, I can't hold him yet, but I could touch him right now. Soon. Soon.

"Hello, Mr. Swanson. I'm kind of surprised to see you."

"I had to come." Swanson saw this momentarily puzzled Molina, then he said, "You should be worried," indicating the other cars.

Molina's shoulders bunched briefly under his black coat, drawing it tight. "I know these people. They're my relatives. They don't do anything, especially not at her funeral. I had to explain it to my friends." He nodded his head a little to the right at the feds grouped nervously around him.

"It's a big risk."

"I wanted to see her father again. Angie's dad and me. I wanted to see him close." Molina's expression was savage and musing. Swanson felt depthless hatred brush by him.

Molina tried to scratch his nose with his handcuffed hands. He had no more interest in Swanson. He said toward the casket, "I would've got something better, they let me do it." Then he turned to go.

In front of him and the feds guarding him, the young men and Angie's father flowed on coiled muscles from the cars toward the gravesite.

A fed swore. "What do you know," Molina said.

The two groups faced each other, Molina still near the casket, his hands clasped together in a metal prayer. He turned to Swanson, his face bright with brute pleasure.

The old man marched straight ahead, while the younger ones paused. One of the feds called out, "Stop right there. I don't want you any closer."

An adjuratory hand was raised, the fed holding it up like his own form of benediction. But the old man ignored it and marched forward, his gaze set on Molina. Most of the words were caught up in the wind and Swanson only heard him say daughter, killer, murderer.

Then the old man shrieked, "Your own child hates you. She hates you. She couldn't come to her mother's funeral because she's afraid of you." His fury became incomprehensible in Spanish.

The first fed tried to push the old man back, but even as he went on venting his inconsolable and unappeasable grief, he lurched by, into the second rank of men around Molina. Molina didn't move much, only raising his head a little, showing his greedy triumph.

As Angie's father was pulled backward by his arms and his coat, he strained forward, his profiled neck and face taut like steel. With a terrific lunge, he threw himself toward Molina and spat at him. The white spittle landed on Molina's black suit. He made no move to wipe it away.

The four younger men rushed toward the gravesite making whoops and shouts as they did.

"We gotta stop them," Swanson said imperatively, moving to grab one of the young men who twisted, cursed, and flung his head around trying to see who was holding him.

Weyuker and several of the feds flailed around the casket perched over its resting place. The two undertakers crouched down on the other side of the hearse, hands clutching the fenders for protection and support.

Swanson stumbled, felt an open hand pound the side of his head. He swore and punched out, the man he struggled with grunted loudly. Suddenly, Swanson had the terrible fear of being shot with his own gun. He felt it bumping, being painfully pressed into his side each time he thumped into the other body.

"Everybody freeze! Everybody down!" commands shouted.

Only seconds had passed. He could see that two of the feds held guns out at the ready, pointed into the writhing bodies.

Sluggishly, with sullen reluctance, the bodies untangled and sank to the earth. The black sunglasses had been knocked away. They're just kids, he thought. He heaved breathlessly. I'm way out of shape, way, way. He felt for his gun. It was still there.

"You, too. Down. Right now," inflexible demands, the gun pointed between where Swanson and Weyuker stood breathing heavily.

"I'm a cop. What do you think this is?" He angrily pointed to his badge.

"I want you down," the fed ordered again.

"Oh, for shit and shinola," Weyuker cursed, dropping down. One of the disheveled young men chuckled.

Swanson also lay down against the earth. It was damp and cool, smelled dark, full. He jerked his head up. Molina must be safe, he must be all right. Four feds hustled back to their cars, Molina among them, a stocky figure bobbling awkwardly.

Swanson saw feet approach him.

"You got some ID?" the fed demanded, towering over him.

"Right here, in the coat, I'm reaching in, see I got a gun." He slowly opened his overcoat as he sat up and gave the man his wallet.

"Where the fuck is Santa Maria County?" the fed asked. He holstered his own gun.

"Up north. I'm here with that detective."

"How come?"

"I was a friend of the deceased."

"Get up." He was briskly motioned to his feet. He stood, brushing bits of grass and dirt from his overcoat. Weyuker was also rising, his toupee slightly askew. The others, the young men and Angie's father, were being herded back to the black cars. Only her father resisted. "How can you protect him? How can you do that? He's a murderer, he murdered my child. What gives him that power. . . ." The voice trailed off as he got into the car. His face appeared at the window. "This is my child's funeral. You can't throw me out of my child's funeral because of him. This is my own child, my only child."

The first fed, who Swanson figured was in charge, called over, "If you and your party are not out of here in two seconds flat, sir, I am going to place all of you under arrest for disturbing the peace and assault on a federal officer. Now, get yourselves and your familes out of here. Do it now."

He turned to Swanson. "What's this bullshit?" he asked coldly, taking Swanson's wallet from the other fed.

But, Swanson couldn't let Angie's father go like this. He ignored the fed and ran to the black car, its motor revving, its horn braying a challenge to the feds. He spoke into the open window.

"I cared for Angie very much. She was very brave."

"Who are you?" the bitter, hard old man asked.

"I was a friend of hers, Mike Swanson. From Santa Maria." He pulled off his badge and handed it to Angie's father.

The old man took it slowly, like a holy relic. The feds shouted and the young man in the driver's seat urged something in Spanish. Angie's mother leaned against the backseat window, her eyes open, quiet, distant. "Santa Maria," the old man repeated. "Her letters. All of them from Santa Maria. I know you."

Oh, Lord, Swanson thought, hoping none of his sick understanding showed on his face. "Did you write back to her?" he asked, fast, breathless.

"Every week a letter from her. Sometimes we wrote, we called her. She was lonely. She talked about you."

It was as simple and terrible as that. Swanson didn't want the old man to know how Molina had discovered Angie's new, secret location. Somebody in her family had spoken carelessly at someplace or sometime and the secret of a lonely, brave woman passed to a listening, searching Molina. Did I warn her about her own family, he tried to think through the haze and revulsion. How do you warn her about her family?

It was the future that mattered. He seized the idea. "I just took all the legal steps," he said, still breathless. "Molina's going to be brought to trial in Santa Maria in six days. I want you to come and see justice done."

"I am justice." The old man slowly handed back the badge.

"Six days in Santa Maria," Swanson said passionately.

The car was moving slowly away from him, the horn still sounding its futile defiance. He watched the black cars speed down the cemetery's roadway.

Weyuker walked over to him. "I talked us out of it," he said, irritably pointing at the feds.

"You're a little messed up top," he said, taking back his wallet from Weyuker.

"Shit and double shinola." Weyuker gently put both hands to his head and began shifting his hair very cautiously.

"Wind it up," called the agent in charge, making a wide circle in the air like a cattle driver. The remaining feds jumped into the blue sedan. Molina must be safely tucked in the white sedan. The two undertakers, gathering up the overturned chairs, straightening the wrinkled baize like huffy sorority sisters after a drunken party, were alone at the casket.

The feds were leaving, the sedans backing up, onto the curb and the green lawn, turning rapidly to leave the cemetery in the opposite direction from the funeral party. Tires squealed.

There was a final reason, Swanson suddenly saw, for his compulsion to be here. It was to see Molina at last. The white sedan was retreating up the roadway.

Leave Molina with something to think about, worry about, make him feel a little of what Angie's father and mother were feeling.

He knew that Molina had to be watching, from the sedan's rear window, handcuffed, protected, smugly secure.

Swanson was the third man to raise his hands that morning at Angie's funeral.

For the retreating sedan, he held up five fingers of one hand, and a single finger of the other. Six days.

CHAPTER SIXTEEN

Susan said, "Put a pin in it, Michael. You're too excited."

"I can't slow down. I feel wired, I'm all jumpy." He paced restlessly from the office window back to her. "I was close, this close to him," he held his hand out, "and we had this civil little chat. You know what scared the shit out of me? I thought, Jesus, don't let any of these crazy Mexs do him before I get my hands on him."

"I'm surprised Weyuker showed up at the funeral. It must have been on his own time."

"He said he wanted to pay his respects. Maybe he was checking on me, like he's worried I'd do something crazy or something." He laughed, his head giving a snap. "I've got Molina, Sue, got him nine ways. That was what was so great." He was gleeful. "This little asshole is acting so tough? He's got his two pricks out there, he got Rolly, he got Angie, he's going to get me. And I've got him."

"Try to calm down, Michael," she said. "Take a deep breath before you have a fit."

It was mid-afternoon, and he could hear the other members of the unit joking and arguing about their cases.

"The bad part," he said, "was the zinger from Angie's old man. I didn't have the heart to tell him. It works out with what Max said about Orepeza digging to get Angie's location himself. She gave it to him, her folks, too. Man." He brooded only for a moment and then the exuberance broke through once more. "I feel good, you know? It's not perfect, but hell, it's good to feel good finally."

Susan was sobering. "Nothing more has come over on Rolly's killing. They're doing a photo lineup with those two, Alves and Rivera. We have no word on them. They could be anywhere."

He was equally sober, and confident. "It was them, maybe just one of them. They followed Rolly. They were watching and he was on his own. Six days, we get Molina, zap, he can't communicate with those pricks anymore. He's deaf and dumb. We'll get them along the way."

"That leaves us with Fran." Susan sat in a designer chair. Since she was a supervisor, her office was larger than his, books and awards crowding the walls along with posters of art shows. Ferns filled the rest of the space.

"How good is it?"

"Bobby is convinced by the lie box answers. There was clear dissembling throughout, but especially on the answers dealing with money and property. It's her, Michael, let's face that fact."

"Kind of tough. Even kind of tough to get mad at her somehow."

"I checked with the county credit union. Fran's had about two hundred dollars automatically deducted from her paycheck for the last year."

"Where'd it go?"

"She's got a personal savings account at Santa Maria Federal. She and her husband have a separate joint checking and savings account at another bank."

"So this is her stash?"

"That's what I think. I'm getting a warrant typed up for it now. Then we'll find out if she's got any kind of cash there."

"Where's she now?"

"At home. Joe suspended her. He's still more interested in getting her out of the office than getting her in jail. For now anyway."

"Anybody talked to her?"

"Like a statement?"

"Anything."

"No, not since the word came from Joe to stay away."

Swanson had been surprised that no news crews were around when he returned to the office. Gleason had held a morning press conference and neatly allayed all significant interest in Angie's murder. The investigation was continuing, leads were being checked. It sounded thin and unconvincing until he sprang the new information that she had been the victim of a robbery. Her wallet had been stolen. One suspect was talking. That made the story far less interesting. There was no mystery.

"I'll go see her," he said shortly. "She'll say something to me."

"You can't Mirandize her." Susan got up from the chair. She folded her arms and blocked Swanson's pacing. "We're not going to arrest her yet."

"I'll find out what she did, Fran'll open up. You know she will."

"Yes," a resigned, sad admission. "We probably won't be able to use anything she says to you."

"But, we'll know. That's what counts, that's Molina's game, he plays in the background, he pulls strings, he makes threats. I'll know how."

"All right," Susan said, "call me, please? I'd like to hear. Maybe I'll tell you what Judge Haata called me in court yesterday."

"Anybody home?"

He said it again, knocked twice more on the front door. All of the curtains had been drawn in the house, but there was a car in the driveway. Swanson repeated his name.

Susan was right, he was too excited and it was impossible to notch it down. The fight at the cemetery started it and now he couldn't contain his impatience. Six days would be hell like this.

"Anybody there?" he said again, a fist harder on the front door this time.

It was a square, single-story brown house, on a street of brown houses. Fran and her husband lived in the flats, a development of new homes that appeared overnight with strips of grass unrolled like carpet over the dust. Frail young trees were stakebound on every front lawn. An old man, his pants pulled nearly up to his chest, stood stooped, watering the tree on his lawn next door. Every so often he glanced suspiciously at Swanson. Mid-afternoon on a weekday and nobody around.

He was about to knock again when a woman inside the house said, "You can come in," and locks were turned. The door opened a fraction and stopped.

"Franny? You there?" Swanson pushed the door open completely.

"Come in and shut the door."

The voice came from someplace far back in the inky-dark living-room. It was Fran, but he couldn't see her.

"It's like a cave in here," he said. "Where are you?"

"Don't turn on any lights, just sit down and do whatever you're going to do."

"Just talk, that's all."

"I don't care." The voice was weary, empty. It seemed to come from a pit of absolute black in a corner. He groped his way toward her, knocking his legs on the chairs, fumbling over the furniture.

"Let me just let a little light in, I'm going to break something of yours the way I'm going."

"No lights. You get out of here if you turn any lights on." There was vehemence in her voice. And something else. He couldn't quite tell, but her voice sounded different, thicker and rougher.

"Okay, let me just find someplace solid." He felt around the edges of a chair and sank slowly into it. He was facing the blackness. "I want to talk to you about Hector Molina."

"I don't know him," a husk of breath, almost elephantine in its thickness.

"How about your brother. He's up at Folsom. How about

moving him into protective custody? Nobody's going to hassle him there, nobody can hassle you."

"What're you talking about, Swanson? What about my brother?"

"He's doing the upper term for breaking into a house at night, right? Didn't somebody tell you he'd get hurt if you didn't help them? I can understand that, Franny, it's not so terrible, you want to help your own family. I'd do it." Angie's dead, Rolly's dead, we're in hiding, and still it was impossible to hate the shy, fragile woman sitting someplace in the dark. Maybe it was because she seemed to be a victim herself, set upon by so many violent hands.

"What's my brother have to do with anything? Is that why they fired me? Because my brother's in prison? It wasn't a secret. I thought nobody cared."

He tried to see her, but only made out an outline, a source for her voice. "Angie Cisneros is dead because of what you did," he said gently.

"I didn't do anything," her voice exploded. "Everybody says I did something and I didn't. I didn't."

"You've got a special bank account. I know that's where you put the money Molina gave you. He wasn't asking big stuff, was he? I mean, his pal, Orepeza. He asked. He wants a couple of badges, what's Angie saying, what could it hurt to tell him, right?"

"I don't know them. None of them."

"What's the bank account for, Franny?" This was like hooking the confused customer at the car lot. Don't raise your voice, draw them on, notice this feature, look at this style, and then they'd be saying, yes, yes before they knew it.

"It's my business."

"The bank's giving up the records. I know there's going to be a lot of money there. See, Franny, all I want now is for you to tell me what happened, so I know, so I can see how much Molina had and what he doesn't have."

"Don't keep saying that name. I don't know him. I don't

know anything about him. I never even met that woman, Bonny handled her. I didn't take any badges." The thick, husky voice was sharp.

"He's going on trial. We're bringing him back and we've got a witness and all the evidence. You need a friend to stand by you." He was soft, sincere, and it was almost the truth.

"I don't want to talk anymore. Leave me alone."

He slid out of his chair and toward the voice in the blackness. He crouched on one knee and reached out. "It's over now. You need a friend to help you. You got to trust somebody now." He put his hand toward her.

"Leave me alone."

He touched her arm with his fingertips, then pressed to stroke her.

Her scream of pain made him twist backwards and almost fall over.

"What's the matter?" he said, standing up quickly.

"Just leave me alone," moaned, imploring.

"I'm going to turn on a light."

"Please, Jesus, no, no."

He fumbled in the dark, heard her moving away as he caught the base of a lamp, hands riding along it until he found the switch and punched it. An amber cone of light fell around her empty chair. She was huddled in the corner, back bent to him, head down. She was crying.

"I only want to help you," he said, because he was the cause of her shame. "Let me help, please." He put his hand on her shoulder.

She huddled away, then turned suddenly.

"I was hiding money," she shouted, swollen lips heavy on each word, "for me, so I could get away. I took the money from the travel vouchers, I took witness fees, I put it all in my bank account, for me. So I wouldn't have to stay here." She used her good arm to wave at the faint, spotless living room. "That's all I did, no badges, no money, nothing. Just for me, to get away."

"I'm going to take you to a hospital." He swallowed. It hadn't been him, it wasn't his petty questions that bothered her.

It looked as though her right arm was hurt. She held it pressed to her side. Her lips were swollen, some bits of dried blood left that she hadn't cleaned off. One eye was shut in puffy flesh. It was a gargoyle's face, a misshapen idea of Fran. Why did it have to be her, why always the weakest ones, he thought. Anybody else and his heart would have been as stony as the face of Angie's father. But even knowing her guilt and responsibility for a cruel death, he almost forgave her.

"Right after he found I couldn't go to work," she said, "right away he started in, so I don't care what you blame me for, I don't care what you do. I don't care."

He put his arm around her. It shouldn't be like this, he thought, wanting to hate, and failing, his excitement gone. "It's okay," he said uselessly, "it's okay."

Swanson and Di walked along the sidewalk holding hands, talking in alert confidence. It was a windless early evening and two girls ran by, giggling, and across the street a short caravan of boys on skateboards drifted into the failing light. Every few steps, Di dropped his hand and looked away, reaching for him again. He brushed a stray eyelash gently from her face.

A plainclothes cop walked in front of them. Another followed behind them.

"Well?" he asked.

"What?"

"What do you think about taking the kids to Palm Springs for a week?"

Di tightened her hand slightly. "It's not fair to involve my mother or my sister. We wouldn't be any safer, would we? This man could still find us."

"It'd take time. You'd be safe." He felt her hand loosen, fall away. He was running headlong into some inner wall of hers, futilely rebounding from it. "Honey, after today I don't know what's safe around here. After that thing at the school, you're going to be stuck in the house now. Almost all the time. You'll be like prisoners."

She walked a little closer to him. "So I'll teach the kids at home, that's sort of fashionable. Finish them out this semester, then maybe we want to think seriously about teaching them full-time," she smirked at him.

"I'm not joking."

"I'm not, either."

"This is all temporary, you know, making the best of a bad situation. Things'll go back to normal. Look, you want me to talk to whatshername Crossland?"

Di shook her head. She was dressed in slacks and a light shirt, her hair pinned up. It was the simplicity that made her appealing. She was at peace, he saw, clear and resolute and hard to budge. "No," she said, "it was time for me to leave. This might be a blessing. I loved my classes, but it was time. I wasn't going to get moved up or given any better assignments."

"Because of me."

"You're so self-centered," she mocked mildly. "It was me. Like the time I had them do two acts from *Midsummer Night's Dream*. I never heard the last of that. Too ambitious, too much, too soon, too this, too that."

A jogger strained toward them, both he and Di tensed as the cop ahead slowed slightly, head following, hand held toward his coat.

Swanson wanted to touch her every moment and hated when they walked apart even briefly. Make her see what was coming. "If you stay, honey, you'll have to start lying to everybody. Just like I do. It might be dangerous for our friends to be near us." He looked at her. "How's that? You comfortable with that?"

"Are you?"

"You look around," he jabbed his finger, "we know people in almost every house on this street, all around here. Right now, one of them wants to come over, say hello, talk about Brownies or soccer or who's a good babysitter, we got to tell some lie, keep them away. We can't let them get near us."

"You said it's only for a week."

"I got to keep lying because Gleason's out on a limb and he's done a lot for me. Anybody asks me about Angie, I say it's a robbery. And Fran, she's a thief for now. We get Molina back for trial, it won't be so bad because he's the one everybody's going to watch. Yay, Joe you stick it to a kid killer. Gleason needs the protection now or this comes back at him when he runs again."

"He's asking a lot."

"He can't ask. I'm just doing it for him."

Di glanced to her right. Someone waved across the street, a pair of clippers held high, a small pile of cut twigs and branches at his feet.

"You better hope he doesn't want to say hello," Swanson said, low.

Di waved back. She made a finicky, diffident tug at his collar, answering him. "I see the whole thing, I do. It's like right after my dad died, I had to get a job." Her feet scuffed along the concrete as they walked.

Her voice was subdued, without sadness or rancor, reciting facts like her height and weight. "So I got a job, office work, files and typing, whatever, over on Lyle Street downtown."

"Who with?"

"It doesn't matter. It was only part-time. I worked until eight every night, I got paid every week and we needed the money, you know, we weren't going to starve, but dad didn't leave the whole world for us. So, anyway, I was usually the last one there with the guy who ran the office. Just us, it got dark and he started asking to take me home. I said no. He started getting insistent. I told him I didn't want him to bother me. He didn't say anything for a few days, just cut me out. Then, when we were alone again, I was getting ready to leave. And then he grabbed me and gave me this big, wet kiss." She shrugged to show how lightly she took it. "And he kept trying to get his hand in my blouse. He had a bad stutter, he always had spit on his mouth. It was a mess."

"Who was it?" Swanson demanded.

"Mike, it was almost twenty years ago. You want to go beat him up?"

"Yeah, I want to beat him up."

"The office's gone, he's gone. I don't know where. It was that place that sold wholesale photographic supplies on Lyle."

He put his arm around her. "The old son of a bitch."

She moved gently under his arm, familiar warmth. "Nothing happened. He wasn't very good at anything, even going after me. I wasn't scared, I was angry. I gave him a shove, he knocked over a light stand display, made so much noise he got all excited and started stuttering and he went and hid someplace. Well, I just left. I didn't go back. I couldn't tell my mother, not the way she was acting, not then. At least I didn't think I could tell her. Maybe she wouldn't have cared very much. Anyway, what I did was stay out until eight for the next couple of weeks until I found another job. When she asked about the money I was sup- posed to bring home, I said I spent it, you know, bought things for myself like records. I loaned some to a boy." She was clear and intent. "I'd say anything to protect my mother then. I lied to her. I let her think I was selfish because I had to. I don't mind lies or being cooped up or having men watch us. I'll do what- ever keeps us together."

"You won't go," he said with dismayed certainty.

"No," she said.

They turned a corner, heading away from the house, having walked two blocks in the dreaming spring night. Back home the kids were watched by two city police officers. He didn't tell Di how that made him feel, knowing that Hannah and Frank Tice were locked up in the basement of county jail. Santa Maria could spare the police to protect his family, but not them. Since she would not leave, he couldn't let her know the confu- sion and shame he carried because his job and children meant special privileges. It was like an extra ration of water on a lifeboat.

"I believe you and me and the kids will be protected," she said. "That's the point of faith. I know we will."

"Don't start now. It doesn't make sense to me, it doesn't work. He keeps us safe," Swanson pointed ahead, "and him," behind to the cop placidly walking. "Good people still have bad things happen to them. We're not immune. I've seen it."

"I'm sorry, Mike, I didn't mean to make you mad. I wish we could talk to each other about it."

"We can't. We never could."

"If I could only understand why you don't think there's a God or any point thinking there's one."

Swanson was curt. "He exists, he doesn't care. He makes a sad little woman work for a killer. He lets that killer murder a helpless, brave woman. He makes us prisoners. That's why I've got a real problem with him."

"We'll do what has to be done. We'll see how that works. I hope it will." He watched her eyes and face become opaque, dim, growing into the spreading gray opacity of the evening.

Behind them, the cop said casually, "Probably shouldn't go much farther." Swanson didn't want to see him. The restless gaze, checking every person who came near, spoiled the fragile, fading illusion he and Di were taking a stroll after a hard day. He rejoiced and was appalled that Di wouldn't leave.

They turned back and Swanson's beeper whined loudly, like a razor scraped on a blackboard.

CHAPTER SEVENTEEN

Molina picked up a finished matchbook and critically looked at his work. It was good, not as good as some of the others, but the instructions were all there. He put it down on the upper right-hand corner of the small desk in his cell. There were three matchbooks. From the left-hand corner he picked a virgin matchbook and opened the cover.

The morning routine was going on, metal carts rattling along the chipped floors, men laughing and cursing at one another. The worst thing about a jail or prison, anywhere, was the distracting noise. He could shut it out, after years of practice, as cleanly as turning down the volume on a radio. Emerald silence filled him.

The desert air, as dry and vapid as the inside of an ancient tomb, fluttered a distant breeze through his cell. It was whitely morning outside, the hot clean implacability of the desert. Just the time to get work done.

Molina stopped and massaged the fingers of one hand slowly. He would hate to leave this cell. Not that it was particularly nice or special, but an attachment grows, however unwillingly, to any place we have lived in and planned in. So it was here. He had been here over a year now. He knew the crevices and shy quirks, like a new bride accustomed to her husband's ways. Perhaps he would marry again, someday. Massingill might even agree to free him, someday. Life was endless possibilities.

Over his whitewashed desk he had hung a picture of the Madonna, robed in pastel blue and white, with great fleshy white lilies hanging adoringly around her. Her eyes were fixed on the observer in the most abject, sorrowing expression. This was the Madonna of the Crucifixion. Whenever he wanted to weep, Molina merely thought of this picture and the Madonna's sorrowing eyes. The tears came.

He picked up a new pen, and put in a new nib from the collection he had acquired for his calligraphy. Massingill encouraged it as a useful hobby. Massingill had warned him last night that the chances of being extradited to California were very good. He must be ready to move. They exchanged hard, angry words, nothing irretrievable, of course, because no matter what happened, he still needed Massingill. Prepare yourself, Massingill said, we're going to fight it in court, but we could lose. Molina tested the new nib and then inked it. Make ready.

He bent to the matchbook cover. Its little gray oblong was beginning to sprout dark spots as Molina worked in the morning's pure white light, the light of inner clarity and certainty, under the changeless sorrow of the Madonna. He moved the nib precisely, as he had learned at DVI and then Folsom. He could print up to thirty-two characters per line, almost as small as an insect's tiny footprints. He could print a page inside one matchbook. And there were four this time, four sets of instructions to be handed out and followed when he was taken away from this cell and no longer able to pass them along one by one. He was circumspect in what was said over the phone. He assumed his calls were now being overheard. Massingill's edginess leant force to the possibility.

He rarely said much to visitors or on the phones anyway. It was to tiny scraps of paper, insignificant bits easily hidden or overlooked, that he committed his thoughts. Like these matchbooks.

A matchbook for Orepeza's sister, Elisa, in Los Angeles. Two matchbooks, with very specific instructions and threats, leavened by pleas and promises, for his hesitant contact in Santa Maria.

A final one for Alves and Rivera. Kill Swanson. Kill his family. Kill them all. Kill Max.

He stilled an urge to hurry. He had visitors coming soon, the girls. The matchbooks had to be ready for them. They were wives of men who worked for him, who could carry these little matchbooks where he directed. On paper these women were substantial people. They owned property everywhere Orepeza had bought it, putting restaurants and land in their names because men on parole can be stopped any time by any policeman. The wives came and went as they pleased.

A fly, black and droning, appeared in the cell, lighting first in the window, which overlooked the sandy yard and then off into the fearful expanse of the desert. Molina raised his head to the Madonna. He sighed and two fat tears glistened in his eyes. He wiped them with the edge of his sleeve and went back to the matchbooks. The fly rose in humming certainty and circled Molina, hunched low over the matchbooks, engraving in fly's letters the orders he wanted carried out. He didn't notice the fly, or perhaps simply couldn't hear its low, plaintive buzzing as it adoringly circled him.

"Call me Ernie." Molina's lawyer stuck a stiff card in Swanson's hand. They stood in the nearly empty Department 16 of the Superior Court, in the white-concrete-and-glass courthouse across the street from Swanson's office. Alone with them was the bailiff, spooning cough medicine into a paper cup at his desk.

He's all pink, Swanson thought, like a little pink balloon all covered with clothes. That's what he'd tell Di about the man who had yanked them away from their evening walk. Gleason had called to break the news. Molina's lawyer was going into court the next morning to get a temporary restraining order preventing his transfer from Nevada to California.

Less than eighteen hours later, many spent at the office trying to meet whatever Ernie Grignon threw at him, Swanson held his card.

"Call me an optimist, my wife says I'm the last optimist anywhere." He moved his arms as though calling a runner safe at base. "So I'm so optimistic this morning, I believe you're going to see the light of reason and reach an accommodation with me and those Justice Department guys."

He pointed at the back of the courtroom. Three men had come in.

"I thought you've got a motion," Swanson said.

"Well, we can always talk? Can't we? I can withdraw this old motion here and in return you can drop your extradition request for, say, one year. After one year, well, you can bring my guy into your county. We'll take things as they come then."

"I'm going to bring him here now."

"Rush, rush." Grignon was dressed in a blue-and-white seersucker suit with a blue dotted bow tie. His round pink face was shaved closely, with a reddish patch on his lower cheek where he had cut too hard. Swanson thought if he scraped further all he'd hit would be more pink, like shaving pink dough.

"I had a client, so anxious to get his day in court he took a swan dive from the third floor of the jail, landed right in front of me as I was coming to visit him," Grignon imitated a diver. "Broke his legs, his ribs. I says to him, you can't even escape right from jail. That's the vice of haste. You do everything all wrong, like you're doing. There is more than enough of old Hector to go around, believe me."

He waited with a smile.

The bailiff coughed loudly and swore.

Swanson didn't know the men in the back of the courtroom. They were whispering and joking with each other.

"I got one," he said to Molina's lawyer.

"Okay."

"Knew this lawyer once, only did DUI cases. He came to court in suits with these little cigarette burns in them, he looked like he didn't take a bath, he kind of whined at you when he wanted a deal for some guy with a .23 b.a. who'd just run over three nuns in a crosswalk."

"I know the type."

"And the best part, this guy's office. You call. It's a garage. They're fixing cars. Sometimes he's there, sometimes he's not. The mechanic took his messages." Swanson stopped. Grignon looked eager.

"I think I'm missing something. I don't see the point."

"You remind me of him." Swanson turned and sat down at the counsel table.

Grignon gave a horsey snort, with a smile.

The Honorable Douglas Pizer popped from his chambers and clumped onto the bench. Sour, hard of hearing, Pizer had once ordered his bailiff to close the doors so Swanson couldn't leave the courtroom. He was checking to see if he had grounds to hold Swanson in contempt. He called Swanson a clown. Not the best judge to have been assigned to.

Pizer wouldn't look down from the bench. He tossed the motion and Swanson's response from one side of the bench to the other. "Call your witness," he barked to Grignon.

"I'm an optimist," Grignon said to Swanson, and rose.

Nothing's too good for the little prince. Give him whatever he wants. Etchells stirred himself and peered through the meshed glass of the door into the visitor's room. There he is, the little prince and his harem, Etchells saw acidly. Two of them this time, pretty good looking this time, not like the coyote meat he had in a couple of weeks ago. Of course, through the door like this, you couldn't hear anything they were saying to each other, no, no. That would be unkind to the little prince, Humberto Cazares. It would invade his privacy. There were strict rules for the little prince and Etchells had gotten burned by the warden for violating the one about not annoying him. Asked the little prince too many questions, that was the sin he committed. Everybody was supposed to bow and scrape, not ask questions like he would to any other prisoner in the joint. Old Humberto had some juice with the warden. Keep the little prince in Security Housing, practically with a whole floor to himself and special details. Humberto Cazares my ass, Etchells thought again, as he always did on the days when he had to nursemaid this very special prisoner. He's some kind of fucking snitch.

No taping the little prince. No opening his mail except on direct orders from the warden, and then only with the deputy warden present. No cavity searches for his visitors either, coming in or going out. All you could do was to take a look inside the visitor's room every so often to make sure one of the harem wasn't spreading her legs, reaching inside and passing a shank to the little prince. Although why Cazares would want out of this pampered prison setup, Etchells didn't know.

Whenever Cazares had the harem in, that's what Etchells and the guys called them, there was a lot of hand holding and kissing and passing of matches and cigarettes. Cazares wasn't big on smoking, but he sure had matches and cigarettes to pass out to these babes when they came. Etchells saw Cazares take one babe's hands, push his scarred face into hers like he was trying to eat her fucking tongue. Etchells turned away in frustrated disgust. For a guy in about the most protected custody in Nevada, this Cazares sure had enough women who would come to see him once, sometimes twice a week. There was one, his wife, kind of chunky but cute, she used to come all the time, brought a kid once, but there was some kind of fight about the kid and Etchells didn't see her again. The wife, she used to show up regularly on time. It was hard to tell if she got along with the little prince. They did a lot of kissing, though. She hadn't been around for some time.

Sometimes men came. Usually, though, it was women, dark haired, young, and generally tough looking, but then others like these two today, real sweet.

He ran the metal detector over them himself before they were taken into the visitor's room where the unfiltered desert sunlight whitened everything. He wasn't that old, not even fifty, but these two with their reddened cheeks and mouths giggled when he complained about the cramp in his back, just trying to make conversation, then off they pranced to wait for the little prince to be brought up.

There it went.

He saw the matches and cigarettes going to one of the girls. She laughs, takes out a cigarette and lights it. He's kissing the other one, too. Same style. He finishes. And now she gets her pack and matches. These are carefully stowed in her purse. I checked that purse, he thought savagely, and she isn't bringing anything in for him.

He looked at his watch. Time was almost up. The little prince was always good about that, like he had some schedule to keep. He never got caught chatting or doing something. Soon as he'd gotten his smooches and given away the smokes, he just sat there and the harem got up, smoothed the lines out of the dresses or straightened the jeans and pranced up to the door to be let out, like I'm a damn employee in some damn hotel.

Etchells still held the book he'd been reading between glancing at Cazares and his girls. His finger had grown icy, the blood cut off holding his place. Maybe next time, honey, he thought, I'll have to run that detector up around your legs, maybe you'd like that and I don't care what the warden says about not bothering Cazares or his damn visitors. Maybe I'll even have to march you over to the prison hospital and let that half-wit inmate tech spread you out for an X-ray just to make sure you're not carrying stuff in for the little prince.

Sure enough, right on time, the tapping, knocking, giggling arrogant summons came from inside the visitor's room. Etchells smiled. Let them wait. He slid quietly into the chair just to the side of the door and let the rapping grow more impatient. He opened his book, the blood rushing back into his numbed finger.

It was a good story, old-fashioned Western with good guys and bad guys. He pushed his glasses down his nose, listening with pleasure as the knocking increased in force. Now he heard one of the girls calling out. Sorry, honey, the door's locked and I'm going to let you sit there for a minute while I finish a little reading. The little prince had been kind of jumpy since he came back from whatever trip they let him out for this time. It was hard to tell with him, but he was mad as hops about something or real worried. Etchells didn't have to ask him and risk getting in trouble. He could see it in the way Cazares moved, the way he talked.

Never saw a prisoner get taken out of the joint so much, even a regular snitch. He must be Super Snitch.

He sat reading, the pounding on the door almost like music. Good guys and bad guys, he thought, the old West. Not like now. Nobody had any trouble telling the difference between one or the other in those days.

"Mr. Rau, how long have you been with the Justice Department?" Swanson leaned against the empty jury box. He was so tired it was like sitting in molasses, heavy and overpowering. The court's clock swept down to two and clicked.

"Off and on for about fourteen years. I was in private practice in San Francisco for several years." Straight backed, middle-aged, with a small black moustache, an impassive witness.

He made a startling contrast for an hour during Grignon's brisk examination. The pink balloon, the banker.

"You said you're responsible for the Molina case?"

"I'm one of those responsible. The Task Force on Organized Crime actually has three members, including Mr. Massingill."

"But, you," Swanson now pointed, "your special responsibilities include coordinating the transportation of this witness when he comes to California?"

"Yes, that's correct. I make the arrangements for getting him out of Nevada State Prison and transporting him to whatever jurisdiction here in California will be conducting the trial."

"What sort of arrangements?" Swanson idly drew on a pad he laid on the railing of the jury box.

Rau sighed reflectively. He had a worn look that some men get after years working in a large department, as if his only individual mark was an engraved pen set. "Well, there's the internal prison transfer. We have to get him from his cell to whatever transport we're using. We've got to present some excuse for moving him."

"Because he's under an assumed name with a false prison jacket?"

Rau nodded deliberately. "It's all part of the security program for him. So, what we've used in the past is family emergencies, a parole hearing, things like that."

"How is he moved inside the prison?"

"You mean from the inside to the outside?"

"Yeah, physically moved. How do you take him from one place to the other?"

"Objection, please, your honor." Grignon slowly stood, stopped, held one hand out toward the judge, "Relevance, your honor, lack of relevance."

"What's the point?" Pizer said loudly.

"I'm trying to find out what precautions are taken, your honor." Swanson pushed himself away from the jury box, "I want to find out what kind of risks the Justice Department normally exposes this man to."

"Overruled." Pizer sounded unhappy.

Grignon sank down.

"How is he moved?"

Rau now had an idea where Swanson wanted to go in his questioning, but there was no way to meet Grignon's objection without revealing it. Rau was planning his answers.

But Swanson had one surprise for him.

"He's got the usual complement of staff," Rau said carefully, "two or three guards, armed, of course. He's in handcuffs and sometimes a belly chain."

"You think he's an escape risk?"

"Well, part of it's for show. The other prisoners have to believe he's what they think he is, a tough guy."

"Is he an escape risk?"

"I don't think so."

"Never?"

"Well, I don't think he likes being in prison."

"You can say it. Hector Molina's an escape risk, isn't he?"

"Every prisoner is."

Swanson glanced at Pizer, but as usual it was impossible to tell what was going on behind the heavy glasses and the owlish squint. "Guards who escort him are armed with guns and rifles?"

"Shotguns are the weapons used, I think. I really don't know."

"But Molina's not given more of an escort than any other security housing prisoner who'd be moved, is he?"

"No. That would make him stand out. We treat him like he's one of the prison population, nothing to make him seem different."

Grignon sat hunched forward, like an inquisitive child.

The bailiff burped quietly from his medicine and the clerk got up to answer the telephone ringing in the judge's chambers. It was all stupefying, this ritual, and yet so much hung on its outcome. Swanson felt a little better. He had just made Rau expose his own weakness.

"Isn't there always a risk of trouble when inmates are moved in prison?"

"Yes, I guess there is."

"Other prisoners might try to free them? Help them escape? Overpower the guards?"

"Any of that, I guess. I really don't know."

"But any time a prisoner is moved, for whatever reason, if he's going to the prison hospital for a stomachache or being taken to testify in a major gang trial, there is a danger from the other inmates, right?"

"Ordinarily, I imagine there is."

"This isn't ordinary?"

"We're talking about a very special prisoner."

"The other inmates don't know that, do they?" Swanson said very briskly.

Rau hesitated for a moment. "No. They don't."

"You know what happens when a prisoner is taken across the yard or through a cell block?"

"Generally."

"The guards have shotguns at the ready? Inmates have to press themselves against the wall when the detail goes by, right?"

"Sure, sure."

Pizer squinted tightly at Swanson. It wasn't exactly a smile, but he seemed pleased.

"So, it's accurate to say that nothing you do for Hector Molina when you take him out to testify increases or diminishes the dangers faced when any prisoner's moved?"

Swanson didn't think Rau got into court very often; he had the caution and bloodlessness of an office jockey. He was trying to find some way around answering the question as Swanson wanted him to.

"I guess in a very loose sense that would be true." Rau puffed his cheeks.

"Be specific if you have to, Mr. Rau."

"I was only going to say that Mr. Molina is a special prisoner so other considerations get factored in."

"Because he's special you expose him to risks more often than most other prisoners, right?"

"We try to minimize every possible risk."

"But, he's moved more often, isn't he? Didn't you just say he's special and he gets taken out to testify?"

Rau shook his head. He wasn't irritated or angry, merely uncomfortable that he was still a witness and out in the open. "He is moved more often."

Swanson sat down and fought the urge to yawn. It was amazing that he could feel fatigue when so much depended on what he did in the next few minutes. "It's fair to say," he began gently, "that when you, and by that I'm talking about the Task Force, weigh the risks of moving Molina against the testimony, you come out on the side of taking the risks? That's the way it is, right?"

"It's never that cut and dried."

Swanson bolted up. "Give me a time you decided it would be too risky to move Molina and you let a case fall apart without him."

"Objection." Grignon also stood up, a pink flush on his face. "That's argumentative, your honor."

"Sustained," Pizer agreed.

"All right, Mr. Rau," Swanson walked to him, "are the risks of moving Molina from Nevada to California any greater if he's extradited as opposed to traveling to California to appear as a witness?"

"I think so."

"Why?" Swanson knew the answer and knew Pizer wouldn't like it.

Rau puffed his cheeks again for a moment. "Well, because in an extradition situation, Mr. Molina would be out of federal custody. I don't feel he'd get the protection we've been able to provide."

"The state can't do it as well as you can?"

"I don't believe so. This is our area of expertise." Rau tried to grin. "We've been at it for a while."

Pizer snorted.

Swanson liked the sound of it. He'd gotten Rau to say that the risks didn't matter as long as the feds thought they were getting the better part of the bargain and nobody but them could protect Molina. The question of irreparable harm coming to Molina, the whole point of trying to block his extradition, had been nullified.

The last doubt, the key weakness in Rau's appearance, remained to close things off.

Swanson went to the clerk's desk. A matchbook lay there, tagged with the court's identification as Defendant's Exhibit A. He held it up. "You believe this death threat is serious, don't you?"

Rau nodded emphatically. "That was given to the U.S. Attorney by the protected witness. We do take that kind of threat seriously."

"He's got a lot of enemies?"

Grignon frowned and touched his bow tie several times. Pizer couldn't understand this shift, either. Swanson sounded like he now agreed with Rau.

"As I said on direct, Mr. Swanson, this particular protected witness has taken a terrific risk. He's got three or four gangs out for his blood, literally. He's got a contract out that will stay out. We have to take this kind of death threat seriously."

"Which gang sent it?"

"Beg your pardon?"

"Where did the threat come from? You've got to have some idea who's telling your special witness he's going to get killed."

Rau sat silently for a moment. "No."

"No what?"

"We don't know the exact source of this particular threat."

"There've been others?"

"I'd rather not specify."

Swanson appealed directly to the judge. "Your honor, please direct the witness to answer my question unless he's claiming some kind of privilege."

Grignon held a white handkerchief in one pink hand and moved it across the table in front of him. "With the court's permission, I don't understand the purpose of this inquiry."

"I do," Pizer said loudly. "Please frame an objection if you have one, Mr. Grignon."

"Well, your honor, the district attorney is going into an area that is remote to our hearing today. The question is the clear and present danger to this witness today. Immediately."

"Mr. Swanson? Response?"

"Nothing, your honor."

Pizer squinted tightly. "Mr. Rau, are you claiming any privilege on behalf of the government?"

"Confidentiality, your honor," Rau said apologetically.

"All I want to know is if there've been other threats like this, your honor. He can keep the rest of it to himself."

"I understand your purpose, Mr. Swanson, don't repeat yourself." The judge shook his head and leaned to Rau, "Answer his question, sir."

Rau sighed deeply. "Other threats? Yes. There have been others."

"Communicated to you solely by Hector Molina?"

"Yes."

"How many in the last few years? One? Two? Ten? A hundred?"

"Nothing like ten. Maybe five or six. I don't know exactly."

Swanson walked to Rau. On other occasions they might have worked together and been part of the same effort. Cross-designation among prosecutors happened in Santa Maria so that a deputy district attorney could also go into federal court as an assistant U.S. Attorney. But not on this case. Molina had them chasing each other.

He held the matchbook up for Rau. "You don't know if Hector Molina wrote this himself, do you?"

"That's silly."

"You don't know which person or gang sent it, right?"

"Yes."

"So anybody, including Molina, could have written this and given it to the United States Attorney?"

"I cannot, for the life of me, see one good reason why a man like Mr. Molina would do such a thing."

Swanson put the matchbook down on the clerk's desk. She smiled up at him briefly. "What happened on those other occasions, the other threats?"

"I don't understand."

"Objection. Three-fifty-two material, your honor," Grignon said promptly, "without revelance today and very time consuming if I have to go over it again."

"Overruled. Answer the question."

Rau crossed his legs and frowned. "Please repeat it."

"Absolutely. Did you take some kind of action on those other occasions when threats were passed from Molina to the Task Force?"

"Certainly. We tried to increase his security, we took measures to safeguard him."

"Did those measures involve granting him more telephone privileges? More access to things he wanted? Moving him to other cells?"

"Yes, they did."

"And this time?"

"It involved transferring him to another jail."

"Doesn't that say that Hector Molina is calling the shots in his case?"

"Of course not." Rau laughed genially. It sounded ridiculous to him.

"Tell me, Mr. Rau," Swanson shrugged easily, "if you wanted to manipulate the witness protection program to get more things from it, wouldn't you use phony threats? I'm asking hypothetically."

"If somebody's unscrupulous, there are all sorts of ways to jack a program around. But," he smiled again, "we've been doing this for a while. I have a pretty good idea what's real and what isn't."

"Sure you do." Swanson picked up the matchbook for the last time, holding it so Pizer had the best view of it. Grignon folded up his white handkerchief slowly into smaller and smaller squares.

"You're so sure Hector Molina is playing fair and square with you, you never had any analysis done of this matchbook, right? No ink testing, no microscopic examinations, nothing at all to determine if Molina might have written it?"

Rau shook his head. "Of course not."

Weyuker had a small mirror lying flat on his desk in the Homicide Bureau, and he was just barely able to look critically at the way his new hairline sat on his forehead. So it wasn't perfect. It was an improvement. Sarah couldn't complain about it.

Sokol tapped him on the back. "You still taking a week starting the twenty-fourth?"

"Believe it. Got the wagon loaded and we're driving down to L.A. then renting a boat." He turned his head a couple of times.

"Looks like a frigging mop," Sokol said. He had a file card in one hand. "Okay, so you and the woman get out of here. Why don't you take the twenty-eighth instead?"

"Fuck me." Weyuker slid the mirror back on his desk and shifted his gun around at his waist. He belched contentedly. "I ain't switching with you, I ain't taking any time for you, I ain't changing my vacation, Ricardo, periodo."

Sokol wagged the card in the air. "Just four little days later, amigo. I need the extra days."

"Last two times I got burned. I take a vacation last year, no, year before last, I come back and they've transferred me from Narcotics to Fradulent Documents. Hot shit. I take CTO for three days in January and they transfer me from Bad Checks to Child Assault. Then I say I'm going to take a vacation so they give me Homicide, like I only get good assignments when they think I'm leaving."

"I don't get it. I thought you liked it here."

"I do. Jesus yes. But, those other times I switched with guys. Every time. Every time I switch I get burned on assignments and I don't want to get out of here."

"You're paranoid, bud."

It was early afternoon and the bureau was relatively empty and quiet, before the other detectives and the whole troop of secretaries and cops came in from shift. Weyuker leaned back in his chair, hands clasped behind his head. He sucked in his non-existent gut and thrust out his nonexistent chest. "Sorry about that, but I can't do it. I got my wife all primed, I got the kid set up. It's go on that day or my ass."

Sokol stuffed the file card into his shirt pocket. He put his hands in his pockets and bobbed his head. Obviously he was bored and didn't want to be anyplace where he could shatter the inertia of the moment. "Anything happened with that beanhead and his pal?"

Weyuker shook his head and yawned. "They're both doing nothing."

A kid in blue jeans hurried in, dropping bundles of letters and manila envelopes on the various deserted desks. He darted to Weyuker's and tossed a few folded-up flyers and envelopes at him. He kept his eyes on the floor. When he was out the door, Sokol said, "Brain dead, I'm telling you. Hire the helpless."

Idly, Weyuker poked at the mail. He came to one flat yellow manila envelope and paused. He looked up at Sokol. "I got to get some work done."

"Who doesn't."

"I really do have stuff to do."

"All right." The other detective reluctantly shuffled to his own desk. "Think about the twenty-eighth, will you? It'd make my day."

Weyuker slipped his thumb under the flap and gingerly opened the envelope. He glanced at Sokol, who was on the phone. From the envelope he took out a single stiff piece of cardboard on which two matchbook covers, cut off neatly and taped carefully, had been fastened.

Someone had printed HI AGAIN at the top of the cardboard. He felt a heaviness in his throat and brain at the sight of the too-familiar tiny letters neatly ordered on the matchbook covers. It was the same heaviness that came over him when he stood by the white-sheeted thing in the coroner's office. He hadn't told Swanson about this personal, furtive visit right after Angie was killed. It wasn't me, he tried to tell whatever remained of her. I didn't know about this, he pleaded with the unforgiving, almost inhuman white form lying in front of him.

Not again, he thought as he began reading slowly, with disbelief, what was being demanded of him. This is the last thing I need, Weyuker could hear the words in his mind, I'll leave you alone after this. The last thing. No more.

He caught his own face in the mirror on the desk and pushed the mirror away, fearfully.

"Further argument?" Pizer called to Grignon, who had thrown himself limply back in his chair.

"None, your honor."

"People?"

"No," Swanson said. He wanted to make his next call home to Di to find out how she and the kids were. Three times a day, in what was becoming an inflexible routine, he telephoned them.

Late in the afternoon. The burnt-orange-colored walls of the courtroom closed out the daylight. It could have been four in the morning.

"I'm going to make my ruling now on your motion, Mr. Grignon. I don't think it requires any further research by me."

Go. Go, Swanson thought. He grimaced over at the bailiff who grinned back in sympathy. The Honorable Douglas Pizer was never hurried in his own courtroom.

"I do not find that you have carried, by a preponderance of the evidence, your burden of showing that irreparable harm would come to the prisoner if the extradition warrant issued by this state is duly executed in the state of Nevada. I make a specific finding that he's moved all the time by the federal authorities into California. And I fail to find any evidence presented to me that indicates this prisoner is going to be more at risk if he's brought back into this county to stand trial."

Pizer spoke from the notes he had been jotting through Grignon's last two witnesses, federal marshals who moved protected witnesses from place to place. Now the judge dropped the page of notes. He scowled as he usually did. "My decision is to deny your motion for a temporary restraining order, Mr. Grignon. The extradition warrant will be honored forthwith as far as this state is concerned. Maybe you'll get a different view of things from Nevada."

Grignon blubbered his thick lips softly. A smile instantly appeared on his pink face. He rose. "Thank you for your promptness, your honor."

The bailiff rose. Pizer rose. Swanson slowly stood up. There would be no problems from Nevada. Molina would be handed over in five days. He would meet his oath to Hannah and Frank.

"Excuse me," Rau and his two associates stood at the rear of the courtroom.

"Mr. Rau?" the judge squinted tightly and called out.

"I just wanted to advise this court and the district attorney that we will be filing for immediate relief in the Eastern District."

"You do what you have to."

Swanson threw his pad down angrily.

"And, I also, your honor," Grignon smoothed his shirt with a smile and a slight bow, "will be filing an immediate appeal of the court's order directly to the state Supreme Court. The appeal is being delivered by me personally tomorrow."

"Please say hello to everybody." Pizer exhaled quickly and disappeared back into his chambers. The door closed loudly.

Suddenly, Swanson had no time. One attack he could have met, but simultaneous assaults in the state and federal system would freeze the extradition solid. It could take months of delays and hearings to get it moving again.

Grignon was beside him as he left the courtroom. "I told you, I'm an optimist," the other attorney said agreeably. "Always keep trying, keep pushing in there. Push, push, push."

Something hard and decisive was needed now. Swanson strode by Grignon, an idea springing into his mind.

Weyuker parked carelessly, taking up two spaces, forgot to lock the door or set the brake and had to go back to do both. It's never too late, he said to himself, you'll figure something out. The words writhed over his brain in little black letters.

His wife's box-like office was set flush on the side of a supermarket and said TAX RETURNS in white-outlined blocks. People moved around the supermarket but nobody seemed to notice the tax office or two other side stores that sold Taiwanese toys and shoes.

I just took money. I didn't do much. I didn't even tell Orepeza much. The badges, hell, they wanted badges for some rip-off, and that's all I ever thought. It was just money, that's the worst I did. I'm owed something after all these wasted years, big joke thinking you can stop evil or any of it.

Weyuker's thoughts flew, frantic and unrestrained. He was justifying and condemning all at the same time. When he went into his wife's office, he slammed the door behind him, automatically muttering he was sorry.

"You said you'd be ready," he called to his wife.

"Only a minute more. Almost done, almost done," Sarah Weyuker sang out. She sat behind a plain brown desk heaped with papers. The only other desk in the office was bare. A putty-faced man in a Hawaiian shirt sat in front of her looking dejected. Around them dust danced in light slashes, agitated by an old metal-bladed fan straining on top of a row of pale-green file cabinets.

"I'm taking vacation time for this," he said. "I'm here right on time, you said you'd be ready. Let's go, okay?"

She looked up from the papers, her pencil held as if to stab down. "So shoot me, Dick, I've got to finish with a client." She said blithely to the man beside her, "We talk like this all the time."

Her graying blonde hair hung down to her wide shoulders, partly covering a bright coral shell necklace. "Sit down for a second, I'll be finished." She sucked air in, grinned at the dejected man who, dog-like, watched and listened. Her pencil ran down the papers and she shook her head.

For a moment, Weyuker stood, hands half-cocked irresolutely in his pockets. He was choking in the dusty, warm office. His throat ached with every breath and she wouldn't get up and leave. It was a simple thing. He relied on her word. She thought they needed a new car, the kid was going to college, trade in her old one. But she let him down, still sitting there, false words, false trust.

He watched her, then leaned over the file cabinet on one elbow, his right hand flicking out at the dull steel blades whirring and pushing thick air onto him. One small fall from grace, like looking away from the road for an instant after a lifetime of vigilance, that's all it was. Take money once from this guy Orepeza. Why? He didn't know. It was as if his concentration failed, faltered, and he started sleepwalking, only bolting awake when those matchbooks came to him and he sat, still and dumb and horrified at his desk. He tore them up, flushed the tiny pieces and washed his hands. I've got to do what he says. Weyuker reached out, barely aware of his fingers drawing back, jabbing closer to the blades.

The entreaties bore in on him. He says this is the last thing, it's all he wants now, and I'm free and clear and it's all over, Weyuker thought. It's never too late, I haven't gone too far.

Even as he reached for the idea, the white-sheeted, faceless thing lay before him. One woman dead, not my fault. I didn't tell them where she was. Another woman, down at the D.A.'s office, arrested, and that's not my fault. But the tiny words threatened, and Weyuker knew the white-sheeted form blocked any way back for him. He could only go forward and try to find his way out.

There's a way out, he said again and again. It's never too late. I could kill him, even. Pukes like him get killed and nobody asks anything very hard. Or maybe just do what he says and he won't bother any of us again.

"You're going to hurt yourself," Sarah called out. "Would you stop fidgeting?"

"What?"

"Don't poke your hand into the fan. It's distracting."

"I don't have a lot of time," he snapped back, "I got things to do."

She sighed and said something conciliatory to the client, who tilted his head in agreement, pawing several papers into one hand and stuffing them into his baggy white trousers. He lumbered past Weyuker, shutting the door with a faint, defeated whisper.

"Now, Dickie," she said, as if he was a child, "what's the matter? You've got some hair up your ass about something."

"I said I'd come over. You said you'd be ready. It's your idea to get a new car. So I counted on you."

"It's not the end of the world." She swept pencils and bits of things from the desk into a drawer.

"I just expected a little loyalty."

"What are you talking about?" She came over to him.

"Don't I deserve some consideration? You tell me one thing, you do something else."

Sarah's mouth turned down faintly, a frequent indication of the boredom she felt lately. "I'm very, very sorry. It was inconsiderate, but let it go, Dickie." She flipped off the fan, the dust spinning in the light slowly, hanging suspended.

It's not you. Not you, even if my being a cop bores you and

cops bore you and going to cop parties bore you. It's something else, he thought, a secret. I've got a secret to keep. "We'll take my car," he jangled his keys.

"We can take mine. I don't mind."

"I took the trouble to drive over here, special for you, we'll take mine."

"I give up," without any heat. "Something didn't happen at work? Nothing's wrong?"

"Like what?" They stepped out onto the asphalt, the vacant toy store and its dusty, unwanted cheap metal displays bearing their reflections in the window.

"They didn't change your vacation again? I mean, I think you need a vacation. I know I do."

They got into the car. "Everything's the same, we're going. It's all set." He turned to her. "I do a lot for this family. You don't know all I've done."

Sarah Weyuker closed her eyes and lay against the seat. "We both work very hard, Dickie."

He started the car, his hand moving without guidance. "There are things you don't know about."

"I don't want to hear about all the silly people and silly things they do. Year after year you try to straighten their messes out. It doesn't go away. There's always more and it's always the same. If somebody has to do it, I'm glad it's you. I know you." She smiled at him. "Now, calm down, let's talk about something more pleasant."

He thought about the bank accounts she didn't know existed, the messages that came to him written in tiny black specks. He swung into another lane, Sarah asking him about the new car. What color? Did a stereo radio matter much? His hands and feet moved mechanically, his mind occupied with its chant. It's never too late, he said, trying to conjure solidity and truth from magical repetition. There's a way out, it's never too late, just do what he wants now, it's never too late, Weyuker thought in hope and despair.

CHAPTER EIGHTEEN

"They can't see this far, this damn far in front of their own faces." Gleason held his hand out, quivering with anger. He stomped around his office and raged freely. "Brother Claude won't even pick up the phone when I call now. He's too busy. He can't talk. He's got my message, but he can't come now, he's got something else doodly-squat to do. I do not understand these people. No, I do not."

Susan stood at the large windows that overlooked Santa Maria's busy downtown. At the far edge of the city, almost lost to view, a black crop-duster dipped and swooped to earth.

"What about it?" Gleason demanded of her. Swanson sat brooding on the sofa.

She turned from the window. The black crop-duster's distant, whining pitch sounded like an insistent fly. "I hated having Fran arrested, Joe. I know it had to be, but I hated doing it. She still had on all these bandages and even though I tried to make it as inconspicuous as I could, we had the usual gawkers standing around when we came out of her house."

Clean sweep, Swanson thought. Even the right things feel like fumbles in this one.

Gleason flopped down in his chair and winced as he banged his cast against the thick leg of his desk. "We got a halfway decent case against her going in, Susie. Enough for a holding order, get her set for trial. You put on the bank records with her bribe money, access to the badges, Mike's informant, the way she acted after the lie box even if we can't use the results. She'll cop to the badges before trial." Gleason was unrelenting. "Somebody like her, somebody you trusted, they always cop out when it comes down to it. If she has a hard time, it doesn't bother me at all."

"Well, it bothers me," Susan said with a dry snap. "I felt like the lord high executioner this afternoon marching her away."

Gleason bent over his cast to massage his ankle and upper leg. He adroitly moved the cigarette holder from one side of his mouth to the other and puffed furiously. "No deals for her. We aren't going to cut anything."

"Joe, we made deals with Mike's snitch, we can deal for Fran, my God."

"She's different."

Susan folded her arms and glared at him, into his wounded pride and unslaked grief. "How?"

"She was one of us."

Swanson barely heard them arguing. He had his hands deep in his pockets, his legs straight and motionless in front of him. Over the angry voices hung the curving drone of the crop-duster, and when he looked out over Gleason's shoulder, through the window, he could just see it dipping into the black sawtooth edges of the palm trees.

"The first priority here," Gleason sank back with a small groan, "is to get busy with responses we can take to court. Susan, you and Mike are going to the Supreme Court. Get in there and get that appeal denied tomorrow."

Swanson sat just below the wall full of diplomas, citations, photos, and plaques from Gleason's thirty years as a public man. His life was nailed to the wall. In his high-backed chair, smoke writhing and twisting around him, Gleason was outlined in the late afternoon's fiery light.

"Somebody's going to have to take care of the federal writ," she said. "I can get one of our cross-designates to be there."

"Good. Exactly." Gleason nodded. He looked at Swanson. "You have two cents to put in? We're talking about your case."

"They'll beat us in court." Swanson didn't look up.

"Bullshit," Gleason said.

"I think we've got a good shot." Susan knew he had something on his mind.

"They'll keep us bouncing back and forth from state courts to federal. It'll take months in court."

Gleason tossed his cigarette holder into a marble ashtray so hard that it flipped onto his desk. "You can't block an extradition forever, goddamnit, even these guys are going to lose." He snatched the holder up.

"No," Swanson said. He seemed to be staring at his shoes.

"No what?"

"Let's kidnap the son of a bitch," he said.

"Look, dude, I had this warrant out for six fucking years. I lived at my own fucking house and they never even checked. You think they going to find us now? We could walk into the fucking jail our own selves and they wouldn't even know who we are. It's the truth."

The troll wobbled his head and splayed his hands out energetically. That was when Nancy figured these two guys were parolees or something and she didn't want to wait on them anymore, but nobody else could take her station, so she was going to have to bring them their food anyway.

Two of them, in the back table, facing the door and the dinner crowd at the bar. It was the usual crew, nurses from down the street at Santa Maria Community Hospital, some construction guys, everybody else in shorts because it was a hot night. Real dim in here because Asa was too cheap for a few lights and the place glowed from the video games and low-watt phony Tiffany lamps. Everybody was nice to Asa since he had his stroke and his face was frozen in a half sneer, but that didn't change the fact that he had always been cheap.

God, dinner was noisy. And then these two came in. The troll, a short guy with a little beard, and the jock. The jock seemed to follow along with the troll, not the other way around. Every time she came over to take their order, hastily put some water down for them, it was the troll doing the talking and the jock kind of dumbly, unhappily nodding. He didn't seem to like whatever the troll was saying and she could see him blowing air out his mouth in frustration.

But they were parolees, Nancy was sure. Couple of Mex ex-cons. She balanced four plates, burgers and tuna salad, and slipped them to other tables. She didn't want to go back to the two in the back. They were creepy and she didn't even know what they were so worked up about.

She was at the table alongside theirs.

"I don't want to stay here," the jock said. He drummed his fingers on the table. "We ain't getting no money, right? We ain't got no friends here, Ray."

"I got friends, in jail. A couple. Somebody can take care of business."

"So I want to go."

The troll was touching her arm. She yanked it away.

"We got to hurry," the troll looked deeply into her eyes. He must have been five feet tall, max, and he was kind of scrunched up. "Can you get our stuff faster?" He smiled at her. That was bad.

"I'm hurrying. This is the busy time." Nancy spun away and back to the bar, to the kitchen. Asa watched her. He was joking with some construction guys.

So she tried to hurry it up. Get their order out and maybe she could go on break and somebody else would have to wait on them.

Their order was up and she grabbed the hot plates, chicken fried steak and ham with gravy, and pushed out of the kitchen, almost bumping into Asa doing his surprise checks to make sure nobody was eating his food as they were cooking. Jesus, he was so cheap.

Nancy heard the troll even over the laughing and the loud

talk from the tables, over the pinging and bonking from the video games, like his voice was in a tunnel of silence for her.

"I like this place," the troll said, with that smile. He was kneading the jock's shoulder soothingly. "We're like invisible here. We can play games."

"I'm not going in the jail."

"It's done already, like that fat guy, okay? Done, over, forget it. I got it covered sideways, every way."

"No money."

"So it's like for the fun of it, okay? The invisible men. No-body sees us, okay, but they get these footprints where we been."

"A snitch is the lowest thing. You got to be in deep, deep badness to snitch."

She was setting the plates down quickly even as the troll, who didn't look up at her, said to the jock with fierce, terrible intensity, "Yeah, but Max's different, okay? He was one of us, man."

The silence ended abruptly and the other sounds flooded over her almost with a shock. She backed away. The jock was dubiously eyeing his pink slab of ham in its brown gravy pool.

The troll said something to her with that smile.

"What?" she said, still moving back, into the familiar, reassuring bar.

Knife in one hand, fork holding the steak down as he slashed at it with intent, brutal strokes, the troll looked at her, "I said, thank you, sweetness."

Nancy hurried away. They were talking again.

Chapter Nineteen

Dinner was over. They ate in the dining room now instead of the kitchen because there were too many windows. Mike and Di cleared the table. In the living room, watching TV, the two cops on this shift would eat, at different times, in about an hour.

He stood with Di at the sink, scraping the dishes.

"He's not doing very well, Mike. He's moping around and I can't get him to tell me anything. I ask him and he either won't talk at all or he says it's nothing."

Swanson could see Matt still sitting at the table, idly playing with a spoon, lifting it, dropping it. Both Lizzie and Meg had gone into the living room and sat in front of the TV, as though the two strange men in plainclothes had always been there. He saw one cop, in great secrecy, slipping a Lifesaver to Meg. Di normally forbade candy.

"I better do it tonight." Swanson rinsed the last plate and put soap on the whole stack. "Early morning again tomorrow and probably we won't get back until eight or nine."

"It's still a secret?"

He grinned. "I don't want to get your hopes up."

"Now I'm going to go crazy."

"You'll survive."

"I will." She put down the sponge she'd been using to wipe the counter, "It's Matty who worries me. Take him out. He didn't get out all day." She held him closely.

"You're doing better than I am." He kissed her slowly. "You're the brave one."

"He'd like to be with you."

That stung Swanson, but he tried not to show it. He hadn't been much company or support for any of them. "Okay," he said.

When he told Matt they were going out for a while, his son didn't move. Then slowly, as if rousing himself, he followed Swanson. One of the cops, Randy, got up.

"Stay put," Swanson said easily, "We're not going far. I'll keep an eye out."

"One of us should come with you," Randy said apologetically. His partner looked away from the TV interestedly.

"Not this time," Swanson said firmly. He took Matt by the shoulder and they stepped outside. He could hear Randy, crackling and garbled, coming over his walkie-talkie to the patrol car on the corner. Swanson waved and he and Matt turned down the other side of the street, away from the police and the reminder that they were locked up inside their own home.

"Warm," he said as they strolled down the sidewalk.

"It's okay," Matt said.

Swanson secretly moved his gun more completely under his sport shirt. Weyuker had arranged a small waist holster for the gun. At least with his shirt pulled over it, it was out of sight.

They walked in silence toward the opposite side of the park. A glittery disk of water was before them and swans and geese honked brazenly on it. A few couples strolled by the trim lake. A pickup touch-football game was going on in the center of the park. Swanson pretended to be interested. "Ooh. Fumble. Did you see that? Perfect toss, fingers just barely around and he fumbled."

Matt said nothing.

"You get a chance to practice any today? Get some kicking practice in?"

"Nope."

"You got to keep up your kicking, Matt. Next game you're going to be right in there."

"Next game I won't even have a team to play with. I'm not even in school now." The voice was angry and forlorn at the same time.

"It'll change." Swanson and Matt had come to the edge of the water. Fat geese swaggered by them. A man crouched nearby throwing bread bits into the water and the swans glided quietly and swiftly toward him. An azure night sky and heavy warm breezes brushed over them. He was watching everywhere, each man or woman anyplace near them. And he never let Matt get farther away than arm's reach. If he had to, he could wrap himself around Matt in a moment.

Otherwise, he had to act as though they were no different from a week before. "This isn't going to last long. So you practice tomorrow, okay?"

"I don't have anybody to practice with."

Swanson was about to ask about Matt's many friends. But he caught himself. Other people who came close to the Swanson family were at risk. Di could only talk to Robin over the telephone. No kids for the girls or Matt to play with in their long, endless days in the house.

"Look, Matt, you're a big guy. Some things can be changed. Some can't. Not right away. Right now I can't change the way we have to live. You have to understand that."

Matt looked at him, fully, for the first time since they began walking. "Why don't you quit your job? You could do something else. We could go back to school and Mom could get her job back. You could do lots of different things."

"I might quit my job," Swanson said. There were too many people who depended on him not just for their peace of mind, but their lives. Justice exacted too great a price sometimes. Di and everybody else had to pay along with him. "Right now I've got to finish a very important case. I started it and it's my responsibility to finish it." There was no way to deflect Molina from him. Resignation wouldn't change his involvement in the Tice killing. It wouldn't save Frank or Hannah, either.

"If you really wanted to quit, you could. You always say you can do anything you really want to do. You always tell me that. So why don't you do it?"

"I'm doing the best I can."

Matt walked ahead, away from the lake. This hadn't been a good idea at all, Swanson realized. He had no answers that made sense. He had obligations and none of them ran in the same direction.

Matt stopped and bent down.

"I found a football," he called to Swanson. Silhouetted behind him the touch game was still going on raucously.

"Throw it," Swanson said. He braced himself as the dark bullet shape hurtled from Matt, high in the air.

It was a partly deflated football, with what looked like a dog's teeth marks in it. He ran his fingers over it trying to get a grip. The faded jock syndrome, he thought.

"That tree and that tree," he pointed at two tall elms near the lake, "are my goals. Try to get past me. It's your ball, Matt, run it out."

Matt hesitated, then poised, waiting for the ball.

Swanson threw the ball quickly. The light faded, washing everything into purple and black, and the park was now ringed with yellow lights like a necklace.

Matt ran at him, the ball protectively tucked away. He bobbed and moved, trying to match Matt's surprisingly swift evasion. For an instant they stood opposite each other, frozen in alertness. He saw Matt's determination. Soccer, baseball, Matt played them all with a panicky persistence and Swanson, deep down, knew Matt didn't like the sports very much. He only did it because it was expected of him, exhorted from him, forced on him. Di sometimes said Swanson was too much of a Little League father. But he thought life was like that, flat out, played hard. Like now.

Then the instant passed and Matt broke to the right, moving

with agility. Swanson called out in annoyance as Matt ducked past him to the tree goals.

They did it again, Matt sprinting out to catch the high, lazy passes, high-taunting as he ran with pleasure. Swanson was out of breath very soon, panting and lumbering with slower moves. For those minutes, it was just the two of them in the park and the only thing of importance was catching the ball and trying to run it past the arbitrary and transient goal of two trees.

They were both lightly sweating when he saw it was time to go. Matt held the football like a proud trophy. He had gotten by Swanson every time. He cantered a few paces ahead as they walked back toward home.

"I didn't think you were that fast," he complained, as Matt grinned and jogged back to him.

"I'm faster. I wasn't trying, I wasn't."

"Don't say that. Makes it worse."

Under an arching vault of trees they walked. "Dad," Matt said, then paused.

"What is it, champ?"

"Everything will go back to the way it was. It's not going to be like this forever?"

He put his arm on Matt's shoulder. "It's going to change real soon. Maybe even tomorrow," he said incautiously.

"We have a plane?" Swanson asked Weyuker.

"We have a plane and a pilot, guy from Modesto who's in the sheriff's reserves over there. That part's okay."

"The Carson City deputies meet us on the ground?"

"It's going to go bang, bang, bang, Mike, believe me. We land at ten-ten, something like that. The cars are there, we hit the road, we're at the prison in twenty-five minutes they say. Maybe less, they give us some speed."

They sat alone in the reception room at the jail. Max urgently wanted to see Swanson. It was nearly eight-thirty and only the evanescent, almost imaginary noises of men locked away in the depths of the jail convinced him there were other human beings around. The hard jail lights fell unforgivingly on them.

"I talked with the warden," Swanson said, grinning. "He says he'll be happy to get the little pecker out of there. He's been a pain ever since the feds dropped him in."

"I don't know about it," Weyuker said, worried. "It feels kind of loosey goosey."

"It's real simple, Dick, we're just going to pick up a California prisoner, that's all. We've got a signed warrant, we've got everybody on both sides of the state line cooperating."

"I've never done anything like this," Weyuker admitted. He got up and sneezed loudly. "Hayfever's got me, too. Out of nowhere this afternoon." He sneezed again, explosively, in the empty room. "The whole thing makes me a little nervous."

Swanson nodded. It made him nervous, too.

"You'll get over it as soon as we're in the air. Flying along, all that beautiful landscape below you. It'll be great."

"I hate flying." Weyuker dabbed at his nose. "We've got some fucking toy Cessna, room for you, me, a deputy and the pilot and Molina. I asked the pilot, he says, and he thinks it's funny, he says you feel every air pocket there is, we'll fly so low. Man, I'd like to stay at home."

"You're a Nevada sheriff for two days."

"Fanfuckingtastic," Weyuker said sarcastically. "We get over there I'm going to see how many of those casinos I can shake down."

They sat without speaking. Swanson had spent the afternoon with Susan and Gleason arranging the details of Molina's sudden move to California. Coordinating it with the police agencies in two states, two jails, getting the transportation to and from the airports, deputizing Weyuker and another cop, only made clear how many missteps were possible in the brief hours of the move. Making Weyuker a deputy sheriff in Nevada gave him authority to act there if something went wrong or somebody questioned their right to take custody of Molina.

For the whole time, from the moment they left Santa Maria

until they took off from Carson City with Molina in custody, they would be running ahead of Grignon and Rau.

He glanced at Weyuker. Lately, the detective seemed more subdued, as if fastened on an inner preoccupation. Maybe my imagination, Swanson thought. Weyuker sniffed gently and sighed. He was lost in his own thoughts.

"They're taking forever with Max," Swanson complained to break the oppressive quiet.

"Always," Weyuker said.

"Is Dufresne up yet?" he called over to the duty officer's mirrored booth.

Clicks, pops, the faint sound of paper rustling and the P.A. snapped on. "Someone's going right now."

"These guys are unbelievable," Swanson complained to Weyuker. He stood up. "I get gripe calls from Max every day. I've got to hold his hand about something. Then I pump him a little. 'Max,' I say, 'how'd Hector let you know what to do?' 'Oh,' he says, 'couple times we got letters.' 'From Hector?' Max says, so big deal? So, I asked him, 'Max, didn't you think some-one's maybe reading this letter?' Max tries to look foxy about it. 'No. See, the envelope's got a phony address. It isn't coming to anybody special. The real address is the return address.' 'That's yours?' Sure, of course. Molina sends out letters, he never gets any, the prison people are looking at the address, not the return. Max says Hector's tried dummy ones, no problem."

"Pretty stupid," Weyuker snuffled.

"So, I get something else from Max yesterday. This's going to hurt Massingill. I ask Max, 'You had a couple face-to-faces with Hector.' 'Two times,' Max says. 'Must have been important, Big Ralph makes you go to see Hector personally.' Max is coy now. 'Well . . .' 'Tell me, it's part of the deal.' So Max says the first time, couple weeks ago, Hector gives them an assignment, this biker named Shorty Harris. The bikers want to make an exam-ple of him, he's selling and not turning the money over, he's fucking around with somebody's woman, I don't know. The bikers, Max says, didn't want it laid on them. The cops, this is over in Vacaville, they know there's bad blood, so it's got to be new talent taking care of Shorty, everybody knowing who's really behind it."

"They do it?"

"Max says so. Vacaville's sending me a file, like I don't have enough coming in suddenly. Max swears he was just the lookout, another guy did the shooting."

"His pal Lester?"

Swanson shrugged. "As usual, Max won't give up Lester on anything. But, it's good enough to burn Molina. It's a face-to-face contract. Max can lay it out for Massingill."

It was another piece of good news, Swanson thought. He was buoyed by the results of the photo lineup in Bakersfield, too. Both Alves and Rivera were picked out by the bartender at the Barrel Club.

Weyuker pinched his nose. None of this news seemed to lift him. "Anything happening on your inside deal, the gal?" Weyuker asked. "She said anything?"

"All she says is she took money from the office. I've got two investigators checking the places she was, when she could've gotten to the badges, when the bank accounts started getting active."

"But, she's it? The leak's plugged?"

"Gleason thinks the case is going to get better."

"Let me know how it goes." Weyuker took a deep breath, as if collecting himself. "The wonderful world of snitches," he said, half to himself. "I ever tell you about my granny snitch?"

Swanson shook his head. Since visiting hours were over, no one else would be coming into the green reception room, as windowless and timeless as the courtroom across the street.

The detective spoke with covert pleasure, finally diverted from whatever was on his mind. "I had this old granny, she's slipping Mickey Finns to old guys she picked up in bars. Then she'd get them home by cab and roll them. I had these old guys saying they were paralyzed while she pulled off their wedding rings, got their checks, money, whatever wasn't nailed down. These were guys, seventy, all of them, old guys. She was probably even good for one homicide. Maybe two. But, we couldn't make them."

"Was she really a granny?"

"You never saw such a perfect granny. I bet she didn't have any kids, unless she smothered them. She had the white hair in the bun, the little wire glasses, the black dresses, little red cheeks. I swear, you'd run over and hug her. She was real lovable."

"She was a good snitch?"

"Man. We got her over in the Women's Facility and I get a note from her. She's got stuff. So I go over. She tells me all the young girls are coming to her with their problems, where their boyfriends are giving them a bad time, the crimes they've done, full confession. Everybody wants to talk to granny. And she wants to turn them all in for a deal." Weyuker clapped his hands together mirthfully. "Oh, did I get junk from that old fucker. She'd lay it all out."

The speaker crackled to life again. "You the D.A.?"

"Yeah, I'm the D.A." Swanson said, a little annoyed. "I just talked to you."

"Not to me. I just came on."

It was a different voice. "Fine. How's Dufresne coming?"

Weyuker snorted in amusement.

There was a shuffle of papers. "He's up. He's in a visiting room, number four. He's been up for a half hour."

"For Christ sake," Swanson said.

"I just came on," the unseen deputy said grumpily.

Swanson and Weyuker went to the door at the side of the mirrored cubicle. The door buzzed angrily and Swanson roughly pushed inside. They checked their guns in.

"Did beanhead say what his problem was?" Weyuker asked. He had his hands in his pockets and he seemed a little discomfited, as if being in the amber-lit corridor was a new experience. He must have walked through that door ten thousand times.

They walked briskly, through another door. It was a fairly narrow corridor, featureless, stale. Max was probably sitting in the visiting room, getting more anxious as the minutes passed and no one came to soothe him.

"He didn't want to talk over the phone. Maybe it's the food. He doesn't like the menu, I don't know. He's a fucking big baby."

Weyuker was beside him. He was about to say something as they turned toward the large rooms set aside for special visits. Swanson heard the first shouts, the first feet running. "Get the goddamn fire extinguisher," he heard somebody cry out.

Down the hallway, he saw deputies darting into one of the visiting rooms, the last one, the door opened wide.

"Jesus Christ, it's a fire," Weyuker said hoarsely. From the doorway, in lazy thick gouts, curled heavy smoke, clinging like a vine to the ceiling as it climbed. Swanson began running.

Somewhere a bell clanged riotously and antic figures pushed by him, shoved him aside as they surged into the room. He forgot about Weyuker. He smelled the stinging smoke of turpentine coiling around them, the whizzing white clouds of the fire extinguishers aimed into the center of the smoking mass in one corner of the room, chairs piled around it in a small bonfire.

"There's a guy in there," he heard, the deputies shielding their faces and arms as they tried to get nearer to the oily, pluming orange flames that rose from the piled chairs and whatever lay beneath them. Twisted ropes of fire reached even higher as the extinguishers were turned on them.

"I can't see anything," Weyuker shouted. He edged forward, retreated, one arm up, coughing harshly. Voices cried out and Swanson pushed into the wildly moving mass of bodies, fighting to the front where the flames and shouting were most intense.

"Get him out!" he shouted, or thought he shouted. He wasn't able to hear anything when he saw the crouched blackened thing under the piled burning chairs as the flames parted momentarily around the incandescent heart of the fire. "Get him out of there, he's in there. Get him out!"

Weyuker was pulling him back, one arm around his waist. Swanson didn't notice. Everything was consumed in the roaring bright center of a silent abyss.

He stood with Weyuker and Bracamonte, the stocky little jail commander in a creaseless olive uniform, in the center of the soot-grimed, blackened visitor's room. A charred table, legs ending in whittled stumps, lay on its side, skeletal. Otherwise, the room had been cleared. It was now an empty maw, caustic smelling, the black walls and floor shiny with water.

Swanson stepped on a piece of ash deliberately and it crumpled soggily. "You got to shake down the whole place," he said to Bracamonte, "Find every shank, every stash. Get me your visitor's log since Max was brought in. You know the gang members, associates? Find out where they were."

"The place is in lockdown," Bracamonte turned from Swanson to Weyuker in testy self-justification. "Was he shanked before?" He raised his chin toward the place where the blackness was deepest and the fire had been its most fierce.

"Jesus, I hope so," Swanson said.

"The guy was a puke. But he didn't deserve this, no he didn't," Weyuker talked to himself.

"Everybody knew he was a snitch," Bracamonte began, flaring over the as-yet-unspoken accusation. "Anybody has access to these rooms. I got trusties, visitors, anybody walking by."

"He was a protected witness. You should've watched him," Weyuker said furiously.

Swanson cut off Bracamonte's already forming obscenity. "You know who brought him up? You know who left him here? I want those names. I want to talk to those guys."

"I got the names, I talked to one guy already, I'll send over the report." Bracamonte broke off a strip of sooty veneer, cracking it into pieces in his hands. "It was a mix-up, shift change, getting ready to button up for the night when you called over and wanted him brought up. Somebody went to sleep at the switch, what can I say? I'm going to discipline their asses."

"You screwed up." Weyuker's arm shot out at him. "You can't even watch one goddamn snitch."

"We don't have time," Swanson said sharply. To Bracamonte, "Get all that stuff over to me early as you can. I'll be back tomorrow afternoon." He was stunned, trying desperately to fix on the job for the next morning. Only a few hours, he thought. "Put some extra people around the Tices, all right?"

"Sure, they're safer downstairs. Only staff sees them." Bracamonte barely controlled himself, twisting his head around the ruined room. "I got nearly double the population here I'm supposed to. I got other fucking people to keep an eye on. I got this place damn stable for all the damn things I'm doing." He said this to Weyuker, then stamped from the room, the brittle curled linoleum crunching under his feet.

Swanson knew a long night lay ahead.

Weyuker stood, furiously following the jail commander's squat figure. Action now was the only redeeming quality left for them both.

He grabbed Weyuker's shoulder. "We'll get Molina," he vowed.

CHAPTER TWENTY

It was barely dawn, only the first tentative thready glow through the still-closed blinds. The radiant clock by Di's side of the bed said five forty-eight.

"You want some breakfast?" she asked.

"I'll eat at the airport." He went on dressing. Di was nervous watching him. She hadn't seen that look for two years, just before he started drinking and everything threatened to crumble around them.

"It's easy for me," she said. She had on her blue robe, his gift from last Christmas. Standing by the door, she kept out of his way. He moved around the room, from closet to dresser to the bathroom, with a deadly mechanical preoccupation. What was so wrong now? What had gone so badly that he wouldn't even talk to her all through the night when he woke up again and again?

He was brushing his change into one hand, putting it in his pocket. She was even getting used to seeing the gun, which vanished completely when he slipped on his light gray coat.

"You're not quite ready." She gently adjusted his tie and

smoothed the shoulders of his coat. He still felt solid, reassuringly so. "Can I do anything?"

He shook his head. He wouldn't look at her.

"What is it, honey? I want to share whatever it is with you."

He took a deep breath and kissed her. Now he looked at her deeply, as though staring into her. "Stay inside today until I get back. Don't go out for anything, don't let the kids go out. Stay here, stay safe."

"I will," she said slowly.

"Sorry I got you up so early." He gently lowered her arms and kissed her hands.

"I thought you were leaving at seven. This is okay, though."

He nodded, and gazed around the room, the closed windows and the lights making it seem as if night eternal held them. "I'll get back as quick as I can."

Almost coyly, he left the room without a goodbye or a farewell embrace. She saw him go quietly to Matt's door, open it slowly and go inside. He was only in there for a moment, and then he hurried down the hall without raising his face to her.

Di stood in the bedroom doorway, more perplexed and uneasy than ever before. In the early morning stillness she saw Mike go into the girls' room. He's saying goodbye to all of them, she thought suddenly. When he came out, he quickly went downstairs.

The whispered voices of the two policemen and Mike came to her through the growing distance, the front door closed stiffly and the car started outside.

She could hear the policemen moving around downstairs. The pale morning light washed up to the bottom of the stairway. Something's happened, she thought.

She glanced toward Matt's room. He was in such a hurry, she thought, he had to leave so early, and he stopped to see each of them before he left.

Behind her was the rumpled bed and the faint, lingering astringency of his aftershave.

★　★　★

It was called St. Gregory's, but Swanson didn't care what the name was. He parked in front of the church and went in. It was just before six.

Scattered throughout the whitewashed interior were a dozen people, all sitting in drooping, flickering expectation. Swanson found a pew and sat down. He tried to calm himself. Rainbow light broke through the stained-glass windows on the east side of the altar and dotted the white linen with red, yellow, and green abstractions. He had a meeting at seven with Gleason, then Weyuker at the airport immediately afterward. This was the right thing to do, the only thing, and it would cut away the baleful presence hovering over him and everyone who depended on him.

It wasn't his church, and he didn't know any of the proper words. He lowered his head, his hands held between his knees.

Without thinking, he bent forward and knelt.

The instincts of an old acolyte. Reverend Busch always said, when in doubt up there at the altar, kneel down. Everybody else will join you in a minute anyway.

When no prayer came with kneeling, no thing beyond the fear and sickness from what he had seen, he remembered carrying the heavy processional cross on Sunday morning. Behind him came the choir, singing to the loud triumphant sonorities of the organ. Carry the cross stiffly, don't let it lean or tremble, all the way around the church and up the steps of the chancel. The old man and his mother were there every Sunday. For five years he carried that cross unwaveringly.

Someone cleared his throat, and a priest entered without ceremony and came to the altar. Swanson looked briefly. The few other people stirred hopefully. He didn't bother to join them when they stood up or crossed themselves.

He and the old man had a great fight one Sunday morning. It was just before he went to college, a month or so. Suddenly the cross was nothing more than a weight and the whole thing a pointless ritual. The old man swore, then grabbed him, but Swanson was bigger and pushed him away. What the old man really believed was uncertain, but he would have been very embarrassed if his son abruptly stopped going to church. Bad appearances. Bad for business maybe. Bad manners.

Swanson never went back to church until he married Di and then only for her. It had no other significance.

Until this morning when he had to come here, even if the prayer remained inchoate and the only things he could not banish from his mind were the smell and the fury of the fire.

You came here to seek strength and sometimes resolution. And to propitiate a sense of failure so deep it threatened to paralyze. No matter what had happened before, he couldn't fail today.

Swanson sat back in the pew, his eyes closed, his mind traveling over the worn words of the liturgy echoing in the whitewashed emptiness. On his way out he dropped money into the collection box.

CHAPTER TWENTY-ONE

The little plane ploughed ahead through turbulent transparent air, into a morning as clear and bright as a teardrop. Every so often the plane dipped, its engines groaning.

"Only another forty minutes," Swanson said.

"I'm walking back. I swear." Weyuker had lowered his face into his hands.

For the first time that morning, Swanson chuckled. Flying with Weyuker to Nevada gave form to the cryptic prayer he had tried to make. The pilot and the Santa Maria cop sat in front, he and Weyuker immediately behind them. A last seat remained empty in back. He planned to put the cop there on the flight back.

"This'll make you feel good." Swanson almost had to yell over the plane's incessant engine drone. "Gleason's keeping an open line to the prison. Soon as we have Molina, he'll know and get everything ready for the homecoming."

Weyuker nodded unhappily. His pale face was whiter and his toupee almost garish by contrast. He kept shaking his head. "I never made a good gang case from the joint. You ever get a good one? So Bracamonte gives you everything. Even if we find out who poured turpentine on Dufresne, it's going to be rough getting witnesses, something to back it all up." He looked out his small window. "Last one I did, I had three fucking guards come and say they saw one puke shank another puke. Recovered the knife, too. We had X-rays. We get to trial and the jury thinks the guards are all liars and the inmates were like these proud rebels that got set up."

"We got to find out. Molina did it. I want to know how."

Weyuker lowered his head again so all Swanson saw was a sun-reddened neck, the knobs of his spine. He groaned with the plane as it fought the invisible air currents. "Mike," he said, head up a little, eyes abashed, "Mike, I don't know if I've played everything right on the case."

"Join the club. That's what I've been telling myself the last couple days."

Weyuker was earnest. "I'm going to make sure it comes out right. I promise that. I'm going to do anything I can."

Swanson tried to leaven Weyuker's pale seriousness. "You and me working it, we got a good shot. You have a bad night?"

Weyuker nodded. He popped a couple of Dramamine pills, swallowing hard and looking bilious. "Sarah says I have to have a good breakfast, always. Every morning she makes me eggs and something, the winter she throws in cereal. I eat it. I ate it today. Took some allergy crap, too." He looked again out the window. "It's all floating right behind my eyes."

"I couldn't get anything down," Swanson joked truthfully. Below them lay a brown crinkled land, the hardy tufts of trees dotting the dryness irregularly. They'd be in Carson City by nine-fifteen with any luck.

He looked at his watch.

"What time?"

"Eight-forty, about. Right now the warden's probably breaking the bad news to Hector and telling him to get his ass in gear."

"He's going to yell for Massingill?"

"Warden won't let him have any phone calls. He's out of there as far as they're concerned."

Another deep glide, the plane changed pitch and dropped lower, then rose suddenly. Weyuker put his hands over his eyes.

Swanson couldn't help laughing. It broke the tension and the cop even turned to see what was funny. They all laughed.

"I ever tell you when I jumped a guy in Department 15?"

Weyuker dumbly shook his head, grimly swallowing and watching the fleeting land beneath him, the plane's cruciform shadow passing over it swiftly.

"Oh, it was a royal fuck-up," Swanson said enthusiastically, his face brightening, "right after Sid DeBerry went on the bench. Sid's a great guy, good prosecutor, but he was so goddamn nervous when he hit the bench he couldn't decide anything. Everything went under submission. A basic four-fifty-nine prelim took a week."

Weyuker turned a wan face to him.

"I'm in there on a real bad actor. Career criminal prelim, four counts robbery, two counts burg, armed allegations, he was going for a whole fuckload of time."

"Put off his appointments until the year 2045."

"You got it. So he's brought out, Sid's sitting up there, and this asshole, his name's Boatwright, jumps over the holding tank rail, he's going to sprint right out of court."

"Fucking pole vaulter." Weyuker whistled in admiration.

"Boatwright's getting up speed, so I just stepped in front of him, did a quarterback sack and he goes down, screaming his head off, on top of me. Sid sees this. He fumbles around there under the bench for the emergency button to get every other marshal and deputy sheriff into court. Only he's so goddamn flustered he hits the wrong button."

"Wrong button?"

"The doors of the courtroom blow open and instead of a dozen armed, crazed deputies, I see all these lawyers from the indigent criminal defense panel hurrying in, trying to beat each other for what they figured must have been the world's biggest damn case. Sid hit the button to call lawyers across the hall from the panel. So I've got this maniac going bananas on top of me,

I'm trying to hold him, and these poverty-row defense lawyers are reporting for duty."

"Oh, Jesus."

"So Sid's bailiff has finally gotten his gun out. He's shaking as much as Sid. He's got the gun pointed. Sid's yelling, 'Shoot! Shoot!' while this mother's on top of me and I'm trying to yell, 'Don't, don't shoot.'"

Weyuker laughed. Some color had come into his face. The cop was half-turned in his seat listening, too, with a wide grin. Just like the old days, Swanson realized, like everything was fine again.

Grignon strode down the wide hall on the fourth floor of the Supreme Court building in San Francisco. He was a little disappointed that it was fairly drab white plaster and linoleum, and there were no resonant echoes on marble. But he was here. It was almost nine a.m. and he had his new leather briefcase gripped tightly. He swung it a bit jauntily because it was a fine morning.

He had found a place to park only a block away. That was a miracle. He had arranged everything with Massingill. That was a miracle. He was going to see a justice of the California Supreme Court, and that was the greatest miracle of all. Actually, he probably would never see a justice, but a member of the Court would have to approve and sign the order he had with him.

With a little awe, he had glimpsed the Court's great blue-draped room where oral arguments were heard. Ranged in a gently curving semicircle were the seven high chairs of the justices. It was like a silent temple, the Great Seal of California its central icon against the blue drapery behind the chairs. He was both frightened and inspired.

Now he tingled. Everybody had said Molina would be a terrible client, all the federal entanglements, the gang threats, the years of problems to sort out. But Molina was unfailingly polite, always open. And here the case had come and he had come with it, to the Supreme Court of the largest state in the nation.

He was going to have his way. His papers were beautifully

pleaded. A stay would be granted on Judge Pizer's denial of his motion. All he needed was a stay. There would be time afterward to file more papers, more motions.

The clerk's office was like any court clerk's office, only much larger and located on the other side of the building from the Court's chambers. A wide public counter was laden with boxes of forms and the latest decisions from the Court.

He presented himself proudly. Nine-oh-two by the ornate clock on the wall. He saw still more white plaster. No majesty about it.

"I've come to get an emergency stay on an extradition warrant. My name is Ernest Grignon. I called yesterday."

"Yes, Mr. Grignon," said the slim young black woman. "I understand. Do you have your moving papers with you?"

"Of course." He proudly opened the briefcase, his wife's insistent extravagance. Everybody else was snide about the Molina case. They called it the Grignon Full Employment Act because he could, in theory, bill the government forever for legal services connected with Molina's representation. But Regina wanted him to bathe in his good fortune. She bought the briefcase for his Supreme Court debut.

The young clerk took the papers and stamped them, filing them. She handed two endorsed copies back to him.

"It's an emergency stay," he said. "It requires immediate action."

"I see that," she smiled. "It's already been assigned."

"I'm very pleased."

"The Court is in morning conference now." She looked at the clock. Nine-oh-four. "It's an unusually heavy calendar, so they'll be a little while."

"It will be heard this morning?"

"Oh, definitely. I'll make sure these go to the justice who will handle the case right now."

He remained standing at the counter. There were seats around the room, and more clerks moving leisurely with stacks of papers. One came by with a large handcart stacked high with file boxes.

"It will be a few minutes," she said.

"I'll wait here." He smiled and found a seat, his pink hands folded on top of his briefcase.

Another sip of the too hot coffee. Massingill made a face and held his cup away from him, but didn't slow his pacing. "Tastes like axle grease and it's hot as a pistol."

Rau sat in one of the pale overstuffed chairs. He nibbled on a fingernail. The only way, though, he showed worry was by sucking on one side of his lip, making it slightly swollen.

"Take it easy," Massingill said. "Grignon will get his stay. We'll get that damn subpoena for the records quashed, too. I keep saying that to myself."

"You're jumpier than I am."

"You're sore about getting nailed yesterday."

"I got hometowned by a deputy D.A. and a half-wit bench-warmer," Rau said.

Massingill slowed a little. He had paced up the length of his office, back to the small kitchenette in the rear where boxes and books that couldn't go anywhere else were haphazardly stacked up. "It's always this case, isn't it? Always the same apple cart that's about to tip over."

He dragged out another cigarette, lit it, and blew twin plumes of smoke. "I keep saying, I know the man's mind after all this time working with him, sweating with him, digging the truth from him. Then I get all of this dumped on me and I don't know what's going on. I swear I don't right now." He aimed the cigarette at his wide desk littered with white and yellow papers, little pink phone messages, and office memos.

"Well, there's nothing really definitive." Rau sucked his lip.

"Not the point. It's the trust. I have to trust Molina, just as he's got to be able to trust me. What I've seen, what the D.A. has sent over, I'm not sure I can trust Hector."

"It may not be a question of trust anymore, Claude," Rau said carefully. "We've come an awfully long way with Molina. We're very far in."

"I know, I know. But that's what it is for me." Massingill

blew on his coffee again. He couldn't concentrate on anything this morning. "Now Swanson's prime snitch's killed. I don't know how I can put that question to Hector."

"There are only two main issues. As I see it. One. Is he doing a valuable job for us? Okay, we both know that answer. Two. Is there anything the D.A. has alleged that can be linked concretely to Molina?" He looked inquisitively at Massingill.

Massingill was at his desk, hands running over the reports and photographs Swanson had so maliciously supplied. "Proved as either a substantive crime or something that could be used as impeachment against him when he testifies?"

"What exactly can a defense attorney do to us? What's the worst?"

"Okay. Let's do that. This dead snitch knew the moneyman. The same moneyman named by Hector's wife. The man Orepeza. The snitch also knew Molina's location. He named Raymond Alves as one of Hector's accomplices. Alves is ID'd as the responsible in the Bakersfield homicide."

"The guy, Rolly?"

"Who's also a witness to a murder we know Hector committed. And now the snitch himself is dead."

"We can break it down," Rau said, tapping his finger under his nose. "No testimony from this snitch. Inadmissible utterly and completely, can't come from any written statement or anybody who talked with him. Cross it out. The Rolly murder can be anything you want. It's not a link to Molina. Orepeza's gone. Inadmissible material entirely from Hector's late wife. So there are no crimes chargeable at this time against Molina. There isn't even any admissible impeachment. Anybody tried to bring any of it in, any of it, Claude, we'd get an order *in limne* from the judge and the jury'd never hear it."

Massingill frowned. "All we've isolated is that people who could hurt Hector are dead."

"Well, it's still a question of viewpoint in that sense. Any of these homicides are explainable in ways that suggest Hector's not a factor at all. Robbery, one victim was a known snitch, another was vulnerable because she was his wife." Rau paused.

"His wife's the only one you could tie to him. Only, in the sense that his enemies got to her when they couldn't get to him."

"He was seeing an Aryan Brother," Massingill said, "the dead snitch. Why was he doing that?"

"That one, well yes, we'll have to ask him. But, why Hector saw this guy and what the guy did afterward, hell, they're nine miles apart in terms of proof. The snitch could've been playing both Hector as a pal and his buddies in the AB."

"We still vote Hector a member in good standing." Massingill raised his coffee cup.

"Based on what we've gotten so far, Hector can keep testifying until there's nothing left to say."

Massingill nodded, his eyes falling on the large twelve-line telephone on his desk. All the lights were out. All the lines were ready. He and Rau were waiting for one dark light to brighten, the call from San Francisco that Molina wouldn't be brought to California.

"I've been trying to see this from Swanson's point of view," he said, putting his coffee down on the Rolly investigation reports and the long phone message of Max Dufresne's death, "but I can't do it."

"It's turf," Rau said flatly, "always has been. He wants his little piece."

It was nine-oh-five and Massingill stared at the papers. "Sometimes, between you and me, I ask myself. I say, have I made some gargantuan error?"

"He's the only game in town," Rau said.

Massingill trailed his thin fingers over the telephone, as if willing it to ring. He took another swallow and grimaced. At this point, his reputation and career were inextricably knotted into the success of Molina as a witness, a trusted and reformed man.

"Where'm I going?" Molina asked without raising his voice.

"Santa Maria, California," answered the assistant warden who stood with him in the lime-colored holding cell. There were no blankets on the bunk's solid rectangular mattress.

Nothing on the walls, no soap, toilet paper, or cover on the concrete floor. Molina was dressed in his dark suit.

"I want to call my lawyer."

"No calls. Just be ready. You're out of here in an hour." The assistant warden turned to leave.

"I don't want to go to Santa Maria. It's a bad place. This can't be legal."

Molina hadn't raised his voice at all. He strode futilely around the cell.

"Hector, it's as legal as it's going to get. Two special deputy Sheriffs are going to come here and escort you all the way to California. Now, I guess you can make your complaints from there." The assistant warden was outside, the barred door slid shut. Two officers stood outside, one watching into the cell, the other staring down the corridor.

"I'm not supposed to be moved." Molina was at the bars. He looked a little fearful. "Does Mr. Claude Massingill know about this?"

"Hector, I couldn't say."

"You should tell him."

"Well, I think you can take that up with the authorities later."

"You call him now. I want to talk to him."

"I said, no calls. I meant no calls. You are no longer the responsibility of the people of Nevada or this prison or me. Or the warden. He says to tell you goodbye. He'd like to see you off, but he can't come himself."

"I'm telling you I've got a right to speak to my lawyer or Mr. Claude Massingill, who's the U.S. Attorney in California."

"I know who he is. I'm sure he'll be glad to see you again."

Molina watched the assistant warden, dressed in that cheap poplin suit, hands in his pockets, start walking away.

"What time is it?" Molina called out.

"Little after nine. They're supposed to be here around ten. I'll say my goodbyes now." He half-saluted. "Enjoyed your time with us, Hector. You're always a pleasure."

The two officers remained fixed as knights keeping watch.

Molina sat down on the lumpy, cool plastic mattress and waited. He thought of the Madonna briefly. He thought of his life until that moment.

He thought that a change of scene might do him good.

Swanson was already opening the plane's side door before the engines had stopped. He saw two Carson City Sheriff's squad cars driving across the tarmac toward him. They had landed on a side runway. A rusted Quonset hut, several other small planes, and an old Army bus crowded the otherwise limitless space that began where the runway ended. Like a ribbon of order laid down on the immutable desert.

The pilot was beside him, polishing his sunglasses and blinking against the light. "Where do you want me?"

"Right here. We'll be back by eleven at the latest and I want you ready to go right away."

"A-OK," said the pilot. He watched the squad cars pull up.

Swanson and Weyuker went to them. The introductions were made quickly.

"I understand you're a temporary deputy? So's your associate?" the sergeant in charge pointed at the cop with Weyuker.

"Duly authorized to carry out the laws of this county." Weyuker showed him the papers.

Swanson was impatient. "We can do all this on the road, guys. Let's get in gear."

The sergeant, a man as thin as Weyuker, but brown and solemn, nodded. "If you men want to ride with me, we'll take the lead and get you there in no time."

"Go," Swanson said, jumping into the front seat of the first squad car.

For the dozenth time in as many minutes, Grignon looked up from the opaque court decision he was reading. It was nine-thirty exactly.

People had come and gone from the clerk's office. He had overheard three dates being made, a young woman being bawled out for some sloppy filing, snatches of talk about cars, TV shows, and people who worked at the Court.

He stood up. He went to the counter again. The young black woman looked up.

"Excuse me, it's been nearly half an hour. I know that's not very long, but do you have any idea?"

"It's Conference morning," she said apologetically, "they're still talking."

"Could I talk to whoever is reviewing my motion?"

"No, I'm sorry."

He glanced unhappily at the court decision. He was almost finished. It was about some intricate interpretation of municipal water grants. There was nothing else to read.

"Is it necessary for you to be here until your motion is decided?" she asked. Nobody else noticed him at all. He wanted to tell them who Hector Molina was, how the United States Justice Department was behind him, but Massingill wouldn't appreciate such boasting.

"I have to be here. It's very important that some action be taken this morning."

"I'm sorry. I can't do anything else." She returned to her paperwork.

"Do I have time to get a cup of coffee?" he asked. His mind rested on the vivid image of a chocolate doughnut as well.

"You could," she said, "but you know what would happen if you left the building."

"They'd come back."

"They'd come back," she agreed. "It always happens."

"Thank you." He sat down again. He vowed not to look at the clock or his watch. No matter what.

He picked up the water rights case.

"You folks on a tight schedule?" the sergeant asked Swanson. He was pushing the squad car up to sixty-five, the brown, white, and blue desert landscape rushing by them. Weyuker and the cop sat in back. No one had said much.

"Pretty tight," Swanson said. He was trying not to think

about two things. The first was Di alone in Santa Maria, and even with police protection, exposed. The second thing he fought to obliterate was a great fire, and a black shape in its center. Speed and motion were all that mattered now.

"I could run the siren, get the lights going," the sergeant offered. He drove almost negligently, one hand draped over the wheel, the other hanging limply out his window, and he seemed to be looking at Swanson more than the road.

"I wouldn't mind a little more speed."

"You ever been out to our prison?"

"Nope," Swanson said. He didn't want to watch the sergeant drive. It was a little too unnerving. Although there was virtually no traffic, the buildings looked small and distant against the indomitable brush and sharp hills. They had gone through Carson City so fast it seemed a ghost town.

The sergeant had a sly gleam. "I guess you figure this is pretty important."

"Yeah. It is."

"I know this guy's going back on a first-degree murder charge."

"Two."

"You think you'll kill him in California?"

Swanson shrugged. "I don't know. It's hard to say. We're going to give it our best shot."

"He didn't kill anybody in Nevada, did he?"

Weyuker said, "Naw, he specialized. Everything happened in California."

"Too bad. I'm keeping an eye on a couple out at the prison. We're going to kill them pretty soon. Got one a little while ago."

Swanson grunted. Life was a good deal less complicated here.

The sergeant chortled. "I shouldn't say killed. I should say, we're going to be carrying out the order of the court."

He sped up and hit the lights.

Swanson wondered, for the first time, what he would do and say when he saw Molina.

* * *

The door to Massingill's office opened again. Rau stood there.

"Has he called?"

Massingill shook his head. He had taken off his coat and un-buttoned his vest. It was a rare demonstration of his tension.

"It's ten o'clock, Claude," Rau said. His patience had worn thin in the last half hour. "Let me get a federal judge."

"The first question you're going to get is whether we used up all our state remedies. And you won't be able to tell him."

"For this kind of stay we don't need to exhaust our state appeals first." Rau ran a handkerchief around the back of his neck even though it wasn't wet. Massingill kept his large office quite cool, like a florist with delicate flowers on ice.

"Whether we do or we don't, we're still going to get asked. I'd like to stay clear of all that. He's only been there a little while."

Rau shook his head. "I'm just nervous. I shouldn't be. There's no real rush."

"I think there is."

"How?"

"Swanson got the extradition warrant in record time. He's got a burr under his saddle about our friend."

Rau grinned ruefully. "That he does."

"I think he'll try to get Molina out of Nevada as quickly as he can."

A few minutes after ten, Swanson's squad car drove up to the main gate of Nevada State Prison. Squat older buildings, dun colored and ringed with barbed wire, sat in the desert sun.

"We got a nice gift shop," said the sergeant. "The guys make everything. Ships in bottles, blankets, some awful nice things."

"No, thanks." Swanson covered his anxiety. Up until the moment they drove back out of these gates, Molina's move could be stopped. Every moment was endless.

Weyuker got out with him. The sergeant stayed in the car, the motor running. "Ugly place," Weyuker said, low. "I thought Q was ugly. Folsom's ugly, but this is really bad."

"Thanks," the sergeant said.

The other squad car had pulled up behind them. A guard in a sharply creased uniform came out of the building to the right of the gate. He carried a shotgun.

"Morning," Swanson said. "We're here to pick up a prisoner." He pointed to Weyuker. "This man is a member of the Santa Maria, California, Police Department. He's been made a special deputy in the Carson City Sheriff's Department. The prisoner will be turned over to him."

The guard shifted in his highly polished shoes. "We got him ready. Let me see your marching orders." He held out his hand and Swanson gave him the warrant and their identification.

The sergeant was whistling merrily.

"How do you want to handle this?" Swanson asked.

Without looking up, the guard, his hair flat and black said, "Got an escort made up. He's in a holding cell and we'll just go bring him out. I'll show you where to move your vehicles."

Swanson looked at his watch. "I'd like to get going."

The papers were passed back. "Follow me through."

The guard waved at the men in the high guard towers and at the gate. Swanson and Weyuker got back in. The double row of gates swung open, creaking, and they drove through into the main yard. The guard with the shotgun walked slowly ahead of them, sometimes using his right hand to indicate that they were to turn.

As always, Swanson was keenly aware of men watching him. From the tiers of barred windows, from the guard towers, from dark corners he couldn't even see. The small procession moved ahead and around corners several times.

No one spoke. The sergeant whistled softly through his teeth and laconically brought the squad car to a stop at the rear of a large mustard-yellow building decked out with ventilator holes and an incongruous white-and-red awning over its wide double doorway. There were several large garbage bins full of old vegetables and boxes to one side.

Swanson said, "I'd like to go in."

The guard nodded. "It's okay with me. Assistant warden's

going to be in charge and I'll turn over the prisoner to your partner, okay?"

"That's fine."

"Where is everybody?" Weyuker surveyed the dusty, deserted inner square formed by the angles of several cell blocks. From the building with the bright awning came the low whir of fans and the sound of doors opening and closing.

"Everybody's locked down while we do this little move," said the guard. He shifted his shotgun and unlocked the rear door.

"You wait here," Swanson said to the police sergeant, still sitting in his car. He nodded and half-saluted.

The door was open. Swanson saw a large kitchen, gray metal stoves, huge vats and utensils, all temporarily abandoned. A great pile of lettuce stood beside one or two sinks.

"Tell me how it's going to go," Swanson said. Somewhere, faintly, a man laughed riotously.

"We bring him here through the kitchen, out to your car. The holding cell's next door and this is the safest way out, we got the most control over it. I don't mind where you walk when we're escorting him, but I don't want you to stop or say anything if you don't have to. I'd like to get this over and done with as fast as I can do it." The guard was about thirty and he had the nervous woodenness some men get after working for years in a prison. Swanson didn't think the guard felt as nervous as he did.

"You lead the way," he said. The guard nodded and they headed into the kitchen. Vague smells of onions, grain, and beef soup clung to the place.

Through the brightly gleaming gray corridor, down a flight of narrow stairs and then up again, into what Swanson guessed was the cell block alongside the kitchen, they walked single file, the guard in front, his shotgun held at the ready, followed by Swanson and Weyuker and the Santa Maria cop. The sounds of a prison were missing, as though cleanly shut off. They didn't see anyone.

"Are you worried about moving this guy?" Swanson finally said, as they stood under the white light at another heavy locked door the guard opened.

"Yeah." The guard had the key in, turned the lock, swung the door, all with one hand in a quick, practiced motion. "I'm really icy-dicey about it."

As quietly as he could, Grignon got up. "I'm going to take a short walk," he said. "I'll be right back."

The young black clerk smiled at him. It was ten-ten.

He held his briefcase firmly and huffed with irritation. How long was he supposed to sit there? Nobody told him anything, nobody cared. It wasn't as if he was some jackass filing a notice of appeal. He was here on an emergency review. Some attention should be paid.

He was going to make sure attention was paid.

He marched back down toward the Supreme Court chambers.

Before coming to the Court's doors, he went into a smaller set of doors, along a short hall. The brisk snap of typewriters told him he was heading in the right direction. He could still hurry this along. It only required personal presence.

The secretary looked up. "Yes?"

"I have an emergency matter. It's being reviewed and I'd like to know how long it will take. They didn't know at the Clerk's office." He passed over one of his cards.

"Do they know you're waiting?"

"I told everyone I'd wait for the decision. I'd like to know what's happening."

It was a quietly set-up office. A burly man in a sport coat lounged in a chair, reading a newspaper. He glanced up thoroughly.

"You're welcome to wait here."

"I'd like to talk to someone."

"I'm sorry. The Court's in conference."

He smiled, annoyed. "I'd like to talk to the man or woman who is reading my motion. I'd like to see that person."

"I'm sorry. I can't let you go back."

He gripped his briefcase. Couldn't let him go back? He marched forward. Beyond this office was the labyrinth of law clerks and assistants who served the justices. One of them was even now wasting time. He could make his case more forcefully in person.

"I'm just going to make a few points."

The man in the sport coat was suddenly, immovably in front of him.

"No. You can't go back."

"I'm an attorney. I've got a client who's in great danger and I want to talk to someone about what's being done."

"You can wait here. I'm not letting you through."

There was no way around him. He hadn't realized there were Supreme Court guards.

He relaxed a little. "Well, I don't want to cause any trouble."

He hefted his briefcase again. The secretary watched him suspiciously.

He left quickly. Time to call Massingill and tell him it was going to take longer than expected.

Massingill had the phone, but he said nothing. He nodded slowly when Rau asked if it was Grignon.

"Well, I certainly do understand," he said. "You stay there on top of it. Give me a call as soon as you get a decision." He hung up.

"So?"

"Grignon's flustered because it's taking a while."

"God, the guy's a case."

Massingill leaned back in his chair. He opened a fresh pack of cigarettes rapidly. "Get the wheels rolling here," he said to Rau.

"Got it." Rau was already heading out. He paused, worriedly. "It's after ten. They're all going to be on the bench by now."

"Can't be helped. Either you or Grignon's going to get that damn Santa Maria denial shit canned in the next hour," Massingill said firmly. "I am not going to have Molina upset."

"How are we?" Weyuker asked. They walked past a two-tiered row of cells. The men inside hooted and small globs of spit splatted on the concrete around them.

"Right on time." Swanson didn't look up or around him. He only wanted to keep the small group moving.

They went through a final series of double-locked doors. "You know why cons have naked women tattooed on their backs? Where they can't see them?" Weyuker talked loudly enough so that anyone could hear him.

"I know why."

Weyuker went on brutally. "They do it so they can look at something while they buttfuck the guy they're on top of. I love cons. Really. I love them."

They were in a small cell block. Six cells, all empty but one. Molina sat in the cell, on the bunk. He looked like a child in his black suit. Two guards watched Swanson talk to the assistant warden, who had thinning brown hair and wore glasses. The assistant warden handed papers to Swanson, who gave them to Weyuker. "He's yours now. Free and clear," said the assistant warden.

The guard with the shotgun stood aside as the cell door was opened.

"Stand back, put your hands behind your back and don't say anything," he ordered.

Swanson thought Molina might do something, lash out in a hopeless escape effort, anything. But, Molina simply got off the plastic mattress on the bunk. He clasped his hands behind his back, like a teacher about to lecture his students. He faced the wall.

Now that they were going to take him, Swanson wanted Molina to make some kind of move. End it here and now, with witnesses who could be relied on. Who would mourn or question the death of Molina in this place? He clenched his teeth painfully.

Molina, handcuffed, turned around. The two guards had him by each arm, pulling him forward out of the cell. He was holding back a little, resisting slightly so they had to work at bringing him out.

"Hey, is this legal?" he asked.

Swanson nodded.

"I think you're kidnapping me or something."

"Come on, Hector. We've got a plane waiting."

Molina leaned backward. He was at the cell door. He was sweating a little, twisting and turning his arms to make it harder to hang onto him. "Plane? What plane?"

"Just take it easy," Weyuker said. "Everything's okay."

"You gotta let me call my lawyer. I think this is some kind of trick. You guys are going to pull something." There was sweet panic in his voice and Swanson liked it.

The assistant warden stepped to Molina. "Listen, you're going out of here now. You can make a lot of noise if you want, you can do whatever you want, but your ass is out of here. You want to do this easy or hard or what? I don't care."

"You're witnesses," Molina said, his voice rising a little. "I'm being kidnapped. These guys are doing something."

"Let's go," Swanson said.

"You're my witnesses. You know what's going on," Molina said, but he stopped holding back. His muscles relaxed. He breathed tightly.

With Molina in their center, the line moved back through the prison, through the howls and laughter, spit and a few bits of paper hurled down at them. Molina didn't look up. In tense, rapid order they went through the kitchen, still deserted, to the waiting squad cars.

The assistant warden stood under the festive awning like a father seeing a son off to camp.

Molina, hands behind him, stopped at the car door. "I can't get in like this. I can't sit on my hands."

Embarrassed, the guard with the shotgun opened the cuffs. Molina put his hands in front of him and was cuffed again. He nodded as though satisfied. A quick glance at the assistant warden, the buildings. "What about my stuff?"

"Don't worry about it. Get it to you in a couple of days."

"We give you everything," Weyuker said. "You'll like it."

Swanson slid in front with the sergeant, who kept looking curiously in the rear-view mirror at Molina. Weyuker tapped him.

"We're all in."

The squad cars turned around, driving quickly toward the main gate.

When Swanson looked at him, Molina seemed to have lost his fear. He idly watched the prison buildings go by, almost bored by it all. The sound of Molina's voice startled him. They were at the two main gates, opened, the highway beyond it and the desert whiteness everywhere.

"So how you been, Mr. Swanson? How's everybody?" Molina asked.

The law clerk handed Grignon the papers. They stood in the guarded section of offices behind the Supreme Court's great room. Each justice's chambers were back there. He looked at the small green slip clipped to the top of his motion.

"Interesting case. Sounds a little wild," said the clerk.

"It's got everything, believe me," he mumbled, trying to find the box checked off on the green slip.

"Feds, state, murder, protected witnesses, man, I loved it. I'm going to listen to you guys argue."

He found it. Beside the word GRANTED was a small red check mark. He groaned in relief. A further notation said that the Supreme Court's order was temporary and that a full hearing would be held in forty-eight hours.

"I told my wife, I said this is a lucky day. I told her that before I came up here. Thank you," he said, taking the clerk's thick hand, "it pays to look at the bright side."

Rau heard the grumbled, muffled voices and a moment later the courtroom door opened. Judge Harry Sinclair ambled slowly from the bench toward his chambers. He yawned and then grinned when he saw Rau sitting by the clerk's empty desk.

"You know you're not supposed to come back here. You're going to make me look bad." The judge was still grinning.

"I've got something hot, judge. You're the logical one to take it." Rau had known Sinclair for ten years when they were both in the same anti-corruption unit in the Justice Department.

"Well, hell you better bring it in." The judge looked at his watch, then at his clerk, who stood holding a newspaper and cup of coffee for him. "We're taking a fifteen-minute recess while your boy tries to find an AWOL DEA agent." He cackled.

Rau followed the judge. "You're going to love this."

"I ain't getting in." Molina shook his head as he stood by the plane. Its engines' liquid drone made his voice faint. A dry, frivolous breeze came off the desert and played dustily around the tarmac.

"You're getting in," Swanson said, "and you're going to shut up. The game's changed. You better get used to it."

"It looks too small."

"I'm not arguing with you." He nodded to the cop who began pushing Molina into the high hatchway.

Molina struggled briefly. "I never been in one."

"You're scared?"

"I don't like it."

The cop and Weyuker hesitated. He sounded truly frightened. Another small plane taxied down the runway, then like a bird flushed from its covert it suddenly shot up, rising with aquiline grace into the blue sky.

"Look, I don't give a rat's ass if we have to tie you up and throw you in," Swanson said. He thought of his murdered witnesses and the bright fire. He thought about Di keeping away from windows.

"So you tie me up. I saw a guy once in the back seat of a cop car. They had him down. He was all handcuffed like me." Molina stared at Swanson. "I saw this guy kick out the back seat. You think he'd like it if somebody's kicking the back of his head?" he leaned toward the pilot, who was fiddling with the controls.

Swanson looked at Molina's eyes. It was like staring at two ball bearings in oil. He had his gun out without even willing each movement that made it possible. Weyuker said something cautionary. Swanson held the gun near Molina's face.

"I could shoot you right here. Be the end of everything for me. No more hassles, no more bullshit. You ran. You were running into the desert."

"I got handcuffs on."

"So what."

"You can't shoot me."

"Believe me, I've got cases and cases that say I can. You're a very dangerous felon. You're an escape risk. Get in. Don't make any noise, don't do anything. Just sit there."

The pilot, oblivious to what was going on, shouted out, "We got clearance now. They want us to go now."

The cop had one arm on Molina; Weyuker stepped to his other side. Swanson held the gun tightly. It would all be over. Jesus. That's all it would take. He slowly put the gun away.

Molina shook off the cop's arm. "I'll get in," he said. His heavy shoulders shrugged under the dark suit. He climbed into the plane and sat by his window. There was no sign of fear.

Swanson felt sickened at himself and Molina. It was some act. The guy wasn't scared, he was just pushing, testing, seeing what would happen.

Even as the idea sharpened, Swanson jumped into the plane next to Molina, the cop squeezing back to the tiny rear seat. Weyuker gave a high sign to the pilot as Swanson pulled the door shut and secured it.

As the plane turned, gathered speed, and droned down the runway, its tail lifting and wings straightening just before flight, Swanson felt a tremendous exhilaration take hold of him.

He tapped Weyuker on the shoulder. Weyuker turned.

Swanson winked at him.

First the call to Massingill out of the way, then a lightheartedness that comes from being freed from daily routine, even briefly. Grignon stood by the telephone booths on the first floor of the Supreme Court Building. Very dreary looking place, like all government buildings, faded, bleached, rubbed, and cheap. No grandeur or majesty. But, he'd won a good battle by careful argument and persistence. He glanced at the people who came by, stopping at the elevators. He felt more significant than any of them.

What to do? Where to go? He could be back home in no

time, San Francisco wasn't far. He idly jingled the change in his pocket, tinkling and jangling as he thought.

Maybe a celebratory lunch? The more he thought, a pink, bulbous man, jingling his coins, the more he knew he should go home. Take the rest of the day off. That would be the ideal way to celebrate.

He brought out some change and counted it. Enough for a long-distance call. He sat down and pulled the door shut.

It didn't matter that the Supreme Court had given him forty-eight hours. Between them, he and Massingill could come up with a sufficient number of writs, appeals, writs again, appeals again, to delay any extradition for months and months. Perhaps indefinitely.

His wife answered the phone.

"I won," he said ebulliently. He jiggled a little on the small seat in the phone booth. "Baby's coming home."

Massingill ate an early lunch at his desk, as he usually did. A cigarette smoldered acridly beside him in a full ashtray. He read the *Wall Street Journal* and ate potato salad and tried not to think about Hector Molina at all. It would be great, he thought, to forget about him for one day. Tune out Molina's hopes and fears, his loves and lusts.

Never again, Massingill said to himself, no snitches anymore, no matter what happens, no matter what kind of case I've got to give up. No more like this.

He took a drag off the cigarette. It was a big, beige, empty office through the smoke of his cigarette. This was what it meant to be top of the line in your chosen profession.

A quick, perfunctory knock, and Rau came in, a sheaf of papers waving before him.

"Sinclair had an orgasm, he liked this so much." He slapped the papers in front of Massingill.

"Grignon got a stay."

"So we're covered."

"You care to make a trek over to Carson City tonight to tell Hector what's happened? Tell him I'm still looking out for him."

"I don't mind going." Rau smiled with self-satisfaction. "I feel pretty good right now."

"It was basic brain death," Swanson said to Weyuker. He talked loudly and slapped Weyuker's meatless shoulder every so often. "I mean, this guy managed to piss off every juror before the trial even started." For the first time since they got into the air, he spoke to Molina. "Hector, you must've had some bad lawyers, right? Some really stupid guys?"

Molina nodded slowly, thoughtfully. He sat like solid black coal. He made no complaints or comments. Behind him, the cop had closed his eyes, his mouth slightly open.

"You ever represent yourself?"

"Once."

"How'd it go?"

"I hung it up. The D.A. dumped it afterward." Molina spoke without any pride. It was a fact, no more.

Swanson wouldn't talk about the Tice killing or Angie or anything else. He was surprised that he felt so willing, suddenly, to talk to Molina at all. He imagined it was the feeling a hunter must get after a long chase and a successful kill.

Molina seemed bored.

"You never had a defense attorney this bad," Swanson said over the plane's loud harmonic hum. "He gets to juror nine or ten, I don't remember, and he says to her, 'Now, you know if you're selected to sit on this case, you will not be able to talk about it to anyone?' She nods. So far so good. He says, 'You won't be able to go home at night and have any intercourse with your husband if you're selected as a juror. Do you understand that?'"

"Bullshit."

Swanson talked fast, with exuberance. "So this woman just stares and stares and stares. He says, 'You do understand what will be expected if you're a juror?' She stares and she finally says, 'You mean I can't have any intercourse with my husband when I go home?' He looks real serious at her, 'None. Not during this trial. No intercourse with him or anyone else. Except your fellow jurors during deliberations.' Now she looks up and down at the other people sitting in the box. Then she looks at the judge, 'No way,' she says, 'I want to be excused.'"

"So?"

"So we all stipulated and got her out of there. She was going to have her intercourse and I didn't want her to worry about it." He laughed with Weyuker.

As they were laughing, Molina said, "I had a trial, this old homeboy came in against me."

Swanson and Weyuker stopped in mid-laugh, as though the plane's engine had suddenly shut down. They both looked at Molina.

"He had handcuffs like this," he held up his wrists, "and they wouldn't take them off. He was a security problem." Molina smiled briefly.

Swanson watched.

"Okay, he's testifying? He's got his hands cuffed and it looks like he might be a bad guy. His lawyer didn't like it. The judge told him, screw you, I ain't taking this guy's handcuffs off. Tell him to keep his fucking hands under the witness stand so the jury can't see them."

"So?" Weyuker asked.

"Anyway, we get into it, my time comes, I get this guy going about some shit he'd done, and he got pissed. Man, he was mad. He got so mad, you know what?"

"What?"

"He pulls his hands out, he started shaking his fists at me, these handcuffs right in front of the jury. I laughed my ass off."

Swanson chuckled. "You made him do that."

"Damn straight."

"You're a remarkable person, Hector."

"I am. No shit."

Weyuker grinned. "I think it's pretty funny. Guy's so stupid he can't even remember to hide his handcuffs."

Molina had turned to Swanson, his face intent. "You don't like me."

"You're kidding, Hector."

"I mean, it's not just this stuff now, you know what I mean."

My wife, my children, my witnesses, my snitch. I do know, Swanson thought, staring at the intent face. Weyuker was looking idly out the window. It was as though only he and Molina were in the plane.

"No," Swanson said, "it's not what's happening now. It's the kid you killed."

"You know him?"

"No."

"So how come?"

"You don't understand?"

"No, I don't," Molina said sincerely. "You would always come after me? No matter what I do for you guys? You want to get me or something?"

"Why'd you shoot him?"

"Why?"

Suddenly, it was important for him to see into Molina's mind, if only to wash away some of his own bewilderment in the face of evil.

Molina repeated the question again. Then, "You know what? I don't remember. Why? It's his fault, okay? He was jacking around, doing something. That's it."

Swanson turned away. Jesus, he thought, even when evil acts out the first immemorial crime, it eludes us in the mundane. He just forgot why he killed Donny Tice, that's all.

"I didn't do anything to you, man. Can't you give me some credit for all the good stuff I been doing? They're after me, man. I put myself way out for you guys."

"I can't make the Tice kid go away."

"So I never get off the hook?"

Swanson shook his head. "No."

Molina hawked, cleared his throat and shook his head in mild amusement. "I got a question for you."

Swanson waited.

Molina's expression was benign. "Is this really legal? This whole deal?"

"It really is."

"No shit?"

"You're not going back to Carson City."

"I didn't think so." Molina nodded. It was a detached inquiry, as though about someone else. Swanson wondered what
it would be like to push him out of the plane. "It doesn't matter that this is like, against my will?"

"Not a bit."

Weyuker glanced around. Ahead of them was blue sky, like a
china cup upended at the horizon.

"Someday, sometime we should talk more about this thing.
Get into it." Molina nudged Swanson with his solid shoulder. A
passenger on a bus jostling another passenger.

"Maybe we will."

"We will. I know it. We'll really get into it."

The pilot called out, "Just crossed into California, gentlemen."

Twenty minutes later they landed in Santa Maria. It was over,
Swanson thought, a dark morning transformed into a bright
day as inexorably as the movement of the sun in the sky. Sometimes prayers, even the unformed ones, do get answered. No
hitches, no problems, only the immensely satisfying sight of
Molina walking ahead to three squad cars and the small jail bus
waiting in front of the airport terminal. Men in uniform
waited by the vehicles. And as inexorably as everything else,
Molina moved toward them, the cop holding his arm.

Swanson walked ahead when he saw Susan talking with
some of the cops.

"That's him?" she asked as the slower group approached.

"Nobody else."

She put out her hand. "Congratulations, Michael. It was a
terrific idea."

"I feel better," he said as Molina, the cop, and Weyuker
walked by.

She whispered to him, "Joe's put your other guy out at the
branch with special protection. He doesn't know anything happened to Max. You've got him left."

"Narloch won't talk. Not to me."

"Things have changed."

Molina stopped before the jail bus. He shook his head and Weyuker tugged at him. Swanson went to them.

"What's going on?"

"I got to use the bathroom," Molina said. "I didn't get a chance all morning. I got to go now."

"In a half hour," Swanson had the bus doors open.

"I'm going to have an accident. Maybe my lawyer can get one of those habeas corpus things going because you're denying me toilet facilities."

"Get in," Weyuker said. He shook his head because his toupee had become itchy in the warm sunlight by the terminal. "First you didn't want to fly, now you don't want to drive. I'm tired."

"Let him go," Swanson said. He knew the kind of trouble such a writ could cause and the delays that would occur as it was examined slowly in federal court. "Take a couple of these guys and use the men's room inside."

"Whatever." Weyuker jerked Molina toward the terminal. He had two cops follow them and the little group marched into the building.

"He's not stupid, is he?" Susan said.

"No. A lot of things, but not that."

He only had to put Molina into custody at the main jail. Then see Hannah and Frank Tice and tell them it was almost over. Then try to twist Les, using his dead buddy as the lever.

Then his wife and family, and it had to go in that order now.

"These long days are killers," he said to Susan. They waited with the remaining cops.

"Take a look inside." Weyuker directed one of the cops into the men's room in the terminal's lobby. Curious people gave them a glance and hurried away and the stocky man in black, his hands clasped in front of him, shifted from one foot to the other.

"Hurry, come on," Molina said.

The cop returned a moment later. "All clear."

"You guys wait here and keep everybody out while we're in there."

The cops took up stations at the men's room door as Weyuker propelled Molina hastily inside.

Molina looked around rapidly, still moving, his dull eyes on two bolted windows over five sinks. He pulled Weyuker around the side of the stalls to the urinals. They were shielded from view if anyone opened the door. The terminal's P.A. murmured. The voices of anonymous travelers flowed by the door.

In the shadows, Weyuker in front of him, now nervously biting his lip and fooling with his toupee with one hand, Molina arrogantly held out his handcuffed wrists.

CHAPTER TWENTY-TWO

Seven minutes had passed and they watched the takeoffs and landings of several planes. The cops talked low to themselves. Swanson was about to say something to Susan when a cop came running out of the terminal.

He turned and began running to the terminal, knowing there was only one reason, Molina.

Behind him, the others followed.

In those fleeting instants as he ran, he saw people inside the building staring, gathering, and pointing around the men's room, heard the P.A. calling for airport security. The others, including Susan, were right behind him, two cops rushing ahead through the men's room door.

I've done all this before, he thought, all of it. I'm repeating everything.

In the men's room, a cop bent into one of the stalls, the other cops chattering, pointing, one standing precariously on two sinks and starting to push himself through the window over them. On the floor just below it, what had been a nail file, thin, bendable, the handle taped, the end needle-pointed, the sides razor-like. The cops stood around it.

Another case flashed into his mind. A murder scene, motel living room, man shot in the head leaving a sine-curved arterial spray on the carpet. Swanson entered, the cops standing around an overturned cheap metal chair. It was laughable. A nail file, a cheap chair. These shallow things with such importance.

Dick's dead, Swanson thought numbly. One more.

He heard Susan telling them to check immediately the wide fields and groves surrounding the airport. It had only been a few minutes, he had to be nearby. A handcuffed man in a black suit ought to be seen easily.

He jammed into a cop, and got halfway into the open stall.

"Goddamnit, Mike, goddamnit," Weyuker said as the gag made out of his own shirt was quickly untied. "He had a blade, pulled a blade on me, goddamnit. Went through the fucking window."

"I see, I see," he tried. Weyuker's gun was gone. Molina had gotten it somehow.

Weyuker's bony chest was lightly sprinkled with freckles, his face red and sweaty. He held moist, fevered eyes on Swanson. "Had my back to him, Christ Almighty, had a fucking blade," he said in anguish. His pants were down about his ankles, effectively holding them tight. Both hands were pulled awkwardly to the shiny metal bar on the stall's wall. Swanson realized it was reserved for the handicapped. Weyuker, a cop jiggling and puffing to free him, was handcuffed to the metal bar.

"It's okay, Dick, don't worry, let's get you out," he said gently. Weyuker pressed his reddened face down to his confined arms.

Susan stood beside him. "At least he's all right. My God, my God," she shook her head.

It was then that Swanson noticed Weyuker's freckled bald head.

Molina had taken the toupee.

CHAPTER TWENTY-THREE

"Didn't they search him?" Gleason asked.

"They said they did." Swanson sat at his own desk, empty coffee cups and his crumpled jacket near his white, restless hands.

"You didn't."

"No, not a second time. It's my responsibility."

"It's mine," Gleason said harshly, braced on a new thick cane, sunlight planing around him, his face dour, his stance belligerent. "It's still my office and I'm responsible for every case that goes through here."

"For Christ sake," Susan snapped from her chair, "that's over. Maybe it is your fault, Mike, or the yahoos in Nevada. The point is, he's a fugitive now. He's got Weyuker's gun. We've got to keep our eye on what's important."

"Weyuker didn't put up much of a fight," Gleason said.

"He didn't want to get shanked in a men's room. He feels like shit." Swanson couldn't forget Weyuker's bitter shame as he was uncuffed and he dressed, pulling his clothes back on with quick, imprecise motions. "Dick was at the sink, washing his hands. Mirror's over the towel machine near the door, so he couldn't see Molina behind him. Molina's at the urinal, Weyuker's got his head down, washing his hands, eyes away for a minute, and he's got a blade on his neck."

"I'm just not very impressed with the way he handled himself."

"What was he supposed to do, Joe? Start swinging? Molina's got twenty pounds, solid, on Dick Weyuker. He's got him pressed against the sink, he's got a blade in his neck. You tell me, Weyuker's got a real good choice about what to do. He moves, he shouts, Molina's got that shank in him so fast, that's it. Even with handcuffs, Molina might get the gun if Weyuker went down, so you get a shoot-out when the other cops come in." For the first time since Gleason called the council of war, Swanson's voice rose. "He screwed up. I screwed up. I mean, this wasn't my idea of how things should go," Swanson said too loudly. "I've seen the damn blade, you could hide it in your damn shoulder seam, put it on your arm, anyplace. They could've missed it in Nevada. This wasn't a solo screw up, Joe."

Susan broke in, "Stop taking shots at each other. There's no good point. He's probably still near Santa Maria and the striking thing about all this is that he didn't hurt Weyuker. He could have easily, but he didn't."

"So what?" Gleason threw a butt to the floor and stepped on it.

"It's significant when a man like Molina can inflict injury and he doesn't."

"I can hear Brother Claude saying exactly the same thing. Oh, can I hear him. He's got to know what happened by now." Gleason stamped his good foot in irritation. "So everything's coming right out in the open, a fugitive, the drug business, the witnesses, every bit of it."

"I can say something." Swanson restlessly fidgeted with a paper cup. "We're bringing a wanted felon back for trial, someone smuggled a weapon, lay as much off on myself as you want."

"It all comes back to me," Gleason said. "I'm the one making any statements. That's my first rule. Nobody says anything in public, because if I'm going to get the heat, I'm going to do the talking." He had an edge to his voice. "All right, I'll talk to Massingill shortly, then something public. Is there anything else we've got to go over right now?"

"I think he had somebody waiting for him." Swanson looked at Susan. "He planned this. It wasn't spur of the moment, hey I've got to go. This was setup."

"Well, that's one item I can throw back at Brother Claude when he starts making noise about his pride and joy getting away."

"I don't know how he did it." Swanson shook his head. "The day, the route, nothing went out of here."

"He could've grabbed someone outside, got their car, got away that way," Susan said.

"People notice things like that. I haven't heard anything."

Gleason lit another cigarette in his holder. His face had the same sadness, tinged with anger, that Swanson had seen when his son was killed. As if Gleason, who built and fought and survived, hated to confront forces that mastered him. "I'm going to get some kind of cockamamie statement out," he said. "Then I'll handle Massingill and the whole blessed Justice Department." He stood in the doorway, poking the cane at the floor, looking down.

Swanson got up. Gleason wanted to say something and was having trouble doing it. With his own sadness, he suddenly knew what it was. Susan avoided looking at him.

"I don't know how it happened, Joe, I honestly do not see how this fell apart. Not this way. I'm looking back at it, running it over again, and he was play acting." Swanson wanted to wipe away Gleason's unsaid judgment. "Being scared, mad, the B.S. at the plane about his court stuff, all acting. He knew he was going to get away when we landed. And he set up all these witnesses along the way. We grabbed him, right? We jammed him into a plane, right? He's so terrified he's got to escape—that's how he's going to play it."

Gleason leaned on the cane and looked at the floor. There would be no anger shown, only the terrible, true pronouncement from someone Swanson admired. "I'm very disappointed in you, Mike," he said.

"I know," Swanson said. He had nothing else to offer.

He had to call Weyuker. "You know the first thing they're going to ask," he said. "They'll say, you should've taken someone with you into the restroom."

Weyuker snorted. "Where's he going to go? I got guys all around the terminal, two guys right outside the door. I checked the place out before we went in. Jesus. What else was I supposed to do?"

"I'm not second-guessing you, Dick. You just have to be ready with that answer when the questions start. We both look bad."

"Jesus," Weyuker breathed. "We got one witness, possible. An airport food handler may have seen Molina going out the men's room window. If it's him, he went across this connecting road, he's running, down a drainage ditch, over to the side of the highway. There's all the trees on that side. Guy thinks he saw a car there. He had somebody else."

"How'd he get the word, Dick? We plugged our leak, she's over in county jail."

"Right now, I don't know."

"It's got to be back in Nevada. Somebody there gave him the time, where we'd be coming from. They could've worked it backwards, there aren't any other airports."

Weyuker sounded beat, "Sounds possible."

"How you doing?"

"Okay. I feel kind of naked. I feel like some people who shouldn't are maybe thinking this is funny, but I'm okay."

"Did he say why he took it?" Swanson knew Weyuker understood.

"No, he just took it. He gets me cinched in, and I feel so bad about that, Mike, I can't tell you. My own cuffs, my gun, sitting there like a fucking dummy for everybody to see. I got my report to do, guys handling the escape part, asking me questions. There's talk I.A.D. is interested."

"What's Internal Affairs want?"

"Jesus, I don't know," Weyuker snorted. "Guy's in my custody in the goddamn restroom, so they're thinking it's interesting. I don't hear anything definite."

Swanson wanted to help Weyuker very much. Official doubts reflected on him as well, and he was stung by Gleason's words. "Look, your way out is detail. You tell them every damn little detail and that makes your story work. Like, what happens, the first thing you and Molina get in the restroom?"

Weyuker was quiet for a moment. He cleared his throat. "I say, 'Go on over there, hurry it up.' I stand there, he kind of has trouble with the zipper, he never looks back at me. I see he's settled in, so I go to the sink."

"Why?"

"Jesus. Had some sticky crud on my hand, something from the plane. I started to wash."

"Molina said anything?"

"Naw. Just taking a whiz. I figured he was telling the truth, he had to go bad because he was there for so long."

"What kind of soap you use?"

"What?"

Swanson repeated the question. "Detail, Dick, did you have to wet your hands? Put powdered soap on them? A liquid, what?"

"Powder, that gritty shit."

"Okay. How long did you wash your hands?"

A pause at the other end. Swanson couldn't hear any sounds. Weyuker must be in a phone booth. "Ten, fifteen seconds. I wasn't making a career out of it."

"Okay. You rinse them off?"

"Yeah. Both hands."

"So you had the water running?"

"Yeah. Sure."

"So you didn't hear Molina finish?"

Another pause. "Jesus, I guess I didn't, I think about it now. I didn't even hear a flush."

Swanson took a deep breath, "See, what I mean, Dick? You

say everything in detail, small as you can, fill up as many pages as you can in their report. Next thing, what happens?"

"Next thing I got this point in my neck, like right below my right ear, pressed hard. I knew what it was, I could feel it starting to go in."

"What's he say?"

"Take my gun out, put it on the sink."

"Your hands wet?"

"Sure."

"You dry them?"

A long pause again. "Probably. On my coat, I guess. I mean, they wouldn't be wet, I gave him the gun."

"Tell me why you gave him the gun."

"He was going to stick me with whatever that fucking thing was he had at my throat," Weyuker snorted.

"Why'd you think he'd stab you?"

"Are you kidding?"

"Tell me why, exactly, Dick."

A deep breath, then, "He's got his body against me, I'm right on the edge of the damn sink, he's pressing down, like this ton of cement on my back. He's strong, he could slip that shank in me like butter. Jesus, Mike, what am I supposed to say? The guy's a fucking killer, he's got me so I can barely move my arms, he's ready to cut my throat."

The rising anger and panic in Weyuker's voice were what Swanson had waited to hear. "Okay. You tell I.A.D. that, just like that."

They spent ten more minutes covering the minute or two that elapsed from Molina picking up the gun from the sink, letting the nail-file blade fall to the floor, holding the gun as Weyuker unlocked the handcuffs, his own gun held by Molina's heavy arms and clasped hands, the murderous end of a tapering V, then putting Weyuker in the stall. "I tell you one thing," Weyuker said at last, "he pushed me around, sat me down, he wasn't even working up a sweat. He wasn't jumpy, either. These guys, you know, they get jumpy, they sweat, they talk, they get rough; Molina was all business, no talk except when he told me what to do, no roughhouse. Just left me there a stupid asshole."

"Lay it all out for I.A.D.," Swanson said. "You're just a careless jerk, like me."

"Should've shot the little fucker."

"Next time."

"We'll get him back," Weyuker said emphatically.

When they hung up, Swanson was left with his own sense of catastrophe. Weyuker could work away his shame and failure managing the search team at the airport. I'm here, Swanson thought, cracked up on the rocks.

He hung up his jacket behind the door, on top of a raincoat that had easily been there for a year. He looked around his office. Every move from one office to another meant boxing up the leavings of years of old cases and carting them along. Some of the boxes and books were still piled up, untouched, from the last move to Special Investigations. On his desk, two studio photos of Di and Di with the kids. In a corner of his blotter, where he had to see it, was a picture of Angie, laughing, taken at a birthday party.

He sat down and began to work. It was his way through the failure and shame.

Pen in one hand, the phone crushed to an ear, he started with a call to the warden at Nevada State Prison. The warden was less than receptive to the proposition his staff had been lax in searching Molina. He went on for some time about how much of a pain Molina had been and the eternal federal interference that went with him. Since Molina was no longer a federal question, the warden was going to send over any of the documents Swanson requested.

Next came Bracamonte's reports, with attached Polaroids of the corridor and the burned visitor's room. Clipped to them was the autopsy report. Swanson read it quickly, searching for one small reprieve. He found the section. The condition of Max's lungs, his nasal passages, the oxygen content of his blood and various other signs pointed to the fact he had been alive when the fire was started. Swanson put the report down. Unconscious, depressed fracture of the occipital bone, a nonlethal stab wound in the upper chest, but Max had been alive.

There was no solace. The thing had been done as cruelly as possible.

The years of reading, absorbing, using reports like this came to Swanson's relief. He uncapped a red marking pen and carefully underlined the salient words. Alive. Alive.

He was not going to be inundated by the failure. He went on, Bracamonte's interviews with four deputies who were on duty. Max was brought up from his secure cell at 8:03 P.M. and placed in the largest visitor's room, the door locked. At 8:10 the shift changed. There was traffic near the room for fifteen minutes, some staff, some inmate. Bracamonte would have all the names soon. The fire was discovered at 8:37 and brought under control ten minutes later.

The accelerant used to ignite the fire and keep it burning was, as Swanson smelled, turpentine. One of the constant chores at the main jail was painting and repainting the walls and doors. The turpentine came from a storeroom one floor below. The room was still secure when checked, so Swanson believed the turpentine had been taken out during some regular use.

More names to check. Two inmates gave vague statements about people loitering near the visitor's room.

He wrote out investigation requests for his staff and the Sheriff's office. Who was using the paint within the last two days, names and records of men in cells near Max's. Who had gang references of any sort? Who came from Los Angeles? Were there any active gang cases within the D.A.'s office?

He stood up to make a series of phone calls, holding the phone and walking a few steps with it. He talked to several nearby police departments and prosecutors. If Molina wasn't alone in his escape, which looked certain, his presence would create some disturbance in the gang world in neighboring counties. Swanson wanted to know of any change in activity, particularly among the men whose names he had sent over from Angie and Max. He was about to make another call when the phone rang. It was Massingill, from Sacramento.

★ ★ ★

"You're in direct violation of a federal court order." Massingill had trouble speaking. "You were prohibited from removing Molina from Nevada."

"I didn't know about your damn order."

"The order was still in force and valid. I'm going to get an order to show cause here, Swanson, you'll have to appear. You'll be found in contempt."

"Look, I had every right to bring him into my jurisdiction. You bring me in front of a federal judge, I intend to tell him everything about Molina and the evidence I've got."

"Where is he?"

"I don't know."

"You do know."

"What are you? Out of your mind? He escaped. He pulled a knife on one of our detectives and he escaped. And it's starting to shake out he had a car waiting for him."

"I don't believe it. You've got him."

"I don't have him."

"This whole scheme has been designed to unlawfully transport a protected witness. I think you've got him somewhere in order to evade the court's jurisdiction."

"He's an armed fugitive."

"Molina told me he's being held against his will. He said you've got him under restraint."

"He's *talked* to you? When?"

"Twenty minutes ago. He said he had been forcibly taken from Nevada State Prison by you. That is unlawful." Massingill was in cold fury. "A California law-enforcement officer has no authority to do that—"

Swanson interrupted quickly. "Where is he?"

"You've got him," Massingill yelled. "I don't know where he is."

"If I've got him, why didn't he tell you where he is? How the hell is he making long-distance phone calls to you?" Swanson stood, feeling impotent rage.

"He didn't know where he was, he didn't have any time to

talk. He said you're holding him. I believe him. You unlawfully
took a protected witness into custody, you won't tell me where
you've got him, you've violated a federal court order. Now, I'm
directing you to produce Molina this afternoon."

"I can't," Swanson shouted, "he's gone."

"He says you threatened him. He wouldn't get to California
alive. He says you talked about throwing him out of the plane,
for God sake."

I thought it. I never said it, Swanson thought. "I don't know
why he called you, Massingill, but Molina's lying about everything. He escaped from the custody of our police. You want to
hear that from the officer he stripped and left in an airport
bathroom? He's got a gun."

"I know the whole history of your personal problem with
this case." Massingill was controlled and deliberate. "And I'm
swearing to you, if Molina is killed in your county, I'm going to
have the Justice Department charge you and anyone I can find.
Don't you see what you've done? I've got trials that are sham-
bles now. I can't go on any of them. I've got a dozen murderers, organized gang leaders who'll be cut loose. It's your fault.
Your goddamn personal attitude destroyed everything."

For some time Swanson sat trembling, his hands tight on the
chair. He had to find Molina.

"Looks like a squished cat or something. Looks ugly." Ralph
Orepeza's sister Elisa made a face and poked the toupee Molina
had dropped on her bare thigh.

Molina nudged it with his finger. "Kitty, kitty, kitty. See, it
knows where to go." His hand slipped the toupee between her
legs. "That feels good, betcha. Like that."

Elisa squirmed a little and sighed. "You telling a lot of lies on
the phone. Why you doing that?"

He didn't stop. "Messes them up, makes them run around.
They don't know what's going on."

"You tell me a lot of lies."

"I never lie to you." He bent lower and kissed her belly. Her
eagerness to get into bed surprised him. It must be the legend

of the outlaw. Even as she drove from the airport, constantly jabbering, that mouth always going, trying to watch him and the road at the same time, her hands holding the wheel, then one dropping away to touch him, like he was a hitchhiking Martian. Her brother always knew she was hot after him. She came to the prison more than anyone else, even Angie. She had been good, he thought, to keep Orepeza in line.

"I don't mind, you tell me lies. Nice ones." She moved her leg over his.

"I don't lie to you, you don't lie to me." He didn't like the way the blinds made the motel room so dim. He wanted to watch her. "You hear from Ralphie, you're going to tell me?"

"Oh, I'll tell you."

He threw the toupee against the wall. He could barely see her dark hair, dark mouth, her breath close to his face. "I'd like to see Ralphie again," he said. "I still got business with him."

"He's scared, you scare him. He doesn't even tell me where he's going in Mexico." Her eyes were closed.

He kissed her. There was pleasure in the simple sensation and nothing more. At least at one time he had loved Angie. Elisa, who would marry too late or not at all, he didn't even like.

He was impatient to get moving, but she held onto him. He hadn't risked so much with a fradulent escape, putting himself literally in the open, to spend his time in a dark motel room with her. Because of what Angie had done, and Orepeza had done, and Alves and Rivera had so far failed to do, he was in federal custody for no reason. He had no money and his orders weren't followed. Swanson and the others were still alive. Whatever was wrong, and Orepeza's sister just brought stalls from Alves and Rivera, demanded personal attention. It was worse in some ways than the first gamble to get himself into the witness protection program. At the worst he was still part of the NF. Now he had cut himself off from them, set them upon him forever. But, now he had no choice. Fix the problems and get Massingill to take him back. Do it quickly.

"I hated that place," Elisa said. "I didn't like going there to see you. I hate prison. You looked so unhappy. I'm glad you're here."

"I like it here."

"You do?"

"Sure. I wouldn't be here if I didn't want to be."

She was almost petting his arm. They hadn't gotten under the covers, but her strenuous movements had pushed them to one side. He would have to find another place to stay. Orepeza's sister wouldn't work out at all.

"Let's do it again," she said, still stroking him.

"I want to find the guys. I got to move."

"Once. Not so long this time. I promise."

"I got to see them," but thought Alves and Rivera could wait a little if it would keep her satisfied. He needed her very much. "Okay," he said, moving to her.

"One little, leetle thing."

"What?"

"Get rid of that thing first? It's so creepy. I know it's on the floor there, like it can see me. I don't want to step on it."

CHAPTER TWENTY-FOUR

Swanson couldn't stay in his office after talking to Massingill. He had to see Les so he drove out to the branch jail, the Santa Maria Correctional Center.

It lay near the edge of the county, along a bone-dry expanse of abandoned rice fields, as lifeless as the Nevada desert he had flown over. The single-story buildings were made of cinder blocks ringed by double rows of fences. Les and Max had been more heavily guarded downtown, but out here it was harder for anyone to come near. Inmates in blue shirts and jeans, faded and washed into supple flaccidity and stamped with numbers, painted some of the dozen buildings inside the fence or worked out in a small yard. The Correctional Center was for short timers, generally, men either waiting to be sentenced and taken elsewhere or low-level offenders. Drunk drivers repaired bicycles and farm equipment in the shop alongside stupid drug dealers and killers whose victims lived.

He checked in at the main building and left his gun. A stale griminess clung to him from the day's business. Weyuker could find his salvation in tracking Molina. He could find some hope in turning Lester.

The Security Housing Unit was a separate cinder block building with its own fence and gate and another deputy sheriff to check in with. This one had been there for two years and liked it. Some guys did. There was very little to think about.

Swanson read down the rosters for the Correctional Center Panthers and the Jailhouse Devils softball teams prominently hung by the door to the single block of cells in the building. The deputy returned from verifying his ID and walked him down to Les's cell.

It was the last one, the largest and least accessible.

"Leave you to it," said the deputy cheerfully. He opened the door and Swanson went in.

Les lay on his back, legs straight out, hands behind his head. He was methodically chewing gum, with slow perfect bites.

I'm going to get to you, Swanson swore, and you're going to give it all up. If I don't get anything else this goddamn day, I'm going to get you.

"You care your buddy's dead?" Swanson asked. He leaned against the bars of the cell door.

Les's eyes shifted slightly, but he didn't move or stop chewing.

"I was there when Molina had it done. Saw the fire. You knew that, right? Hector set him on fire. Used turpentine to get it going good. Max wouldn't have burned without something like that. Kind of like a ghetto cocktail. Lye, hot water, honey. The honey makes the lye cling to the skin. It's kind of amazing the things you can do with stuff around the house."

By his side, Les had year-old *People* magazines. He had his shoes off and white socks on and every so often he wiggled his toes. Beside his bunk there were the usual sink and toilet, a frameless picture of an androgynous Jesus, and a small folded pile of clothes, nothing else. Whatever he read would be searched, brought to him, taken out, and searched again. He ate alone and exercised alone. But he was still alive.

Swanson tossed two packs of cigarettes onto the bunk. Les glanced at them, stopped chewing, carefully took out his gum and wrapped it in the piece of foil it came in, and got out a cigarette. He put it in his mouth. He looked at Swanson.

"Hold it," Swanson struck a match, holding the flame to the cigarette. Les had sneakers with no laces and trousers without a belt. All utensils came in and went out. Unless he stuck his head into the toilet or banged it against the wall or tried to smother himself by swallowing his sheet, there was no way to commit suicide. It was a waste of time to be so nervous about that, Swanson thought; Les would never kill himself. Despair, that had been more Max's line. Swanson watched Les inhale. "Cigarettes are easy, you're going to have trouble with the matches."

"I can take it or leave it." He pushed the two packs of cigarettes to the floor.

"Max used to ask about you. He wanted to know how you're doing, things like that."

"Guy's a riot."

"He didn't give you up. I had you anyway, so Max said he wasn't going to give you up. On that contract in Vacaville? Max left you out. Right to the end."

Les coughed once and dropped the lit cigarette to the floor. Swanson stepped on it.

"You saw how they did him?" Les coughed again, stared up.

"The last part, I did. Just read the autopsy report and he was still alive when they burned him. There was scorching in the lungs, which is what you get when you inhale flame, smoke. Hector wanted it that way, I bet."

"Max was a snitch."

Swanson laughed. "And you're not, right? That's the deal? Well, Lester, big fucking deal." He leaned toward the man staring up on the bunk. "Hector isn't giving a rat's ass whether you're in here bending over for me, or playing big con and telling me to go to hell. You get it? It doesn't matter! Max snitches. He dies. You snitch, you don't snitch, either way, Hector's going to kill you."

Les snorted. He partly rolled onto his side, legs drawn up a little.

"He's out. You know that? You hear back here in this armpit that Hector's running around again?"

"He's in Nevada."

"Not as of high noon this date." Swanson barked his words out, "He was brought here for trial and he escaped."

"No shit?"

"No shit, Les."

"The man is a certified genius." The news actually seemed to please him. He grinned; his hands went back behind his head and he lay on the bunk as relaxed as if in a hammock in his backyard.

"He's going to kill you."

"No."

"You think you're safe here? I thought I could keep Max, my witnesses safe," and my family, he thought desperately, "but Molina's made a believer out of me. He wants you all. He's going to get you."

"I'm not a snitch."

"You are, you asshole. What about your sorry buds in the AB? You're a fucking Aryan Brother rollout, that's all, and that's lower than a snitch, isn't it? You gave up your brothers so you could go in with a taco bender." Swanson felt Les's hot hand close over his face in a quick, brutal motion. He was shoved back to the bars of the cell and fractured light filled his vision when his head banged hard against the metal. Les was swearing at him. He couldn't see. He couldn't breathe, so he kicked out blindly, struck something and suddenly the hand was gone. Les leaned down for an instant, his leg twisted slightly. Swanson pushed him violently, joyfully releasing the fury he wanted to vent on Molina.

Les stumbled backward and thumped onto the bunk on his back, his head cracking against the cinder block wall. He swore again. Swanson thought he'd jump back off the bunk.

But he didn't. He curled forward, both hands holding the back of his head as if he was trying to roll into a ball. He groaned twice and rocked back and forth.

"You finished?" Swanson said, "Is that it?"

Les rocked once more and uncurled himself, sitting with his hands hanging down. He swore at Swanson. "I was just having a little fun. Can't do much around here."

Swanson stayed near the bars. Les was lean and smart. He could have come again and it would have taken some time before the deputy near the front of the cell block heard anything. All he wanted was his displeasure registered at the crack about selling out. Now was the time to educate him.

"Remember the S.H.U. at Folsom?"

Les nodded.

"All you sorry gang jackasses were in Security Housing. The prison within the prison. You know that was a joke."

"Sure it's a joke."

"I had three cases from the Shoe after you got out." Swanson carefully moved toward the sink and the ambivalent Jesus intently gazing upward. "Three kiester stashes, buck knives. Not shanks; knives you buy outside."

"Who had them?"

"ABs."

Les grinned.

"That's why Hector's going to get you. If you can bring store-bought knives into the prison, you can do just about anything."

"I know the man."

Swanson kicked at the cigarettes on the concrete floor. "Here's the situation. If Max was alive, I'd be ready to take you into court. We go to trial and you get the death penalty."

"I know."

"Max is dead. Hector's loose for the moment. Somebody's got to testify against him. That leaves you. I wouldn't be here if there was any other way I could think of to get him."

"Snitch him off like Max? Max's always cheating. He does things wrong and he wonders, hey, why's everybody dumping on me? He's got good points and bad points, but he does bad things when it's cosmically bad," Les plumped his flat pillow, "and that's not me."

But you're talking, Swanson exulted, for the first time, you son of a bitch, you're talking about Max like he's still alive and that means I've got you. You cared about him.

"I told you how I saw it," Swanson spoke flatly. "I didn't like

Max, but he was better than you are. You're better than letting Hector get away. What I can't figure out is why you'll let Hector kill your best friend, kill you, and you won't fight back. Doesn't make any sense. You see how it makes sense?"

"Because," Les said it as though Swanson was an imbecile, "I'm not going to give you anything."

"Me? We talking about me all of a sudden? I'm talking about you," Swanson pointed, "and Max. You've got the power to hit back at Molina. I'm giving it to you. Right now. This second. Tell me you'll come into court and I'll deal this minute. I walk out of here, you might stay alive for a month, a year, you know how long it can take. I thought I was talking to a different guy, he's going to take care of his own beef."

"I am."

"Then get Hector for your pal."

One more compromise was always possible. There was, with luck, another more egregious offender just one rung higher on the ladder. Deal with whoever was below him. Sometimes it was possible to avoid doing the vilest thing, but he knew that was no longer possible in this case. The man who shot Angie four times in the head was the only witness available. Over the years Swanson had worked out compromises that were between good and evil, and then, like this time, between evil and evil. The choice was never unaffecting. It simply had to be made.

Les looked up at him.

CHAPTER TWENTY-FIVE

Molina parked Elisa's rented car just in front of a sign at the Motel 6 that advertised free Jacuzzis for "traveling businessmen." He changed clothes at her place and wore a short-sleeved green-checked shirt and black jeans. It was five in the afternoon and hot and he was tired, but a shower helped.

"We'll get something to eat after I see these guys," he said to placate her. "But you stay out here. You watch out, okay?"

"I want to come in."

"I want you to stay here."

"I didn't get any lunch, I got to wait for you, I want to come in."

"It's your fault you didn't eat. They don't know I'm coming?"

She shook her head.

"So stay here and we'll go eat after."

No question about it. Orepeza's sister would not be good to have around at all. She had to be on her way back to L.A. as soon as possible. She didn't look bad, he admitted, head in one hand on the car window, long dark hair hanging straight down. Like a dark-haired Madonna, a pouting, spoiled Mary.

He kissed her shoulder. "Watch for me, okay? It's important. I don't want to get surprised in there."

"Sure," she said grumpily, without looking at him.

Molina climbed the outdoor stairs to the second floor of the three-story motel. A fat woman pushing a cart of jumbled sheets and cleaning brushes looked at him without interest. She stopped at a door and pounded on it.

He strode past her, past numbered doors, windows with the curtains drawn. Once a bunch of guys he had briefly worked with had set up a speed lab in a Motel 6. They rented three rooms and began cooking. The ether fumes coming from the third room grew so strong that they made several guests walking by outside faint. The cops were called. Sometimes the capacity for sheer animal stupidity amazed him, and he liked to think that one of his strengths was enough experience never to be amazed at what people did.

He knocked on the door.

The television game show loudly braying inside suddenly went silent. He knocked again. A thump, a curse.

"What?" came the shout. Little Raymond. Very annoyed.

He obviously couldn't tell who it was.

"Cleaning your room now," Molina said.

"Shit, go way. Do not disturb."

"Open it, Raymond."

The door opened instantly. Bright-eyed, frantic, in a T-shirt and briefs, Raymond grabbed his arm. "Jesus, man, get in here." He pulled Molina inside.

One yellow lamp burned. The television scattered its own flickering rays over the Taco Bell cups and greasy papers, parts of newspapers, and clothes around the room. Molina quickly listened and looked.

"Where's Cisso?"

"Out. Gone. Someplace." Raymond waved his arms and scratched his nose suddenly. He began hyperbreathing as if running laps.

"When's he coming back?"

"Couple minutes. Just to the store, man, for supplies. We're low. He wanted to get out, check things out, look around." Raymond was bright-eyed watching him. "God, man, you got out. Shit. I was thinking, hey, he's going to do it, he'll make it. Then I go, no way, man. But, you did it."

"Any left?" he didn't take his eyes from Raymond.

"Hey, yeah," with pleased surprise. "Not much, but some for you. Last batch from the biker boys. Crank," he ground out the last word hard and slow.

"Don't use anymore."

"What?"

"You're all messed up," Molina cleared a place at the bureau by sweeping all the paper plates, bits of old food, and beer cans to the floor. He sat on the bureau. "You haven't taken care of things, okay? Do whatever you want to after, okay? Now I want you to tell me why things aren't taken care of."

Raymond, all small and tight and brown, like a feral child, bounced on the bed. "We got that white boy Max and the fat old dude. It's all being handled, man," bounce, bounce, bounce, "we got a problem, you can fix it you're out now, hey it's great to see you, man."

"What problem?"

"See, Cisso and me, here we are. We got expenses here, we can't get out because all the other dudes you want are here, yeah? See, there ain't no cash. The biker boys don't give us nothing free. Pay. Every motherfucking thing, pay, pay," bounce, bounce, bounce, "so Cisso and me we got to wait for you to tell them to pay us. Or you got to pay us. Ralphie's gone, yeah? We got enough to get through some of these dudes, but it ain't enough. We got nothing left for us, we got to jam out of here. There's expenses, man, other guys, things to do. We got to have more bills before we get to these others. They're tough, not like Max and the fat old dude."

Molina slid off the bureau. He put a hand on Raymond's stick-thin brown throat and began squeezing. The bouncing stopped. Two small hands grabbed his. The bright-eyed face was slick, terrified, furious. Molina immediately thought that

holding a speeded-out little shanker like Raymond was like in-
tentionally seizing a writhing snake.

"Where is Cisso, right now, this second?"

"The store, fucking robber store Seven-Eleven or something
couple blocks."

"When's he coming back?"

"Soon. A second, right now."

"He in this with you?"

"Hey, it's no fucking big deal," the eyes like nails on him,
"we do everything. Trust me, man, trust me it's money, Ralphie
didn't give it to us."

Molina let go. Raymond scrabbled toward the bed's head-
board and balefully gibbered at him. It was all complaints,
driven by the speed and his own juices, and it made Molina a
little sad to see a homeboy so lost. Everyone assumed Cisso was
the worst of the two because he was bigger and took care of the
wetter chores. But, it was Raymond who had the will and the
viciousness. And even he couldn't control himself enough to
wait until everything was in order before tanking up and taking
the rough methamphetamine ride.

"Sorry, Ray, I haven't worked out all the shit today. Tough
day for me." Molina turned the sound back on the television,
flooding the room with bells and applause and squeals.

Raymond gradually sank to the bed, his feet kicking, then he
was up, jumping around the room, "It's okay, no big deal, because it's no big skin off my fucking ass, man, I tell you how it
is. And that's no shit, all one hundred percent, ninety-nine, nine
percent pure truth. Money. Money."

"I'm going to get it."

"I knew you would, no doubt, ever, ever," and he went on.

"How long you and Cisso staying here?"

Raymond looked at him, bewildered. "Until it's over, wrap
it up."

Molina shook his head. "They going to find you here, you
stay long."

Molina was genuinely startled, although he didn't show it,
when Raymond hopped onto a bed and began doing a rapid

little jig. "They never find us, man, we stay here forever. It's like I tell Cisso, we're like invisible, they walk right by us." He thought this was very funny and giggled, along with the laughter from the television.

"Couple days, I get you the money."

"Then I take care of the whole thing, choo, choo, choo," he aimed off rounds from an imaginary shotgun.

"Take care, Ray. Tell Cisso I say hi. I see you both soon."

Raymond jumped high, and fell back onto the bed, laughing. "King of the mountain, man, like always."

CHAPTER TWENTY-SIX

Tonight it was Larry and T.J. from SMPD playing babysitter inside, and Swanson had the drill down perfectly. Ask how they're doing, talk about cops and D.A.s they'd all know, joke about the situation, ask if they need anything. Larry and T.J. had been on duty before, so they knew the drill, too.

It was dark outside. Di was upstairs with Matt. Swanson felt so clumsy and leaden, but better, after the quick trips to the garage and the bottle he'd brought on his way back from the Correctional Center. When in doubt, go straight for vodka.

He sat at the piano bench while Lizzie impatiently thumped through the two pieces she'd learned that day. Things might be going badly but piano lessons were forever. Teacher came by twice a week. Meg began banging on the low notes to get his attention.

"Don't do that, honeypie, let Lizzie finish and then we'll do yours." He stopped her by taking her hands.

Meg paused without liking it.

"That's all, there's more practice but I didn't do that yet," Lizzie said, immediately launching into another round of simple chords and melodies.

"Well, that's just fine. I really liked that."

She kept playing but glanced at him with an odd expression. "No, you didn't. You didn't like it."

"You're right. I didn't."

This made Meg laugh and start playing scales. T.J. was making his quarter-hour check over the walkie-talkie. He and Larry were at the center of the living room, cards spread over the coffee table. Swanson got up and made himself dizzy.

"Get you guys anything?" He cocked an inquiring finger at them.

"Maybe some coffee on your way back," Larry said. He used to be a bailiff and, like Swanson, had grown a little softer and grayer.

"You stay here and practice, both of you." Swanson gently tried to untangle Meg's hands from his arm and his leg. In the last few days he noticed she was frightened whenever he left her. What was Di telling her? "I'll be right back, just going to the kitchen, stay put." He put her hands back on the piano. Lizzie went on, primly ignoring them both. Swanson stroked Meg's hair. She watched him, every step, as if he was going to disappear in an instant.

Her look made him feel worse suddenly, and he went through the kitchen quickly, fumbling at the door to the garage. The kitchen was lit cheerfully, the dishes washed, everything in order as Di always made it. What a miracle, he thought bitterly, she can keep the place clean, and get the kids piano lessons like nothing was happening. At least one of us can do something right. She's keeping the family running.

The kitchen was connected directly to the garage. He flipped on the light, opened the car door and sat down, the bottle resting against the brake pedal. The car buzzed because the door was open, then stopped. Swanson drank from the bottle slowly and waited for the heavy warmth, the forgiving mist.

For a moment, seeing him in the front seat of the car, tapping his hand and knee to the rhythm of music on the radio, Di thought he was relaxing. She didn't understand why he would have come out there, but he looked at ease. Not like when he came home haggard and angry. Then she saw the vodka bottle, watched it come up, tipped back, lowered. He went on tapping, the music echoing thinly in the garage.

"What are you doing?" she asked. She stood beside him at the open door.

"Well, hiya kiddo. Just minding my own business."

"I don't want you to do that."

He ostentatiously screwed the top back on the bottle and reverently laid it on the brake. He turned the music down a little. "I was done anyway. You want to sit down?"

"No."

"No," he said more slowly.

"Don't do that anymore," she said. "I can't do everything myself in this family. I need you."

"I think you're doing one hell of a fine job."

"Things didn't go the way you wanted to today. Moping around doesn't make them any better. It doesn't change them."

"Thanks for that insight." He was scowling at her. At once she felt fear because he had done that before, the other time when events had taken their own course and he was unable to do anything about it. "I don't think I need your advice."

"Are you going to stay out here?"

"Maybe."

"Come back inside."

"Later. I got things to do out here." He half-turned in the seat and gestured at the garage. "You go on."

"I saw Joe on the news. He was talking about the escape, this man Molina, trying to bring him here for trial. Is that it? What you didn't want to tell me about yesterday?"

He half-laughed, coldly, emptily.

"You must be disappointed. I understand. But you can't simply give in. You can't do this."

"I can't?"

"I'll have to take the kids."

He half-laughed again, then, "Anything else on the news?"

"Like what?" thinking at the same moment how ridiculous

they must look, threatening, badgering and bickering, to the beat of the radio. After twelve years, she knew what he said beneath the words and the actions. He was wounded, deeply and painfully, and his shield against further blows was petulant self-pity.

"Fire over at the jail. Prisoner getting burned to death. No big item probably. Joe didn't mention it, I bet."

"I don't think he did. Maybe there was something.

"Let's not drag each other around," she whispered, "let's say what we mean." If ultimate meanings were sometimes clearer to her now, the signs to them grew more obscure. Mike's words hid too much, his childishness angered her even as she recognized its cause. The scowling face was his, but coarsened. He thought the world would always come out right for him. Big Mike could do a little tinkering here and there, talk his way around, and the world's various travails would easily give way. She imagined his shock at finding out the truth.

"My prisoner, who he was." He shook his head, eyes closed a little, then opened on her. "My snitch. I saw the fire, saw him in it. All I've done, Di, is make things worse. Everything worse."

"Not us. You haven't done that." She tried to penetrate his shell of resignation. "No matter how terrible these things are, I refuse to give these people power over me or my family."

"You want to hear what it was? I got pictures at the office, you want to see them."

"Mike, Mike, it must have been awful to do this to you. But that's what they want, to sicken you, frighten you. You can't fight them. But that's when you've got to fight harder." She held his wrists, locking him to her, as if to yank him physically from the escape that frightened her more than anything else. Stay with me, she called out to him, don't leave now. She let go of him, his hands dropping.

"I'm fighting back." He smiled at her, deceiving and cold, changing the station on the radio to easy-listening strings and woodwinds. "Got to keep my sense of humor."

"Do you hear what I'm saying, Mike?"

"You're standing right in my ear, sure." He pulled his wrists free when she took them again. "You would've laughed, you saw Weyuker in that bathroom, no toup, all tied up. Scared the hell out of me for a minute, but afterward, he looked funny. I mean ha-ha kind of funny. I thought, gee, I don't have to worry about Dick. I'd be okay if I didn't have to worry about you—" he started ticking off fingers in front of his face, "—the kids, God bless them, my pals the Tices; I told you about this asshole Lester Narloch, he's a pal, too. I could be okay if I didn't have anybody hanging around."

"Come back inside." She bent to him.

He sat there, still talking, as though alone. "I was just wondering, does Molina ever wonder? I mean, does he think he might make a mistake, he's doing the wrong thing? I guess that's the difference. He doesn't worry. That's his edge." He slumped. "He doesn't have all these people to worry about."

"I love you," she said, trying to comfort him and rouse him from his stupefying pity.

"And God loves me. I don't want to hear any of that crap now. Spare me, okay?" He turned the music up very loudly and reached for the bottle again.

"All right," she turned, seeing him last in the car's interior light, a pale nimbus over him. He drank once more.

The radio's plastic noise riotously played up to the door as she closed it, shutting him and it in the garage. If he thinks he's failed, she thought, so have I.

CHAPTER TWENTY-SEVEN

The road was very rough, rutted on either side of the car so that Molina had to hold the wheel tightly to stay in control. A constant dull rumble and sudden, startling bang from stones hitting them carried over Elisa's constant chatter. One thing, she was never inconspicuous. With that voice going on and on and on you could find her in a crowd. Somehow, Molina didn't remember her talking so much when she visited him in the joint. Maybe she stored it up.

They drove through a dirt track, barely wide enough for the car, running between what seemed to be two high dark-green walls, the very tops of the pines merged together somewhere near the sky. The air was sharp, electric.

"You should do it yourself." She chewed another Tic Tac in a single, hard crunch. "Forget about that little shit Raymond. I hate him, he stinks, he never cleans, always wears the same shirt, I bet he never changes anything. That little shit. Money." She shook her head rapidly.

"I can't do it myself."

"Honey, I tell you, you got to take care of that little shit. He and Cisso think they own it all now. Believe me, I know them. You don't see them for a year. You got to let them know it."

He shook with the violent jerking of the car, "I do anything, cut anybody, anybody gets hurt, I'm out of the program forever."

"So?"

He really didn't want to explain it all to her, but she had a stubborn streak that made things hellish if it wasn't turned aside. He should have left her in town. But he wanted her company, so that made no sense. "I got to let Raymond and Cisso take care of everything. I got to get back in with Massingill and the Justice Department. Let them worry about me."

"It's so great in the joint?"

Molina almost thought he could hear the clattering inside her head when she thought.

"Better than being out in the open. I got no time. I got to get my money from these guys." First Swanson, he was the worst, then the other two. When it happened, he'd be safely in the protective arms of Massingill and everything would be like it was before Angie and Ralph pulled it all apart.

"You don't have to go back inside."

"Where else do I go?"

She nodded her head, glanced out the window. "Somebody could be with you, you stayed out."

"Who? You?" He slowed the car as they came to a crude fence posted across the road.

"I wouldn't mind," she said. The idea didn't strike him as funny as it ought to. There was something about her he felt drawn toward, even though she was willing to betray her brother, perhaps because of it. He thought about his own kid. You're supposed to love your kid, feel some connection to her, the blood link humming. He felt nothing, heard nothing. Only to Orepeza's sister beside him did he sense any closeness.

He left the engine running and got out. Large warning and NO TRESPASSING signs, some printed, others poorly home-made, were tacked on tree trunks and the fence. Orepeza's sister had her head out the window.

"Raymond says this way?"

"Smokey's out here." Molina unwound a coil of wire from the fence and lifted up the section blocking the road. "He's still buying from the bikers so he knows the way."

"Hey," Orepeza's sister called out in greeting.

Molina looked up as a bearded, slouching man holding a shotgun ambled to the front of the car. He wore dark glasses and a brass earring.

"Going up to see Smokey." Molina wiped his hands. "I'm Hector. He knows I'm coming."

"Hector who?" The man held the shotgun easily.

"Hector Molina. You guys and me been doing business a couple of years. Me and Ralph Orepeza in Santa Maria. Smokey knows me."

"I don't know you."

"I don't know you, but I know Smokey and I know how to get up here."

In the brief spaces between their words, Molina felt an oppressive silence crowd stealthily from the green depths. It was morbid in all that forested silence. It made him nervous.

The man coughed and spat abundantly. "Shit, go ahead, end of the road, you run right into it. If you're not okay, then it won't make no difference, cause this's the only way out."

"I run with a lot of the brothers." Molina rattled off names and crimes for a moment. "I keep in touch."

"I know Shorty," the man said. The shotgun relaxed toward the pine-needle-blanketed ground. "I know him from Vacaville."

"So I catch you on the way back," Molina grinned, getting back into the car. Orepeza's sister sucked on a Tic Tac and watched the man through the windshield.

The car moved slowly past the fence, like a needle into an artery. The man shambled into the trees and disappeared.

Orepeza's sister began talking again as they jolted up the road. He cut her off. "He didn't know me."

"He's got no mind, you could see, big dumb guy, no brains. He guards everything?" She went on until Molina said something. "What?" She turned to him.

"Who's Smokey working with, these guys never heard of me? What's going on?" For one of the rare times in his life, he was worried, as though a great block of masonry had inexplicably appeared in front of him. His thoughts froze. It was easily as bad as those moments when he couldn't stop himself from doing something he knew was dangerous. Like I want to do it, just to see what happens. Get tired of thinking everything all the way around.

They entered a small clearing. A blue circle of sky hung over it, torn by the ragged sharp tops of the pines. In the clearing were two campers. There were metal cylinders near one and several cardboard boxes and crates. Another bearded man with an immense belly sat beside the door of one camper. He was cleaning the bottom of a very old boot with a large folding knife. He stopped as Molina pulled up.

Elisa made a face. "Supposed to smell like that? I didn't think that little white stuff, little powder, little pills would stink so much." She held her nose.

"That's what my money smells like." He tried thinking of one thing, getting the money, getting back to Massingill. There was no time for anything else.

He noticed three other men at the edge of the clearing. He took a deep breath. It smelled like a towering pile of babies' diapers, ammoniated and ripe. It was a stench, a brassy color.

"Hey, where's Smokey at?" Molina called out. The man scraping his boot pointed the blade at the other camper. "How you doing?" he sauntered toward the camper, pointing at the men near the clearing. Elisa stayed in the car. He heard the doors lock.

The medium-sized white camper was streaked with rust. Molina knocked on the door and called out. He felt no fear, even though there had been surprises all this journey. He was in charge.

The door opened.

"Officer Robinson," Molina said.

"Jesus, they let anybody come out here." Smokey Robinson smiled widely. He looked old with brown hair and wrinkles.

His jeans had stains on them and his short-sleeved shirt bared arms ridged and reddened to the elbow, as if the flesh had melted and reformed poorly. "Get in here, you asshole, we got to talk," he said, pulling Molina in by the shoulder.

Molina saw the car, Elisa huddled in it, the men watching her, him.

He was getting used to the smell, the stink of phenyl, even though it was stronger inside. An alarm clock rang and Smokey darted suddenly to the other end of the camper. "Got to check my soufflé out," he said, adjusting several gauges over a large re-action flask. Next to it was a round vat, capped, tubing coming from it, heavily insulated like the flask. Molina didn't have to check. The smell came from the dark syrup in the flask, and the three others like it stewing in the camper.

"You keep watching," Molina said. "I don't want to blow all over the trees."

Smokey straightened. "I got to keep half an eye on the cook-ing. I learned my lesson." He rubbed the burned, congealed red flesh of his arm. "Last week again, almost, this close." He made a small space between his hands. "Could have been very messy."

Molina perfunctorily looked around. The interior of the camper was like a wizard's chamber, misted condensers on small Bunsen burners, vacuum dryers and pumps for taking the syrup and distilling it, heaters to keep the liquids at the right temper-ature. In the midst of the tubing, glassware, bottles, and chemi-cal stains were some balled-up shirts and two chairs, a counter with papers and a half sandwich, three beer cans. A calendar from the California Highway Patrol was tacked over a too-large splash of dried chemical.

Smokey's name was Jeffery and he got nicknamed when he went to prison for grand theft.

"It's a good place. I couldn't smell anything until we were al-most here," Molina said.

"You get back here, it's like you're on a desert island. No-body comes around, you see anybody who does, scare them off. You drive these campers away, you're gone and you just set up someplace else. This is the best. Forget nailed down houses, apartments, buildings. Stay mobile. Move fast, stay loose." He rolled his shoulders.

"They still give you that shit?" He pointed at the calendar as he tried to figure a way to get his money from Smokey. It suddenly felt as though it would be difficult.

"I'm in the computer. I bounced out of the CHP, I go to the joint and they still forward my mail. Calendar every December. So I put it to some use. Been having little accidents with this new equipment. Scares the shit out of me sometimes." He sipped from a beer and laughed.

Smokey doesn't want to talk about the money. The thought was sharp and clear. "Guys outside are all new."

"Had to be." Smokey tapped a cool, empty flask. "Things changed so fast."

"Like what?"

"Thing with your wife, all that talking. Guys thought you were blown." Smokey fidgeted a little. He had a twenty-year man's soul, on or off the CHP. He would always sound like a bureaucrat even if he was in the middle of nowhere cooking speed for bikers.

"Everything's exactly the same," he said too hard. Maybe he'd been locked up too long. He'd lost his edge, the sureness of control. It slipped away so easily. "You told them, I bet."

"I said, Hector's got this set, we're set, but I couldn't make them do it. Orepeza runs, like I said, everything was changing so fast."

Molina sensed the tension. Smokey was tight as a drum, the red fingers spread along a flask, eyes darting to the clocks. He was all false friendship and chat. "You didn't change the p-two. Still stinks. You didn't go to ephedrine."

"Can't get it. It's no major deal, I don't mind the smell, it's easy enough to get p-two now."

Phenyl-2-propanone, ether, acetone, phenylacetic acid, methalymine, a dash of this, a drop of that, slowly simmer, separate, and serve. Smokey knew the step-by-step recipe for methamphetamine by heart and fiddled with it in a little black cookbook he kept.

"You still get twelve for a pound?" Molina asked. He was feeling tighter by the moment. The sharp stink burned.

"Eleven on a bad day, the guys have moved it around thirteen or thirteen-five a little north, like Stockton, Sacramento sometimes. It averages out." He patted a small stack of carefully wrapped bundles, translucently white. "For a while everybody was hot for rubbers, put your stash in a rubber. Now everybody's using balloons."

Finally they were talking about the money. He counted the bundles. There was about fifty thousand dollars worth of speed in the camper. Smokey was always a good cook. He could do his work in two days so that in a decent week, no time off, he might produce close to two hundred thousand dollars worth of drugs. Then it was off the the ABs and bikers for distribution. Nothing fancy or expensive.

"I need my money. I want you to give it to me." He stood near Smokey, close enough to smell the beer and see the ruined face. A man was decaying in front of him.

"No problem, Hector, I got cash in the other camper. Do my serious living there."

"You got a hundred seventy-five?"

"I got like eighteen thousand."

"I want the hundred seventy-five. That's a discount from what you owe me since Orepeza split."

"I give you what I got." Smokey was visibly nervous, glancing again and again at the three alarm clocks scattered through the camper. "I don't have bucks like that. I'm just the cook."

"It's what you owe."

"Not these guys. It's all different, it's a whole new thing we got going out here. These guys are in it for themselves."

"How much they got here?"

"Like now? We're low, nothing much. They got maybe sixty, couple guys got it."

Molina knew this was where the break happened. Another man would call it quits and stop and that would be the end of it all. Or he could push ahead. It was a question of willpower.

"Get me the money, Smokey. I need it and it's mine."

"Whatever I got, I told you. Look, this isn't the same deal, same people, same anything. There's no money for you. Not from this deal." Molina heard the clocks ticking, saw Smokey staring at them, as if waiting.

Molina took out the gun. "I want you to bring it to me."

"That's a cop's gun. .38 Colt King."

"Go get everything they got."

"Jesus. Take this, fucking Alves can move it." He reached around and gathered up two of the white bundles.

For a blinding instant, Molina surged with a primal, explosive urge to kill Smokey, smash the place. He was the center of a fireball that rose, reaching defiantly toward the blue sky. His arm flashed out, the bundles snapped from Smokey's red fingers, split in the air and, like white spume, fine snow covered the counter and shirts.

"Jesus, Jesus, Hector, I don't have it. I can't get it," Smokey waved his hands, motes of powder drifting around him.

He didn't hear anymore. Waves washed deeply through him. He swung the gun barrel into some glassware. Tubes and a spray of glass scattered with a tinkling cry. He was at the stewing liquid, black-brown muck in its pampered incubator.

"Jesus, Hector, come on, Jesus." Smokey pulled back, trying to get to the door. White powder settled on him.

Molina stopped, staring at the flask. An alarm clock rang and he breathed heavily, controlling himself. Smokey hurried to one of the flasks and fooled with the heaters.

"I'm going to get that money," Molina said. The explosive burst calmed him, gave him the familiar purity of vision. He felt like he could see to the center of the earth. "Or I'm going to take this whole fucking thing apart. Your guys on the street, the guys in the joint, I'm going to take everybody down."

He heard the deep sputtering of motorcycles outside.

"I'll talk to them. I'll try something, but you got to see it's different. Nothing stayed the same, I'll lay it out," he chattered.

"Shut up. What're they doing?"

"I don't know."

"Tell me, Smokey," almost gently, the gun pointed into the ruined face.

"They want to turn you in. They're going to give you up."

"To who?"

"NF. They got the local lieutenant all bothered. Want to collect on the contract."

Molina smiled. "How's it go? I want to hear."

Smokey deliberately stepped back slightly, bumping into the counter, his heavy flanks sagging to it. "I told them it was stupid. I said, don't count me in, I'm out. I have a debt to this man."

"Okay."

"I'm supposed to be out of here already." He looked nervously at the alarm clocks ticking. "You come out. They wait until you get to your car, two of them going to grab you. I don't think you were supposed to bring anybody."

"I wasn't."

"You're supposed to be alive, they hand you over."

"Sure, that's how you want it. Make a big noise so everyone knows what happened to me." Molina lowered the gun. "Somebody coming here?"

"Couple hours, after dark." Smokey was working on his panic. "They didn't tell me, maybe twenty minutes before you got here. They kept me in the dark. All I'm in for is talking to you, and walking out so you'd follow me to your car and you'd be thinking about the speed, doing business, that like." He tried a smile, but the effort was weak. "I wasn't going to do it. I was going to tell you anyway. I'm not brave."

Molina looked at his gun. "They think I'd show up here without anything? What's the idea?"

"Hector, I swear, these are not the brightest people I've ever worked with. I mean, you have some prime idiots out there." The old cop talked with disdain. "I believe they figured to cold cock you or something brilliant like that while we're talking, while you're busy with me out in the open."

The motorcycles went on roaring, then quit, like tribal drums abruptly silenced before an attack.

Molina found the treachery amusing. Angie's death hadn't

fixed anything. He no longer mattered outside except as a reward and then, a painful, illustrative execution so the word and honor of Gilbert Villagrana would be respected. He felt like a man on the highwire experiencing his first taste of real giddiness.

"Tell them it's okay," he said to Smokey.

"It's okay?"

"They can have me. I'm going to walk right out. What're there? Five, six of them?"

"Eight. Everybody's got a piece."

"Tell them. From here."

He looked around the camper again as Smokey shouted through a small vent near the ceiling. He didn't care what Smokey said or the answering curses shouted back.

Elisa began squealing in high, thin bursts.

Smokey said to him, "They think you'll help her. Maybe deal."

"They can have her. Tell them. I said I'm walking out." He pushed Smokey forward to the back door. The camper was slightly off center, so they tilted downward, as though on a rough sea.

"Jesus, let me turn the heat off."

"Car's right outside. You walk, get in with me. You fuck up, these assholes are going to have to make this shit themselves."

"You want my hands up?"

Molina gently poked him with the gun barrel. The door opened and they stepped out. Smokey was talking again, placating, explaining. He saw five men, some bearded, all dressed in dirty blue denim and coats, their gang colors faded, torn, stained. Elisa was pressed against the car door by the fat man Molina had seen cleaning his boot. He held a snub-barreled gun to her ear.

Molina pushed his gun into Smokey's ear as the fat man began swearing at him, the belly pressing undulantly into Elisa as though he was trying to wobble her through the metal car door.

"Open the car doors," Molina said. "Both of them. Put her inside." At that Elisa's squealing rose.

The fat man leaned tighter into her. "Fuck you, I'm going to shoot this bitch, I swear, you don't fucking let go of old Smokey there and chuck the beaner gun here."

Molina twisted the gun so that Smokey cried out. "See what I'm doing here? See that?" He ground the barrel into Smokey's ear again, and the sharp cry cut through the voices around Molina.

"I'm going to shoot the bitch. I'm going to shoot her." The fat man jiggled angrily, the denim jacket shaking around him. His knife bumped against his leg.

"You going to be all by yourselves, nobody to cook for you." Smokey's red arms shot up in reflex.

"I got to check that stuff soon," Smokey shouted. "It's real critical now." He twisted his head a little.

The fat man, Molina presumed, was the leader. No one else ventured to do anything unless he went first. Now the undulant body moved back from Elisa, the gun came from her ear. The fat man's tongue lapped quickly on the patch of black moustache under his nose. Molina kept walking with Smokey toward the car.

"Open the doors, open them, do it," Smokey cried.

Elisa stopped squealing and pushed her hands at the fat man, cursing him. He didn't take his eyes from Molina. The tongue, mindless and darting, kept reaching for his lip. "Open the doors," Molina said.

The fat man opened the passenger side with one hand, Elisa slid in, across to the driver's side and opened it. "How about that, buddy boy?" asked the fat man. "How about we do something together?"

"Get the fuck out of the way." Molina pulled Smokey in with himself, the gun still at him. Look at them, he thought, the eyes, stupid, vicious. Not like the cons he talked to at Folsom, at DVI, who watched with fascination, with attention, as he told them what a few bold men could do outside the joint to become rich and feared. But, something had happened. He hadn't made a single wrong move. Angie's death was necessary, his escape was compelled by the situation, the witnesses had to be obliterated so he could go on. Step by step, each one singly made sense, yet in sum they left him here, fighting his way out, loveless and alone.

"Shut up and start the car," he ordered Elisa, who lashed out a final time toward the fat man, leaning backward. The other men, like apes in a primeval encampment, looked at each other or the car, their guns lowered. "Pull forward slowly, we got to drive around to get out," he said. He sat with Smokey in the back seat, the gun hard in his ear.

"I can drive. I been driving fifteen years, I can get a fucking car out." She stomped too hard on the accelerator and the car jumped forward. "I'm going to take a couple of these guys on the hood," the car bumping on the brown rocky soil, circling the campers, the men furious as it passed by. The fat man's mouth was working busily, one hand raised with the gun a part of it, a shot fired off into the sky.

"Put it down, would you, I'm not going to do anything, Jesus." Smokey pulled his head from the gun. "Do whatever you have to, but I got to get back here quick."

"They can take care of things."

"I'm the cooker. They don't know anything. They'll blow everything."

"They all should die," Elisa yelled. She drove too fast down the rutted, tree-bound road.

"You want to work with these guys?"

"I got to go where the action is. It's strictly migrant labor."

He held the gun loosely on his lap. Elisa called down every bane and disaster she could think of.

"I thought you were staying in the car," he said angrily, "what happened?"

"The fat guy, he points a gun at me, what you think I'm doing? You think I sit there so he can shoot me? I got out fast so this fat guy can try to feel me up, the whole place stinks like hell," and she started swearing again.

"Slow down," he said. She was driving so fast that he could feel the underside of the car shaking with the potholes and roughness of the road.

"I'm getting out of here, I don't give a shit about anything, I want to get out of here," she emphasized the last words over the car's rumbling.

"They ain't going to follow us. I can hear them. They've got some kind of session going, trying to decide what to do," Smokey said nervously.

"Slow down, you're going to hurt the car," he reached over her shoulder, the gun sliding off his lap to the floor. He grabbed the wheel and she swore at him.

"I can drive."

"I said take it easy."

He sat back and picked up the gun. Smokey watched with ill-concealed concern. Molina held the gun for security, like an anchor. You could do everything right, things that hurt and made you want to scream, and still find out that it didn't matter. He thought of Flaco. Did Flaco really have to die? He could have stayed at the top in the NF and it wouldn't have been very different from this. He shook his head. Not so different at all.

The bright point was Massingill, like a silvery harbor at the end of a turbulent journey. A little care and he could still make it back to that harbor. He still had people and Elisa was willing to do anything.

A new small thing glittered brightly in his mind, then went out. What if I didn't go back to Massingill? That was something to think about.

Smokey stirred, nervously looking out the window, at him, at the protectively held gun. "I feel real bad about this, Hector, really do. It's bad all the way around, shouldn't be. I got something you might use, get some cash."

"What?"

"There's an Iranian kid, down in Stockton, wants somebody to hit his father. Old guy's a general or something like that in the old days. Took a lot of money out with him, lot of it."

Molina looked at Smokey, the new idea fading for the moment. "What?"

"He said, there's this kid, Iranian kid in Stockton," Orepeza's sister shouted.

"You listening?"

Molina nodded.

"I can't hear," Elisa called when they were at the fence again.

"Keep going, straight through," Molina said.

"How far you taking me?" Smokey watched the last marker disappear behind them in a thin, quickly dissipating curtain of dust.

"Tell me about the kid." He looked at Smokey, the fine white dust flecked over him here and there. Could you get off just having the stuff fall on you? Nobody had ever thrown twenty-four thousand dollars worth of speed over himself to find out.

"He's a kid, well, about twenty-six, I hear. He's got the word out that he needs somebody to take out his father. Very fast, he's impatient, he wants the old guy's money or something. Within the week would be good. He's so stupid, he's asking around. He keeps asking like that he's going to get a cop and a setup, and he's going to jail."

"Okay," Molina said. He forced himself to listen. Smokey was shyly offering a bone.

"The kid's only deal is that you got to get the old man to sign over his power of attorney or his bank accounts, whatever he uses to keep the bucks. Then get rid of him."

"How much?"

"Right now he says fifty thousand."

"So it doesn't sound like a big deal."

"It's not. No bodyguards, no funny stuff. The old guy, this old general, he's got a Persian restaurant out in the new part of town. I'll give you the kid's name."

"Stop here," Molina said. They were still in the forest, but the rutted road was giving way to a paved stretch winding along a high ridge.

Orepeza's sister slid over to the passenger side. "I don't want to drive anymore," and she suddenly began crying.

Smokey passed a folded slip to him. His nervousness now that they had stopped irritated Molina. "You write too neatly," Molina said after quickly looking at the name and phone number Smokey had written. "It's like me. They get you in court, anybody can read it."

"Bad habit. That's the way they taught us to write reports. Look, this is as good as I can do, Hector, a quick thing, fifty thousand. I'm sorry. Really."

"You think I'm pissed?"

"I don't know."

"I'm not. You did everything okay."

Smokey sank inward a little with relief. His helplessness made Molina momentarily sad.

"How come you don't want it?" Molina held the slip up. "Or those assholes, back there?"

"Why? Fifty thousand? It's three days work back there, no risk, no deals with outsiders. I don't want waves."

"Okay. Get out." Molina got out, too. He stood for a moment looking back into the green heart of the dark forest.

"Sorry," Smokey said, "it's the best I can do." He gave out a whipped-dog grin, glad to be alive, glad to be going back to food and shelter, glad in the feeble inchoate way of an animal. He half put out his hand to Molina, drew it back, pushing it deep into his pocket. He began walking down the brown, rutted road, slapping the traces of white powder off of himself as he went. Distantly, like a man starting to bring up phlegm, Molina heard the sputtering motorcycles.

He got back in and drove ahead. The gun lay on the seat between him and Elisa. As soon as they were moving, she grabbed him, her face against his arm. She was still crying.

"I'm scared," she moaned. "The fat guy, he says, he goes they're going to keep me. They get you, they keep me like their slave."

She clung to him. A formless impulse made him stroke her leg, comforting. He didn't know why he wanted to do it.

"We got things to do," he said to her, "I'm going to call this kid. You like ten percent of the fifty? It's going to be real easy, no trouble."

"I'm staying with you, you go anywhere, I'm going."

"Sure, that's okay. We both got to do it," he said soothingly. His heart pounded quickly from the excitement. It was better, he suddenly reasoned with himself, if he had a use for Elisa, a utilitarian purpose so that the fearsome impulse to touch her could be denied. I don't love her, he thought, I just need her, like the car. No more.

He thought of something and laughed.

"Tell me," she said tearfully.

"Nothing, I got an idea, crazy idea maybe." He let his breath out merrily, feeling fine. "Sometimes things don't come out like you think, the way you figured it's supposed to be. Maybe it's time for a big change, like."

"Change what?"

"I don't go back to the witness program maybe. I see Smokey and these guys? They couldn't sell me out, right? They fucked it all up. It's like a sign, like I'm supposed to forget about them and do something completely different." He was pleased with the notion. She was sniffing, asking him questions and looking out the windshield, appeased and thrilled, like him, by the unstoppable speed and forward rush.

CHAPTER TWENTY-EIGHT

Weyuker slouched in his chair. Across the table in the interview room were Stan and Ollie, at least that's who they looked like, murmuring to themselves, pointing at things in the file folders they both held.

"I've said it all." Weyuker tried to get comfortable. "You got something new we got to talk about?"

Stan always took the lead. "Not new. Couple of old business items."

"I got cases, guys, just ask and let me go." Weyuker was horrified when Internal Affairs called abruptly fifteen minutes before and wanted another session. He had barely made it through the first one, leaving the building, finding sanctuary in the deserted jurors' parking lot down the block, where he stayed for an hour. He didn't recall how he got through those fifteen minutes between the summons and coming into the interview room. It might even be the same room he and Swanson had used on the dead guy, beanhead Dufresne. There was a bitter rightness in that.

"We got a lot here." Ollie pointed to his statement. "I mean, you've gotten the whole thing pinned down."

"I'm surprised you didn't count the tiles," Stan chuckled.

"I didn't count them."

"Yeah, well, everything's here, one, two, three."

"So what else?" Weyuker asked.

Stan took over firmly, that silly smile on his face. Only Weyuker was in shirtsleeves. Stan and Ollie had their coats on, I.A.D. identification prominently showing. "Is there something going on in your personal life?"

"I don't understand." He moved in the chair, hoping he wouldn't shiver.

"Well, here we got a thing where a cop with a long, very good record slips up. My first idea is, this cop's not paying attention. So is there something on your mind?"

Weyuker shook his head. "Everything's fine."

"You worried about some bills, a loan, your kid, your wife even. Sorry, you know. . . ." Ollie was apologetic.

"There's nothing. You guys look at my cases? Anything wrong?"

"No, no. They're great. See, that's the thing. I see this big glitch here with a prisoner and I can't get it together." Stan's little fingers struggled to lock.

"All there is, maybe, is that fire the night before at the jail. I stayed there, the D.A. and me stayed there until close to midnight, we're up again early to go to Nevada." Weyuker thanked Swanson's insight about the detailed statement. Internal Affairs was looking for an excuse to let him off the hook. "I felt up to par, no question. Maybe I was a little down."

"Yeah, you're tired, you can maybe loosen too much," Stan said. He and Ollie bent to their folders. They were taping the whole thing and Weyuker was sickened by it. The real torture of his betrayal was that he couldn't tell anyone, not Sarah or the kid. Not Swanson or any D.A. or any cop he had ever known over the years. It stripped you entirely, left you naked with only the betrayer himself to turn to. *I must have been out of my fucking mind,* he thought.

"So what we have," Stan was direct, "is the knife. You're positive it's not a knife from the outside?"

"Positive," Weyuker said. It was clear from the way he made the nail file look.

"That's weird."

"No, it isn't."

"They swear they strip-searched this asshole before giving him to you," Ollie said. He consulted his file. "Yep. That morning they poked and pried."

"Well, they missed it," Weyuker said.

Stan glanced at the tape to make sure there was enough left. "They could have. Maybe they're covering themselves. So, tell me, where you think he had it?"

"Someplace in his coat, he didn't have to work to get it. I didn't see where he had it, I'm guessing. Like he stashed it in a pocket, along the lining, someplace like that."

Ollie shook his head in wonder. "He really lucked out, didn't he? He's got his shank ready, he's got somebody to pick him up outside, and it all just falls into place when you're with him."

"Fuck." Weyuker felt actual indignation rise from somewhere. "You think I gave him a fucking knife?"

Stan was unmoved. "The second guy at the prison, he swears to me today that Molina was clean."

"Well, he wasn't. He had the knife." He was sick again. They weren't easing off at all, only boring in harder for some reason. His strongest defense was that long initial statement, a collection of every nail and crack he saw during the investigation afterward in the washroom. And the undeniable fact of every cop's experience that no search was perfect.

"You didn't search?" Ollie asked.

"No, I didn't." He tried to maintain the tone of indignation. It masked his real fear.

"Didn't you think it was a good idea?"

"I figured they already did it. They had him a lot longer than I did and he got a goddamn shank through."

"See, that's what Larry and me are chewing on here." Stan gave that smile again. "Because this guy had to think, okay, I can get this through, the shank I mean, if somebody doesn't check me out. He had to figure somebody, you, the prison guys, was going to let him walk through."

"How about I just gave him the knife."

"Yeah," Ollie said with a slow grin. "Sure."

"Maybe I fucked up, I should've searched him, but it's done all the time. I'm not the only one."

"Nobody says you are. It's a knot to untie." Stan stretched out his arms along the table, feline and cold. "Like you're having all that bad luck."

Weyuker said nothing.

"They given you a new piece?"

He nodded. He hadn't kept much down since yesterday and the emptiness in his gut made him dizzy.

"Hope you get the old one back," Ollie said.

"Yeah, me too." Weyuker stood up. "Anything else? I don't have anything else to tell you."

"No, no, go back to work." Stan gestured casually. "We'll call you. Remember, it's standard procedure when an officer loses his weapon and/or a prisoner. We got to go through it."

"Doesn't bother me." Weyuker grinned sloppily and managed a slow, painful walk out of the interview room, hearing Stan and Ollie talking to each other but missing the words themselves. They didn't want any answers, he thought, sickened; they wanted to look at me again.

He kept walking until he was downstairs in the empty locker room. The next shift hadn't come on and he was alone with the brown ranked metal lockers and rows of benches. He banged into his own, working the lock quickly. Familiar things filled his locker, another pair of shoes, jacket, some case files that shouldn't have been kept there, family pictures, metal studded knuckles, and a small club from a case he didn't even remember, junk stashed away. He pushed it aside. In the back, covered by the jacket, was a .38 caliber pistol, a gun he'd recovered three years ago from an unclaimed Cadillac. It was an unauthorized weapon; he was not entitled to it.

He took the gun out of his locker. It needed bullets, and he'd get them on his way home. He wrapped the gun in the jacket, putting the bundle under his arm and heading back upstairs. He did have a new gun in a belt holster, but it was his official weapon.

For what he was thinking of now, the outcast .38 had no rival.

CHAPTER TWENTY-NINE

Swanson waited until the last moment before he left his office and walked upstairs to see Gleason. There was no point, he thought as he dragged himself laboriously up each step, condemning yourself the day after, or the late afternoon as the case might be, for going through three-quarters of a bottle, passing out in the front seat of your car, waking up because it was cold, and managing to haul yourself like cold death to bed. T.J., he dimly recalled now, asked if he needed a hand. No, thanks. Up to bed, tiptoeing fearfully past the kids' rooms, shoes off, shirt opened, pants off in the dark. Di was either asleep or ignoring him.

She was right, whatever she said exactly. All he remembered was crowded together, a tenement of words, jumbled, contradictory. You'll only make things worse, that came through. What she didn't tell him was how to assuage the thirsty little demon who at least brought some release from the situation.

Perhaps Gleason and Massingill had the answer, and that's what the meeting was about. He had the flash sweats from the two-floor climb, and he held himself against the stairwell door for a while before risking more. Two Misdemeanor Bureau secretaries on break passed him without sympathy.

Swanson went on, passed the main outer office where Gleason's secretary sat behind a wide, almost bare desk. Only a spray of red and yellow flowers in a tall vase cluttered it up. She was older, addlepated, and had been with Gleason since before the beginning. Her hair was permanently fixed, as though frozen, in the same sweeps and curves.

"Hi, Mabel," Swanson said, trying to move his sluggish legs quickly by her desk.

"Hello, Mike," she replied, brightly and slowly.

He smiled, gave a sign that he was heading for Gleason's inner office, and made it past her. Her major function, as everyone knew, was to block, by physical means if needed, people whom Gleason did not wish to see or hear.

Along the inner corridor, carpeted and quieter than the other floors, were the chief deputy, the three bureau chiefs, the office administrator, more secretaries. Nearest to Gleason's office was the trophy wall, pale brass golf awards, tall baseball awards, plaques, and a long sepia-tinted photograph of Gleason and all the investigators in the office dressed in a rugged 1870 style, rifles in hand, hitching post in front of them, staring woodenly into the camera and the past.

He was a little late for the meeting. When he opened Gleason's door, Massingill was talking pleasantly. The U.S. Attorney held a cigarette to his side and breathed a leisurely cloud of smoke.

"I told Claude I'm glad he took the trouble to see us."

"Mike probably doesn't share the feeling."

Swanson said, "Something's going on when you show up," as he dropped to the sofa, waiting coolly for whatever Massingill had to say.

Massingill nodded. "Yes, something is going on."

"You have a cold, Mike? You want some aspirin?" Gleason leaned over to him. "You got an allergy all of a sudden?"

"I'm surviving," he said, feeling anxious and weary, wondering what was going on. Gleason watched him, and the dour rancher in dark glasses was running some kind of act for his benefit, or Massingill's. The benign good fellowship was nonsense.

"Let me get down to cases." Massingill picked up a marble ashtray and slowly ground out his cigarette. "Molina's been in touch with me again, this morning."

"I don't believe it," Swanson said angrily. He instantly forgot about his weariness.

"We're keeping this friendly," Gleason said, "because cooperation is the only way we'll get anything done. Go on."

Massingill kept his eyes on the ashtray. The long legs were twined, reaching from his chair to Gleason's desk. A very big cricket, Swanson thought. Massingill also seemed beat, but he spoke evenly and authoritatively. "Molina is on his own. I apologize for my remarks the other day," he nodded without looking directly at Swanson, "and he wants to turn himself in."

"When and where?" Swanson demanded.

"He thinks some guarantees are important first."

"Such as?" Gleason, very pleasant.

"He wants to turn himself in to federal authorities, preferably the Marshal—"

"Because you run those guys," Swanson snapped.

"Hold it down, Mike."

"—or the FBI," Massingill continued, "but on no account does he want the Santa Maria Police, Sheriff, or District Attorney involved in any aspect of his return to custody. No cover, no transportation, no personnel. He's convinced harm would come to him."

"Are you just presenting his demands or do you have some opinion?" Swanson said.

Massingill looked up at him. "I have an opinion. I think he's right. He'd be foolish to get anywhere near you."

"Well, I can't agree with that, Claude," Gleason smiled. "If Mr. Molina acted as he's supposed to, why he could balance an egg on his nose and nobody involved in law enforcement in this county would disturb him in the slightest."

"Joe, with all respect to you, the events of the last couple of days say you're completely wrong."

"Why doesn't he walk into the FBI office?" Swanson put it sharply. It was as if Massingill had neither understood or even seen any of the reports, photos, or rumors about Molina coming to him since Angie was killed. What more does he need?

"Something could happen on the way."

"So he's still in this area?"

"I'm not going to say."

"You're going to withhold the location of a fleeing felon?"

Gleason didn't intervene and waited for Massingill.

"I don't know his precise location." Massingill leaned to Swanson. "But if I did, you bet I'd withhold it from you."

Gleason sat back, then rubbed his eyes. "Fellas, decorum? Go easy, please."

"Where does he get this attitude," Swanson stood, asking Gleason bitingly, "like I'm responsible?"

"You are," Massingill cut in bluntly.

"I'm out of here, Joe." He started for the door.

"You're part of this and you're staying," Gleason said. The acting was put aside. "Now sit down, and I don't want to hear any bullshit."

Swanson hesitated, compelled by his anger—and by the recognition that Gleason was accurate—to throw it back at Massingill. He sat down once more, determined to make Massingill learn.

The U.S. Attorney took out a yellowed handkerchief and polished his glasses slowly, huffing on them with his breath. He spoke between frosting and wiping. "The other guarantee Molina wants is an agreement you won't prosecute him on any charges arising from his escape. It seems fair to me, given the way he was brought here."

"It's Weyuker's call," Swanson shook his head, "not mine."

"You file the charges. You have the authority to do whatever you want." He settled his glasses on his face again.

"Weyuker got tied up."

"What Mike is saying," Gleason carefully lit a cigarette, "is we have a firm policy. Officer victims are listened to very carefully."

"You're still the charging authority."

Swanson broke in, "What do we get out of all this? I mean, you've got his demands, you bring them over here, and what do we get?"

Gleason nodded. "I was a little unclear on that myself, Claude."

"Simple and to the point." Massingill's thin fingers drummed on the armrest, he untwined his long legs and sat up very straight. "No federal investigation into your handling of Molina's extradition, no grand jury investigation into possible abuse of authority, and I will promise not to pursue any order to show cause in the violation of a federal court order."

"You want to go back to the way it was?"

"As much as possible." Massingill really did look beat, and for the first time, Swanson detected a reluctant tone when he spoke about Molina. He felt the dampness under his arms, around his neck, the spongy aftermath of indulgence. He wondered if Massingill ever got drunk, blind and mindless. "You taken a look at what I've sent the last four days? You talked to the other prosecutors I told you about?"

"I did."

"Our jail commander and the Sheriff's Department tell me they've decided a guy who worked as a painter, a trusty at the jail, he's the guy who stole the turpentine. He's in on a twelve-oh-two-one."

"Possession of a sawed-off shotgun," Gleason said helpfully.

Swanson looked at Massingill, half-turned from him. "This guy, his name's Carera, from San Jose. He was buddy-buddy with Raymond Alves couple years ago in their purse-snatching days. So Alves makes a phone call, Carera's calls aren't monitored. Maybe it was a favor, maybe a straight contract, I don't know."

"Are you going to arrest him?" Massingill asked shortly.

"We're working on it."

"You can't yet."

"Not yet."

Massingill nodded.

"You've got bank records and statements from Angie Cisneros and Max Dufresne. Your security for Molina was so open he could've sent out anything, if he wanted to do it," Swanson said. "I've got the shooter in his wife's killing turned. He's going to say that Molina ordered Angelica Cisneros killed."

"None of it's decent, admissible," Massingill answered with slack conviction. "To accept what you've been saying, the evidence has to be direct and credible."

"You let Molina go on, there won't be anybody alive to give that kind of evidence," Swanson said.

Massingill was no fool, even if his instinct now was to preserve Molina; the sheer bulk of accusations against his witness must give him doubts. Even doubts which could not be voiced publicly. Swanson thought he and Massingill were alike in some ways, united in their perplexity. He had done everything that should have been done to bring Molina to trial. Yet in doing these things he had caused death and misery and placed people he loved in peril. Massingill too, seeing a just and unimpeachable triumph, had done all the right things to bring it about. Now the terrible doubts.

"You have a timetable?" Gleason asked briskly.

"I want to get this done in the next forty-eight hours."

"You do?" Swanson was sarcastic.

"Molina does, too. He's vulnerable now. He feels exposed."

Gleason spoke to Swanson, "What's it going to be?"

"I thought this was your decision," Massingill protested to Gleason. "What's the point of this meeting if you won't decide?"

"It's my case," Swanson said, grateful to Gleason because the easiest choice would be to take it from him. I'd probably do that, he thought, if I was sitting there.

"I don't second-guess my deputies," Gleason said. He took the marble ashtray from Massingill's side of the desk and clattered it empty into the wastebasket. "I did it once, first year I got here, and you never saw such a bollixed-up trial. I'll give Mike advice, but I'm not going to go over him."

I know how disappointed he is, too, Swanson thought. He takes the responsibility in the election. "What do you think?" he asked Gleason.

"Well, my general view is if you've got a body in custody, you've got something to fight over."

Massingill nodded. "At last."

Swanson said to him, "There're some people I'd like you to meet."

He sent Massingill down to his car and went back to his office for his coat. Then, because he had to, Swanson called Di.

"I got out before you were up," he said. He held his coat in one hand.

"I know."

"Fed Meg. Cleaned up some orange juice she spilled. You didn't even know it happened."

"I couldn't tell."

"Everything okay? What're you guys doing?"

He could hear her warning one of the kids, then she came back, "We're in the dining room doing verb conjugations. Meg's napping upstairs." She was rueful. "I'm not concentrating completely. You all right?"

"Got somebody waiting outside in the car."

"You better go."

He tried to mend without reminding either of them how embarrassing he had been. "I'm sorry, Di. I wasn't exactly all myself last night. What I was saying—"

"I know what you meant, I know you're sorry."

"It was all wrong, I didn't mean it. Believe me, it was just everything hitting me at once."

Her answers were perfunctory, not genuine, he thought.

"There's a man walking a dog outside, in front of the yard. Matt and Lizzie are watching him."

"Big deal," he said, "I'm missing something here."

"It's like being on the other side of an aquarium, Mike, being the fish looking out. I've been thinking about it all day. And I've been thinking about last night."

"I mean it, I'm sorry, forget what I did or said. I'm not drinking at home, not outside. I'm done."

"No, it's not that. I've been thinking I'm responsible."

"How could you be?"

"We could have gone anywhere after you finished law school, and I insisted we come back to Santa Maria, as though there was some magic because we both grew up here. You wanted to go someplace new, and the idea started preying on me after last night. We wouldn't be like this somewhere else." She said it easily, but the idea obviously bothered her.

"It's got nothing to do with us moving back, honey. It just happened. It could've happened anyplace. It just happened here, to us."

"I don't really accept sheer accidents," she said. "Things are more purposeful for me."

God's plan, he thought sourly. He doesn't play dice, it all has a logic. "Don't worry about that, Jesus. We're all together and that was your idea and I'm so glad you had it."

"I want to get our lives back," she said firmly. "I don't intend for us to go to pieces."

"We're staying together, I'm not going to do anything to mess that up. We're doing okay."

"Keep saying that."

"I got to go," letting the coat hang open so he could slide into it. "Love you," he said. Finally, that knowledge frightened her as much as him. There was no end to where it might go.

"They came out yesterday, soon as the news broke about the escape. We don't have enough coverage for them. Cops are checking more closely, I've got a number for them to call, but we can't put a full watch on them."

"Like you have?" Massingill's acrid nicotine smell followed him as he walked toward Tice's Market. Old people sat on the benches across the street at the senior citizens apartments, several solemnly eating from brown bags. Frank had immediately put up large signs advertising pork roast and celery sales when he got back. The market's doorway was a cool dark gape in the white stucco building.

"I got kids, and that's the only reason." He glanced at Massingill alongside. "You married?"

"Not for three years almost."

"Kids?"

"We were in the process of discussing it."

"You really don't know how the Tices feel or I feel knowing our families are threatened."

"I came because I want to show I'm willing to go an extra step for you," Massingill said. "We're not enemies, Mike, whatever you think."

Two little girls rushed loudly by. "Tell them whatever you want," Swanson said.

"I don't have anything to say to these people."

"Then just look at them."

Swanson hadn't tried to convince Frank and Hannah to stay in custody. He had no more promises or pledges to make. He had kept none of them.

He saw Frank first, behind the counter, ringing up a small pile of groceries for a plump little brown woman who kept plucking at her purse as he totaled her purchases. Three other people, two women and a husky redheaded kid, were in the aisles.

"Hi, Frank," he said.

Frank Tice looked up. "Hannah's going to be back." He click-clicked the price of another package of jello into the cash register.

"This is the U.S. Attorney handling Molina." He pointed at Massingill leaning on the ice-cream freezer.

"Hello, Mr. Tice."

"So?"

Frank Tice didn't pause in his work. He's got a gun right there, under the counter, Swanson thought. Tice's thick, rough features looked up at the woman as she scratched in her purse for money and he began putting her groceries in a bag.

"You've got a good business, Mr. Tice," Massingill said. He went through the twitchy motions of finding and lighting a cigarette.

"You got to work, you're going to keep it. I got to be here, got to work."

"Thanks for your time."

Tice looked at Swanson. "You going to give him the grand tour?"

"He knows what happened."

"He's here, show him. Take him around. Take him in back, show him the storeroom. My boy died there."

"I know. I'm sorry." Massingill stood, slightly stooping, ill at ease because Tice's expression was angry. "My office is going to do everything to make sure justice is done in your case."

"He says that," Tice jerked his head at Swanson. The woman gathered up her bag, frowning at them as she left. "You guys, you don't know what it means anymore."

"Sometimes it takes time."

Swanson suddenly felt the same uncomfortable tension that bothered Massingill. He thought he was over it, but simply being near Tice revived it. There was nothing to say. And the absence of any words left men like him and Massingill fearful. They both knew what justice meant for Frank Tice and his dead boy. The problem was that neither of them could bring it about.

"All right," Tice said tonelessly. "You've been here, we met, and that's all there is."

"I will be doing everything possible—" Massingill began.

"All right, go away. Go."

Massingill's cigarette was tucked in the side of his thin lips. He nodded. He walked to the door.

"Tell Hannah I was here," Swanson said.

"You're coming tonight? Nine?" Tice's questions were tart.

"I'll be here."

"Then you tell her. Tell her any damn thing. We're going to do what we're going to do." He stared into Swanson. A kid was at the counter with a six-pack of Coors.

"Okay, Frank." He halfheartedly waved.

Out through the cool dark doorway into the sunlight, the street and trees. He didn't say anything, nor did Massingill, until they got back to the car. Massingill coughed several times and tossed his cigarette out the window.

"I wanted you to see them," Swanson said.

"I've met victims before."

"They're his victims."

"The trouble, Swanson, is that you pretend we're after different things. You're the white hat. I'm the black hat. I make compromises. No question. No apology. You make compromises. You made one with the shooter, Narloch? So who's worse in that balance? Molina because he killed fifteen?"

"You don't have a right to give away the Tices or me or my family," he flared angrily.

The car was rank with Massingill's stale smoke. He took off his glasses as he had in Gleason's office, his face suddenly tinier and pinched as he squinted involuntarily, blowing and wiping and polishing. "All I'm bound to do is go after the worst offenders if I have the chance. If you want justice, so do I. But, if I'm not after justice, neither are you." The hesitant tone returned to his voice. "We're prosecutors and this is the way the world works." He said it without emotion. Then, "If I believed Hector was orchestrating a massacre, I'd get out. I'd get him out."

"I gave you the evidence. That's what's he's doing." Swanson's alcoholic logginess had finally burned away. Massingill had learned nothing by meeting Frank Tice and seeing his pain.

"You've raised some questions," Massingill said, putting his glasses on. "They may lead . . ." He faded briefly. "Look, I've also got to investigate the possibility the killings, the banks, all of it, are an NF scheme to kill Molina or smear him so he's no good as a witness."

"You can't believe that." He was dumbfounded.

"It makes as much sense to me as what you've claimed," Massingill said emphatically. "I've got to check it out and eliminate it as a possibility before doing anything irrevocable. There's too much at stake."

He went on, saying that the proof of Molina's good intentions was his fervent desire to surrender, turn himself in. A man who killed, escaped, all the things Swanson charged, would run and keep running. He wouldn't try to come back.

He's talked himself clear, Swanson thought. Massingill's

done a better con job on himself than Molina ever did on him. The thing now was to get Molina back in custody. Any way possible.

"Tell him it's okay," Swanson said gruffly. "The conditions are okay."

Massingill had one arm cocked out the window, holding the car roof. He expelled a relieved breath, nodding. "What was that about going back there tonight? I didn't catch it exactly." The long thin body sat angled.

"I made one promise to Frank Tice I can keep," Swanson said.

CHAPTER THIRTY

Molina waited while the waitress brought Elisa her second beer after she went through the first one like it was a Dr Pepper, one gulp and gone. His first was half down. The dark-haired, stiff kid sitting beside him in the booth would sip his own beer every so often, make a small face, and shake his head a little.

"You want something else?" Molina asked.

"It's fine, it's okay. I have a sick stomach." The kid was very straight-backed, sharp featured. He had on a polo shirt, white pants, and a blue windbreaker.

"I don't know why I'm so thirsty." Elisa downed her beer. "Mind?" She smiled at the kid and slid his to her.

"No, please, please," he said. He was probably in his late twenties. They sat in a phony red-leather booth at the Café Majestic. The place was crowded, most people eating dinner, some just drinking, like them.

"You want something instead of the potato skins?" Molina asked, concerned.

"When I have the sick stomach, I don't eat. Mineral water helps me. I don't know what I have."

"You're too young to have a bad stomach," Elisa said.

"I've been through too much. Too much."

The kid was already easily impressed. Molina had shown him the .38 Colt King and described two hits he had made years before. He talked knowledgeably about various prisons and that made Behzam, the kid, light up. Knowing the floor plans and the hierarchies in prisons was strong recommendation, apparently.

"I love that way you talk, you know, good English, but different. I love that accent, you roll the words around." She made a gargling sound.

"Farsi makes me do that. I have a vocal coach and he promises no trace in a year. Two maybe. I have so much else on my mind."

Molina nodded sympathetically. "You don't have to talk loud. I can hear you over the music."

The kid, Behzam, blushed. "I'm so nervous."

Elisa patted his arm. "Don't be nervous, don't be nervous. Everything's going to be all right."

"I believe that, yes. I have found the right man."

Molina drank a little beer and grabbed a handful of popcorn from a bowl sitting on the table between them. Behzam took a couple of kernels and delicately picked them apart. Elisa craned her head around trying to find the waitress again. "We're going to hold, okay?" Molina said to her.

"I'm very, very thirsty tonight."

"No more right now." He smiled at her, strict and dead. Sometimes she was a terrific pain and he brought her along because she might keep Behzam a little loose and make things go more easily. But a disturbing feeling was churning in him. He didn't like it. The idea of feeling any affection for her repelled and frightened him.

"Grouch and grump," she sighed heavily, then patted Behzam again, smiling at him. "You don't want to be grouchy."

"What are you going to give me about your old man?" Molina asked.

Behzam reached to his lap and brought out a manila envelope. "I have his picture and the documents you must make him sign. And his address, his home, the restaurant. My set of car keys."

"Say 'guy' again. I love that sound." Elisa grinned.

"Guy," Behzam said shyly.

"I could listen to that all the time, you shouldn't change it."

Molina opened the envelope and took out a postcard-sized photo of a bald, severe-looking man in a solid blue suit. Heavy, solid himself. This was a general. Not like the guy he knew who called himself a general. Maybe that's why Gilbert Villagrana was a fraud, he had no army. He was a general with only a gang.

"He is a very greedy man," Behzam spoke emphatically, without hesitation or shyness. "My father is very greedy, very selfish. I talk to him for many months about giving his money to his children. He has a lot of money, he brought a lot of money with us when we left Iran."

"He looks cheap." Elisa peered closely at the stern face.

"It's not fair he should be so greedy. Not fair to my sister or me."

"She doesn't know about this?" Molina riffled through the other things in the envelope, bank authorizations, a revocable trust form, a deed.

"I am the revolutionary in the family," Behzam said.

"You know, you look like someone, just then, you sit up real straight." She wagged her finger at him.

"People say I look like the Shah's son."

"You brought something he wrote?" Molina looked out at the crowded restaurant.

"I have a letter." He passed it over.

"Isn't this exciting?" She squeezed Behzam's arm. He blushed again.

"I've never met people like your husband," he said with a small, nervous smile, "or you, Mrs. Negron."

"It's all an act."

Molina couldn't read the letter, but there was enough to make out the handwriting.

Behzam took another sour sip from his beer. "Why do you need this letter? Do you understand it?"

"Well, I got to know if he's screwing up his signature or doing something funny when he signs these things." Molina tapped the envelope.

"Ah," Behzam said. "Mr. Negron, how soon will this be done?"

"Tomorrow. I don't want to drag it out."

"That is soon. I understand."

"Is that a problem?"

"No, no, no. It's hard for me to imagine."

"You don't have to imagine anything. I do all that."

Elisa waved for the waitress. "I'm dying."

"That's it."

"I can do four fucking beers," she snapped. The waitress came by, scooped up the dried bits of potato skins, and got the order.

"Last Monday, I go to my father, for myself and my sister. I tell him we can't succeed in this country on the allowance he gives us. I have to see him in his office, in the back of the restaurant. He keeps his uniform there, an autographed picture of the Shah. He makes me stand in front of him, like a lackey."

"A what?" Elisa leaned into his face.

"A servant, a stooge, a flunky. He treats me like a flunky."

"That's tough," Molina said. He closed the envelope. The old general sounded a little like Angie's father. Maybe an East L.A. barber and an out-of-work Iranian general would have stuff to talk about.

"Of course, he turned me into a revolutionary."

"What kind?" She looked impatiently for the waitress, then smiled fast for him.

"I haven't decided yet. It's a matter of principle."

"You brought money."

Behzam nodded. "But my father is very stubborn, very greedy. He refuses to give me anything so I can succeed in this country. I can't even work in the restaurant. I must do everything myself."

Molina nodded, watching Orepeza's sister. He had to watch her. In a way, he dreaded going to a motel with her later. It was growing harder, after an adult lifetime of counterfeiting emotions, to dredge up the pleasing frauds. He didn't even know why he liked this woman.

The kid furtively, as though he'd seen it in some movies, put his hand in the windbreaker and took out another envelope. He glanced around and gave it to Molina. "I will give you the other half as we discussed."

Movie talk. "Great, like I told you. I'll call, everything should be taken care of. You'll get these things signed, you'll pay the rest and we go on our way."

"Twenty-five thousand?" Elisa bobbed her head and slapped a palm on the table. "You got that from your allowance?"

Behzam was confused. "I had to sell some things, too. This is not easy."

"You want to meet some American girls? You want to marry an American girl?"

Molina reached over and held her hand very tightly. "That's it. We got to go." He stood up, making her rise with him. Behzam sat watching, puzzled.

"I want to take my beer," she protested.

Molina pulled her out of the booth. "I'll call you tomorrow, afternoon probably."

Behzam nodded, he looked at Elisa attentively. "I'm so nervous, but I think everything will be okay."

"He carry a gun?"

Behzam shook his head, a kid alone in a red booth. He had his hands clasped in front of him. "He has no enemies in this country."

Molina circled the restaurant twice, the Golden Crescent, with a small fountain gushing red, blue, and yellow-lit water in front of it. A night wind had come up and green flags planted throughout the shopping center rippled and snapped.

"Probably the only Iranian restaurant in Stockton," she said as they drove by the second time. "Good business, look at that. They got a line inside. What do they eat?"

"Goat eyes."

"When I was a kid my mother made this thing, you cut half a cow head and you cook it. Barbecue it." She shut her eyes and shuddered. "I can't eat that stuff."

The first pass had been through the neighborhood where the old man lived. No traffic, nice houses, Orepeza's sister complaining about having to pee, so he had to cut it short and get her to a gas station. They were working on rental car number two since he first saw her.

She poked through her purse. "You going to come by here in the morning, he comes to work?"

"When he leaves the house. Not here, you got traffic, cops, a whole zoo."

"I'll wait at the motel."

He shook his head. "You got to come."

"I can't do anything." She made a whine. "I don't want to be around." The whine turned into a sulk.

"You can drive. I'm going to take his car."

"He looks like an old fucking hardass, it's going to take a long time to get him to sign that stuff. I don't want to be there."

"He's not signing anything."

She tossed her purse down. "What?"

"You think I'm going to sit around waiting for this guy to sign all that shit, this motherfucker old fucking general? I'm going to sign it."

She watched the fashionable stores go by. It was a cold night, surfeited with his cold purpose. "It's going to go fast?"

He nodded. "Real fast."

Swanson heard Frank Tice drop something, swear, and drop something else in the storeroom. "You need a hand?" he called out.

"I got it, I got it," the snapped reply.

"Last year," Hannah said, "I made him go through the closet, the hall one at home. For years, he says, just stick it in there, it'll be fine. Then the door wouldn't close. We had to put a brick in front of it." She shook her head. She sat behind the cash register. The whole place was vividly lit, empty except for them and the babysitting squad car outside. The cops insisted on following Swanson. "He went to open the door to clean the closet and ka-boom! All over the hall, fishing stuff, his shoes, boxes, I don't know what."

"My wife's real conscious of too much clutter, three kids all over the place."

"You could get very crowded if you weren't careful. How is everybody?"

Swanson got it off casually, "Doing all right. Cabin fever for the kids. They want to get outside."

"It's very hard for them to stay indoors." She nodded.

Frank came into the front of the market carrying a .22 rifle. "I knew it was back there, I put it there special." He sighted along the gun, ran his hands over it. "This was Donny's, his fifteenth birthday present."

"I don't know anything about guns." He thought Tice wanted to see his revolver, so he took it out. Hannah glanced at it, then looked away.

"After Donny was gone," Frank said, "I used it for those cats that used to come around, you know, hide out in the garbage in the alley, a dozen, maybe?"

"There were a lot of cats," she said.

"I cleared them out."

"Well, we're ready for them," Swanson said with bravado. He meant it as a joke. Frank nodded seriously, like a minuteman, holding his squirrel gun against the advancing enemy.

"We're going to take a look around," Frank said to Hannah. He squared his shoulders.

"Be right back," Swanson said.

She half-smiled and got up. "I'll make some coffee?"

"Thanks."

"Don't wave that around, Frank. I told the guys outside you'd have something, but don't make them nervous."

"I know how to hold a rifle, see, like this, easy. So you're ready." It was impossible for Tice to say anything without sounding truculent.

They walked back through the market, the empty, bright aisles, out back into the alley. High streetlights shone down on them. A car sped by at one end of the alley.

"Didn't think you'd come," Frank said.

"I promised."

"You did."

They walked slowly up the alley, past garbage cans and fences. "Couple of days, one way or another, it's coming to a head." Swanson had his hands in his pockets, brushing the gun on his waist. What were they doing? Like the wild West, high noon in an alley? Two fools who couldn't make anything work right, hoping to feel a little better by a charade.

"You come back tomorrow night?"

"I'll try. If I can."

"You got your own family, your kids to worry about. I think we'd do okay, you know, handling things together."

"The cops are trained for this stuff."

"But we got the interest," Tice said vigorously, "it's personal for us."

At the street they turned, walking to the market. Swanson felt better, even playacting, than he had since Molina's escape. If he wasn't with the Tices he'd be home, with Di, the lurking threat and failure building each second.

"Frank," he said hesitantly, "you're in trouble, you're family's in trouble. In danger. What would you do? How far you going?"

"Protecting them you mean?"

"Yeah."

"There's nothing I wouldn't do. Nobody I wouldn't walk over, anything, do anything, whatever I had to do for my family. That's what I should've done that day, he came here I let myself walk first, I let Donny go last."

"You didn't know what was going to happen."

Tice held the rifle tightly, his face shadowed, hard, and guilty. "I should've stayed last, make sure everyone else was safe first, not left him all alone back there."

They hadn't stopped walking and the market was in front of them, the squad car visible across the street, the wind humming coldly through the new leaves in the trees. Swanson wanted to say something, but he couldn't find any ideas that weren't false, empty, banal. His remorse was small compared to Tice's immortal sense of betrayal.

"Cold," he said.

Frank was thinking, remembering, his hand on the market door. "Couple of days something happens?"

"Molina's turning himself in. Whatever he's got in mind for us, he's got to do it before then. That's my guess, that's why he escaped, take care of things personally."

"I get down on my knees and I pray for that. Let me see him one more time." Frank Tice swung open the market door roughly.

CHAPTER THIRTY-ONE

Weyuker left his car on the side of the levee road, tilted steeply toward the stunted trees, vines, and low brush that started about fifteen feet below and spread, in a dark, unkempt tangle into the night.

"Whoa," he said aloud in surprise, the first thing he'd spoken in an hour. He had fallen to one knee getting out of the car on the passenger side, startled by the angle downward. He clumsily wobbled upright, then sat back against the car. About nine or ten by now, he figured. He wouldn't look at his watch. Didn't really matter what time it was. Sarah started to complain about now, when he didn't call, then she'd make it known to him when he did. She wouldn't wonder where he was much longer. Certainly by morning everything would be clear.

He slid on his pants to the road's shoulder. The dirt slope gradually fell away into the trees below and Weyuker, with a sad, resigned sigh, slid down, feet first, using his hands to slow him, feeling the pebbles and dirt, hard and dry.

He hit a gully, unseen in the darkness, sitting down in it. It had about a foot of water in it, coldly shocking him. He swore aloud, splashing out of the gully, his shoes soaked, the water dripping down his legs in cold, fingery trails. Shakily, he stood up. Overhead, his car perched as though looking down on him, the passenger door hanging open. Above the car, thin black lines of telephone wires sliced across the crescent moon and stars. He rubbed his hands together and the moist dirt fell from them. It smelt like dried apples at the base of the levee. It was cold, dusty.

Weyuker pushed into the trees, using his arms to thrust the brush aside, hearing a twig or branch catch his coat sleeve, ripping it. After work, desk left neat and tidy for the last time, a few drinks well, more than a few, at the Pine Room with other cops. Then to the gun store three blocks away where he was an old customer, pick up a box of ammunition for the .38 and he was off. Driving around, driving until he was east of the city, out toward the line where the farmland started and the river was held back by levee roads.

This is stupid, he thought disgustedly, pausing where he could see a little ahead. Nobody here, no point in going so far. He heard things, now that he had stopped crashing through the brush. A faint, high whistle of wind, the jostling of branches, quick scurrying nearby. And like a distant reminder of life, the train calling, rising, gone.

He fumbled in his pocket. "Woof," he said aloud. Then again. A solitary human voice sounded so pathetic and lost at night in the woods. He tried to whistle, but his lips wouldn't form correctly. He only made an insipid spluttering sound.

Out came the .38. He could barely see anything, even with his eyes growing used to the shades of dark among the trees. He couldn't really see a good tree trunk, so he just sat down where he was, legs out in front of him, back bent to the task, the gun and bullets in the space between his legs. He loaded the gun carefully, thinking about each bullet as it went in.

It occurred to him that he was engaged in the most profound activity of his whole life. Nothing up until now came close. He wondered about Sarah, deciding it was for her that he left the car intact and came away. Don't mess up the car so she can't use it.

As a cop, Weyuker had quickly learned to wear different faces. There were ones for civilians that ranged from the sympathetic, through hearty, to cold. Another set of faces was for pukes. Little variation in them. Then there was the face for people you didn't know if they were civilians or pukes yet.

D.A.s got another face, and Swanson, he was different. Mike got something close to the real thing, if there was a real thing left now.

Other D.A.s, they were friendly most of the time, but they weren't you. They didn't know what you thought.

The family got another face, the one where he was head of the house or something. A face for Sarah, one for the kid, May. This was a puzzling and mysterious area because Weyuker wanted to be honest with his wife and daughter, yet he knew very well that in all their married life, he had rarely shown Sarah how he felt.

And friends. He grimaced and loaded the final bullet, snapped it in. Sat there with the gun resting easily on his thigh. Some friends were civilians, not many. There was a face for friends, good cheer, bullshit, reserved for the ones you went boating or drinking with. Good friends.

The final face was for other cops, who no matter what personal differences separated you—even like those two assholes in I.A.D.—still knew the routine, as you did, that required the faces. They were the true friends and family, who knew each other and saw each other. So many different faces, slipping into each one without thinking by now.

In the last four weeks, Weyuker had never come out from his concealment, even with other cops. The tension of his false front was unbearable, and when he couldn't even talk to Swanson, it was time for it to stop.

You think I'd ever hurt a cop? Molina had asked him as soon as the handcuffs came off in the airport bathroom. My best friends are cops.

Weyuker found himself talking to Sarah, then Swanson, without making a sound, confusing who he was talking to sometimes. He got up and started to walk again, looking for a better place, buying a little more time. He had the gun in his hand.

My first mistake, he said, was this guy Orepeza. He comes up to me at lunch right outside the department. Orapayza, that's how he says it. He knows me, the Tice case, he knows Angie is up here. He calls her that, Angie, like they're old pals. Comes right out, he'll give me twenty thousand for whatever Angie's saying. First time, I told him, fuck off, take a bribe, for what? I should've busted his ass, I don't know why I just let him walk away.

Weyuker listened, glancing around.

He was on a path, narrow, but used. Who goes down here? he wondered. He kicked out at the low brush, the air heavier with a chill spiciness. Sarah, I never thought it was a killing; just, like, they wanted to know what she's saying so they can stay clear. I'm talking about Angie, the one I saw in the coroner's office, night I came home real late. I swear to God. And then couple weeks, Orepeza would like a couple of badges, something he can use. What? I ask. Scare some people, he says. Sure, I say. Who gives a fuck, pukes scaring each other, maybe even a rip-off. More money, nothing much to do, nothing really you could say was bad. So, hell, Mike, you guys got them sitting there in that geek's office upstairs, hell, I took two, and Orepeza's happy and I don't care because that was another five thousand.

I got paid for the badges. We used to meet, me and this puke, near the old cannery. He's there, I drive by, chat for a minute, I'm gone. So he has the badges and she's killed and that's all for me. No more games, man. Orepeza's showed me that match-book, first time I saw those little letters. He writes to me, Orepeza says. Maybe he'll write to you.

Weyuker looked around himself. There was a beer can, crushed and disintegrating on the ground, and what looked like a sanitary napkin farther along. He was weary, he had gone as far as he wanted to go.

He sniffed because the exertion and allergy made his nose run. He passed a clumsy hand over it. Feel that wind, he thought, like down in L.A. with you, Mike. Goes right through you and it's spring, too.

In his career, he had seen only four suicides. Two by gunshot, one by poison, and one by hatchet. The hatchet guy had taken three blows to his head and he couldn't remember the victim's real name because almost as soon as he got there and the other cops started figuring it out, they called this guy Harry Headache. That's all he could remember now, standing in the wooded thickness holding the gun—Harry Headache. He sure was a determined guy.

What's the joke going to be for me? he wondered. He didn't know. It depended on so many things out of his control, how he fell, how he looked after a night lying there, what the cops thought about him once everything came out. Suddenly he didn't think there would be any jokes after all.

So, the last thing he wants—Weyuker pushed himself up to a rough tree trunk, his damp pants clinging coldly to him—he tells me how to contact Orepeza's sister, how she'll be waiting for him. Weyuker had started shivering and this irritated him.

All I want, Molina says, is to get away, start again, the last you'll see of me. So I don't believe this at first, but after Angie he's got me good and he reminds me on this little matchbook.

Weyuker stood, head against the tree, his teeth trying to reach each other spastically. Mike, he said, I thought it was a way to get clear, really, the only way. I can't just kill the guy at the airport, he knows it. Somebody else he's got knows about me. So I try to argue with him. Weyuker trembled, teeth loudly, brittly chattering. I got the handcuffs off, I still have my gun. I say, you're not going to use this. I'm telling him. So he says, Cops are my best friends, like he's thought ahead of me. You're my protection. I don't want them after me because I hurt a cop.

He takes off, Weyuker remembered starkly, maybe he really wants to get away, get clear himself, that makes sense and after seeing Angie, I wanted that.

Rolly, he ran, he did that himself. I would've protected him like I protected the Tices, or you, Mike. Nothing's going to happen to you, your family. Rolly and the snitch, none of that's mine. Pukes killing pukes. He fumbled with the memory of the fire.

That was bad. Nobody should die that way.

He had the .38 in front of his face, in one quick motion. No way to keep I.A.D. or somebody from finding out. I was crazy, I thought getting Molina away would change everything. Mike, you'll find out. You're going to, you keep looking.

The conventional wisdom said that putting the gun over your heart or to your temple was too risky. A momentary jerk of life at the last minute, a shudder, and you ended up alive, crippled, worse even, lying in the woods until you bled to death. The sure way, barrel in the mouth, one sudden trigger pull.

How about that Harry Headache, he was a determined guy.

Weyuker tried to squeeze some of that intractability into his own movements. He was supposed to say goodbye to Sarah. He dutifully offered a hope for her happiness and a vow that he loved her.

He concentrated on raising his hand to his mouth before he was conscious of it, the gun ready. His arm felt frozen, heavy. It trembled slightly. He made a strangled cry of frustration and fear. What else? Say you're sorry. He did, several times, trying at the same instant to rush his other iniquities into the plea. He felt wounded already, his head falling forward.

"No," he said aloud. "No. No," repeating it, opening the .38 and letting the bullets fall out, hitting the ground with soft, invisible thuds. Mike and his family were still in danger, so were the Tices, and he could try to protect them. His redemption lay there, not in this place.

Weyuker put the empty gun in his pocket, sinking down to his haunches against the tree. The wind was around him, sharp and quick. Overhead, the crescent moon in a cloudless sky, split thinly by wires. Redemption had nothing to do with it. He was only a coward, which was why he had not turned himself in after Angie was killed and why he fooled himself into believing Molina would actually run and take all the terrors away with him.

Back against the tree, Weyuker cried bitter, shivering tears.

* * *

Molina sat bolt upright in bed. He was naked and shivering. Through the drawn blinds at the window came the hard mercury vapor light from the hotel's parking lot. Maybe the window was open a little and the cold wind made him shiver.

He got out of bed. Elisa was on her side, legs pulled partway to her chest. She made a gently rising hillock, wrapped in covers and snoring slightly.

He went to the window, fiddling his hands under the blinds. It was closed, the air-conditioning off, the air motionless in the room. He put his hand on his arm. It came away wet. He was sweating hard. His heart was beating tightly, like a pressure driving in on his chest. Something's happening to me, he thought, something new.

He got back into bed, still shivering, curling himself against Elisa for warmth and security. A door slammed far away, and he heard people laughing, phantoms floating derisively through the cold night.

It was like the night he killed Flaco, when the world seemed to stand still for him. I'm not going back, he thought, knowing it was this revelation that beat in on him exuberantly, ferociously. I'm going to take her and go to Mexico and get Ralph and get the money. Ralph won't like it, the ways I'm going to make him tell me where the money is. A new gang, he would find them one by one, as he had before. More of the money into businesses. He would make himself into a power wherever he ended up, politicians this time working for him. He could deal directly with drug suppliers, using all he had learned in physical persuasiveness.

It was this new vision that so excited him he couldn't sleep.

She snored, a gasp, pressing her hips to him. They had made love again. He put his hand out and touched her hip, fingers sliding over the warm flesh beneath the covers. Not since the early days with Angie, right after they were married, before the kid was born, did he feel so close to a woman. I'm a real old con, he thought, wondering, delighted and aroused; I get laid and I fall in love.

He wasn't going to tell her yet. There was a great deal to do in the morning and she shouldn't be distracted.

He pulled the covers off her gently.

Check-out time. The night visions roaming brightly through his mind. Get the rest of the money from the Iranian kid today, pay Raymond and Cisso. He wasn't going to pursue Ralph and a new life leaving Swanson and the mess here to haunt him.

"Let's go, let's go." He clapped his hands. The rumpled bed reminded him of their lovemaking, a sign of his new dynamism. She was in the tiny bathroom, dumping little bars of soap into her purse, taking some glasses and a towel. Over breakfast they'd gone over the details for the morning. Like we're married, he thought.

"Just a sec, okay, okay, I'm coming." She darted from the bathroom, zipping closed the large purse. She scanned the room with an anxious, absentminded glance. "What am I forgetting? I'm forgetting something."

He reached into his jacket pocket and pulled out something clear plastic and dangled it in front of her.

"Wear gloves," he said.

CHAPTER THIRTY-TWO

The first thing he heard in the morning's spooky stillness was a door slamming close by. Slight pause, must be locking it, maybe even jiggling it to make sure, then he heard the crunch, crunch of shoes across the gravel of the driveway. The old general was coming for the car. Time to go to work at the restaurant.

Molina didn't move from the floor of the backseat. He lay stretched out, his feet turned a little against the door. It was actually nice down there, clean car, old BMW, maybe 1964, '65. Behzam had a key so he had a key. He counted. One-thousand, two-thousand, three-thousand, the feet crunching, the tread firm, hurried. This was a guy with a busy schedule; Behzam said his father was always on the go.

He had the cop's gun out as the driver's door opened. Felt a bulk slap into the seat, grunt, cough and the sound of a key impatiently thrust into the ignition. The car rumbled, turned over, and started. The old guy always waits to let it warm up in the morning before taking it out, he's more cautious and loving with the damn silver BMW than me, Behzam said as he rattled out all the ins and outs Molina needed to know.

The bulk moved and so did he.

"Back out," he said, gently pressing the barrel into the fleshy, startled cheek.

"Hello? Yes?" A momentary surprise. Molina saw the old general's face freeze solid quickly. A little disturbing he recovered so fast. Maybe Behzam's description was too rosy. The old guy might put up a fight, even with a gun in his face. Behzam said he was a negotiator, he liked to talk, wear everybody down.

"You're Mansour Riahi?"

"Yes. You want my money? I give it to you. In my front coat pocket, I open for you, hand it to you."

"Nope, nope, just back out like you're going to, I'll direct you."

"You kidnap me?"

Molina kept his voice conversational, just pressing the gun a little more tightly each second. "Your daughter Giti, she wants to see you."

"You've hurt her?" Now Molina worried that using the daughter as bait was not such a good idea. He sensed the old guy tensing up, and even cocooned in a heavy navy blue overcoat, the old general Riahi was a big man. The last thing he wanted was a struggle here in the driveway.

"We're going to her, she'll be okay you just drive carefully like I say. You don't and you get hurt and so does she."

The muscles on the old man's jowled face were tight. He turned slightly and put the car in gear. Molina slipped right behind him, their cheeks almost together, the cold gun metal between them. "Back out, good, okay now hang a right and go to the first light. We're going out toward the port."

"I know short cuts."

"Just go my way."

"I have employees, they will worry and call my home. My wife, she will call the police, she probably saw you."

Molina kept his eyes on the street. Anybody glancing into the car when they came to a stop would see two heads, like they were talking. Very hard to make him, he knew, from the shadow and angle into the car. "Your wife left you four months ago. You live alone. Don't bullshit me, Mansour, I know you. We're going to get you to your restaurant before anybody gets antsy."

"Is my Giti all right?"

"In the pink. Left up here at the intersection." They swung from the residential streets onto a main business drag, more cars around them, everybody rushing to get to work. Molina felt much better as the old routines came back, like they'd never been in doubt. Some things, he thought pleasantly, you never forget.

"My neighbors, somebody saw you. You going to have trouble later, is it worth doing this? If Giti is untouched, I give you my wallet, I write a check, and you can just leave."

"I used to wonder about that." Molina watched the street names flashing by. Time to turn soon. "Guys with these fucking stockings over their faces, ski masks, all that bullshit. You ever get stopped with a stocking in your pocket, they got you. Most guys don't go around regularly with a ladies' stocking, couple holes cut in it. And ski masks? Shit. You're in the mountains freezing your ass off, it's okay, but you got one downtown here, okay? It's going to look a little strange."

"I have not seen you very good. You look like nothing."

"So what I've found is, you take a handkerchief, plain old white hankie, ball it up like you're blowing your nose, and you hold it there, kind of move it a little, nobody notices anything. What're they seeing? Big white ball stuck in front of your face. No fucking ID at all. They pick you out, a show-up, a line-up, your lawyer he gets that ID canned first time in court. Believe me."

He rubbed the gun on the old man's cheek. "Get on the freeway northbound."

They drove onto the freeway, elevated so that Stockton spread around them, pearly and iridescent in the misty morning's sunlight. Now he's thinking, Molina ran through it, what he can do, things he might say. Maybe off the wall stuff, swerve into the concrete embankment, jump out, wave his arms, scream for help. Now he's seeing the daughter. Now he says, forget it.

The trick was pretending the guy's head was made of glass, you could look at it, like the inside of a watch.

More directions and off the freeway, the old guy driving very carefully, thinking, I'll do this so nicely, so calmly, everything will be okay. I'll be so reasonable, I'll do anything, give up anything and then I'll be fine and my kid will be fine.

Along the embarcadero, untouched by any civic renovation, wooden pilings and rusting ships and the smell of dried muck. Before going to the motel, they'd scouted along here, past the few businesses on to a dead end where a high, rust-dappled concrete bridge soared overhead like an atheist's vision of a cathedral. The sun broke through the mist, a little after seven-thirty, and hung immovable in the seamless sky.

"Now, what you're doing next is pulling over, right there, see the other car? The Accord? Right along here." Molina sat back for the first time. Elisa leaned against the trunk of the car. She waved and smiled. Like we're going sailing, he thought.

The old general parked and remained motionless. "What should I do? Where is my Giti?"

"Just get out. Just stand there."

Molina slid out fast on the other side in case the old guy felt like slamming the door on him or something like that.

"Hello," she said to the old guy.

He stood beside the car, hands limp at his sides, head straight up. "You have demands?"

"Walk back, couple feet, that's good, good. Stop. Sit down, knees up, hands around your knees."

He sat on a slope of dirt and brown, dead grass. Like a picture, a study in gray, black, brown, and blue.

"Give me the papers," Molina said to Elisa. She had on her plastic gloves, crinkling when she handed the envelope to him. She watched everything with a wide-eyed, golly-gee look. Not afraid or horrified, just interested.

He held the gun on the old general and at arm's length, gave him the envelope. "Sign those things, okay? That's all. The kid is safe, you go to the restaurant, it's all over. Simple as that."

Out came the trust documents, the other bank authorizations. It took about five fast seconds for the old general to see what he was holding. He started saying something very nasty in that rolling, glottal sound Behzam made, only Molina couldn't understand a word of this. In another second he flung the papers away. Elisa nipped after them, gathered them up.

"Tell my son he's a serpent, I disown him, I renounce him. Tell him he gets nothing," and after that he was off making those funny sounds she liked so much. He half-rose, angry, staring at Molina.

"Stay down," Molina cracked sharply. It was isolated here, but things were getting out of hand. "You don't want to sign? You want your daughter in trouble? Can be done."

"He wouldn't hurt her, the coward. He would hurt me, tell you to do that, I'm certain."

He reminded Molina of Angie's father, at her funeral. The same combative superiority. What a family this old guy had raised, his son and daughter hiring to have him taken out. He sure wasn't going to help, though.

"Okay," Molina said a little wearily, like he was tired of it all, and was going to give up. "I'm clearing out. Tell him you didn't cooperate."

"You must not hurt my Giti."

"No, no, that was to get your attention."

The old guy listened, half-believing, half-suspicious. The sun was warmer. He must be getting hot in that big heavy coat.

"See, okay, we're going to leave, I don't want you to watch the way we go, okay? So I want you to turn around, face the ground, okay?"

"You're leaving me?"

"Got to take the car."

The old guy's stern look was relaxing a little. Then, from nowhere he asked, "What is that on your hands?"

"These? Dishwashing gloves. Your hands don't get red and rough. Come on, turn around." The gun waved for effect.

The old general grunted, shifting on his knees so that his face was toward the dirt embankment, broad back and gray head to Molina and the ocean. "You want to clear some of that junk? Get the weeds and stuff," he ordered.

"What?" the old guy turned his head, puzzled.

"What?" Incredulous that the old guy had the nerve to ask questions.

"I don't know why you want me to do this."

"Because I'm telling you to do it. That's all. Use your hands, just make it clear, down to the dirt. Like that. Good, great."

He took a look at Elisa. She held the envelope to her chest tightly, watching everything. Again, he felt the twinge. She was now an accomplice in everything. He had joined them together as surely as if married. I want her, he thought, no acting, no joke.

The old guy's dog-like motions ceased. He had swept the dead grass and weeds away. He faced a patch of brown earth.

"Okay, stay there, count to two hundred slowly, don't look around, you hear anything, just stay there, you understand?"

Nod. A sigh. He was thinking about what he'd do to Behzam. Must be.

As he spoke, Molina came to the old general's back, pressed the cop's gun to his head, at the joining of his skull and neck. One shot, very loud in the morning.

Even as he shot, he stepped back. The body moved forward suddenly, then fell to its side, rolling a little on the slight slope. Arms flung around himself in a final embrace, the old general lay, half-face-down in the grass.

"Oh, my God," Molina heard Elisa say. Not sick or frightened; in wonderment. As though she'd seen a total eclipse.

He was at the dirt patch, poking it, squinting, trying to find from the small spurt of dust where the exiting bullet had gone. "If you do it right," he said aloud, "should be right here. I'm not going to leave it." He twisted, digging around. "Fuck. I can't find it. It went right here someplace."

He stood up. She was looking inquisitively at the body. "It's not so bad."

"We got to take him."

"Take him?"

"I can't find the bullet. They find him here, they match it maybe to the gun." He put the revolver in his coat pocket. He had on a safari-type jacket with deep pockets. She bought it for him.

"Go open the trunk. His car." He tossed her the keys.

She nodded, walking and opening in slow motion. He didn't know what she was thinking. She didn't seem disturbed by it.

He straightened out the arms, rolling the body on its back. No, it wasn't bad, he thought, you got blood to watch out for, but the bullet coming out made only this strange puckered hole in the forehead, just below the hairline.

She came back to him, standing at the feet. "Help me get him over there, we got to get him in the trunk."

This was not easy, flopping around, getting the heavy old guy the few feet to the trunk, hoisting his upper body inside, watching out not to get too close, pushing the arms in, taking the legs from her and bending them so he fit. Slam down the trunk lid with a solid sound. He was panting a little.

"How you doing?"

"I'm okay," she said, "it wasn't like what I thought."

"Most things aren't." He had his hand on her neck gently. "You follow, back about a block. Go to that mall, couple miles."

"I want to stay with you."

"We'll talk about it, we stop to eat." She almost embarrassed him. Brown eyes and a face that looked so delicate in the morning's freshness.

He was gone a long time. When he came back to their table, she stopped picking at the pineapple slices in the fruit plate.

"That number? It's his scuba club." Molina sat beside her. "They put me on hold, they had to get him out of the water. So he finally comes on the line, he says, okay, okay about four times and then he's going back to take his scuba lesson because, he says he doesn't want to do anything unusual. He always takes a scuba lesson at eight on Thursday morning."

"He's cute, kind of."

"Cute? I don't think so."

She smacked her lips, sitting back with a satisfied look. "Where we going when he comes back with the money?"

"Out of here. Back to Santa Maria."

"Why we going back there?"

"Take care of Raymond and Cisso. Finish my business."

She pulled closer to him. "No, I guess I mean, after. After that, where?"

He enjoyed teasing her like this, acting noncommittal because it drove her crazy. "I don't know, maybe you go back to L.A. What do you think?" He fished through the fruit plate and found some pieces of orange.

"I don't want to go back. Why don't we go someplace, like together? You showed me things, you want to stay together. I know you do."

"I don't think so."

"You do."

He shook his head, eating more orange. "No, no. I think you go back to L.A. I'll see you sometime."

The marina cafeteria was only a little occupied, a couple of businessmen out for breakfast, the waiters leisurely fixing table settings, boats moored right outside the fern-and-brass-adorned picture windows. He was having fun, too. She was expectant, selfish, petulant, he saw that. She meant giving up the hope of security with the feds. But he wanted that, with all the single-mindedness that had made Gilbert Villagrana take notice. There was one regret, he admitted. Out of the witness protection program, not testifying for Massingill, he would have to find some other way to even things with the Nuestra General. I killed one general today, he thought gloatingly, I can wait to get another.

"I'm staying with you," she announced, holding him tighter, like she could physically attach herself.

"How about like this." He appeared conciliatory. "We live in Mexico. I'm in business, big again. We find Ralph. You think you'd find him, we're together?"

"Sure, sure, I could find him probably. He'd come to me, I could get him to come. He doesn't have any other sisters, just me. He'd come to me, yeah."

"Okay," he said with satisfaction, "okay. We do it."

She was kissing him, saying things. He seized her face in one hand, drawing her head down to his mouth. He pressed his mouth to her, then began whispering to her, tensely, in virile obscenity.

Anybody passing them, leaning together at the little table early on a workday would think they were truant from some boring jobs.

They met Behzam outside at nine. His hair was slicked back from the water. This time it was topsiders, canvas pants, and a green windbreaker. He was a little white when Molina told him everything. He started nodding, saying okay, okay, and looking at the sky. Orepeza's sister smiled at him.

"Here, your keys." Molina handed him the car keys.

"I don't want them."

"Okay." He took them back and threw them into the softly lapping black-green waters of the marina. "Let me have the rest of the money."

Still white, shuffling but getting hold of himself, Behzam gave Molina an envelope. "I would like the material she has." He pointed at the manila envelope. She held it by the edges and let him have it.

"He really a general?" Molina counted the money, flipping it in the envelope.

"In the Air Force, yes. The materiel command."

"Behzam, I tell you this is short like almost ten thousand," keeping his voice even.

"I thought I would write you a check."

"Behzam, you won't write me a check."

"I don't have any more money."

"Oh, Behzam," she said.

He put the envelope in his pocket, nestled with the cop's gun. "You still got your car?"

"Of course. I must have a car."

"You should sell it, Behzam."

"How am I going to have transportation?"

"You know what I could do to you?"

The kid suddenly swallowed, took a few steps backward and almost bumped into Elisa. "I will write a check. I will give you a security note."

Molina knew the kid was scared, whirly about hearing his

old man was actually taken care of. Either Behzam was very tough or very stupid, and nothing so far had demonstrated any toughness on his part. There was no maneuvering room with somebody this stupid.

"He didn't mean it," Elisa said. "Come on."

"You know what I'm doing?"

The kid shook his head, trying to see which way he could run. But he was thinking about the papers in the envelope and his dead father and how running would call attention to himself, so he waited, indecisively.

"I'm thinking," Molina said.

"Yes?"

"The papers are signed, everything's okay?"

"Yes, yes, they are fine."

"You shouldn't conduct your business this way. It's not fair, is it?"

"I'm so sorry. I will try to make it up. I will send the balance to your address."

"No, no, Behzam. The right way to conduct your business is fair, first thing. Then there's nothing to fix. No bad feelings."

"I do not want you to have bad feelings."

"I think you are sorry," Molina gave Behzam's shoulder three solid whacks. "Okay, Behzam, you remember what I told you. You be fair from now on."

He looked back at the kid once, still standing on the hill overlooking the marina, touching his stomach tenderly, then studying the forged signatures, undoubtedly figuring out how he was going to use all that money.

In the car, driving back to Santa Maria, she said, "You were very sweet. And fair's fair. You signed the papers, so forty thousand for bogus papers is okay, isn't it?" Very coy about it.

"Old Behzam's going to last a fast five minutes, he tries working shit like this on his own. Smokey's right about him. They're going to snag him fast."

"He'll tell about us." Alarm colored her voice.

"He says, a guy named Negron hit my father for me. He says,

I paid him forty thousand. What? No weapon, no fingerprints, no shit anyplace. Nothing they can fuck with."

"He could pick you out. And me. He would do that, wouldn't he?"

"It's uncorroborated. It's like this guy who paid to have his father killed, he says, this is the guy. He did it," Molina snorted. "Really good. They can really work with that."

"We should go now, keep going to Mexico."

He was adamant. "I got to finish this shit in Santa Maria." He had to explain the world to her. "My first rule, rules to live by, is you make as few enemies as you can. You don't start fights over nothing, you don't give guys shit, get in their way for nothing. Don't make enemies if you can. Second rule, you got to take care of a guy, you do it clean, no shit left around. Nobody should know it was you. Like this old general? Classic. All business, no fucking with it. You see me with old Behzam? I could've fucked with him, he held out, but I didn't. Just keep trucking."

"Behzam," she said, "he's around."

"Sure. No Behzam, and then they really look for us, somebody else helping him. They got Behzam, who's read the papers about me, they're going to say, and they got everything. This guy Behzam, he shoots his pop, he says this other guy did it, not me. Some other dude did it. Cops always make fun of you, you tell them that. Some other dude, they say. Like who?"

"We should forget Santa Maria. Makes me feel funny going back." She sucked in her breath.

"So my third rule, this is the one you got to follow, whatever, is if you got to take out some guy, get somebody else to do it for you. Always. Unless nobody's around, like this old general. The second rule, you can mess with that. Sometimes you want everybody to know who did it, make a big show. Then you get two, three witnesses, make them watch, scare the shit out of them. They tell everyone." Which was exactly what he told Raymond to do to Max. A big show.

Molina deliberately turned the wheel, making the car thrum-

thrum over the bumps dividing the lanes. "But I want to get clear of these two charges."

"They won't find us."

He remembered the plane and Swanson. "This guy, he's got something about me, I don't know. He's going to follow me. He's got these two charges, they're not my fault, you look at them, but he's going to keep coming. And I've done so much for those guys." He was momentarily bitter, though not very concerned about Massingill's animosity. It was Swanson he couldn't comprehend or fool and therefore could not leave behind.

She agreed that the feds had no gratitude. "I got the paper at the marina. I didn't read it all, but they got you. They got this story here, they go, escaped prisoner and all that."

"Read it to me." He was expansive. "I tell you what those little bumps in the road are?"

She rooted around in her large purse. "I don't know."

"Like road braille, you know how to read them, they give you directions, tell you where to go."

She started reading the article, a broad smile on her face. Quoting the D.A. Gleason about bringing him back for trial, two murders, not a bad article. She stopped whenever she came to his name and read that part again. Nothing about Swanson in the paper.

Remember your rules, he thought, and clean everything down to the bone.

Time for Swanson tonight.

CHAPTER THIRTY-THREE

"Your honor, the People oppose a bail reduction for this defendant," Swanson didn't look down the table at Fran, dressed in jail blues, one arm in a cast made for a child, "for several reasons. The crime she's charged with involves a high degree of dishonesty, abuse of trust. Her promise to make appearances in this case means little without a high bail to insure it."

Judge Pizer, once again, squinted down. "Defense?"

Swanson sat back in his chair as Fran's public defender rose. It was late and the courtroom had only one remaining spectator, a courthouse regular in a ratty red sweater, chin down on his chest, eyes closed. Pizer's bailiff was already going over to wake him. Swanson recalled another regular who came to many of his trials. Always sat third row, two seats in, if possible. Always fell asleep before noon and after three o'clock. One day, they all walked out of court for lunch, leaving the old guy slumped over in the third row. When they came back for the start of the trial at two, he was still in the same seat, slumped over. He had been dead most of the day, as far as anyone could tell.

He glanced back. Pizer's bailiff was poking this regular out the door.

Fran's public defender was speaking. "Your honor, can we take care of my recusal motion first?" she asked. "I don't think it's appropriate to address bail before you decide if the D.A. should even be here."

"You brought it up," Pizer snorted.

"Yes, your honor, but I think we're doing these things backwards."

"Your honor," Swanson broke in, "if the court decides my office should no longer prosecute this case because of a conflict of interest, you cannot rule on the bail question this afternoon."

"That's true," Pizer said loudly, snidely. When he saw Fran from time to time, Swanson noticed, even Pizer's harsh manner gave way a little. She still had bandages on her face and she sat perfectly motionless, as if startled into immobility.

Her lawyer was named Kehlet, relatively new in the P.D.'s office. Why she was given Fran's case, Swanson couldn't understand.

"So we're doing the bail motion first?" asked the public defender.

"I'm doing it. I don't know about you."

"Your honor," said Kehlet, her fingers splayed and arched over her papers on the counsel table, "all we have today is a charge of grand theft, in the amount of seventeen thousand dollars. Normally, as this court knows, a defendant like my client would be out on her O.R. and probably get an offer of plead to the charge with a promise of no state prison at the outset. Why the D.A. is insisting on a high bail, going so hard on this case, is a clear demonstration of bias. The D.A. is treating my client differently from others charged like her. There isn't an offer in this case."

"Is there?" Pizer barked.

"Not at this time," Swanson said.

Pizer grumbled loudly.

"This bias is the basis of my motion to have the Attorney General take over this case." Kehlet sat down. She was staring over at him.

"One thing at a time," Pizer said irritably. "Mr. Swanson,

does your office have some intent to file additional charges? Is that your reason for asking bail to remain as set?"

I can't tell him about the murder charge, Swanson thought. Ask me again when Molina's in jail and Joe looks a little like a hero. He weaseled. "We're exploring other charges. We don't have any more charges to file at this time."

Pizer grunted. He knew a weasel when he heard it. "Bail is reduced to twenty thousand dollars," he ordered.

Swanson stretched his legs under the table. Fran looked over at him blankly.

"Now, this motion to recuse the District Attorney of Santa Maria County and bring in the Attorney General," Pizer said gruffly. "Where's the Attorney General?"

"Your honor?"

Swanson closed his eyes. The public defender hadn't brought over an assistant attorney general to speak up and say if his office would even think about taking the case.

"Mrs. Kehlet, we can't proceed unless I hear from the Attorney General." Pizer fought a yawn. Although he would stay on the bench for hours on end during a trial, bringing everyone else in court to a squirming desperation, Pizer did not like to stay beyond five. Get the business done during business hours, he said.

"Can we put this over, your honor?" Swanson stood. "Tomorrow maybe? The public defender can have somebody here from the Attorney General's office."

"Yes. Tomorrow at ten. Have somebody here, Mrs. Kehlet."

She glared at Swanson. "I thought that was the D.A.'s responsibility, your honor."

"No, Mrs. Kehlet. You're making the motion to excuse the D.A. It's your responsibility. Good night." Not waiting for his bailiff to say court was adjourned, he simply walked off the bench. The marshal came for Fran, head sunk low, sitting and talking with her lawyer.

He swung tiredly from the courtroom, into the empty corridor, grown very still at that hour. The commotion of people paying fines, getting married, getting divorced, applying for licenses, waiting to get into court, coming from court, jurors and defendants, cops and lawyers, was gone. The day's rapt self-absorption ended, lawyers with briefcases, clients alongside, the long line of drunk drivers outside Department F, dispersed. A courthouse was unlike a factory that made cars or shoes when it came to the end of the day. Nothing was made in a courthouse over the days and years, only human entanglements interwoven and usually indissoluble filled it. A courthouse at the end of a day wasn't merely empty, Swanson thought, it was sepulchral.

The high-glossed floors, cigarette butt-littered, scuffed and dirty, resounded as he walked out to the broad white plaza in front of the courthouse, shaded by a wash of decorative trees, the wide fountain, its abstraction of a stone statement in the middle, dry. Even the buses that waited in front all day had departed.

Like all good people should, he thought.

But there was a great deal of work left for him. He had seen Narloch again that morning and the transcript should be ready. Weyuker, looking like death warmed over, left reports from two other counties about Alves and Rivera. LAPD, at Swanson's direction, was using their Fugitive Detail to check Molina's former addressess. He had called Angie's father to ask his help. At least it gave the old man something to do, and Swanson had a half-submerged wish that her father find Molina and thus reckon their accounts rightly. And there were calls from the state Department of Justice to return.

The D.A.'s office was nearly as empty as the courthouse, and he passed knots of lawyers, purses, briefcases, papers in hand, going to their cars. He found Susan watching Mary Tyler Moore on the small television. Dropping his files on her desk, he leaned against the window, feeling the sun press back on him.

"Massingill call?" he asked.

She shook her head, watching the little black-and-white figures before her, daintily picking up a cheese cracker. Susan never offered them to anyone, and Swanson knew if he ate one, she would immediately replace it.

"I'm not waiting for Massingill." He pressed his head back to the window. "I got people looking all over, but I bet Molina's still here. That's why he hasn't called Massingill. He's going to turn up when he wants to turn up."

"Anything Joe needs to know about today?"

"Bail got dropped on Fran."

Susan sighed. "Don't tell him today. Do it tomorrow."

"What happened to my weenie wagging judge this morning?"

"Well, I went over on that, we discussed it, and I put it over for two weeks." She smiled at him. "You can have it back."

"Thank you."

Her postponement of the Haata case actually made him optimistic. Susan hoped, as he did, that he would be able to handle it by then. Molina would have reached some resolution.

A thought struck him. "You doing anything later?"

"I think I'm between engagements."

"Come on over for dinner. Di'd like to see you." We could all use a little breather, someone new instead of our police buddies and each other over the tense dinner table.

"Well, all right. Thank you, Michael." She hastily finished the last cracker.

He pushed himself away from the window, his shirt and coat stuck to his skin with sweat. "Great," he said, picking up the files again. "Off to work."

Susan was most reluctant when Meg had to go to bed finally. The adults were strewn around the living room on the floor or the sofa, the children amongst them, carrying drawings or toys to display.

"I'll watch her," Susan said to Di.

"No, thanks, she's really getting overtired." Di stood up.

"I'll take her." Swanson scooped Meg up. "Say good night to Susan."

Meg, still holding a small furry thing that didn't have a head anymore, said, "How old are you?" as she faced Susan in Swanson's arms.

"Well, how old do you think I am?"

A short, calculated pause. "Eight."

Susan and Di both laughed. "I'm a little older, but not

much," Susan said. "Good night, precious," to Swanson's back, the little girl draped over it, waving.

Di looked over at Lizzie and Matt, studiously trying to remain unobserved and unobtrusive and creep past their inviolable bedtime. I told Mike we were in an aquarium, she thought, but it sometimes feels like a jail. She knew that was inapt, too. A jail meant punishment for a wrong and they had done nothing. It was more like a quarantine, as though they were diseased, without fault, without cure. Always morbid by the end of the day, she thought. She tried to be cheerful when Susan said, "You seem to have everything in hand."

"I do? I never think so."

The watchful cops indoors were discreetly off in the kitchen. Di could hear Mike arguing, playfully, with Meg about brushing her teeth.

"No, really," Susan said, adjusting herself on the couch, careful to avoid Meg's drawings at her feet. "I look at how you and Mike are taking things, and I'm amazed. I couldn't do it."

Di turned to Matt. "How are we handling things?"

"The worst time I've ever had." He said it plainly.

"What do you think, Lizzie?"

"Oh, I don't care," she said without looking up from a doodle.

"You've heard from the experts," Di said. Mike banged the bathroom door shut and Susan winced. She's not used to the sounds of a family, Di thought. Di took in the room. Matt was reading, head low, while Lizzie drew and colored. Coffee cups on coasters sat on the magazine-covered table in front of them. It was a perverse domestic picture, ideal in form, but arranged by fear.

"All of us downtown think about you," Susan said. She seemed to crave something from Di. You're welcome to it, if I can give it, Di thought. "Michael runs around all day," Susan lapsed into a bored tone, "and he's got chaperones whenever he leaves the building, so I don't worry about him. I think about you." The bored inflection fell away when she looked at the children.

"Well, we're getting along. There've been some rough moments, the whole thing is rough. But I've learned a few things."

"What?" Susan was deeply interested.

How much in life is tolerated, she thought, how much, as they say, is taken for granted. I've seen Mike discover limits on how much the world bends; and responsibilities won't excuse collapse. I've seen him struggle, and all the time we've been married, I don't think he ever really struggled, in his heart, with anything. This man Molina, who I hope to God I never meet, has helped Mike become wiser. I hope. I used to think I was self-reliant. It was mostly impatience with other people, my own family. Being together, through this, let me glimpse a little of Mike's world, and he can see a little of mine. That's something.

What Susan wanted to hear was more concrete. Di told her, "I'm going back to the classroom as soon as we get out of here. It's much easier teaching forty strange kids than your own."

Matt grimaced.

"I can imagine," Susan said. She wants to be friends, Di thought. Maybe her idea of happiness is to be locked up with a husband and kids, the rest of the world kept at bay. Loneliness was being quarantined and not knowing how to get out.

"Sometime you'll have to tell me the secret," Susan said. "How you get through something like this. Coping with life's little puzzles." She was arch for effect. "Lay it out for me. I'd really like to know."

"All right," Di said, "I promise we'll do it soon."

When Di opened her eyes again, Mike was gone. She must have dozed. Awake again, she stretched against the pillows behind her on the bed. The open window beside her was cavernous black, falling outward toward the midnight silence where only the rare, quick, broken sibilance of a car rushing by below told her the world went on.

Mike came through the bedroom door. "Remember this?"

He held out a large globular bottle. She didn't have to read the label. "I remember. We used to get it at that Italian market on the way to the river. I think we were the only ones who drank it."

"Well," he handed her a glass, the good crystal, and filled it with red wine, "I felt like some tonight. A touch of the good old days."

She took the glass, held it while he filled his own and carefully settled back beside her in bed. Lesson plans for the kids lay on her lap, and his file folders had been pushed to the end of the bed. They lay, side by side, glasses tilted gingerly. She looked at him. "Tastes just the same. It was nice of you to think of it."

"Didn't I bring this on our first date? I thought I did."

"I think you did, too. You weren't very subtle."

He took a long swallow. "Now look at us."

"We're not doing as badly as I thought."

He drank again, looking at her. "Things could be better," he said.

Sometimes it seemed to her that the great slow river from those long-ago nights had washed them up, first sweeping them along together, then driving them ashore, abandoned. But, as she saw through Mike's supervisor, lives did not fall together inseparably or inevitably. She and Mike, the kids, were the sum of daily choices and actions.

"I'm not going to put any pressure on you, any more than you've got." She set her glass on the night table, beneath the lamp shade so the wine glowed scarlet. "It's easy to get lost in all this."

"I'm not going nuts again. No more." He kissed her deeply and she felt his hand take hers.

"I'm glad we had a different face to look at tonight. I feel sorry for Susan—"

"You feel sorry for Susan?" He let out a whoop. "It's a world's first."

"Don't tell her. She seems lonely."

"She's one of the toughest people I know." He kissed her again. "Jesus, sorry for Susan Utley."

"I'd like to see her when things even out."

"Can't hurt for my wife and supervisor to be pals." He tried to lighten the conversation. "Right now, let's take everything day by day."

As if there were any other way, she thought, as if life were any different. She didn't want to drift into their abnormal troubles. She asked instead, "Did you hear Lizzie cough at dinner?"

"I wasn't paying attention. Don't think so."

"She might be coming down with something. She was coughing this morning. If she gets it, we're all going to get it."

Mike waved it aside. "She looks fine. I didn't see anything." He filled his glass again after she turned down another.

"You're half sleepwalking most of the time around here."

She saw his sad agreement. "Yeah. Well, I never thought a simple murder case would get so complicated. Like you pulled a thread on your sleeve and your coat falls apart." He told her everything each night now, since the monstrous evocation of that man burning to death. In a world grown obscure, it was impossible to say which acts would have personal consequences. You could only do what was right.

She held her empty wineglass. Mike said, "Everything's battened down downstairs. Doors checked, windows locked. Got the porch light on and the front lights. The big light they had me stick on out front looks like a bug motel. The guys were watching Johnny Carson when I came up."

"I don't hear it."

"They got it real low."

"So it's just you and me."

He kissed her again, putting his glass and hers on the night table. A high, thin wind had come up, gently brushing by the house. She wanted to feel the wind at night, drifting through the window.

"You and me for sure." He rolled over to her, the covers coming off, spilling the lesson plans to the floor.

"I'm too tired."

"I'm too tired," he agreed.

They made love more easily and tenderly than she thought possible in the chaos of their lives. The night wind moved over them with the counterfeit sibilance of a great river. It brought darkness and peace and sleep.

* * *

It was the cough that woke her, or the dream of Lizzie's cough. Di lay still for a minute, listening to the subtle sounds of the house. Mike breathed heavily by her. When he did sleep now, it was a narcotized descent, heavy and unhealthy. She got out of bed slowly and quietly, going to the bathroom, taking down her blue terrycloth robe, slipping into it.

Barefooted she walked softly down the hallway, past Matt's room, silent and closed. At the other end of the hall, the girls' room.

From downstairs she heard faint voices, whether the policemen or the TV, she couldn't tell. These two guys were very tidy, even bringing a small cloth to wipe off smudges. She smiled at the idea.

She didn't know the exact time. It was that midregion, though, somewhere between night and day, when the darkness is most secure and the world swathed in shadow and whispers and voices may not be real. She got to the door, pushing it open, carefully, quietly.

So far so good, as she went in. Lizzie wasn't coughing. Meg was sound asleep in her bunk bed. She noticed that the bedroom window was open, the flowered curtains gently waving in the night wind, beckoning to her softly.

The shape was crouching over Lizzie, hunched over her, dark and immaterial, like a wraith or dream. She had taken several steps into the room before fully registering the alien presence. Who is it? What's he doing? She opened her mouth to shout.

At that moment, the shape straightened up. A little man, face in shadow, eyes very big, teeth split wide in a smile at her. He put a hand to his mouth for silence. His other hand reluctantly left Lizzie's hair. He was touching her head, like he was petting her. Di went sick with fright. Shout, shout for them, they're just downstairs, the thought shot through her mind.

Then died.

Impressions assailed her even as the little man was at her. He wore a T-shirt, arms bare. In the moonlight, he gleamed. Sweat. A sheen of sweat covered him. More. In his hand, the one that touched his mouth for silence, something hard, cold, shiny. In the moon's crescent ice sliver through the open window, she saw what it was. Knife. Knife blade.

Oh, God. He came down the roof, climbed in the window so silently he didn't wake the girls. Scrabbling over the roof, out of sight of the police, into the house, out of sight of the men downstairs.

He reached up, pulling her hair back, quick. Face pressed to her ear. Slick, hot, his skin against her face and neck.

"Shut up, shut up," soft, swift whispers, guttural and low. Hard to understand. "Out, out, real quiet," directing her, the skinny hot arm snaking over her shoulder, the hand moist, digging its nails into her cheek, the fingers pressing her mouth closed so tightly her teeth cut her lips. Around her throat, the blade brushing.

She moved back out of the room; he was pushing her, whispering constantly, muttering. Stick-like, brown against the white of his shirt. Get him away from the girls, get him away from the knife. Out of their room, she shuffled with him.

They were in the hallway. She started to breathe heavily, a strange lassitude falling over everything. The shock was too great. The monkey creature exhorting, cursing, pushing at her too unreal.

"Asleep? Still sleeping?" urgently, viciously demanded. The little body pressed to her. He seemed all quivery, wet.

The hand relaxed slightly so her voice could come out. "Who?" she said. They spoke almost in thoughts, the voices so faint.

"The guy, your husband, the guy, the guy," pushing her toward their bedroom.

He wants Mike. He wants Mike, running on a loop in her mind faster almost than coherence.

"He's asleep."

Instantly, the fingers clamped tight again, one between her lips, tasting the saltiness. A hiss of air, through the dark hallway, to the bedroom. What am I going to do? Can't let him have Mike, he can't. He can't get in there with him. With the knife.

She grunted as the monkey-like brown arm flashed from her

mouth, the door opened. The bed dimly outlined, Mike's breathing deafening. I won't let him get any closer.

An instant's tenseness. No closer. One shout. Di yelled and thrust backwards with her body, against the little man at her side. With a bee sting the blade drew past her throat. She was yelling, falling, the little man swearing loudly. A punch as she hit the floor, grabbed for his bare foot as he hopped over her, springing forward in the darkened room. At the bed.

She was getting up, even as the lithe, compact shape sprang to the bed. Running sounds from downstairs, up the stairs. Shouts at the bed, a struggling black mass in the dimness. High pitched, frenzied and wavering, the little man's furious cries.

Mike's single scream.

An ice point exploded into crystalline sound, shattered. Again. Again and again.

Gunshots, she thought.

CHAPTER THIRTY-FOUR

"How?" The word came slowly, awkwardly. The thought behind it was elusive, lost in white desolation.

"You should've seen. Like fucking Tarzan, he's got this rope thing on that big pine in your neighbor's yard. You're always bitching about pine needles all over the place? He must've come in through the alley, he's up the tree, gets this rope tied and does a running start over the neighbor's roof. What'd they think? Cats, they said. Cats always fighting on the roof, all over the block. Like a fucking monkey, Mike, he's onto your roof. I mean, it's got to be one hell of a swing, he could've missed easily. Like a pirate movie, with this knife in his teeth. Christ Almighty, who'd think of that? We figured anybody's coming from the street, not flying through the goddamn air."

"Alves?" harder still. He knew a figure in white, glasses and clean shaven, was intently doing something to his upper arm while he sat on the table, crisp paper rustling under him. Stitching on the arm, like needlepoint.

Weyuker was only a foot or so in front of him, but seemed to recede every so often. He looked pale, bloodless, worn. "It was Alves. Jesus, I'm sorry. I'm really sorry."

"Trouble talking."

"Sedatives and a local so you don't move around," the white figure snapped with efficient indifference. "It's a good wound, penetrating, and I've got to get it back together."

"Dead?"

Weyuker nodded. All white lights and unwelcome odors in the emergency room. "Two shots would have done it. Shit, he's so cranked up he probably still doesn't know he's dead." The bloodless mouth twisted. So upset.

This was the final stage, he knew that much, watching with little interest as the clean-shaven figure bound his arm, taking care with the bandages. "The benefits of flab," he said slowly. No reply. Weyuker watched him, nervous, almost ashamed somehow.

In the vast clarifying whiteness, he saw the thing again. The sudden, wrenching attack. His hand went under the pillow for the gun. Slipped there every night once Di was asleep. All he knew next was that something, taut, atavistic, was on him, and the snick, snick of a blade ripping through the covers. As he shot, he felt the pain in his upper arm. There was no numbness or illusion. The pain was immediate, burning and intense.

He stirred even in the sedated calm. The worst had been all the dark wetness, pushing the covers and the trembling mass off of him. Di was up, running to him. Nothing would suffice to clean that horror away. Or the terrible sound of Meg shrieking from the doorway, as Lizzie and Matt came that far, then rooted to the spot. The cops were already in the room. He and Di barely noticed, so close was their embrace, like children in a very bad dream.

So much noise, so many voices. Then the lights burst on, all shadows banished. He saw Di's red grinning crescent, a thin slightly blooded sign. She held his bleeding arm, telling Matt to get a towel. How could I do this, he thought, how could I let this happen to her?

When Matt returned with the towel, she comforted Meg. He dazedly looked at the familiar room, now foreign and danger-ous. The mattress, partly off the bed, covers heaped on the floor to one side. Red spots spattered along the wall, on the pillows. From the heaped blankets, a brown, bare foot stuck out. From the blankets, red trails like bright scarves pulled from whatever was underneath.

You can go into a room one moment and know all is safe and ordinary and in another moment find it changed by violence. In my own house, he thought.

"She's right out here, right outside," Weyuker soothed.

"What?"

"You were saying, Diane. She's here. She's okay."

The white figure was brusquely tossing bloody bandages, bits of torn pajama, and syringes into a basin.

"A little battered," he said, "but no injury. Except the scrape on her throat. Looks like he couldn't get a grip, I suppose. She's fine." The white figure slammed a drawer.

He had to see her. The words came quickly, too fast, pouring out because he had to get away, out of the blinding, judging whiteness, the insatiable clamor. He didn't even realize Weyuker was talking to him, talking over him, until the detective repeated it several times, looking worn and bloodless.

"Mike, I got to talk to you."

When his leg went to sleep, Massingill tried to unhook his knee from the velveteen chair's armrest, found he could not, and decided to have another drink. Tommy Conn wiped his mouth with a little square napkin, finished a joke, and laughed. He joined Tommy's laughter politely. His brown three-piece suit was folded, loose, as though the body limp in the chair was too small. Ashes spotted his vest. Massingill's cigarette was angled in the corner of his mouth, growing so short he could feel its heat. His eyes burned from the smoke.

He saw Rau come in, shading his eyes with one hand, looking for them in the artificial darkness.

"Here," Massingill called. He didn't move. He didn't feel like moving ever again.

Rau was breathless with news. "Sorry. I didn't see your note until I got back from court. You guys got an early start."

"I thought all of Hector's old friends in the federal government should be at this impromptu wake." Massingill finished his drink. "It's my pre-farewell reception, too." More ash drifted soddenly to his vest. His eyes watered. "Got my work done this morning, more this afternoon, but I've got to take a little time off."

"Hey, we'll straighten it out." Tommy Conn was forever upbeat.

"Chris? What's the news?"

"Oh, well." Rau fumbled as the waiter came by suddenly, made his order, waited for Massingill to make one, and said, "Diaz's attorney's filed the motion for a new trial. Molina's lying, all of it. You can predict the allegations. Our star witness is a perpetual liar."

"They'll all be doing it." Massingill groaned, his leg sliding off the armrest. It tingled, like sparklers going off inside.

"Probably." Tommy Conn smoothed his graying moustache. "Conceivable we can save some of the verdicts, Claude. Maybe all of them. It's a very good argument that whatever, I mean whatever, Hector was up to outside of court is collateral to the testimony he gave in court. Even this fiasco with the D.A. I mean, we say to the court, 'Look, judge, a jury saw this man, evaluated his testimony, believed him truthful after vigorous cross-examination.' Right?"

"We believed him, too."

"I'm just making our argument for saving the verdicts. This other monkey business," Tommy Conn spat into his napkin, "it's collateral. The main evidence he gave was tested in court. You can't quarrel with that." The waiter brought their drinks.

Massingill didn't know if it would work or not. Some of the NF verdicts could be saved perhaps. But there would be no more trials without Molina. There was no way to conceal the ramifications of his foolishness in trusting Molina.

"We have a good shot," Rau said. "It's early to think about resignations." He wouldn't look at Massingill, only sucked his drink fastidiously through the little pink-and-white straw in the glass, denting his cheeks.

Massingill stamped his foot on the carpet. He held his glass in front of him. "Call this a career mercy killing. I'm putting it out of its misery."

"Don't think about that yet," Tommy Conn was at his most irredeemably optimistic.

"It's over," Massingill said. "Goddamn him," and it was as unclear to him, as to Tommy Conn and Rau, whether he meant Swanson or Molina. "I called Gleason and Swanson already. Said I'd do anything. Swanson's got an open account."

"How bad was it?"

"He says he got cut on the arm. His wife got banged a little."

"Jeez," Tommy Conn winced.

"What was the general attitude?" Rau asked.

"Pretty subdued under the circumstances."

"Swanson doesn't want your ass?"

Massingill shook his head. The conversation had been almost amicable. Poor guy, he thought automatically, without much real sympathy. You'd think, Massingill roused his anger, somebody finally getting me to crawl would have said something. Swanson sounded like he just wanted to hang up. Like he had better things to do.

"That all sounds very reasonable. Claude," Rau said earnestly. "You shouldn't be hasty."

For being so wrong? When he heard about the attempt on Swanson's life, it felt like he had come out of a fog. He woke up. For the first time in over two years, he saw the world as it was. And knew he was on his way out.

He brushed the ashes off his vest. "On the bright side, they'll need an interim appointee when I leave. You guys are the seniors. Chris? You'd like to be U.S. Attorney for a while. It might even turn into a permanent appointment."

"Not me." Tommy Conn shook his hands in the air in mock fright.

"Chris?"

He bent to clean the last ashes off his vest and get up. Rau probably has memos in his files saying how shortsighted I was, covering himself. Rau'll survive. He has so far. When

Massingill looked up at Rau, he expected to see a small glimmer of triumph, even gloating.

Instead, Rau seemed saddened and Massingill frowned, bewildered because he could no longer tell if it was real or feigned.

The lunch crowd was straggling in, boisterous, blind, and sleek.

CHAPTER THIRTY-FIVE

"We're alone," Di said to Mike.

"We are alone," he said. They stood on the front step, the door partway open behind them, a policeman beside them. Weyuker was being put in the backseat of a squad car in front of the house. He didn't look back at them. Gleason had just left. For the first time since the night before, the ambulance, lights, cars, and furor were gone.

"I'll tell the kids it's all clear." Mike turned to the door as Weyuker was driven away.

"So we wait," she said.

"That's all we can do." They both went back inside, the policeman, a new face they had never seen, followed, closed and locked the door, and reported in through a small microphone clipped to his breast pocket. No more intermittent reports on the walkie-talkie. Gleason had decreed constant communication in and outside the house.

Di and Mike occupied themselves with as many jobs around the house as they could think of. They didn't talk about the night before. What needed to be said was blurted out frantically at the hospital when Mike, unsteady from shock and sedatives, stumbled to her. They were both frightened and all they could do was wait.

The phone wouldn't stop, and Di gave up handing it to Mike. Most of the calls were for him, friends, colleagues, names she didn't immediately recognize, making him recite cryptic things she knew would take too long to explain now. Other calls she took, from Robin down the street, Frank and Hannah Tice, who hadn't been molested and wanted to know how they were.

After a cheerless lunch, she and Mike sat with the kids around the dining room table. Matt, wan and jittery, Meg and Lizzie quiet and uneasy. We're all right, she told them repeatedly, both your father and me. What you saw was terrible, but it's over and now we're safe. She didn't think they believed her.

She thought of Weyuker with an unconscious shudder. Tentatively, she touched the mark on her throat from time to time, like an angry insect had traced a venomous track. It will never heal, she thought; I'll always remember. It wasn't an injury so much as a brand, the mark of true wickedness passing through her life.

For the moment, the chores filled the time. Garbage to take out, gathering up dirty laundry, picking up and straightening the mess from last night. Matt and Lizzie helped her, Meg trotted hesitantly along with Mike, timidly as though afraid something would spring out at her. Every so often, Mike would lift something, a basket of clothes, a stack of magazines for the garbage, and wince. They held each other spontaneously, often, reassured simply by touch. Mike brought out their old 8mm projector and said they'd look at family movies once the sun went down. It was dusk already, as though they had endured a lifetime in less than a day. Violet and orange shot through the clouds. Each time the phone rang, she hoped it was Weyuker and feared it.

Gleason had arrived first, an hour or so after she and Mike got home from the hospital. The sun was up, midmorning, midweek, deceptively ordinary. Mike was still woozy from the little blue bombers killing the pain. She ached, and felt a paradoxical dryness, as if all the moisture had been leached from her.

"He's here." She shook Mike awake in bed.

"Weyuker?"

"No, Joe."

"I'll be right down."

"I'm staying while you talk."

He rubbed his eyes briefly, nodded, and got dressed quickly.

They both went down to the living room, holding hands. The kids were confined to their rooms. Oh, Lord, she thought involuntarily.

Gleason got up instantly, cigarette holder tight in his thinly drawn mouth. He braced on a cane. He looked older to her, sleepless. There was a moment or two of commiseration and sympathy. Then the knock on the door.

One of the policemen inside the house got the door. Dick Weyuker came in, two more policemen with him. They stayed until Gleason told them to wait outside. Weyuker smiled grimly at her, nodded to Mike.

"Sit down over there," Gleason ordered him.

Weyuker sat on a small rattan chair, Gleason on the couch, cane between his legs, she and Mike standing.

"Joe," Mike scratched his arm without thinking and made a pained face, "I've called Pizer and told him the bail on Fran should be dropped so she can get out."

"He do it?"

"A few minutes ago. He asked who's coming over on the recusal motion."

"Susie's covering while we take care of this." Gleason nervously moved the cane. He tapped the cast on his foot.

Mike wouldn't look at Weyuker's face, she noticed. He seemed to stare at Weyuker's socks. Mike had told her everything Weyuker confessed at the hospital. It was strange to see him sitting there, ill at ease, freckled and thin, a man with a wife, and a daughter about to go to college. His toupee was obvious. He worried about mortgages and loans like they did. She thought of him that night only a little over a week ago, sitting in a kitchen chair, just as ill at ease. He did try to protect us, she thought, I believe he honestly did that. Was the soul always so camouflaged? She had seen nothing that night. People didn't wear sin like a bad suit. Moral corruption was more like a wallet kept closely and hidden.

"Massingill called," Mike said.

"I heard from him." Gleason was angrier and more distressed than she had ever seen.

"If Molina gets in touch with him, he'll set up the arrest and bring us in."

Gleason sucked on his cigarette holder. He leaned forward on the cane. "What do you think's happening?"

"Molina's not leaving Santa Maria, if he's anywhere nearby. Not with me and the Tices alive."

"You think so, Weyuker?"

Hands held tightly by the fingertips, like he was preparing to milk them, Weyuker nodded. "He's got to try for it himself. Alves's dead, Rivera didn't make a move on the Tices."

"Where is he?" Gleason looked at Mike.

"Maybe he's taken a hike, I don't know. I'm sure the idea was to go after me and the Tices at the same time. Alves takes me, Rivera takes the Tices. Nothing happened at their end, thank God. So Rivera either ran or he's got to know things are too tough now."

"How will you find him?" she asked.

Gleason moved the cane top in a small circle. "By accident. If he's still with Molina. When he goes back to doing whatever he did before. That's how we usually pick them up. One robbery too many. One stolen car that's spotted."

"The same for Molina, I suppose."

Mike said, "We've got people looking. Massingill's brought the FBI in because technically Molina crossed state lines." He grinned slightly. "We brought him, but he was planning to escape the whole way. We're looking hard."

Gleason thumped the cane once. "I think he's running. He's getting as far away right now as he can."

She felt Mike tense. "No. My sense of Molina is persistence. Sometimes he's violently impulsive. Most of the time he goes after what he wants until he gets it."

"Excuse me, Diane," Weyuker said formally, "could I have a glass of water? I don't think I can get one myself."

"Stay there," Gleason said.

"All right," she said.

They were not allowing him to move. Mike said Dick had been under arrest since the hospital. She wondered if his family knew. In the kitchen she found a clean glass, surrounded in the cupboard by plastic cups and old grape-juice jars washed out and used for Meg. Ice water for Weyuker, she thought, adding ice cubes when she filled the glass. The voices from the living room were muffled. The two policemen sitting at the kitchen table were reading paperback books. One had his legs hooked to the back of his chair, his back hunched over like Matt.

"I'm against it," Gleason said when she came in and gave the water to Weyuker. He thanked her.

She watched him drink it steadily, without pausing for a breath, his throat working until he emptied the glass and the ice fell back with a silver chink. He held the moisture-frosted glass to his forehead.

"Joe, it's a chance to get him. It's the only good chance," Mike said firmly.

"I didn't hear you," she said.

Mike turned from Gleason. "Dick wants to set up Molina. We'll arrest him."

"How do you do that?"

"He'd come for me. Dick'll play along and tell him where we'll be. Molina'll come to kill me."

"Yes," she said. "I guess he will."

"It's a bad idea," Gleason snapped at Weyuker. "I want to keep Mike a hundred miles away." He waved one hand. "I don't care if he's there." He pointed disdainfully at Weyuker. "But, it's got too many soft spots for you, Mike."

"We can go round and round," Mike argued at his best, using that style she'd seen so often and wished now he was bad at, "and it comes back to Dick being on the money. Molina won't get close enough for us to nail him if he thinks I'm not there.

He's got to see me. He's got to think he can take care of me and probably Dick, too."

"Can you talk to him?" she asked Weyuker in surprise.

He rolled the cool moist glass over his forehead and shook his head slowly. "He may contact me. I don't know where he is. Nobody does. It's up to him if he wants to talk. If he wants to meet, if he wants Mike along because he thinks I'd do something like that, then we can work it."

"You would do something like that," Gleason pronounced.

"Di?"

It was Mike and she knew what he would ask.

"Di, if Molina calls Dick, this would be our best shot at him. He can disappear on us and we'll never know when we're safe or when we're not."

It reminded her of the time he told those policemen to pull the door off a bar. It wasn't, he said to her, the best way or the right way even, to get inside. But it was the way they wanted to do it and right under the circumstances. She asked Gleason, "What kind of protection will he have?"

"Diane, I don't approve."

"You have to do it."

Weyuker answered, "Cops nearby. We can wire Mike, wire me. Soon as Molina's with us, we call for backup and arrest him. They can be on him in a couple of seconds."

"He's going to know you're setting him up," Gleason said. He held his cigarette holder toward Mike. He's afraid for him, she thought. We're all afraid. Mike was right to take the chance and end it now.

Mike folded his arms. "Joe, it's like a goddamn undercover buy. Everybody knows everybody else's going to pull something. Narcs always say buys are setups, don't they?" He finally looked at Weyuker.

"They do."

"Molina'll know, but he'll come anyway. He wants something."

Di, listening, understanding, didn't think it was possible to serve justice in a fallen world without touching corruption and betrayal. It was impossible to avoid the things you hate and fear. She said, "You have to try."

Gleason ran a weary hand under his glasses and Weyuker looked at her gratefully.

"Get him back to his office, at his phone," Gleason said. "We'll see what happens today. Maybe it's a waste of time."

Mike crouched near Weyuker. They were talking about what would be said. Let him set the time. Let him pick the place. Quibble with him over details. You can't do it at exactly the time he wants. Argue with him. Say you won't do it. Let him threaten you. Cave in a little, and let him unload the worst he's got. Let him *persuade* you, Mike said. Ask him for money. Tell him it's not enough. Tell him you'll have a gun, you don't care, you won't feel safe. Tell him you'll give Swanson a good story to get him to come along. Change your mind again. Make him work for it.

"I know how to set up one of these things," Weyuker said.

"Yeah, sure, sure," Mike said sheepishly. "I'm just talking." He had his arm around her. It was the wounded arm and he felt heavy, as though leaning on her.

Weyuker handed her back the glass. "Thanks for the chance," he began to them apologetically.

"Shut up," Gleason interrupted. "He's not carrying a weapon if you go," he said to Mike.

"Joe," Mike was about to argue.

"I'm holding you responsible," Gleason said to Weyuker. It was cold, determined, and final.

On his way out, Gleason limped to her. "I'll do anything," he said, taking her hand. He is innocent, she thought, looking at his weary torment. For all his worldly experience, he had never been touched by corruption this way before.

"Thank you," she said.

Then she and Mike were alone.

It was dark enough at last to put the screen up, hanging from a nail on the living room wall, seat the kids in front of it, the cops keenly watching around the house, and set up the 8mm projector. Blue-black darkness, cleft by the white beam, and memories danced on the screen. Meg at six weeks, staring at the camera, Mike holding Matt for his first swim at the river, the tiny legs futilely kicking, Mike's face screwed up as water splashed into his eyes. She saw herself on a bicycle, bright colored, on their vacation to Yosemite, enclosed by forest. The pictures lie, she thought. You could never save people like that, preserving them from harm or fear or despair. The mutating forms and faces in the white light were not memories of what you had, but what you longed for.

When the phone finally rang near eight-thirty, Mike and Lizzie were raking leaves on a dead autumn morning. At least the movies kept Matt and Lizzie actively interested, usually making fun of each other. The policemen grunted at a blurry image.

Mike took the call and he was gone for a while. This is the one, she knew, the one that will change everything again. He came back, standing by the screen, by his younger smiling image, holding up dead, huge leaves like dried spiders by their legs. The edge of the picture brushed his arm, colored, fluid, impermanent.

"We're on," he announced at last.

CHAPTER THIRTY-SIX

Linked together, the towering blue metal almond silos rose like castle battlements, illuminated by security lights that shot speared shadows down them. It was deserted this late at night. Everybody who worked at the processing plant, at the edge of the city, had long ago retreated home, to bars, to crowds.

Swanson drove slowly through the barbed-wire-topped fence gate toward the great silos. Weyuker sat silently beside him. Behind them, in the darkness, were squad cars poised and waiting.

Railroad tracks ran up to loading docks and several empty cars sat on the siding.

"I didn't know you could just drive in," he said.

"Shit. Who's going to steal a couple thousand tons of almonds?"

Swanson turned left slightly, his headlights flicked off. "Point us back toward the street?"

"Yeah, so he can see the headlights," Weyuker answered. "Park off near the dock, it's dark enough."

He backed the car meticulously into the dark oblong between the loading docks and the low, long tin-sided warehouse. It helped allay his nervousness to concentrate on such a simple task, easing the car with small turns, minute pressure on the gas, braking a little. "This's a great place," he said, finally bringing the car to a stop.

"Molina liked it. Out of the way, quiet, he thinks it's great."

Swanson flipped the ignition key, the engine died and they sat in silence. He was uncomfortably aware of the Fargo unit under his shirt, the tiny microphone just above his heart. He had never worn one before. It was like a leech had attached itself to him, the slight weight of the battery taped to his upper chest. They were listening to him and Weyuker, who also wore one, someplace there in the night. "He can't spot them? I mean, you didn't see anything when we drove in?"

Weyuker opened his door. "They're squared away about as good as you can."

"Maybe they're not there," he joked.

"Don't worry about it."

"What're you doing?"

"Take a quick look around while we got a second, make sure everything's okay."

Self-consciously, Swanson said out loud, "Weyuker's going to check the area. No problem. I can see him."

He watched Weyuker walk a little tensely to the concrete and steel loading docks, barren in the frozen glare under their security lights. Weyuker stepped between the rails just in front of the docks and hopped up onto the concrete platform, as though onstage ready to declaim, a provincial actor in an ill-fitting wig. He looked carefully along the docks, then around them, Swanson watching him examine a steel-shuttered entrance, handling the heavy padlock. Weyuker had on his light tan sport coat, yellow tie, brown slacks. Sometimes he didn't look like he'd been a cop for eighteen years. He looked like a shoe salesman.

Dick Weyuker, who I've known and trusted, Swanson thought. It was hard to reconcile the man gingerly and dutifully going about his job on the loading dock with the weeping, mortified figure confessing last night at the hospital. Everybody deserves a chance to redeem himself, Swanson thought. Maybe he needs it more than most.

"I'd like to hum a little tune," he said aloud in the empty car. He had a desire to say anything crazy, knowing he was wired. He was frightened and excited.

Weyuker, pale, unsettled, came back and got in. He left his door open, one foot dangling out. It was utterly dead around them, isolated and static.

"All clear, far as I can tell," Weyuker said, eyes searching down toward the street.

"They don't even have a security guard," Swanson said.

Who would want all those high-storied towers of almonds? You couldn't steal railroad tracks, either, or the dull buildings around them.

"Hell of a deal," Weyuker said without energy.

"I hope he's on time. Jesus, I don't want to sit here waiting for him." He looked at his watch. It was hard to read. "What time you got?"

"About five minutes, maybe."

"You think he's going to be on time?"

"I never call these deals, Mike. He's going to do what he's going to do."

Swanson let his arm hang out the window. He had his coat open, his gun toward the door in its waistband holster.

"Joe, all I want are deuce trials after this," Swanson said aloud, knowing Gleason listened somewhere in the impenetrable darkness with the waiting and watching cops. "This's worse than getting a verdict."

Weyuker scuffed his shoe in the gravel.

"What do you guys do while you wait?" Swanson asked.

"We just wait."

"Christ."

"I been sitting doing this long enough to take it easy." But his pallor was worse, and Swanson knew Weyuker's hope of putting everything right again was slipping further away each minute.

"Somebody's coming." Weyuker suddenly tensed, leg stilled.

Swanson looked quickly. In the black void between the partly lit street and the bright dock beside them, a car, headlights off, rolled in and gradually slowed to a stop. He imagined the man sitting behind the wheel, staring back, ferocity momentarily contained. He's come to kill me, Swanson thought. It's the only reason he's exposed himself.

"Right on time," he said.

Weyuker moved his head, looking, searching.

"Signaling," Swanson said, flashing his headlights twice. The unseen car responded immediately, two answered flashes, like white eyes blinking in a vast, dark face.

"Get him away from the car," Weyuker whispered. "Let him get away from it."

They both heard a car door open, slam, and the alternating rustle of gravel and weeds as footsteps passed through them.

"It's okay, it's okay," Swanson said briskly. "No problems, see what he's doing." They had calculated Molina would come close, put Weyuker at ease rather than shoot from a distance and risk missing. Swanson wanted him as relaxed, feeling as secure as possible, before springing the trap behind him.

On an impulse, Swanson took his gun from its holster. He held it out to Weyuker. "I never got the hang of shooting. Someday I'm going to have to practice, get good at it," he said for the listeners. Weyuker, as Gleason had insisted, was unarmed.

Weyuker looked at him and took the gun, slipping it into his coat pocket.

Keeping his voice steady, Swanson said, "Coming toward us. We're getting out." He let Weyuker advance a few steps in front of him. It's out of my hands, he thought. Whatever happens, he's got a chance to make up for Angie and the others, and for my family. Only one of us can have the chance.

They walked between two looming red-brown boxcars. In a second, Swanson would see him, stepping into the magic circle of light.

"Okay, like you guys stop. Don't move no more." The voice out of the darkness was edgy, flustered. It was not Molina's voice.

Swanson stopped, whispering urgently, "It's not him, it's not him. Don't do anything."

Weyuker swore suddenly. Almost beside them, fidgeting, looking around with quick, jerky glances was the big guy, Rivera. He made a nervous popping sound with his mouth.

"Where's Molina?" Swanson demanded, as Rivera half-circled him and Weyuker.

"Hey, shut the fuck up." Then, nervously, to Weyuker, "He got a gun?"

Weyuker shook his head.

"You got one?"

Weyuker nodded. He controlled himself with effort.

Rivera turned and swung his arm up in a large circle. He did it twice. Once more Swanson heard a car door open in the darkness. He hoped that the cops, who saw and heard everything, wouldn't try to break in now. He and Weyuker were out in the open, directly in front of two armed men.

"The deal's for Molina," Swanson said, trying to sound upset. "You turning yourself in?"

"Fuck the deal." Molina abruptly was with them, dressed casually in slacks and a safari jacket, jaunty and full of vigor.

"I got a gun," Weyuker finally said.

"Sure you do," Molina said. "Cops always got guns."

"Massingill won't take you back if anything happens." Swanson knew his fear sounded real. He didn't know what to do, where to move, how to get away.

"I want to talk to you about that," Molina said. He looked toward the concrete-sided end of the rail spur a few feet away. "Let's go over there and take care of our business." He pointed. "I got business for all of us."

Jesus, the rail spur was below ground level. The cops can't see us there. What's Dick doing? Weyuker had his gun out and the movement made Rivera tremble, a hand hesitantly pressed to his own coat until Molina cautioned him. Rivera's obvious giddiness contrasted with Molina's bouncy good spirits. He's worse than me, Swanson thought. The urge to shout for help, to bring down all the cars and men waiting for his call, roared over him as they walked. He barely heard Rivera's nervous complaints, lagging a little behind Weyuker, trying to get Molina to let him leave. The hope that Molina actually had a deal to pro-pose came to Swanson even as he saw the trap in thinking it. Molina promised grandly, rewarded greatly, used hope.

"I'm going to lay it all out." Molina spoke sharply to Rivera, "And you're here. You stay with me."

Rivera complied, maybe not the fierce figure everyone painted. It was as though he grew less without the animating ferocity of little Alves. Who I killed, Swanson thought with a flush of imbecile vanity. Maybe he's scared of me.

"I'll stay at the car, we're ready to go, we go whenever you want, you just say it." Rivera patted around for his gun again, right behind Weyuker so Molina had to turn a little to talk to him.

"I said you stay with me." Molina said it with finality.

They were at the spur, everyone tense now, even Molina. Call for help, before they went down there? No time to hide if he did; either he or Dick would be hurt. Wait, wait a little more, something will happen.

Weyuker *wants* to go down there, Swanson thought, startled. He doesn't want to be seen.

"Dick—" he began, Molina alongside him.

"I know what I'm doing," Weyuker said.

"Jump," Molina said.

"We can talk up here," Swanson said.

"I feel better we get out of the open. You're going to be in-terested, you listen, I guarantee it."

Swanson took a breath and leaped down four feet into the rail spur, a stone grave enclosed on three sides. Molina jumped after him.

Weyuker sat down on the edge of the concrete, sliding down almost daintily. The gun was pointed at Swanson. A triangle of light fell over them. Above, Rivera hesitated, his large body shifting, one foot to the other. "I'll watch here, okay? I'll check it out."

"Yeah, you check it out," Molina said, rolling his eyes just a little for Weyuker to show he knew how inept Rivera was.

He thinks Weyuker's played me completely and I don't know what's going on. He thinks he's got it all set. Swanson could only see a short distance down the track, which vanished into blackness beyond the security lights. What have I done, he thought frantically.

Weyuker hadn't lowered his gun. He was still pointing it at Swanson and looking at Molina.

"What's going on?" Swanson demanded. "You can't change your mind. You got to give it up."

"I'm not going back to Massingill's bullshit. That's dead, dead and gone."

"What're we doing?"

"How about we all come out with something? Put the gun down, we're talking now," he said jovially to Weyuker. "No, go ahead. I want you to see the thing like it should be," and Weyuker slowly, with the weight of a great engine in his arm, lowered it. Turning back to Swanson, Molina went on, "He's with me, okay? See, it can be done. I can do it for you. Fuck, I bought Massingill. It's done, that's the kind of deal I can make for you."

"You never bought Massingill."

Molina shrugged, "I could've. You don't think so? What's so fucking great about him? Or you? Or this guy? We're going to do great things, you want to help yourself. A cop, a D.A., we could do some really big things. You believe me?" The words and tone were persuasive, yet it sounded to Swanson as if Molina were imitating someone, repeating a pitch he had heard before.

Rivera broke in. "Okay, Hector, I'm going to the car, okay? Get it started, okay? I got to go to the car, get it ready, okay?"

"Shit, go to the car, wait for me," Molina snapped back, the scarred and pitted face finally set impatiently. It was a lie, what he had said, to make them both relax. Or perhaps Molina simply enjoyed using them one more time before killing them.

Rivera moved away from the razor line dividing the concrete and sky above them. His footsteps were quick, anxiously retreating. Now it was only three of them and Weyuker already had a gun out.

"So, what? You like that? You know we can do it, I can make

you guys very big. You do whatever you want." He moved his hand toward his coat.

Swanson said, "You're busted, Hector. You're busted right now." In that moment, Molina's expression was startled. Swanson lunged forward, Molina driven backward and down onto the rails. He didn't, in the next tumultuous moment, separate the approaching sirens or the red-blue lights reflected off the loading dock from the way Molina struck at him or a violent blow from somewhere at his back that threw him to one side. Molina shouted. Swanson saw Weyuker's gun being pointed and fired; a miniature star flared, and died. Swanson was pressed against the unyielding cold concrete even as the gun fired again. He heard cars braking harshly and Gleason's hoarse cry for him.

Molina's profile was fixed for an instant, hands flung upward toward his throat as Weyuker shot. Red mist rushed to Molina's fingertips. Swanson scrambled, pushing backward along the wall and Weyuker fired again. Echoed, sharp and gracelessly by the concrete, the shots followed him; his feet slipped, slid along a steel rail.

A rustle was all he heard of Molina's half-twisting roll to the grass between the rail ties. Swanson jumped up. Weyuker was already bent over the face-up body. Hands patted the safari jacket rudely, roughly.

"Don't shoot! Don't shoot!" Swanson held his arms in the air, waving wildly as hard, cold lights converged on the spur, firing it shadowless. Gleason called down to him. "I'm okay, Joe. Molina's dead. We're okay," he called back.

He turned as the cops started into the spur, voices roiling all around him. Weyuker retrieved his own gun from Molina's jacket letting Swanson's fall to the ground.

"The son of a bitch," Weyuker said, choked and shaking, "the goddamn son of a bitch."

"Drop it!" an anonymous voice shouted from above them.

"I got it, I got it," Swanson said, taking Weyuker's shoulder. "Let it go, Dick, let it go."

Weyuker, face contorted and without contours in the hard,

blinding light, opened his fingers reluctantly, and his gun slipped off.

"Mike, come out, they're going to give you a hand," Gleason said nearby. Swanson couldn't see him, only made out a dark shape behind the light.

One of Molina's legs was bent at the knee so that it was propped up, like he was lying back, admiring the stars. The crooked leg slowly fell. Three cops were in the spur, taking Weyuker, checking Molina. Swanson knew they were walking, but he only heard Weyuker asking raggedly, "You going to help me?"

Help me. The endless plea. "I'll stay with you. I'll tell them what happened, what he was going to do," Swanson answered. They were out of the spur, beside the loading dock, in the midst of squad cars and cops. The cars were ranged paradoxically, at angles, randomly, cops swarming.

Weyuker was pulled forward by the shoulders, into the center of the seething assembly. He stared back, for a moment, at Swanson. Then he was gone, into one of the cars, a siren whooping suddenly.

Swanson trembled, fought it, lost. Gleason was with him. What happened? How did Weyuker get a gun? Who fired first? Why did you wait so long? The questions were those of a relieved, panicked parent. Gleason's head shook in confusion.

"It was a fair fight," Swanson said finally, carving one certainty out of the noise, brightness, and disorder around him.

Chapter Thirty-seven

"Thanks for coming." Weyuker spoke softly, back against the holding-cell wall, eyes over Swanson, head cocked upward like the poised hammer of a gun.

"I came for Dufresne or Narloch, I come for you." Swanson remained at the cell door. He was aware of a great deal of subterranean commotion in the downtown main jail, men rushing excitedly, war stories already being passed.

Weyuker, the collar of his shoe salesman's outfit open, shut his eyes quickly. "Okay," he said.

"What do you want?"

He walked slowly from the wall to Swanson. He trembled a little, his face was reddened. He held out a small piece of paper. "Give it to Sarah. You don't have to tell her where it came from."

Swanson took the paper and opened it. A series of numbers, in two rows, were neatly written on it along with a bank's name. "How much?"

"Enough to take care of everything."

"She'll know it didn't come from the tooth fairy. It's not yours anyway."

"I earned it," Weyuker's mirthless smile vanished as soon as it appeared.

"You think she'd take it?"

Weyuker shrugged roughly.

"You give it to her." Swanson handed back the paper. He ran a shaking, furious hand through his hair.

Weyuker tore the paper into small bits and let them fall to the concrete floor. There was nothing at all in the holding cell, only a briny drain in the center of the floor, now flecked with white specks of paper. "Now it's nobody's."

"Anything else?"

"I'm scared."

"So am I."

"I bet I beat you."

Swanson moved back from the cell door. The ostensible point of being there was gone, torn up and discarded. But Weyuker still faced him through the bars, across a gulf neither of them could ever span. "I thought I knew you," he said. "I mean, we worked together for years, Dick, days together. This whole case together."

"Nobody knows anybody. You know your wife? Your kids? You know what they're thinking?"

"Sometimes. More now than I did before."

With a dry retching sound, from deep inside, Weyuker turned and moved to the farthest side of the cell. He had a feebleness, both outwardly and inwardly, as though blasted by the heat of an improbably bright star, leaving a husk. Swanson even, at last, felt pity. Weyuker didn't look at him. "It kind of creeps up on you, little bit at a time, and then someone comes along and that's all it takes. For a long time, I swear, it was like I hadn't done anything, like it happened to somebody else."

Swanson understood the feeling. Since killing Alves the night before and seeing Molina die, he thought of himself standing beside himself. He had not yet brought the events into his heart. Gently, he touched his wounded arm. Something had gotten pulled during the excitement and hurt. "Nothing looks the same, you know what I mean? No case's going to. They won't be any fun anymore."

Now Weyuker shook his head. "That's the difference between you and me, Mike, always. It's a game, you think." He shook his head back and forth, a sick animal in pain. "It's not a game."

"I know."

"So it wasn't a total waste."

The outer door clattered, opened abruptly behind Swanson. He started at the intrusion. A deputy sheriff marched in, keys clanging, joylessly efficient. Two more deputies waited. "Got to move him." The deputy unlocked the door.

"Second time tonight," Weyuker said as he was handcuffed again. "I'm getting good at this."

He was brought out to Swanson and they all walked in a bunched, senseless mass. "Thank Di, would you? She's something, you better know it."

"I do."

"Somebody would've made a deal with him again. Sometime, they would've." Weyuker lapsed into their mutual preoccupation without naming Molina at first. "He had too much we wanted."

"Maybe."

"You know it would've happened."

"He's not the point anymore."

"Man, Mike, we got on the little end of things." Weyuker's voice had become quavery, old. "You know what they call a guy who kills his best friend to get ahead, kills his wife, turns in all his friends, bribes, lies?"

"He's not the point," Swanson repeated furiously.

"They'd say Molina was a great man. He's a great man." Weyuker's blind cynicism rose over him like a shroud.

Swanson was going to rebuke him as they got to the next door, but hung back, gave up, when at that same moment, Weyuker turned to him, speaking across the abyss.

"I'm scared," Weyuker said, the door opening for him.

CHAPTER THIRTY-EIGHT

It went on being an unpredictable spring, by turns too hot or cold, too wet or dry, always searching for equilibrium. On a hot day, Swanson and Di sat in the bleachers at Southside High School while Matt's team played soccer on the green field. The blue-and-pink figures, crying to each other, a checked ball flung into the air from one player to the other, had gallant, promising spiritedness. Swanson patted Lizzie's hand, but she shrugged it off, intently watching the game. Other parents and children crowded the weathered bleachers, and like he and Di, broke into resonant cheers whenever a goal was made. It was near the end of the game.

He moved his hand lightly to Di's temple, wiping off a small drop of sweat. She glanced at him wryly, and cheered again. Swanson saw his son dexterously move the ball past defenders. At Di's side, Meg held a cup of warming lemonade in both hands, sipping from it, watching over the rim with grave concentration.

In Molina's safari jacket they found a motel-room key and arrested a young woman, who turned out to be the sister of Ralph Orepeza. She was vituperative, vile, but in searching the room, they found towels from another motel in Stockton and notes that cleared a homicide involving an expatriate Iranian general and his impatient children.

Swanson asked the woman behind him not to kick the bleacher so enthusiastically. The referee, white and pink and tiny on the field, shrilly whistled, arm in the air, and the ball came to him. Both teams faced each other in suspended aggression. The ball fell, and the two teams rushed in, their shouts splintered and full. He lost sight of Matt in the roiling players.

As far as anyone could tell, Joe had been hurt by the news stories that followed Molina's death and Weyuker's publicized arrest. How badly hurt was uncertain, but he was already talking to his old campaign treasurer about the election. No one doubted he would run. Swanson had honored his bargain with Narloch, even though his testimony was unnecessary now. A plea was scheduled from him in a week. In a perfect world, Narloch would in fact serve his life in prison.

Dick Weyuker's case had been assigned to someone else in Special Investigations. Swanson rubbed his forearm over his cheek, drawing damply. He was a witness and could not, even if he wished, prosecute. He had no wish to anyway.

The cheers crashed and rolled from the bleachers as another goal was made, the players below spreading outward on the green field like blue-and-pink smoke. Finally Angie's father and the Tices could find some measure of peace, even if they knew how imperfect justice was.

He saw Matt trotting with his team. Swanson blinked against the afternoon sun. He knew where his skepticism and Di's faith intersected. It was in the certainty that evil always corrupted and the way from that corruption was rarely unstained. Evil played by purposeful rules, just as justice had to. It was a counsel of despair and cynicism to find the one and not the other.

It was worth telling Matt, and Meg, and Lizzie when they were all older and the world began pressing its scornful and brutal history on them.

He would never have survived without Di. He hadn't the strength or foresight to keep the family together, either. Together they were a constant counterweight to Molina's selfish cruelty which destroyed every other family he came near. Di brought them home from the motel. She stopped his drinking when he would have let something like Weyuker's hopelessness drag them all down. She saved his life when Alves attacked.

It was Di's strength that made coming out after Molina's death worthwhile.

Another cheer rose up, and then the people around them stood, cheerfully bickering and teasing. One of the blue-and-pink players broke from the others and jogged toward the bleachers. Lizzie went to meet Matt. She seemed to brood, but that would end when she was back in school next week. He counted her steps as she began a slow decline on the bleachers, her feet barely touching each separate bench, threading her way between the departing parents and children.

Di looked at him. Her hair was combed loosely, her face full of genuine animation. People moved sluggishly past them. "We won," she said with pleasure.

"Yeah." He thought for a short time. "I guess we did."

THE PIPER.

He terrified an entire city. Then he vanished.

No one has heard from him in years.

But now he's back.

And **HE'S KIDNAPPED YOUR SON.**

Turn the page for an advance look at an
exciting new thriller:

PAYING THE PIPER

By

Simon Wood

Coming November 2007

CHAPTER ONE

Scott leaned on his horn and roared through the red light. Six lanes of traffic on Van Ness with the green light on their side lurched forward then slithered to a halt in the same breath. A barrage of blaring car horns trailed after him.

Geary Boulevard rose up on the other side of the intersection. Scott tightened his grip on the wheel and braced for the jarring impact. His Honda sedan bottomed out on the steep incline, but maintained its speed. With the gas pedal floored, the car accelerated and closed in on a slow moving SUV switching lanes. Scott jumped on his horn again. The SUV froze, straddling both lanes to block his path.

"Idiot," he snarled and shouldered his way past the other driver.

Traffic was everywhere, but when wasn't it in San Francisco? He weaved between two cars, jerked out from behind a MUNI bus and still had a stream of vehicles ahead.

His cell phone rang. He snatched it from its holder on the dashboard. "Yes."

"Scott, where are you?" Jane squeezed out between sobs. "You said you'd be here."

Hearing his wife cry split him in two. His own tears welled, but he bottled them for later. He needed to be strong. If he let this overwhelm him, then what good was he to his family?

"I'm nearly there." His hoarse voice cracked in the middle of his short reply.

"Just hurry."

"I am."

He hung up and tossed the phone on the passenger seat next to him.

How could his life have changed so irrevocably? Just twenty minutes ago, he'd been living a normal life. A good life. He was a reporter for the *San Francisco Independent*. He and Jane had a loving marriage—a miracle in this day and age. They owned a house in a good neighborhood in the city, even with its insane real estate prices. It was the perfect place to bring up kids—and they did. They had two great kids.

Had two great kids.

It had only taken a moment to lose one of his children. Some sick freak had snatched him out from under them. How could that happen? He and Jane took every precaution. They'd entrusted their children to a good school—the best they could afford with their two incomes. They'd gone private to prevent this kind of thing from happening. He palmed away the tears clouding his vision and swerved around a UPS truck.

He felt the guilt spreading through him like a virus, attacking his heart and eating away at his spirit. He'd failed his son, Sammy. Abduction was a parent's worst fear, but he hadn't wanted to be one of those parents who saw phantoms on every street corner. Putting bars on the windows and deadbolts on the doors didn't keep them out, it kept you in. But that cavalier attitude had led to this. His worst fears had been realized. Someone had taken his son.

"I'm sorry, Sammy."

A new sensation swept away his guilt. Imagination, strong and invincible, assaulted him. He'd always been able to conjure up images from secondhand accounts. That's what made him such a good reporter. He didn't just relay facts. He told stories—

living, breathing stories. He turned readers into eyewitnesses—transporting them to the actual locations, inserting them inside the people present at the celebration or the tragedy. Now that talent turned on him. From the meager facts available, Scott constructed a nightmare. Sammy appeared to him, his smiling face melting into a scream as the abductor dragged him kicking and screaming inside a van. His imagination blinded him with these false, but true, images. The abduction was true, but the events were lies, just images his fear conjured up. He would know nothing until he reached the school. He stabbed down on the gas again and frightened a hybrid hatchback out of his way.

At the cost of a door mirror snapped off against the corner of a Safeway trailer truck, he made it to the school. Half a dozen SFPD cars were staked out in front. Was that all his son warranted—six patrol cars? Not that these cops were any good now. Talk about closing the stable door after the horse had bolted. Where were these bastards when Sammy was being snatched?

He ground to an untidy halt in front of the cop cars and abandoned his Honda in the roadway. Let the city tow it. He spilled out onto the asphalt, gathered himself up and raced toward the school gate. He hadn't gotten ten feet when his cell rang. He darted back and snatched it off the car seat. He hit the green key on the run.

His antics drew the attention of two uniformed officers protecting the school's perimeter. Seeing him charging toward the school gates, they moved as a unit to intercept him.

Scott put the phone to his ear, "I'm here, babe. It's okay. I'm here."

"That's good to know."

The voice on the line chilled him. Instead of his wife's soft tones, he heard a voice that was harsh, blunted by an electronic disguise. The words came out robotic and demonic. Scott recognized the voice, but he hadn't heard it in eight years. The raw adrenaline left him as swiftly as it had come and he ground to a halt with the cops still racing toward him.

"It's been a long time, Scott. I thought I'd reintroduce myself."

"You've got Sammy." It was a statement, not a question.

"Yes."

Scott feared asking the obvious question, but there was no way around it. "What do you want?"

The cops caught up to him. They bombarded him with questions and threats. He ignored them. He listened to the distorted voice on the line until it hung up.

He lowered the phone. A wave of nausea swept over him, taking his legs out from under him. The two cops caught him before he hit the ground.

"He has my son." Misery clung to his words. "The Piper has my son."

"Jesus Christ," one of the cops said.

SIMON WOOD

PAYING THE PIPER

He was known as the Piper—a coldhearted kidnapper who terrified the city. Crime reporter Scott Fleetwood built his career on the Piper. The kidnapper even taunted the FBI through Scott's column. But Scott had been duped. The person he'd been speaking to wasn't really the Piper. By the time the FBI exposed the hoaxer, time ran out...and the real Piper killed the child. Then he vanished. But now he's back, with very specific targets in mind—Scott's children.

ISBN 10: 0-8439-5980-0
ISBN 13: 978-0-8439-5980-2

To order a book or to request a catalog call:
1-800-481-9191
This book is also available at your local bookstore, or you can check out our Web site **www.dorchesterpub.com** where you can look up your favorite authors, read excerpts, or glance at our discussion forum to see what people have to say about your favorite books.

CAILTIN ROTHER

NAKED ADDICTION

A ticket to Homicide.

That was the first thing disgruntled narcotics detective Ken Goode thought when he found the body of a beautiful murdered woman. But his transfer became the last thing on his mind when more victims turned up—all linked to the same beauty school his sister attends. With time running out, a killer on the loose, and the danger hitting too close to home, Goode has to stop this murderer while fighting his own growing obsession with one of the very women he's trying to save.

ISBN 10: 0-8439-5995-9
ISBN 13: 978-0-8439-5995-6

To order a book or to request a catalog call:
1-800-481-9191
This book is also available at your local bookstore, or you can check out our Web site **www.dorchesterpub.com** where you can look up your favorite authors, read excerpts, or glance at our discussion forum to see what people have to say about your favorite books.

WHAT MIND CONTROL
HAS DONE FOR OTHERS...

—A marketing company used it and created 18 new products.

—14 Chicago White Sox players used it and boosted their scores.

—Performing artists Vicki Carr, Carol Lawrence, and Loretta Swit have spoken about what Mind Control has done for them.

—Colleges and universities have used it to help students study less but learn more.

...MIND CONTROL
CAN DO FOR YOU!

"When persons learn to function mentally at this deeper level, creativity is enhanced. Memory is improved and persons are better able to solve problems."

—Clancy D. McKenzie, M.D., Director,
Philadelphia Psychiatric Consulting Service

"Highly recommended."

—*Spiritual Studies Center Newsletter*

THE SILVA MIND CONTROL METHOD

JOSÉ SILVA
AND PHILIP MIELE

PUBLISHED BY POCKET BOOKS NEW YORK

POCKET BOOKS, a Simon & Schuster division of
GULF & WESTERN CORPORATION
1230 Avenue of the Americas, New York, N.Y. 10020

Copyright © 1977 by José Silva

Published by arrangement with Simon and Schuster
Library of Congress Catalog Card Number: 77-1050

All rights reserved, including the right to reproduce
this book or portions thereof in any form whatsoever.
For information address Simon and Schuster, 1230
Avenue of the Americas, New York, N.Y. 10020

ISBN: 0-671-43343-1

First Pocket Books printing July, 1978

15   14   13   12   11   10   9   8

POCKET and colophon are trademarks of Simon & Schuster.

Printed in the U.S.A.

ACKNOWLEDGMENTS

The authors have benefited from the wise and generous help of more friends, associates, and disinterested critics than they can ever hope to acknowledge fully. A few of them are: Marcelino Alcala, Ruth Aley, Manuel Lujan Anton, Dr. Stephen Applebaum, Robert Barnes, M.D., Joahanne Blodgett, Larry Blyden, Dr. Fred J. Bremner, Maria Luisa Bruque, Vicki Carr, Dr. Philip Chancellor, Dr. Jeffrey Chang, Dr. Erwin Di Cyan, Dr. George De Sau, Alfredo Duarte, Stanley Feller, M.D., Dord Fitz, Richard Floyd, Paul Fansella, Fermin de la Garza, Ray Glau, Pat Golbitz, Alexandro Gonzales, Reynaldo Gonzales, Father Albert Gorayeb, Ronald Gorayeb, Paul Grivas, Sister Michele Guerin, Blaz Gutierrez, Emilio Guzman, Dr. J. Wilfred Hahn, Timothy Harvey, James Hearn, Richard Herro, Larry Hildore, Celeste Holm, Joanne Howell, Margaret Huddleston, Adele Hull, Chris Jensen, Umberto Juarez, Carol Lawrence, Fred Levin, Kate Lombardi, Dorothy Longoria, Alice and Harry McKnight, Dick Mazza, Clancy D. McKenzie, M.D., Dr. James Motiff, Jose Moubayed, Jim Needham, Wingate Paine, Marguerite Piazza, Eduardo Moniz Resende, Rosa Argentina Rivas, Jose Romero, Alberto Sanchez Vilchis, M.D., Gerald Seadey, Nelda Sheets, Alexis Smith, Loretta Swit, Pat Teague, Dr. Andre Weitzenhoffer, Dr. N. E. West, Jim Williams, Lance S. Wright, M.D.

DEDICATION

To my wife, Paula, my sister, Josefina, my brother, Juan, and all my sons and daughters: José Silva, Jr., Isabel Silva de Las Fuentes, Ricardo Silva, Margarita Silva Cantu, Tony Silva, Ana Maria Silva Martinez, Hilda Silva Gonzalez, Laura Silva Lares, Delia Silva and Diana Silva.

JOSÉ SILVA

To Marjorie Miele and Grace and Bill Owen.

PHILIP MIELE

CONTENTS

INTRODUCTION

You are now setting out on one of the most transforming adventures of your life. Each result you achieve will change your view of yourself and of the world you were born into. With your new powers will come a responsibility to use them "for the betterment of mankind"— a Mind Control phrase. You cannot use them otherwise, as you are about to learn.

The city planner of a Western city closed his office door, leaving his secretary alone and troubled at her desk. The drawings for a proposed shopping mall were missing, and a yes-or-no meeting with city officials was scheduled for later that same week. Jobs have been lost for less, but the planner seemed almost untouched by what would have driven other bosses into a secretary-shattering storm.

He sat at his desk. In a moment his eyes closed and he became still and quiet. Anyone might have thought he was composing himself in the face of disaster.

A full ten minutes later he opened his eyes, rose slowly, and walked outside to his secretary. "I think I've found them," he said calmly. "Let's look at my expense account for last Thursday, when I was in Hartford. What restaurant did I have dinner in?"

11

He telephoned the restaurant. The drawings were there.

The city planner had been trained in Silva Mind Control, to awaken what for most of us are unused talents of the mind. One of the things he learned was to retrieve memories that have been squirreled away where the untrained mind cannot find them.

These awakened talents are doing amazing things for the more than 500,000 men and women who have taken the course.

What exactly was the city planner doing when he sat quietly for ten minutes? A report from another Mind Control graduate provides a hint:

"I had an incredible experience yesterday in Bermuda. I had two hours to get on the plane back to New York and couldn't find my plane ticket anywhere. For almost an hour, three of us searched the apartment where I'd been staying. We looked under carpets, behind the refrigerator—everywhere. I even unpacked and packed my suitcase three times, but no ticket was found. Finally I decided to find myself a quiet corner and enter my level. No sooner was I at my level than I could 'see' my plane ticket as clearly as if I were actually looking at it. It was (according to my 'level' sight) in the bottom of a closet tucked in between some books, hardly noticeable. I rushed to the closet and there was the ticket, just as I had imagined it!"

To those not trained in Mind Control, this sounds incredible, but when you come to the chapters by José Silva, Mind Control's founder, you will learn of even more amazing powers of your own mind. Perhaps most amazing of all is how easily and quickly you can learn.

Mr. Silva has devoted most of his adult life to research into what our minds can be trained to do. The result is a 40-to-48-hour course that can train anyone to remember what appears to be forgotten, to control pain, to speed healing, to abandon unwanted habits, to spark intuition so that the sixth sense becomes a creative, problem-solving part of daily life. With all this comes a cheerful inner peace, a quiet optimism based on first-hand evidence that we are more in control of our lives than we ever imagined.

Now for the first time through the printed word you can learn to practice much of what is taught in the course.

Mr. Silva has borrowed freely from both Eastern and Western learning, but the end product is quintessentially American. The course, like its founder, is totally practical. Everything he teaches is designed to help you live more happily, more effectively, here and now.

As you proceed from one exercise to another in the chapters by Mr. Silva, you will pile one success on top of another and so strengthen your confidence in yourself that you will be ready for achievements which, assuming you are not acquainted with Mind Control, you now regard as impossible. But there is scientific proof that your mind is capable of miracles. In addition, there is the successful experience of more than a half-million people whose lives Mind Control has changed.

Imagine using your mind to improve your eyesight. "While taking my first course in Silva Mind Control Method, I began to notice that my eyes were changing —seemed stronger. Prior to this I'd worn glasses ten years through childhood (till I graduated), then again started when I was thirty-eight. Always my left eye was said to be three times the weaker of the two.

"My first glasses in 1945 were reading glasses, but in '48 or '49 I began wearing bifocals—correcting always to stronger. After the course I found that, while I could not read without glasses, my eyes were certainly stronger. Since they were changing so fast, I waited as long as possible before having them checked. I even reverted to twenty-year-old glasses.

"When the local optometrist tested my eyes, he agreed that the old pair would do much better until the new lenses came."

This may seem mysterious to you now, but when you read Chapter 10 you will see exactly how graduates put their minds in charge of their bodies to speed up natural healing. The techniques are amazingly simple, as you will see in the following letter from a woman who lost 26 unwanted pounds in four months:

"First I visualized a dark frame and saw a table loaded with ice cream, cake, etc.—all the things I knew put the pounds on. I drew a large red X through the table and saw myself in a mirror that made me look very wide (the kind you find in a carnival fun house). Next I visualized a scene surrounded by golden light: a table on which all the high-protein foods rested—tuna fish, eggs, lean meat. I placed a large golden check mark on this scene and saw myself in a mirror looking very tall and thin. Mentally I told myself that I craved only the foods on the protein-laden table. I also heard all my friends telling me how fantastic I looked and saw all this happening on a specific date (this was the most important step, because I set a goal for myself). And I made it! Having been a chronic dieter, I find this the only method that has worked."

This is Mind Control—going to a deep meditative level where you can train your own mind to take charge, using its own language of images reinforced with words, bringing results that become more and more amazing, with no end in sight for the person who keeps in practice.

As you can see, this is no ordinary book. It will take you in easy steps first into meditation, then into the many ways you can use meditation until, when you reach the final step, you can do routinely what most people firmly believe cannot be done.

It is a book within a book. The outside book (chapters 1 and 2 and 17 through 20), by Philip Miele, describes the almost explosive growth of Mind Control and how it has benefited many thousands of its graduates. In the inside book, Mr. Silva shares with you many of the techniques taught in Mind Control classes. Because these classes are group experiences led by skilled lecturers, their results are speedier and more spectacular than you will achieve working alone. However, if you follow Mr. Silva's directions carefully and practice the exercises, the results are virtually certain to transform your life for the better—not as speedily, but just as certainly.

There is a special way to read this book: first read it as you would any other, from beginning to end. However, during your first reading, do not begin to practice any of the exercises. Then reread chapters 3 to 14 to get an even clearer, overall picture of the roads you are about to travel. Next read Chapter 3 and practice the exercises in it—and only those exercises—for a few weeks. When you know you are ready, go on to Chapter 4, and so on.

When you reach Chapter 14 you will already be an experienced practitioner of much that Mind Control graduates have learned. To further enrich your experience, you may wish to form a small group of friends who have practiced the same exercises. Chapter 13 tells you how to do this.

CHAPTER ONE

USING MORE OF YOUR MIND
IN SPECIAL WAYS

Imagine coming into direct, working contact with an all-pervading higher intelligence and learning in a moment of numinous joy that it is on your side. Imagine too that you made this contact in such simple ways that for the rest of your life you need never again feel helplessly out of touch with something you always suspected was there but could never quite reach—a helpful wisdom, a flash of insight when you need it, the feeling of a loving, powerful presence. How would it feel?

It would be a peak experience not too different—perhaps not different at all—from spiritual awe.

This is what it feels like after four days of Silva Mind Control training. So far, more than a half-million people know; they have been through it. And as they become more accustomed to using the methods that produce this feeling they settle down into a calm, self-confident use of new powers and energies, their lives richer, healthier, freer of problems.

Shortly José Silva will explain some of these methods so that you will be able to start using them yourself. First let's look in on the beginning of a Mind Control class and see what takes place.

To start off, there is an introductory lecture of about an hour and twenty minutes. The lecturer defines Mind Control and outlines the two decades of research that led to its development. Then, briefly, he describes ways the students will be able to apply what they learn in improving health, solving everyday problems, learning more easily, and deepening spiritual awareness. A twenty-minute break follows.

Over coffee the students become acquainted. They are from widely varying backgrounds. Physicians, secretaries, teachers, taxi drivers, housewives, high-school and college students, psychiatrists, religious leaders, retired people—this is a typical mix.

After the break there is another hour-and-twenty-minute session beginning with some questions and answers, then down to business with the first training exercise, which will lead to a meditative level of mind. The lecturer explains that this is a state of deep relaxation, deeper than in sleep itself but accompanied by a special kind of awareness. It is in fact an altered state of consciousness used in virtually every meditative discipline and in intensive prayer.

No drugs or biofeedback machines are used. Mind Control lecturers speak of entering this state as "going to your level," or sometimes "going into Alpha." In a thirty-minute exercise they lead the student there gently, giving instructions in plain English. In fact all of Mind Control is in plain English: no scientific jargon or Far Eastern words.

Several of the students may already have learned to meditate before coming to class, some using methods that take a few weeks to learn, others after months of determined effort. They are amazed at a simple exercise that takes only thirty minutes.

One of the first things students hear is, "You are

learning to use more of your mind and to use it in a special manner."

This is a simple sentence they hear and internalize at the outset. The full meaning of it is nothing less than stupefying. Everyone—no exceptions—everyone has a mind that can easily be trained to exercise powers that beginners openly doubt they have. Only when they actually experience these powers do they come to believe.

Another thing that students are told is, "Project yourself mentally to your ideal place of relaxation"—a pleasant, calming, remarkably vivid exercise, which both strengthens the imagination and leads to deeper relaxation.

A word about meditation: In everyday speech it means thinking things over. If you set this book aside for a moment and consider what to have for dinner tomorrow, you are meditating.

But in the various meditative disciplines the word has a more specific meaning, referring to a special level of mind. In some disciplines, reaching this level is an end in itself, clearing the mind of all conscious thought. This produces a pleasant calm and goes a long way toward relieving and preventing illnesses caused by tension, as countless studies have proved.

But this is passive meditation. Mind Control goes far beyond this. It teaches the student to use this level of mind for solving problems, little nagging ones as well as larger, burdensome ones. This is dynamic meditation; the power of it is truly spectacular.

We hear more and more about Alpha nowadays. It is one of the brain-wave patterns, a kind of electrical energy produced by the brain, and can be measured by an electroencephalograph (EEG). The rhythms of this energy are measured in cycles per second (CPS). Generally, about fourteen CPS and up are called Beta waves; about seven to fourteen are Alpha; four to seven Theta; and four and below are Delta.

When you are wide awake, doing and achieving in the workaday world, you are in Beta, or "outer consciousness," to use Mind Control terminology. When you are daydreaming, or just going to sleep but not quite there yet, or just awakening but not yet awake, you are in Alpha. Mind Control people call this "inner consciousness." When you are asleep you are in Alpha, Theta, or Delta, not just Alpha alone, as many believe. With Mind Control training you can enter the Alpha level at will and still remain fully alert.

You may wonder what it feels like to be in these different levels of mind.

Being in Beta, or wide awake, does not produce any one particular feeling. You might feel confident or fearful, busy or idle, engrossed or bored—the possibilities in Beta are endless.

In the deeper levels the possibilities are limited for most people. Life has taught them to function in Beta, not Alpha or Theta. At these deeper levels they are pretty much limited to daydreaming, the edges of sleep, or sleep itself. But with Mind Control training, useful possibilities begin to multiply with no end in sight. As Harry McKnight, Associate Director of Silva Mind Control, wrote, "The Alpha dimension has a complete set of sensing faculties, like the Beta." In other words, we can do different things in Alpha than we can do in Beta.

This is a key concept in Mind Control. Once you become acquainted with these sensing faculties and learn to use them, you will be using more of your mind in a special manner. You will actually operate psychically whenever you want to, tapping in on Higher Intelligence.

Most people seek out Mind Control as a way to

relax, to end insomnia, to find relief from headaches, or to learn to do things that cost great efforts of will, such as stopping smoking, losing weight, improving memory, studying more effectively. This is what most of them come for; they learn much, much more.

They learn that the five senses—touching, tasting, smelling, hearing, and seeing—are only a part of the senses they were born with. There are others, call them powers or senses, once known only to a gifted few and to mystics who developed them over lifetimes removed from the active world. The mission of Mind Control is to train us to awaken these powers.

What this awakening can mean was well put by *Mademoiselle*'s beauty editor, Nadine Bertin, in the March 1972 issue:

"The drug culture can have its mind-expanding pills, powders and shots. I'll take mine straight. Mind Control does expand your mind. It teaches you HOW to expand it. It is aptly named because, unlike drugs or hypnosis, *you* are in *control*. Mind expansion, self-knowledge and helping others through Mind Control are only limited by your own limitations. ANYTHING is possible. You hear about it happening to others. And suddenly, you see it happening to you."

CHAPTER TWO

MEET JOSÉ

José Silva was born August 11, 1914, in Laredo, Texas. When he was four, his father died. His mother soon remarried, and he, his older sister, and younger brother moved in with their grandmother. Two years later he became the family breadwinner, selling newspapers, shining shoes, and doing odd jobs. In the evenings he watched his sister and brother do their homework, and they helped him learn to read and write. He has never gone to school, except to teach.

José's rise from poverty began one day when he was waiting his turn in a barbershop. He reached for something to read. What he picked up was a lesson from a correspondence course on how to repair radios. José asked to borrow it, but the barber would only rent it, and *that* on condition that José complete the examinations in the back in the barber's name. Each week José paid a dollar, read the lesson, and completed the examination.

Soon a diploma hung in the barbershop, while across town José, at the age of fifteen, began to repair radios. As the years passed, his repair business became one of the largest in the area, providing money for the education of his brother and sister, the wherewithal for him to marry, plus eventually some half-million dollars to